KING OF THE MOUNTAIN

Nathaniel could stand the strain no longer. He cupped his hands to his mouth and bellowed at the top of his lungs, "Zeke! A grizzly!" Then he retreated several more strides.

Nathaniel glanced over the bear's back, and his hopes soared when he spotted his uncle sprinting toward the bear, a rifle in each hand. He began to think he would survive his first encounter with a grizzly without receiving so much as a scratch, that perhaps the reputation of the species for ferocity was vastly overestimated, when the bear proved him wrong.

The grizzly attacked....

LURE OF THE WILD

In a flash the rattlesnake coiled. Acting on pure instinct, Nate grabbed at his pistols. His left moccasin stepped on a loose rock and he tripped, starting to fall backwards onto the very stones the rattler had been concealed under.

The venomous reptile's tail began to buzz loudly. Nate came down hard on his back, wincing when the sharp edges of several jagged rocks lanced into his body. He pulled the pistols free and cocked them at the same instant the rattler struck.

The snake speared its head at his right foot.

As if in slow motion, Nate saw the rattler open its mouth, saw the snake's long, hooked fangs ready to tear into his skin....

WILDERNESS

KING OF THE MOUNTAIN/ LURE OF THE WILD

DAVID THOMPSON

LEISURE BOOKS   NEW YORK CITY

A LEISURE BOOK®

December 1996

Published by

Dorchester Publishing Co., Inc.
276 Fifth Avenue
New York, NY 10001

KING OF THE MOUNTAIN copyright © 1990 by David Robbins

LURE OF THE WILD copyright © 1990 by David Robbins

Printed in the United States of America.

KING OF THE MOUNTAIN

Dedicated to...
Judy, Joshua, and Shane.

To the memory of Joseph Walker,
Jedediah Smith, Jim Bridger and the rest.

Oh. And to Roland Kari.
We were born about a century too late.
We missed out on all the fun.

HISTORICAL NOTE

This book is as factually oriented as is humanly possible. Contemporary narratives of trappers, mountain men, fur traders and other archives were consulted to ensure authenticity. Certain fictional liberties have been taken in the interests of dramatic licence, which I hope the reader will agree contributes to the excitement of actually "being there."

From the records and evidence available, it is believed that the King cabin was located in what is now known as Estes Park, Colorado, just outside of Rocky Mountain National Park.

The Author

Chapter One

"Out of the way, you dunderhead!"

The harsh bellow made 19-year-old Nathaniel King glance up and to his left; his green eyes widened in alarm. A moment before he had started to cross the narrow cobblestone street. Now he darted back to safety as a speeding carriage rushed past, narrowly missing him, the breeze from its passage stirring his moderately long black hair.

Cackling crazily, the driver of the carriage looked over his left shoulder and waved his whip in the air, apparently deriving perverse pleasure from almost running a pedestrian over.

An impulse to chase down the fellow and thrash him soundly compelled Nathaniel to take several strides after the rapidly departing brougham, and only the realization that he would be late for work prevented him from racing in pursuit. Instead, he drew his heavy wool overcoat tight about him to ward off the chill in the January air, and continued on his way to the accounting firm of P. Tuttle and Sons.

Located several blocks to the north of the New York Stock Exchange, in a stately sandstone bearing a huge sign comparable in size to the owner's view of his own importance to the business community, P. Tuttle and Sons seemed to exist at the center of a swirling vortex of humanity. Passersby streamed past the front window, while an increasing parade of carriages and buggies, wagons and gigs swept past going in either direction. The perpetual clatter of hooves and the hubbub of conversation, punctuated by whinnies and occasional oaths, lent the scene the aspect of a madhouse.

Or so Nathaniel often thought, and he did so now as he paused to gaze at the noisy street. He took one last breath of sooty New York air, then squared his broad shoulders and opened the door.

"My stars! Can it be that young Master King has finally graced us with his presence?"

The sarcastic comment drew Nathaniel around to his right, and he mustered a smile at the sight of his employer, Percival Tuttle the Elder, standing a yard away holding his open watch in his gnarled right hand. "Good morning, Mr. Tuttle."

"Is it really?" Tuttle responded wryly. "And here I thought it might be closer to noon."

"I'm sorry if I'm late."

"Late, Mr. King? No, I wouldn't go so far as to label you late. Tardy, yes. Tardy two days out of every month. Why, I will never know. Not when you only have two miles to travel to work. Yet I know my watch is accurate, and by my watch it is three minutes past eight."

"I'm truly sorry," Nathaniel said, self-conscious of the stares of the other employees, particularly Matthew Brown, Mr. Tuttle's pet.

"If I had a dollar for every time you have said you were sorry, I'd be a rich man," Tuttle the Elder declared dramatically, and snapped his watch case shut. "Fortunately, Mr. King, I practice the Christian forbearance instilled in me by my sainted mother. I forgive you for not arriving on time. For all your tardiness, you're a hard worker. I'll grant you that much."

"Thank you, sir," Nathaniel said dutifully, and hurried to his desk situated against the right-hand wall, near the window.

"There is one thing that worries me, though," Tuttle mentioned almost as an afterthought, although he deliberately raised his voice to attract the attention of the other seven employees.

Nathaniel began to shrug out of his overcoat. "What might that be, sir?"

An impish gleam came into the white-haired gentleman's brown eyes. "If you persist in failing to be on time when you are a bachelor, when you have no responsibilities other than yourself, I shudder to think how tardy you will be after you have acquired a wife and family."

A hearty burst of laughter greeted the remark.

As he had done so many times in the past, Nathaniel smiled to acknowledge Tuttle's profound insight and wit, then draped his coat on one of the wooden pegs in the corner.

"You will, of course, stay six minutes extra this evening to make amends," Tuttle stated.

"Of course," Nathaniel said.

Tuttle uttered a protracted sigh. "When I agreed to hire you as a favor to your father, my dear and loyal friend, I had no notion of the challenge you would present." So saying, he wheeled and walked off to his office.

Nathaniel sat down and considered the mountain of work piled in the middle of his desk. A snicker came from his left, from the plump person of Matthew Brown, and Nathaniel shifted to regard his corpulent rival critically. Brown's desk, in contrast to his own, was as neat as a spinster's dress. "Don't start, Matt," he warned.

Brown ignored the admonishment. "Won't you ever learn, Nate?"

"I've learned enough to know when to mind my own business," Nathaniel assured him, and opened the top file on his pile.

"Irritable today, are we?"

"I have work to do."

"I'm all caught up on mine. I'll help you if you wish," Brown said. He was—unfortunately, as far as Nathaniel was concerned—a mathematical genius.

"No." Nathaniel brushed some lint from his checkered trousers, wishing he were as adept as Matt Brown.

"Why won't you ever allow me to assist you?" Brown asked, his tone implying his feelings had been hurt.

"I'll do my own work, thank you."

"Has anyone ever informed you that you're pigheaded?"

Nathaniel's eyes flashed up from the profit-and-loss statement he had started to study. "Have a care, Matt. I won't take that type of abuse from any man."

"Oh, mercy!" Brown said, placing his right palm against his cheek. "I'm scared to death."

"Do your work and leave me alone," Nathaniel said, returning to the figures under his nose.

"Who are you trying to fool?" Brown persisted, whispering so as not to be overheard by the other employees. "You take abuse from Old Man Tuttle every day of the week except Sunday. Don't play tough with me. Who do you think you are, anyway? Jim Bowie?"

The mention of Bowie caused Nathaniel to lean back in his chair, reflecting on the newspaper article published in September of the previous year detailing the bloody duel between Jim Bowie and Major Morris Wright on a sandbar in the Mississippi River. For several weeks the fight had been the talk of the city. Any news of the frontier typically generated considerable excitement, and the battle on the sandbar had caused more than most.

Nathaniel recalled the details vividly. He read every book, story, and article on the west he could find, and his favorite pasttime was to daydream about the exciting exploits he had read about, the adventures of such famous figures as Bowie and Lewis and Clark. Contributing to his keen interest was the fact that his uncle had departed for the rugged, virtually unknown lands beyond the Mississippi a decade ago, and now lived somewhere in the Rocky Mountains.

"You'd better start pushing your pencil," Brown said. "Tuttle won't take kindly to you wasting his time."

"Mind your own business," Nathaniel said.

"Try prunes. I hear they do wonders for the temperament."

Nathaniel ignored the barb and diligently applied himself to his work. The morning hours seemed to drag by, and he had to resist the temptation to stare out the window at the bustling activity in the street. Tracking down an error in one ledger occupied most of his attention, and while running his right index finger down a column of figures he became aware that someone was hovering over his left shoulder. Startled, he glanced around.

"Hard at work, I see," the elder Tuttle said appreciatively. "Have you found the mistake in the Corben account yet?"

"Not yet, sir."

"Hmmmph. Well, you can take your midday break in thirty minutes."

"Thank you."

Tuttle went to leave, then halted and stuck his right hand in the pocket of his long-tailed black coat. "Oh. Before I forget, there is one more thing."

"Yes, sir?"

"Is there a reason you're having your mail delivered to this office instead of your father's house?"

"Sir?" Nathaniel said, puzzled by the question.

"This came for you two days ago, on Monday, and I misplaced it on my desk," Tuttle stated. From his pocket he withdrew an envelope.

"Who would be sending me mail here?" Nathaniel wondered aloud.

"You tell me," Tuttle replied, and handed the envelope over.

Nathaniel studied the scrawled handwriting on the front, noting the name and address of the sender, surprise and delight etching his features.

Ezekiel King
Fort Leavenworth

"A relative, I presume?" Tuttle queried, obviously having noted the name.

"My uncle," Nathaniel confirmed. "We haven't heard from him in eight or nine years."

"Why would he write you and not your father?"

"I have no idea."

"Well, advise him that as a general policy I do not accept personal correspondence at my business establishment. In this case, though, I'll make an exception."

"Thank you, sir."

"Just be sure to read it on your own time."

"Of course."

Tuttle nodded imperiously and headed for his office. It was a sanctuary that the employees were permitted to enter only on rare occasions.

Nathaniel deposited the letter in the top desk drawer and resumed working. He could scarcely concentrate on the numbers, his mind racing as he tried to deduce the motive behind his uncle's letter. Wait until his father heard the news! Aflame with curiosity, he became conscious of each passing second, and the next thirty minutes went by even more slowly than all the preceding hours. He grinned happily when Tuttle announced that he could take his break, and his fingers flew as he opened the envelope and spread the two crudely written pages on the desk. He began reading eagerly.

December 2, 1827

Dear Nate,

That you will be surprised at hearing from me, I have no doubt. Many a year and many a mile has come between us, and I hope you will still remember your old Uncle Zeke who let you ride on his back when you were a sprout, and who took you to the park on the Hudson River to play.

I'm mailing this to you at your place of employment rather than my brother's. Your Aunt Martha wrote me about your job last January. I don't want Tom to know I wrote you, so please don't tell him or there will be bad blood between us. Again.

Your father never did understand the reason I came out to the great West.

I expect to be in St. Louis in May of '28. Come there. I have found the greatest treasure in the world and I want to share it with you before I die.

You were always my favorite nephew.

If you decide to come, be at The Chouteau House on
May 4. I'll be wearing the red so you know me.

Uncle Zeke

Nathaniel recoiled in stunned amazement at the last portion
of the letter. He reread it again and again, marveling that
his uncle would even think of asking him to travel all the
way to St. Louis, to the very edge of the frontier, to the last
major outpost of civilization, when his father and mother and
two brothers were all in New York, when he had never been
beyond Philadelphia, and when he had his career as an
aspiring accountant to consider. The list of objections grew
and grew. There was his sweetheart, Adeline, and his plan
to eventually marry her and settle down in a house of his own.

How could his Uncle Zeke make such an insane proposal?

Dazed, Nathaniel sat back and mumbled, "Go to St.
Louis? How in the—"

"What's that?" interrupted a familiar voice on his left.

Frowning, Nathaniel twisted and watched Matthew Brown
take a bite from an overstuffed sandwich. "I wasn't talking
to you."

"I distinctly heard you say something about going to St.
Louis," Brown said, his mouth full, a sliver of beef dangling
from the corner of his mouth.

"You were hearing things," Nathaniel insisted. He folded
the letter, replaced it in the envelope, and struck them in
the pocket of his Byronic-style coat.

"Are you planning to visit St. Louis?" Brown inquired.

"No."

"If you go, you're not in your right mind."

Annoyed, Nathaniel faced his coworker. "Is that a fact?"

"Certainly. Why would anyone want to leave the culture
and refinement of New York for the barbaric society of St.
Louis?"

"New York has its drawbacks too," Nathaniel said simply
to be argumentative, although in his heart he agreed with
Brown.

"Oh? What, for instance? Carriage congestion, pick-pockets, footpads, and a little ash in your eyes in the winter when everyone has their fireplace lit? Such inconveniences pale into insignificance when you compare them to the benefits we enjoyed by living in the greatest city in the country, even the world."

"Now you're exaggerating."

"Am I? New York is the largest city in the United States. Do you realize there are one hundred and twenty-five thousand people living here? Why, there are only about ten million people in the whole country. Over one-tenth of the total population lives in New York State. Imagine that!"

Nathaniel gazed out the window at the bedlam in the street and found it easy to imagine.

"Look at what New York has to offer," Brown continued, still chewing as he talked. "There's the opera, museums, and the ballet. Our theaters are the envy of the civilized world. Our newspapers are quoted everywhere. Why, the *New York Evening Post,* the one that William Cullen Bryant edits, is read by the President. Our universities are nationally renowned. Face facts, Nate. New York City is the cultural center of America."

The smugness with which Brown maintained his assertion bothered Nathaniel, but he was at a loss to identify the reason. "St. Louis has benefits to offer," he said lamely.

Brown snorted and almost choked on his sandwich. "Are you jesting? All St. Louis has to offer are ruffians, Indians, and the prospect of having your throat slit."

Nathaniel regarded the fat little man coldly, thinking that Brown wasn't the only New Yorker he knew who seemed to take an inordinate pride in his city, as if New Yorkers were superior to everyone else by virtue of their birthplace. He realized suddenly he shared that snobbish attitude to a lesser extent. New York could boast a culture rivaled by few other cities, but did that culture truly transform its residents into better citizens, better people, then those raised in, say, Boston or New Orleans or even St. Louis? He saw Matthew Brown stuffing more food into that gaping mouth and shook his head.

Brown misconstrued the motion. "What? You doubt you'll have your throat slit if you venture to St. Louis? How can you be so naive? You're read about the frontier. You know what it's like."

"Do I?" Nathaniel wondered wistfully.

Chapter Two

The street lamps were lit by the time Nathaniel bundled himself in his woolen overcoat and started for home. He had performed his work that day in a perfunctory fashion, unable to fully concentrate, his mind adrift with the implications of his uncle's letter. The traffic outside was every bit as bustling as it had been that morning. He turned to the right and flowed with the crowd.

One sentence kept repeating itself over and over, unbidden but irresistible: *"I have found the greatest treasure in the world and I want to share it with you."* What on earth could Uncle Zeke mean? Nathaniel mused. What kind of treasure? Had Zeke found gold or silver? There were many rumors about legendary treasures to be found out west, so perhaps Zeke had stumbled on one of them.

The most persistent legend, a tale every schoolboy learned by heart, concerned the Seven Golden Cities of Cibola. They were said to contain great riches, wealth so great that no man could conceive of the magnitude of the fortune. The seven cities were reputed to exist somewhere in the vastness between the Mississippi River and the Pacific Ocean; they were said to be inhabited by a tribe of fierce Indians. The

Spanish had sent several expeditions to find the Golden Cities of Cibola more than two hundred years ago, but although the expeditions had failed, the legend lingered on.

If Zeke had found gold, wasn't it only logical to assume that he would want to share part of his wealth with someone in the King family? And who better to share the gold with than his favorite nephew? Or so Nathaniel reasoned, and the more he thought about it, the more convinced he became that his uncle *had* made a fortune, and now wanted to mend the rift that had branded Ezekiel the black sheep in the King clan.

Engrossed in his reflection, and eager to reach home, Nathaniel opted to take a shortcut through an alley, a shortcut he might normally take during the day but had never used at night. He was halfway through the gloomy alley, his hands plunged in his overcoat pockets to shield them from the cold, his eyes straining in the dim shadows, when someone stepped from a recessed doorway and blocked his path.

Nathaniel halted abruptly, surprised but not worried, confident his size alone, six feet plus two inches, would deter most pickpockets and robbers from bothering him. "Excuse me, sir, but you're blocking my path," he said.

"Your money or your life."

The gruff words, delivered with an air of impending menace, startled Nathaniel. He knew about the hundreds of robberies that took place in New York City each year, and about the scores of footpads who made their vile living by preying on the innocent and the unsuspecting, but this was happening to *him,* and the reality of his predicament took half a minute to sink in.

"Didn't you hear me, fool? I want your money or your life!" the man declared.

Still stunned, Nathaniel mechanically pulled his hands from his pockets, about to comply, when he detected the flashing gleam of a large knife reflected in the feeble light from an overhead window.

"Don't trifle with me, mister!" the robber warned. "Give me your money now!"

"Go to hell," Nathaniel blurted out, and spun. He saw

the mouth of the alley not ten yards away, and he sprinted toward the opening in the hope that his assailant would not pursue him into the busy street. But he managed only three strides before strong arms caught him from the rear, looping about his hips, and the next moment he crashed to the hard ground with the footpad on top.

Instantly Nathaniel rolled to the right, nearly upending the thief in the bargain. The man clung fast to his overcoat, though, and Nathaniel saw the knife arching toward his chest. He lunged, grasping the robber's right wrist in his left hand, checking the knife's descent, and was clenching his right hand to deliver a blow with his fist when iron fingers clamped on his throat.

The footpad was attempting to strangle him!

Nathaniel bucked and squirmed, but he failed to disarm his foe or dislodge the constricting fingers from his neck. He tried to knee his attacker in the spine, but his overcoat impeded his movements. Frustrated, desperate to break free, Nathaniel felt a surge of newfound power course through him at the thought of being slain by an anonymous thug in a filthy alley.

"Damn you!" the footpad hissed. "Die!"

"No!" Nathaniel roared, and amazed himself by coming up off the ground in a mighty heave of his steely legs. He hurled the robber as if the man were a rag doll instead of a two-hundred-pounder, flinging him against the wall.

The footpad grunted as he hit the bricks, then dropped to one knee.

His fists at the ready, Nathaniel closed in, but the man scrambled to the right, then rose and dashed toward the street. "Hold on!" Nathaniel yelled, and gave chase. Again the overcoat interfered, preventing him from attaining his top speed. He was able to stay within two strides of the robber, though, and both of them burst from the alley without bothering to verify if the way was clear.

Voicing a harsh oath, the footpad collided with another man and both went down.

Not about to allow his adversary to escape, Nathaniel pounced and pinned the thief, his arms around the man's chest.

"Here, here, now! What is this?" bellowed someone in an authoritative manner.

Nathaniel felt hands on his shoulders, and then both he and the footpad were hauled erect.

"Now what is the meaning of this?" demanded a burly constable, who pulled the two men apart and held them at arm's length.

"He tried to rob me!" Nathaniel exclaimed.

"I did not," the footpad responded sheepishly. Revealed in the glow of a nearby street lamp, he was a stout, unkempt man with oily black hair and beady eyes.

The constable released both of them and looked from one to the other. "Now who am I to believe?"

"He has a knife," Nathaniel stated angrily. "He nearly stabbed me."

Smiling sweetly, the robber held up both hands. Both empty hands. "Search me if you like," he said. "You'll find no knife on Bobby Peterson. I'm a man who dislikes violence."

"He's lying!" Nathaniel cried. "He attacked me in the alley."

"Attacked?" Peterson repeated in astonishment. "Why, all I did was bump into the lad in the dark, and the next thing I know he had pulled me to the ground and we were wrestling. I never attacked him."

Nathaniel started to raise his right fist.

"No you don't, son," the constable cautioned. "No more fighting, if you please. Now here I am, on my way home to my loving wife and a hot meal, and I see you two fighting like a pair of cocks. What am I to do with you?"

"But he tried to *rob* me," Nathaniel insisted.

"I just have your word for that, now don't I?" the constable said.

The implied insult staggered Nathaniel. "Don't you believe me?"

"Of course I do. But I can also see where an excitable young fellow such as yourself might, shall we say, jump to conclusions without sufficient evidence."

"This is incredible."

A friendly smile creased the constable's weathered visage. "I'll tell you what. Let's so through this from the beginning again. Then we'll look for the knife you say Peterson had. But let's hurry, shall we? I'm starving."

"And the constable didn't believe you?"

"No," Nathaniel related. "Not after he couldn't find the knife in the alley. He let us go." He paused and added scornfully, "But he did give the robber a warning that he would be on the lookout and if he ever found Peterson had violated the law, there would be the devil to pay."

Adeline Van Buren shook her head sadly, her lovely features downcast in commiseration for his ordeal, her blond hair bobbing as her head moved, her blue eyes fixed lovingly on his face. In accordance with the fashion of dress in vogue all along the eastern seaboard, she wore a dress patterned after the sophisticated Grecian-style clothing so enormously popular in England and France. Her yellow dress had a low neckline, but not *too* low, and a high waistline. She folded her slim hands on her lap and stared at his scuffed shoes and the dirt on his trousers.

Nathaniel noticed, and wished he had changed before coming to see her. He'd already overstepped the bounds of propriety by arriving on her doorstep at nine P.M., a late hour for any respectable man to be calling on any decent woman. Fortunately, her parents thought highly of him and trusted him alone with their daughter. Everyone knew they were planning to wed in a year.

"What did your father say when you told him?" Adeline asked.

"He wasn't home. My father has been working long hours at his construction business."

"I thought January is one of his slowest months, what with the cold weather and all."

"He's busy with the yearly inventory," Nathaniel explained, admiring the shapely contours of her neck and shoulders. "I told my mother, but she couldn't seem to understand why I was so angry over the affair." He sighed.

"That's when I decided to pay you a visit. I knew you would understand."

"I'm happy you came," Adeline said.

Her smile thrilled Nathaniel to the core of his being. He wanted so much to be able to hold her in his arms, to touch his lips to hers and smell the fragrant scent of her coiffured hair. Her beauty seemed almost angelic, and when the time came, he would glady throw himself at her feet and plead for her hand in marriage. So far all they had done was discuss the prospect. Soon, very soon, he would tender the formal proposal.

"There is a matter we must talk about," Adeline stated. "I promised Papa I would mention this to you."

Nathaniel tensed. Her father, a prosperous merchant with three stores in New York City and one in Philadelphia, had always impressed him as being a stern, commanding figure. He counted as a blessing the fact her father and his were close friends. "Mention what?"

Adeline opened her mouth to speak, then developed a sudden interest in her painted fingernails. "How has Mr. Tuttle been treating you?"

"As well as can be expected," Nathaniel replied, perplexed by the question. What did Old Man Tuttle have to do with anything?

"My father went to see him."

Nathaniel's breath caught in his throat, and he couldn't have moved if the house was on fire. He blinked a few times, struggling to compose his emotions, bewildered by the revelation. "Whatever for?" he blurted out.

Adeline looked at him, her eyes radiating all the affection in the universe. "Are you happy working for Tuttle?"

"Happy? Well, I don't know. Contented, maybe. It's a stepping-stone in my career. One day I'll own my own accounting firm. You wait and see."

"And that will take a terribly long time, won't it?"

"Not terribly long. Five, perhaps seven years at the most."

"And what will your income be?"

Nathaniel shrugged. "Who can say? It all depends on how successful I am in attracting clients."

"Will you make as much as your father does?"

"Not that much, but enough for us to live comfortably," Nathaniel answered, feeling uneasy, troubled by the direction their conversation was taking.

"Will you make as much as my father does?"

"Of course not. His income is in the six figures."

"And how many figures will yours be?" Adeline inquired, trying a new tack. "Five?"

Nathaniel said nothing.

"Four?"

"Oh, definitely."

A fluttering sigh issued from her rosy lips. "Nate, I'm accustomed to living in the style my father has provided for me all of my life. We're not immensely wealthy, but we are well off. I like having servants to take care of the menial chores like cleaning and cooking." She studied him for a moment. "Will we be able to afford servants?"

Nathaniel felt strangely deflated, as if his chest had been punctured and all the breath expelled from his lungs. "No," he admitted.

"I see," Adeline said, each word expressed in clipped, precise English.

"I'm confused," Nathaniel admitted. "You've known for over a year about my line of work and you've never raised an objection. Why now all of a sudden?"

"This is not a sudden consideration on my part," Adeline replied. "I've simply been waiting for the proper moment."

"For what?"

"To ask you to go to work for my father."

Nathaniel sat bolt upright in his upholstered chair. "Your father?"

"Why not?" Adeline rejoined stiffly. "In five years you could be managing one of his stores and making ten times as much money as you could by being an accountant."

"Does *he* want me to work for him?"

"Certainly, silly. Why do you think Papa went to all the trouble of seeking out Mr. Tuttle?"

"Why did he?"

Adeline gave him her most radiant smile. "I asked Papa

to do it. He had a long talk with your employer about your career as an accountant.''

''And?''

''And we decided you would be better off joining Papa in his business.''

''*You* decided?''

''Certainly. Don't I have a right to be concerned about your career? As your wife, the amount of money you make will have a direct bearing on my happiness and well-being. I have a vested interest in your future.''

''But I like accounting,'' Nathaniel said softly, gazing absently at the plush lavender carpet, dazed by the unexpected turn of events. First the footpad, and now this. He should have known the day would turn out badly after almost being run over on his way to work. There was an omen, if ever there was one.

''Do you?'' Adeline replied. ''I know you *think* you do, but I have my doubts, dearest. I don't believe you have the proper temperament to be an accountant, to sit behind a desk the rest of your life and fiddle with figures. You have a restless nature, Nate King. You need excitement in your life, and retailing is just the thing to keep you from becoming bored.''

''This is all so sudden,'' Nathaniel complained.

''You do see my point, don't you?''

Nathaniel nodded. ''I see that money matters much more to you than I thought it did.''

''Is that bad?''

''I suppose not,'' Nathaniel responded halfheartedly.

Adeline straightened and regarded him in the same manner a mother would a misbehaving child. ''My father taught me a valuable lesson at a very early age, Nate. As he likes to say, money makes the world go around. Money, darling, is the balm of our existence. Money feeds us and clothes us and provides the pleasures we enjoy. Money separates the superior from the mediocre, and hard workers from the lazy riffraff.'' She paused. ''I would never marry a man who was content to drift through life barely making ends meet. A man who will settle for making less than the highest income possible isn't much of a man in my estimation."

Nathaniel's lips barely moved when he said, "I had no idea."

"So will you give Papa's offer serious consideration?" Adeline inquired eagerly.

"For you, yes."

An airy laugh bubbled from her throat. "I knew I could rely on your good judgment. Why do you think I want to be your wife?"

The question drew Nathaniel's head up. "Why do you?"

"What a silly thing to ask. Because I love you. Because you treat me wonderfully," Adeline detailed, and giggled. "And because you are the handsomeest man in all of New York."

"I knew there must be a sound reason."

"Please don't be upset with me. This is for your benefit, as well as mine."

Nathaniel stared at her, studying her exquisite, elegant form, his pulse quickening as always, regarding her as a prize for which he was willing to pay any price. His brow knit and his eyes narrowed, indicative of the intensity he applied to pondering the issue she had raised, and in his single-minded determination to please her he entertained a wild idea. "What would you say if I could make more money than your father, more money than you ever dreamed possible?"

"Whatever are you talking about?"

"How would you feel if I was rich beyond your wildest expectations?"

Puzzled, Adeline leaned in his direction. "How could you possibly become richer than Papa?"

"Don't you believe I can?"

Adeline laughed lightly and smoothed her dress. "Please, Nate, don't become carried away. I want you to make more money, yes, but we must be realistic about the amount you can make."

Nathaniel reached in his pocket and touched the letter from his Uncle Zeke. Smiling, he removed his hand. "And I tell you that within six months I'll have more money than we will need."

"You're serious?"

"As God is my witness, I would never jest about making you happy."

"And how will you accomplish this magical feat?"

Nathaniel started to reply, to explain about the letter and his belief concerning the treasure Ezekiel had found, until he realized she would never understand, would never attach any credibility to his uncle's claim. Even his own family would view Zeke's letter as the ravings of an eccentric. But he knew better. He remembered the many hours he had spent with his carefree, fun-loving uncle; he recalled the basic decency and honesty Ezekiel had always displayed; he recollected the confidence Zeke had instilled; and motivated by the same impulse that had prompted countless men down through the ages to embark on questionable enterprises, namely the love of a beautiful woman, he came to a momentous decision. In answer to her question he only smiled and said, "Wait and see. You'll be proud of me one day soon. Very soon."

Chapter Three

Nathaniel departed New York City on April 1, intending to travel at a leisurely pace and enjoy "the adventure," as he thought of his trip, to the fullest. He had planned every detail of his departure carefully, and he rode away through New Jersey on a fine mare, with another horse laden with his supplies trailing, at eight A.M. in the morning, oblivious to the nip in the air, his spirits soaring.

The four months since his receipt of Ezekiel's letter had been spent eventfully. He had put aside every cent he could spare for the journey, and combined with the funds he had already accumulated during his employment at Tuttle's and earlier, he now carried the hefty sum of 273 dollars in his inner coat pocket. He had purchased a blue wool cap to keep his head warm, and gone to a tailor to have new wool trousers made, trousers with extra stitching to withstand the rigors of extended periods in the saddle. He had also purchased a new pair of black leather boots, the ultimate in footwear according to the kindly man who'd made them, guaranteed to hold up under the harshest weather.

Nathaniel told no one about his plans. He dropped hints to Adeline, arousing her curiosity to a feverish pitch, but to all her entreaties he would only say that he intended to make her one of the wealthiest women in New York.

Once he attempted to broach the subject of Uncle Zeke to his family at the dinner table. His father immediately announced that Ezekiel had forsaken them to go live in the wilds with savage Indians, and accordingly Zeke was not, and would never be, a proper topic for discussion in the King household. End of subject.

During the four months Nathaniel's emotional state fluctuated between firm resolve and insecure anxiety. Scores of times he told himself he was being a fool. Yet the thought of traveling to the frontier, of seeing his uncle again, and most importantly, of possibly sharing in the treasure Zeke had found, beckoned like an irresistible beacon. The excitement of the unknown also appealed to him, the prospect of encountering strange people and strange lands and having experiences he could one day relate to his children and his children's children. The adventure promised to be a once-in-a-lifetime enterprise and he wanted to make the most of it.

On the night before he left, he composed three letters by candlelight at the small desk in his room. The first was to his family, explaining about the letter from Zeke and expressing his regret for leaving secretly. He assured his father and mother that he loved them, and vowed to return by July at the very latest. The second letter went to his employer, thanking Tuttle for teaching him the fundamentals of accounting and apologizing for leaving the firm in the lurch on such short notice. He also suggested that Matthew Brown would be delighted to handle the pile of work he hadn't finished.

Without a doubt, the hardest letter for him to pen was the note to Adeline. Four pages long, he poured his heart out to her, professing his love repeatedly, and pledged to return at the earliest opportunity. Knowing his father would inform her father about Zeke, he went into great detail about Zeke's letter and his belief that his uncle had amassed a fortune, either in precious ore or by trapping, like John Jacob Astor.

Everyone in New York who could read knew Astor's story. An immigrant from Germany who came to New York

City when he was twenty years old, Astor went into the fur trade in 1787, founded his own company in 1808, and eventually acquired a monopoly of the trade south of the Canadian border. In the process he became a millionaire many times over and the richest man in America.

Toward the end of his letter to Adeline, after vowing his undying affection one more time, Nathaniel added the lines tht would haunt him in later years. "Everything I do, I do for you. Your happiness means more to me than my own, more than my life itself. For you I would risk all. For you I would do anything. If money is your heart's desire, then money you shall have. Think of me always for I will constantly be thinking about you. In three months I will return to ask for your hand in marriage, and I'll be counting every minute until then."

Nathaniel thought of those closing words again as he rode to the southwest from New York, hoping Adeline would cherish them in her heart until next they met. Brimming with youthful confidence, he inhaled the crisp air deep in his lungs and congratulated himself on selecting the Cumberland Road route instead of taking the Erie Canal.

The decision had been a difficult one.

Traveling westward via the Erie Canal had been his first choice. Completed only a few years ago, in October of 1825, the canal linked the Hudson River and Atlantic Ocean with the Great Lakes, providing a much-needed water route into the heart of the country. Three hundred and sixty-three miles long, the waterway was daily jammed with boats crowded with passengers or transporting freight, and there had already appeared editorials in several newspapers calling for the canal to be expanded. For only a cent and a half a mile, passengers traveled at the rate of a mile and a half an hour on heavy boats pulled by horses. The going was exceedingly slow, which proved to be the deciding factor in Nathaniel's decision.

By contrast, a traveler on the Cumberland Road—or Great National Pike, as many referred to it—could move at whatever pace was necessary. Begun in 1811 and funded primarily with Federal money, the road ran from Cumber-

land, Maryland, up over the mountains and across the south-
western corner of Pennsylvania, Ohio, Indiana, and Illinois,
where it terminated at the town of Vandalia, not more than
61 miles from St. Louis. Although not yet completely paved,
thousands traveled its almost 600-mile length each month.
Sixty feet wide where completed, the road included a center
strip to separate the traffic flow.

Nathaniel opted for the National Pike because he could
ride as many miles each day as he wanted, and he would
be much closer to St. Louis at the end of the pike than he
would if he took the Erie Canal. By following the many signs
and sticking to the major roads, he reached Cumberland on
the evening of the seventh day. With approximately a
thousand miles to cover, he was not inclined to push his
horses. Both animals had been purchased at a stable on the
southwest outskirts of New York City, and the proprietor
of the livery had also agreed, for a nominal fee, to store
Nathaniel's gear until such time as the supplies were needed.
Nathaniel had not dared hide any of his provisions in his room
for fear of them being discovered.

Once on the National Pike, Nathaniel began to relax and
truly enjoy his trip. Guilt had nagged at his mind the first five
days, until he'd finally convinced himself that his course of
action was justified. He found the people traveling on the
Cumberland Road to be remarkably friendly. Back in New
York, he had been lucky to receive a curt nod in response
to a hello. But the farther west he went, the more amicable
the people were.

All types of travelers used the pike. Those heading west
formed a steadily flowing river of vibrantly optimistic
humanity, the vast majority en route to a better life in a better
area of the country, where the sweat of their brow would
reap the reward of having their own land and their own
house, where they could prosper and share in the budding
American dream. Or so they hoped. There were travelers
from all walks of life and almost every state in the East. They
went on foot, or on horseback, or in carriages or wagons.
Livestock mingled with the people, primarily cattle being
driven to Eastern markets by drovers from the frontier.

Nathaniel reveled in the journey. He particularly liked the evenings, when he invariably stopped at one of the many comfortable inns lining the road to eat and rest for the night. The stops gave him the opportunity to associate with his fellow wayfarers. He met a farming family intent on starting anew in Missouri, a doctor from Philadelphia who had grown tired of the city life and longed for a change, and a missionary heading for the Old Southwest to "Christianize the Indians." All told, he talked to dozens of fellow wayfarers during the 27 days it took him to complete the trip.

Three incidents of note transpired, two of which he would never forget for as long as he lived.

The first incident occurred at an inn in eastern Ohio, a shoddy establishment where the food was undercooked, the bed uncomfortable, and the manager a slovenly sort who always seemed to have a handkerchief pressed to his nose. Nathaniell had pushed his plate aside halfway through the meal and headed for his room. As he placed his right foot onto the bottom step, the manager suddenly appeared at his left elbow.

"I say, young sir, would you care for some pie?"

"No, thank you," Nathaniel replied, and went up two steps.

"But it's freshly baked tart pie."

Nathaniel glanced at the man, surprised to note a certain anxiety in the set of his chubby features. "Thank you, but no. I have spent all day on the road and I would like to retire early."

"I'll throw in a free ale."

Although tempted, Nathaniel shook his head, bothered by a vague feeling of unease. "Good night, sir."

The manager gave a small bow and backed away, frowning.

Now what was all that about? Nathaniel wondered, and proceeded to the second floor and along the dim corridor. Two yards from his room he halted, amazed to behold his door hanging open several inches when he distinctly recalled locking it behind him earlier on his way down to eat. He eased to the jamb and peered inside.

Looming as a vague inky shadow in the dark room, a burly man was in the act of rifling through Nathaniel's possessions piled on the bed.

Without thinking, angered by the sight of the thief tossing his clothing about, Nathaniel shoved the door wide and blurted out, "You there! Hold it!"

But the thief had no intention of doing any such thing. Uttering a curse, the man spun and charged the doorway, barreling into Nathaniel and battering him aside.

Lunging with his left arm, Nathaniel succeeded in taking hold of the other man's coat. Before he could capitalize on the grip, however, the thief jerked to one side and wrenched loose, throwing Nathaniel off balance into the opposite wall. Nathaniel pushed erect and gave chase, yelling, "Stop, thief! Stop, thief!"

The man never looked back. He reached the stairs and bounded to the bottom, taking the steps four at a stride, then bolted out the entrance into the night.

His pulse pounding, Nathaniel followed to the front door, when he paused to scan the lawn beyond for the pilferer. The earth had swallowed the man whole, and the expanse of green grass mocked him with its emptiness.

"Hear, hear! What's the meaning of this uproar?" the manager demanded, hastening over from the desk.

"A man was in my room," Nathaniel responded, still infuriated, still surveying the lawn.

"What man?"

"A thief."

The manager, his tone laced with the venom of a cottonmouth, snapped, "Not in my establishment, young man."

Nathaniel spun, even more incensed at having his word doubted. "Are you calling me a liar, sir?" He expected the manager to argue the point, but to his surprise the man did an abrupt reversal.

"Not at all. I would never impugn the integrity of one of my guests. If you say there was a gentleman in your room, then by all means there must have been someone in your room."

"He wasn't a gentleman."

"Is it possible another guest might have entered your room by mistake?"

"The man wasn't a guest. He was a thief."

"Was anything stolen?"

The question galvanized Nathaniel into action. He bounded up the stairs to his room and checked his personal belongings. To his immense relief, none of his possessions had been taken. As he finished folding his clothes he heard someone cough behind him and turned to discover the manager.

"I have checked the grounds and there is no sign of anyone who shouldn't be here."

"The thief is undoubtedly long gone by this time."

"Is anything missing?"

"No," Nathaniel said.

"Then no harm has been done," the manager commented. "In the future, though, I would advise you to lock your door. Inns are not farmhouses. I have no way of knowing what type of person may be taking a room for the night. Occasionally someone bad slips in."

"So I see."

"Well, if that will be all," the manager said, and gave another of his courteous little bows. He grinned, an oddly sinister twisting of his thick lips, and walked off.

Nathaniel promptly closed and locked the door, then checked to ensure the single window on the east wall was securely latched. Unnerved by the incident, he pushed the bed against the door and lay down fully clothed on his back, his head resting in his interlocked hands. He stared at the ceiling for over an hour, reviewing the episode from start to finish, and came to the conclusion he must pick the inns he stayed at with greater care in the future. The manager's behavior troubled him, although he couldn't determine precisely why. He slipped into a fitful sleep, and his last thought before he slept was that he should give serious consideration to obtaining a weapon.

The second incident took place a few miles east of Indianapolis, which had been designated the capital of Indiana only

seven years before. He stopped shortly after noon to give
the horse a rest and enjoy a light meal at a quaint inn packed
with other travelers. His dinner consisted of delicious baked
beans, which had been steeped with generous portions of pork
in a big pot left overnight in the ashes of the inn's fireplace,
as was the custom. After eating he went outside to enjoy the
fresh air and the warm sunshine, and it was then, as he
strolled toward the southeast corner of the building, that he
saw them. At first he mistook them for shadows, and not
until one moved did the shock of recognition stop him in his
tracks.

They were seated under the spreading branches of an
enormous maple tree, at the base of the trunk, their backs
leaning against the rough bole, partly ringing the giant
patriarch of the forest that had once claimed the land on which
the inn sat. There were four of them, each with his knees
drawn up against an emaciated chest, each with iron shackles
on their ankles. Their clothes were in tatters, and the grime
from many miles of travel caked their sweating black skins.
Two of the four wore beards; the other two were quite young,
barely out of their early teens.

Nathaniel noticed them when one of the young blacks lifted
a weary hand to lethargically scratch a bulbous nose. He
halted in astonishment 20 feet from the maple and gazed at
them in bewilderment, striving to fathom the reason for their
condition and the shackles. The oldest of the quartet turned
a lined visage toward him, regarding him with the blank eyes
of someone who had penetrated an inscrutable veil and who
now viewed the world as if from a vast distance. Somehow,
those vacant orbs also conveyed the indelible stamp of
incalculable inner torment and sadness commingled in a
singular countenance. Nathaniel looked, and felt an invisible,
frigid wind chill his spine.

"Hey, you want somethin', mister?"

The words, spoken in a peculiar, protracted drawl, came
from one of the six men who were lounging about a wagon
parked a dozen yards to the south of the tree. All six wore
homespun clothes. Several rifles had been propped against
the wagon, and the speaker wore a large hunting knife in

a brown leather sheath on his right hip.

"Why are those men in chains?" Nathaniel asked.

"What's the matter, boy? Ain't you never seen slaves before?" the speaker rejoined, prompting a cackle of mirth from his companions.

Nathaniel turned, noting the man's ragged blond hair, wispy blond mustache, and pale blue eyes. "They're slaves?"

"Escaped slaves, boy. All the way from Mississippi. As ignorant a bunch of niggers as you'd ever want to meet."

Nathaniel had seen many Negroes in New York, although in the circle of his acquaintances he could number only two Negroes he knew personally. Both had been slaves, domestic servants in the house of a man who did business with his father, and both had been freed on July 4, 1827 when the State of New York officially abolished slavery. The pair had stayed on with their former owner, apparently satisfied with the working conditions and the treatment they had received.

Many stories were related in the press about the growing institution of slavery in the Deep South, and the moral and legal aspects were vigorously debated. Other states besides New York, including Pennsylvania, Rhode Island, and the new state of Illinois, had banned the practice.

"Are those shackles necessary?" Nathaniel inquired distastefully.

"They are if we don't want them niggers to light out on us," the man responded. "We didn't trail 'em this far to lose 'em again."

"You're from Mississippi?"

"Yep. We do this for a living, and get paid fair money too. Slaves are always taking off, no matter how decent some of 'em are treated. They're so dumb it's pitiful."

Nathaniel looked at the oldest slave, who had tilted his head against the tree and closed his eyes. "Aren't there laws against chasing slaves across state lines?"

The blond snickered. "You sure don't know shucks about the slave trade, Yankee. Ain't you ever heard of the Fugitive Slave Law?"

The reference sparked a memory long buried, and

Nathaniel simply nodded. Back in 1793, or thereabouts, the Congress had passed the Federal Fugitive Law, which allowed slave owners to cross state lines if necessary to retrieve runaway slaves. He gave the quartet a last glance, then wheeled and hurried to the stable behind the inn to reclaim his horses, filled with an overwhelming urge to put as much distance as he could between the four chained human beings and himself. Until that moment, he had never seriously pondered the issue of slavery. For the remainder of the day he reflected on nothing else.

In Illinois, just over the border from Indiana, the third incident occurred.

Nathaniel stopped at an inn situated a little off the beaten path after he found two others, both nearer to the pike, full to capacity. He bedded his horses for the night, then took a room, washed, and ate a leisurely supper of tasty venison and potatoes. As he concluded the meal, he happened to gaze toward the rear of the dining area and spied an open door. Five men were visible in a room beyond, seated around a circular table, playing a game of cards. Intrigued, he rose, paid for his meal, and walked back to investigate. As he stepped through the doorway all eyes swung toward him. He halted, uncomfortable under their probing stares, wondering if he had committed a blunder by intruding on their game.

"What the hell do you want, whippersnapper?" demanded a bear of a man who wore a cape with a beaver-fur collar.

"I only wanted to watch," Nathaniel replied, putting as much self-confidence into his voice as he could muster.

"This isn't a church social. Go watch the birds play in the trees," the man snapped, and one of the other players tittered.

A third player then spoke, his tone firm, a slight edge to his pronouncement. "Leave him alone, Clancy."

Nathaniel focused on his defender, a slim man wearing an immaculate black suit and a frilled white shirt. The thin man's features were angular, his hair brown, his eyes an icy grayish-blue. He held his cards in his left hand, close to his shirt, while his right elbow rested on the edge of the table and his right hand was lost to view, evidently on his lap.

"Is this sprout a friend of yours, Tyler?" the man named Clancy inquired testily.

"Never laid eyes on the gentleman before," Tyler replied, smiling and nodding at Nathaniel.

"Then what difference does it make to you whether he stays or not?" Clancy demanded.

"If he wants to stay, he stays," Tyler stated with an air of finality, and locked his eyes on the bigger man.

Nathaniel saw the other men stiffen and lower their cards, and he glanced from Tyler to Clancy, noticing the obvious hatred gleaming in the massive man's dark eyes. Tyler sat calmly, composed and relaxed, but Clancy appeared on the verge of exploding into violence. A silent battle of wills had ensued, and neither man seemed willing to back down. Nathaniel inadvertently broke the deadlock by saying, "If I'm causing trouble, I'll be glad to leave."

"I don't give a damn whether you stay or not," Clancy said harshly, finally tearing his gaze from Tyler.

"Then let's play cards," another man said. "This constant bickering is ruining the game."

Nathaniel stood next to the right-hand wall and idly observed the course of the game. Having never been much of a card player himself, he still knew enough to recognize the five men were engaged in a form of poker. He watched as the cards were shuffled and dealt, listened as bids were made and coins tinkled on the table, and marveled at the intensity displayed on all the faces except one. Every player except Tyler sat in a posture of anxious expectancy and hung on the deal of each card. Curses were vented when hands went against them, and although they tried to conceal their elation when they received a good hand, most of them were transparent by their sudden silence or stony expression.

For over an hour the game continued. Tyler dominated the play, winning two out of every three hands, his pile of silver and gold coins and stack of paper dollars growing higher and higher. His slim, elegant hands handled the cards with balletic grace, his fingers flying when he dealt, gliding each card to the recipient with unerring accuracy.

Clancy became progressively surlier as he lost more and more money. Clearly an inept player, he insisted on challenging Tyler again and again. Each loss diminished his self-esteem and aroused his anger, and he began to cast open, spiteful glances at the man in black. He also started fiddling with his brown cape, moving the left flap from side to side. Despite the warmth, he kept the cape on, even though all of the other players had taken their coats off.

Nathaniel was about ready to retire and had stepped toward the doorway when the trouble began.

"Well, you've cleaned me out, Tyler," Clancy declared, throwing his last hand on the table in disgust.

"You play poorly," Tyler stated. He used only his left hand to rake in his winnings.

"You play well," Clancy responded, leaning forward. "Perhaps too well."

The other men suddenly pushed back from the table, giving Tyler and Clancy plenty of space.

"Be very careful."

"Don't threaten me, you dandy," Clancy spat. "I say you play too well."

Nathaniel could almost feel the tension in the room. The other players seemed scarcely to be breathing, as if they were waiting for a great and terrible event to transpire. They weren't to be disappointed.

Tyler placed his left arm on the table, a slow, deliberate, almost delicate gesture. His right hand was once again out of sight in his lap, a fact fraught with significance for all of the players except the irate Clancy, to whom he addressed his next words in a low, hard tone. "Say your meaning straight out."

"I say you cheat."

The players were now statues, rooted to their chairs, their unblinking eyes on the protagonists in the unfolding drama.

"You have insulted my integrity, sir, and I demand satisfaction," Tyler stated.

"I'll bet you do," Clancy said, and laughed, a short, brittle sound, an insult in itself.

"Name the time and the place."

Both thrilled and secretly appalled, Nathaniel listened to the challenge being issued in amazement. Tyler wanted a duel! He knew all about dueling, about the code of last resort for any offended gentleman, but he had never been privileged to witness one. Famous duelists were constantly making headlines. Only two years previously, Henry Clay and John Randolph had engaged in a much-publicized event. Clay, the Secretary of State, had challenged Senator Randolph after the latter had insulted Clay on the Senate floor. Their duel had prompted countless snide remarks and crude jokes because neither man had scored a hit. Clay had sent his shot through Randolph's coat, and the Senator had then elevated his pistol and fired into the air.

"Right here and now," Clancy replied angrily, rising to his full height.

"As the offended party, I claim the choice of weapons," Tyler said.

"Choose whatever you like. I'll be waiting outside," Clancy declared. He stalked from the room like a grizzly bear storming from its cave to do battle.

"Don't trust him, Adam," one of the other players remarked the moment Clancy was gone.

"No," chimed in another. "He's too treacherous."

Tyler stood, his forehead knit in thought. "Renfrew, will you kindly be my second?"

"Gladly, Adam," responded a white-haired man attired in a brown suit.

"My dueling pistols are in my room," Tyler said. "Would you fetch them for me?"

"Certainly." Renfrew hastily departed.

Tyler squared his shoulders and strode from the room, trailed by the remaining players, each man somber and reserved.

Enthralled, Nathaniel followed them, watching Tyler the entire time, marveling at the man's courage. The owner of the inn appeared and remonstrated with Tyler to call the duel off, but the man in black ignored the plea. The news was spreading rapidly, and patrons were flocking to the spacious green bordering the front of the establishment. As he emerged into the bright sunlight and squinted, Nathaniel spied Clancy waiting in the center of the green, standing next to his discarded cape, a large knife in a sheath in plain sight on his left hip.

Tyler waited for his second to return bearing a large black case, then both men walked out to Clancy.

Nathaniel moved through the crowd to obtain a clear view, and watched as Tyler and Clancy exchanged words. He wondered if Tyler was offering the big man a chance to select a second. Whatever the import, Clancy declined and pointed at the black case, saying something that made Tyler clench his fists in anger. The pistols were promptly distributed and the duelists aligned themselves back to back.

"This is horrible," a woman standing nearby remarked. "Someone should put a stop to this."

"If you believe it's horrible, don't look," advised a man dressed in breeches and a white shirt.

Nathaniel tried to take the measure of Clancy. The big man had impressed him as being an uncouth lout, but now he wasn't so positive. Clancy's clothes, while not as refined as Tyler's, were of good quality and clean, his black boots polished.

Renfrew carried the pistol case from the dueling field. He turned and called out, "At the count of three you will proceed ten paces, then face your opponent and fire."

Tyler and Clancy were immobile, each with his right hand next to his chest and his pistol pointing skyward.

"One," Renfrew cried.

A hush fell over the spectators, none of whom averted their eyes.

"Two."

A squirrel in an oak tree off to the right chitterred loudly, apparently peeved at all the noise.

"Three!" Renfrew shouted.

Transfixed by the tableau, Nathaniel saw the two duelists begin to pace. Tyler took measured treads, but Clancy moved swiftly, and the man in black had only gone eight steps when his adversary abruptly wheeled, raised his pistol, and fired.

The booming retort produced a cloud of gunsmoke, and simultaneous with the discharge Tyler stumbled forward as if slapped by an unseen hand. He recovered his balance, steadied himself, and pivoted.

Clancy took one look, saw his doom reflected in Tyler's visage, and threw the pistol to the grass. He whipped his knife from its sheath and charged, bellowing inarticulately at the top of his lungs, as if his maniacal yells could accomplish what his aim had not.

Tyler never hurried. He elevated his pistol slowly, he took aim slowly, and when Clancy had only five yards to cover, he squeezed the trigger slowly.

The ball struck Clancy squarely in the forehead and burst out the rear of his cranium, splattering blood and brains every which way, rocking the big man on his heels for a moment before he toppled over with an incredibly puzzled expression, as if his passage into eternity constituted a perplexing mystery.

Before Clancy hit the ground Renfrew and others were hastening to Tyler's side. After firing, the man in black doubled over and staggered, and he would have fallen if his second had not reached him and provided support.

"Disgusting," commented the matron who had offered the earlier observation.

Nathaniel glanced at her, surprised she had stayed to witness the duel. She gazed at the dead man for several seconds, smacked her lips distastefully, and hurried into the inn.

Renfrew and four others were transporting Tyler inside, holding him as still as they could. A bright red stain had formed on Tyler's shirt, a stain that was spreading.

Upset by the unjust outcome, Nathaniel looked at the man in black as the party passed him. Tyler's face was pale, but his eyes were alert and they focused on Nathaniel. A reassuring smile creased the man's thin lips, and then he was past and being carried inside.

"So much for Noah Clancy," remarked a bystander, an elderly man in the garb of a farmer.

"He always was a braggart and a bully," said another.

"Who wants to bury him?" asked a third.

"I will," offered the farmer. "He's not a fit sight for children to see with his brains oozing out like they are."

Nathaniel lingered at the inn for several hours, waiting to hear the prognosis of a doctor who had been urgently summoned from a small town close by. He listened to other patrons relating the duel again and again and again, disgusted by their callous disregard of the man who might be dying upstairs. All they were interested in were the gory details. He sat in a corner, drinking an ale, listening to them chatter, and came to the conclusion they were the worst flock of vultures he had ever seen.

Only when the doctor announced that Tyler would live did Nathaniel walk to the stable and collect his horses. In 20 minutes he was back on the road, his mind preoccupied with thoughts of dying and death, of justice and honor, and in such a frame of mind he finally arrived at his destination.

Chapter Four

St. Louis.

In 1764 a pair of French fur traders established a trading post on the west bank of the Mississippi River, just to the south of its junction with another mighty river, the Missouri. One of the Frenchmen decided to name the post after Louis IX, a French king who was made a saint, and thus St. Louis had its humble beginnings.

Located in territory originally claimed by the Spanish, St. Louis officially came under French jurisdiction when Spain ceded the region to France.

The transfer gravely alarmed President Thomas Jefferson. The French made plans to send troops to take possession of the territory, and President Jefferson became worried that they would not honor the agreement the U.S. had worked out with Spain concerning the city of New Orleans far to the south. American farmers and trappers who lived west of the Appalachian Mountains shipped their produce and goods by river down to New Orleans. If the French refused to continue the arrangement, untold economic hardships would result.

President Jefferson sent a delegation to France under orders
to make a reasonable offer to purchase New Orleans and the
Floridas. When the delegation tendered their proposal, they
were astounded by the reaction. The French not only agreed
to sell New Orleans, but *all of the territory the Spaniards
had ceded over.* So, for the sum of approximately $15
million, the United States doubled its size and acquired the
city of St. Louis in 1803.

And what a city it was.

Despite all the news reports and stories Nathaniel had read
about the frontier, he was unprepared for the raw, bustling
scene that blossomed before his astonished eyes as he entered
St. Louis on the morning of April 29. First to attract his
attention were the scores of steamboats and barges on the
Mississippi River, enough to almost rival the harbor of New
York on any given day. Grogshops and dozens of taverns
literally lined the waterfront area, and rivermen, fur trappers,
wagoners, and other rowdy types mingled in reckless
abandon twenty-four hours a day.

Rearing above the waterfront area were the private
residences of the wealthy and not-so-wealthy, a curious
mixture of French, American, and even Spanish architecture
that gave the city a distinctive quality all its own. The French
were still very much in evidence, with their regal homes,
Canadian horses, and curious little carts.

As Nathaniel rode into the heart of the city, he was
pleasantly surprised to discover there were several newspapers in operation. He even passed a bookstore, and
promised himself he would pay it a visit soon. There were
also a number of theaters where live plays were performed
daily. All in all, St. Louis was not anything like he had
expected the city would be.

The one element Nathaniel did find, and which he had
anticipated, was the abundant presence of firearms and other
weapons. Nearly every man carried either a rifle, a pistol,
a knife, or a sword. The few who didn't appeared, by their
clothing, to be upper-class city residents. Every frontiersman strolling the streets had his rifle and knife, as much a

part of his attire as his buckskins. Nathaniel had encountered
more and more firearms the farther west he traveled, and
now they seemed as indispensable for survival as the air itself.

Then there were the Indians. Nathaniel had not expected
to discover so many of the red men within the city limits,
and not until the third day of his stay did he learn the reason.
General William Clark, the same Clark who had journeyed
with Meriwether Lewis to the Pacific Ocean and back, was
now the Superintendent of Indian Affairs, and on a daily basis
large delegations of Indians arrived to confer with him.

Nathaniel took a room at The Bradley Hostelry, and put
up his animals at a stable. Once his belongings were safely
locked in his room, he took to the streets and ambled until
nightfall, drinking in the sights and sounds in the manner
of a starved man falling upon a side of roast beef. He couldn't
seem to get enough. There was a vibrant, dynamic, vigorous
atmosphere to St. Louis that thrilled his soul and enchanted
him beyond measure.

That night in his room, as he lay listening to the sounds
coming through his open window, he thought of New York
and compared the metropolis to St. Louis. The comparison
bothered him because he decided he liked St. Louis better.
Both were bustling beehives of human commerce, but St.
Louis was endowed with a robust, undisciplined vitality New
York City lacked. Perhaps, long ago, New York had
possessed the same frontier-style nobility, the same raw
passion for life exhibited by the denizens of St. Louis, but
not anymore. The people in St. Louis were living life to the
fullest; the people in New York merely going through the
motions while waiting to be planted six feet under.

Nathaniel spent the next day much as he had the first,
strolling through the city and familiarizing himself with the
location of various establishments and parts of town. He
found The Chouteau House, one of the premier hotels in all
of St. Louis, and wondered why Zeke would want to meet
him at such an expensive place. He opted to stay at The
Bradley Hostelry to conserve his funds.

Several hours that afternoon were spent browsing through

the delightfully large collection of books lining the shelves at the bookstore. There were bibles, of course, and cookbooks galore. There was a copy of *The History of the Expedition of Captains Lewis and Clark*, edited by Nicholas Biddle, which he was almost tempted to buy. There was a reprint edition of John Marshall's *Life of George Washington* that he found interesting. But by far the books that fascinated him the most were those by James Fenimore Cooper. He had already read Cooper's *The Pioneers*, published in 1823, and enjoyed the tale of the frontiersman Natty Bumppo immensely. Now he found *The Pilot*, a sea novel, and joys of joys, the next novel in the Bumppo saga, *The Last of the Mohicans*. Billed as an outstanding romance of the wilds, the story actually depicted Leatherstocking, as Bumppo was known, at an earlier age, embroiled in battles with the Iroquois. Nathaniel purchased the book and returned to his room. That night he ate a hearty meal and retired early.

For three days Nathaniel spent the daylight hours venturing about St. Louis and the evening hours reading *The Last of the Mohicans*. He made the acquaintance of the owner of The Bradley Hostelry, and of several other folks staying there, and during casual conversations learned more particulars about St. Louis and its history. Mr. Bradley warned him to avoid the taverns and grogshops if he valued his life. St. Louis, it turned out, was infested with the same blight as New York. Cutthroats and thieves prowled the streets after dark. There had even been several kidnappings of affluent citizens, who were returned after a suitable ransom was paid. Nathaniel was astonished to learn that the city did not have a regular police force.

On the morning of May 4 he hurried to The Chouteau House and inquired about his uncle, but no one named Ezekiel King had taken a room. Disappointed, he walked about the general vicinity for several hours, then returned. Again the clerk at the desk informed him that his uncle had not arrived. Troubled by the fact he might have traveled so far for nothing, Nathaniel walked aimlessly until midday. He checked once more, and once again had his hopes dashed.

"You should call again at five o'clock," the desk clerk suggested. "Few travelers like to be on the road at night, and if your uncle intends to register today he'll probably be here by then."

"Thank you," Nathaniel responded. He returned to his room and finished his book, then paced nervously until half past four, reflecting on the consequences if Zeke should fail to show as promised. He winced at the mere thought of going back to New York City empty-handed, convinced he would become the laughingstock of his family. Not only that, but Adeline might well give him the cold shoulder after he failed to deliver on all the promises he had made her. Over and over the same question repeated itself in his mind: Where was Zeke?

Nathaniel hastened to The Chouteau House and learned, to his utter chagrin, that Ezekiel had not arrived.

The clerk nodded at several nearby maple chairs. "You're perfectly welcome to wait, if you like."

A rumble in Nathaniel's stomach reminded him that he had not eaten since morning. "Thank you, but I'll eat a meal and come back. By then he should be here."

"There's a tavern just around the corner called The Ark," the man recommended. "They serve fine hot meals."

"I don't know," Nathaniel said uncertainly.

"They have an excellent reputation, I can assure you."

"Why not?" Nathaniel said with a shrug. "I'll eat there and see you in an hour."

"If your uncle should show up, I'll inform him you've been here."

"Thank you," Nathaniel said, expressing his gratitude, and left. He found the tavern easily, and took a seat in the corner, then ordered a meal of chicken and corn bread. He hardly paid attention to the raucous drinkers, so concerned was he about his uncle, and consequently he experienced considerable surprise when a man abruptly took a seat at his table.

"Hello, there, good sir," the intruder said congenially, with just the slightest trace of a slur to his words, a broad smile on his oval face.

"Hello," Nathaniel automatically responded, the last forkful of chicken halfway to his lips. "May I help you?"

The man wore a fashionable black suit, a fur-collared cape, and an expensive beaver hat. Held in his left hand was a half-empty glass of whiskey. "I saw you sitting over here by yourself and thought you might be inclined to accept some companionship," he said.

"I'm not staying," Nathaniel said, and slid the fork into his mouth.

The other shrugged. "Well, no matter. I simply wanted to share a few drinks and conversation. Never let it be said that Joseph Lowe stays where he's not wanted," he declared and started to rise.

Aware he had unconsciously offended the stranger, and rating the man as a harmless drunk, Nathaniel set down his fork and said, "Hold on, Mr. Lowe. I don't mean to be stand-offish. I have a few minutes to share a drink with you."

Lowe beamed and faced around. "How kind of you. The drink will be on me. What are you having?"

"I could use another ale."

"Then ale it shall be," Lowe said, and bellowed for service. He gave the order and sat back in his chair. "I didn't catch your name?"

"King. Nathaniel King. My friends call me Nate."

"Pleased to meet you, Nate. I haven't seen you in here before, and I know most of the regulars."

"I'm new to St. Louis," Nathaniel divulged. "I've only been here a few days."

"And what do you think of our fair city?" Lowe inquired, and took a sip of whiskey.

"It's quite different from New York."

Lowe sat forward, all interest. "Is that where you're from, then? I've never been to New York City, but I've always wanted to see it. I was raised in Pittsburgh myself, but I haven't been home in many years."

"What do you do for a living, Mr. Lowe?"

"Call me Joe. I'm a speculator, Nate. Land, furs, trade

goods, you name it, I've dabbled in it at one time or another. What about yourself?''

''I was an accountant,'' Nathaniel said.

''Was?''

''Did I say was? I worked as an accountant in New York, and depending on how events develop here, I may be an accountant again after I return.''

''Ahhhh. So you're planning to go back?''

''Yes. Hopefully within a few months. Everything depends on my uncle.''

Lowe glanced around the tavern. ''Your uncle? Is he here with you?''

''Not yet. I'm supposed to meet him at The Chouteau House later.''

Lowe's eyebrows arched toward the smoke shrouded ceiling. ''The Chouteau House? This uncle of yours must be rich.''

''I don't know,'' Nathaniel replied. ''I haven't seen him in ten years.''

''He sent for you, did he?''

Nathaniel stared at the other man. ''Why, yes. How did you know?''

''Simple logic. Here's to your uncle,'' Lowe said, and swallowed some more whiskey.

Nathaniel gazed at the front window, noticing the gathering twilight. ''I should be leaving soon. My uncle might be there by now.''

''I should be leaving too. Why don't I walk with you? The Chouteau House is on the way to the residence I'm renting.''

''Fair enough,'' Nathaniel agreed, taking a shine to the friendly speculator. He paid his bill and followed Lowe out the door, then halted when the other man took a right. ''Where are you going, Joe? The Chouteau House is this way,'' he said, pointing to the left.

''This is a shortcut. Your way we have to go around the corner and down the block. My way there is an alley that takes us almost to the entrance of The Chouteau House,'' Lowe stated.

Nathaniel hesitated, wondering if he could rely upon the other man, until Lowe gave him a friendly smile and hurried on. Chiding himself for being unduly suspicious, Nathaniel trailed after the speculator until they came to a narrow alley. He entered on Lowe's heels, passing a stack of crates propped against the right-hand wall. Three strides farther a hard object jammed him in the spine and a harder voice declared, ''One word and you're a dead man.''

Chapter Five

As stark astonishment will eclipse reason, so instinct will eclipse both in a crisis, and such instinct has at times meant the difference between life and death for the person imperiled. Even as Nathaniel felt the object ram him in the back, an object he intuitively deduced to be a firearm and most likely a pistol, and even though he heard the gruff threat from his rear, he was about to react out of instinct and call out to his companion when Joseph Lowe did a most remarkable thing.

The alleged speculator suddenly whirled, a knife grasped in his right hand, and sneered at the youth. "You heard my friend, lad. Stand still or else."

Shock overcame whatever resistance Nathaniel might have offered, and he stood mute as Lowe pressed the knife against his abdomen and another man came around the left side holding a cocked pistol in his right hand.

"Let's see your money," Lowe directed.

"Money?" Nathaniel repeated, too dazed by the betrayal and abrupt turn of events to think clearly.

"Don't stall, boy!" Lowe snapped. "Your clothes hardly mark you as a pauper. You have a purse. I want it. Now."

Nathaniel sluggishly started to reach for his money in his inner pocket.

"Watch he doesn't pull on you!" warned the man with the gun, a weasel of a ruffian dressed in a gray coat and a green cap.

"This babe in the woods?" Lowe said contemptuously. "He won't resist."

The weasel snickered.

"In fact," Lowe went on, "I have half a mind to teach this lad a lesson he won't soon forget." He balled his left hand into a fist. "You should have stayed in New York, Nate. The East is a safe haven for pampered maggots like yourself. Out here only the strong survive."

Nathaniel's fingers closed on his money.

"Perhaps a broken nose will show you the error of your ways," Lowe stated, smirking.

At that juncture, as Lowe raised his fist to strike Nathaniel in the face, someone else spoke from the mouth of the alley, the words harsh and cracking like a whip. "And perhaps dying will teach you the error of yours."

Displaying lightning reflexes, the weasel pivoted toward the speaker, leveling his pistol as he turned, but as fast as he was, he wasn't fast enough. The thunderous boom of a large-caliber rifle was punctuated by the ball hitting the weasel in the right temple. The impact hurled the man from his feet to crash against the left-hand wall, where he collapsed in a heap, a neat hole marking the ball's entry point.

Lowe looked over Nathaniel's right shoulder, his eyes widening in alarm, and began to back away.

"Try me, cutthroat!" cried the newcomer in a resounding challenge, and the next moment a buckskin-clad figure rushed past Nathaniel, a gleaming hunting knife in his right hand.

Dumbfounded, his city-bred reflexes not equal to the occasion, Nathaniel could only gape as the two men closed. He caught a fleeting glimpse of his rescuer, a pantherish frontiersman attired in the typical garb of those who dwelt on the outskirts of civilization, and then the two men were feinting and thrusting, dodging and twisting, their blades weaving a glittering tapestry in the dusky air, the steel accenting the fading rays of the far-off setting sun that penetrated into the byways of the city.

Joseph Lowe fought with the ferocity of a cornered beast, but all his efforts were in vain. He tried every knife-fighting trick he knew, and each stab, each slash, was parried or evaded with bewildering ease.

Nathaniel saw the frontiersman press Lowe mercilessly, and then his rescuer, who wore a red cloth cap decorated with an odd length of swirling fur, sidestepped a frantic lunge and speared his knife into Lowe's chest.

Lowe stiffened and gasped, then stumbled backwards until he touched the wall, the hilt of the frontiersman's knife protruding from his ribs. He released his own knife and clutched at the hilt, but his limbs were too weak to extract the blade. His eyes wide, fear etched in his countenance, he gawked at his slayer. "You've killed me!" he cried.

"Take your medicine without whimpering, dog," the frontiersman said. "You've reaped your just desserts."

"Oh, God!" Lowe wailed, slipping downward slowly, blood trickling from the right corner of his mouth. "Oh, God!"

Both fascinated and horrified, Nathaniel watched the man die. He had hardly moved a muscle since entering the alley except to reach for his money, and now he realized his hand was still under his coat. He pulled it out and took a deep breath, dispelling the trance that held him. Hushed voices sounded to his rear and he glanced back, astounded to see over a dozen people.

"Help me!" Lowe whined. "Someone help me!"

The man in the buckskins walked over, took hold of his knife, and yanked it free, the blade dripping crimson over Lowe's clothes.

"No!" Lowe declared weakly, and made a sucking noise, as if he couldn't get enough air into his lungs.

Kneeling, the frontiersman looked Lowe in the eyes and started to wipe his knife clean on Lowe's coat. After a minute he stood and slid the hunting knife into a beaded sheath on his left hip.

Only then did Nathaniel gaze at his rescuer.

Like most mountain men and fur trappers who came from the distant plains and mountains to taste the sophisticated culture of St. Louis, this man radiated a raw vitality. His long brown hair, streaked with generous widths of gray, hung to below his shoulders. His blue eyes, as vivid as any mountain lake, regarded the world almost sternly, complementing his hawkish visage. From constant exposure to the sun and the elements, his skin had acquired a dark hue, nearly as dark as any Indian. His buckskins were beaded about the shoulders and down the seams. His moccasins were plain and worn. From the brown leather belt encircling his waist hung his knife and a bullet pouch.

"I want to thank you, sir, for saving my life," Nathaniel said.

A wry grin curled the mountain man's mouth, and he stared at Nathaniel with a curious expression, a mixture of relief and restrained mirth, before responding. "Do you now, Nate? That's nice to hear."

"How do you—" Nathaniel began, then focused on the red cap. A line from his uncle's letter rushed into his mind. "I'll be wearing the red so you know me." He impulsively stepped forward and placed his hands on the frontiersman's wide shoulders. "Ezekiel?"

The mountain man nodded and smiled. "Uncle Zeke to you."

Elated, Nathaniel felt himself taken in a bear hug and squeezed until he thought his back would break. He was abruptly released and inspected as if under a magnifying glass.

"By the Eternal, how you've grown!" Zeke declared heartily. "If that fellow at The Chouteau House hadn't given me a description, I'd never have known you."

"The desk clerk told you where to find me?"

Zeke nodded. "And you're fortunate I came straightaway instead of taking the time to unpack in my room." He glanced at the onlookers. "You let me handle this."

"Help me!" Lowe pleaded.

Nathaniel looked down at the robber, who was wheezing and moaning while more and more blood spurted from his mouth. Lowe returned the gaze with a pathetic, pleading countenance, silently imploring for aid beyond the power of any human agency to render.

"I'll put you out of your misery if you want," Zeke offered.

Lowe tried to focus on the frontiersman, but a fit of sputtering and coughing made him double over. He straightened, blubbered incoherently for several seconds, then suddenly stiffened and keeled over onto his right side, his blood-flecked mouth hanging open.

"Good riddance," Zeke said, and walked to the mouth of the alley. A large rifle was propped against the right-hand wall, and he scooped the gun into his arms and faced the growing crowd. "These men were attempting to rob my nephew," he announced, and pointed at the two corpses. "They were about to harm him when I arrived."

"Let me through! Let me through!" a man at the rear of the onlookers bellowed, and a moment later a portly gentleman dressed in a brown coat and breeches advanced to the forefront. His ruddy cheeks were accented by flared sideburns and prolific whiskers. He stared at the bodies in disapproval, then looked at the frontiersman.

Nathaniel tensed, anticipating trouble over the killings. In New York City, his uncle would be taken into custody and tossed into a jail until a trial could be convened. In St. Louis, where there was no police force, vigilante justice might prevail. To his surprise, the apparently distinguished citizen smiled and exclaimed happily, "Firebrand! Is it really you?"

"It's truly me, friend Osborne," Ezekiel responded.

"What brings you to these parts? We haven't seen you in, what, two years?"

"City life holds little attraction for a man who has learned to live in harmony with Nature," the frontiersman said solemnly.

"Ever the philosopher, eh?" Osborne replied good-naturedly, and glanced at Nathaniel. "Did I hear you say this is your nephew?"

"You did. Nathaniel King, my brother's son."

Osborne nodded. "I'm pleased to meet you, young man."

"My uncle did no wrong," Nathaniel said. "These ruffians were trying to take my money."

"So I gathered," Osborne responded. "Have no fear, Nathaniel. No one will hold these killings against your uncle. Those of us who have lived in St. Louis for a spell know your uncle well, and his word is widely respected."

"Osborne, I would be in your debt if you would see to it that these two scoundrels are disposed of properly," Zeke said.

"For you, Firebrand, anything," Osborne answered. "Will you be in town long?"

"No longer than necessary."

"Are you boarding in town?"

"The Chouteau House."

"Where else?" Osborne said, and chuckled. "I'll be around to visit you as soon as I can."

"We'll share a few drinks and talk over old times," Zeke proposed. He motioned for Nathaniel to come with him, and together they weaved through the crowd and departed.

"Where are you staying?" Zeke asked.

"The Bradley Hostelry," Nathaniel responded, staring at his uncle in awe, hardly able to believe they were reunited again.

"Let's fetch your belongings and move you in with me right away," Zeke said. "We have much to discuss."

"We certainly do," Nathaniel agreed, eager to keep the conversation going. He glanced at the length of grayish fur attached to the back of his uncle's cap. "Is that beaver fur?"

A burst of laughter erupted from the stout mountain man, and he shook his head vigorously. "I should say not, nephew. You have a lot to learn about the animals we'll encounter. Have you ever seen a beaver?"

"No," Nathaniel admitted.

"Have you ever laid eyes on a wolf?"

"No," Nathaniel replied again. "There are few wolves

left in New York. But I have seen paintings of wolves in books.''

''Then take a good look at my cap.''

Nathaniel complied, and after examining the fur for half a minute recognition dawned and he blurted out in amazement, ''It's a wolf tail!''

''Congratulations. Your lessons have begun.''

''But why would you wear a wolf tail on your head?''

''It's not that uncommon a practice,'' Zeke said. ''The *voyageurs* wear them quite often.''

''Who?''

''*Voyageurs*, nephew. Fur trappers. It's a French word.''

''Do you speak French?''

''A little. Out here it pays to learn as much as you can about everything.''

''But why a wolf tail?'' Nathaniel inquired out of curiosity, watching the unique adornment bob as his uncle walked.

''Because a mouse tail would look ridiculous,'' Zeke said with a grin.

Nathaniel had to laugh at the thought of a mouse tail on a hat. ''True.''

Ezekiel cradled his rifle in his arms and moved with a firm tread along the streets of the city, evidently knowing his way about, his sharp eyes constantly roving as he talked. ''There is a story behind this wolf tail. It belonged to old One Eye, the trickiest animal that ever lived. Some years back Shakespeare and I were trapping way up northwest of the Yellow Stone country. Something kept eating the beavers we caught along this one stream. In trap after trap we would find the beaver had been ripped to ribbons and partly devoured. This went on for a few weeks.'' He paused.

Enrapt in the story, Nathaniel hung on every word. His uncle possessed a natural flair for telling a tale, the consequences, most likely, of many an hour spent around a roaring campfire in the company of his friends. ''What did you do?''

''Shakespeare and I tried every ruse we knew to catch the culprit in the act, but nothing worked. We tried snares, double traps, even pits, but the beast helping itself to our catch was too crafty for us. We tried lying in hiding, but the animal always avoided us. Finally, we found a clear set of tracks at one of the kills and knew our nemesis was a wolf, which we had already conjectured. So we decided to dig a hole large enough for a man near one of the traps, and I went into the hole and waited."

"How long?"

"What? Oh, three days, I think."

"What did you eat? How did you survive?"

"I had a pouch of jerked meat with me," Zeke said, a twinkle in his eyes. "Anyway, on the third day this old wolf showed up. There was a beaver in the trap, so the wolf stalked close to it and pounced. Only then, when it was near the hole, did I see how big the beast was and discovered it had only one eye, the right. The left was as pale as the moon."

"And you shot him?"

"Not quite, nephew. I popped out of the hole, or tried to, but the dirt sides were too slippery and I fell on my face not two yards from old One Eye," Zeke related.

Nathaniel imagined how he would feel under such circumstances, and shuddered. "What happened then?"

Zeke looked at him. "What do you figure happened? Old One Eye was on me before I could move, his teeth bared, ready to tear me open."

"How did you kill it?" Nathaniel inquired, agog.

"I didn't. Old One Eye killed me," Zeke said, erupting in laughter and clapping his nephew on the shoulders.

They could have heard him all the way back in New York.

Chapter Six

Seated in his uncle's plush room in The Chouteau House, Nathaniel gazed at the vibrant man he remembered so well from his childhood and shook his head in amazement, thinking he must be dreaming. Zeke's timely arrival had saved his money, if not his life, and in spite of the gulf of years and distance since last they had seen one another, he felt a warm bond with the older man. He gazed at the luxurious accommodations and inquired, "Why do you prefer to stay here? Isn't it expensive?"

Ezekiel surveyed the room disdainfully. "Civilization is difficult enough to abide as it is. Why suffer in a hovel when you can live first-class?"

The remark reminded Nathaniel of the treasure. "You must be quite wealthy."

"You think so?"

"You hinted as much in your letter."

"My letter?" Zeke repeated, his forehead furrowing. "Oh, you mean the greatest treasure in the world?"

Nathaniel leaned toward the upholstered chair in which his uncle sat a few feet away. "What kind of treasure is it, Uncle

Zeke? Have you made a fortune in the fur trade? Did you find gold? What?''

The frontiersman's lips seemed to tighten slightly. ''Is that what brought you out here, Nate? The treasure?''

''I won't lie to you. The treasure is part of the reason I came west, but I also wanted to see you again.''

''I see,'' Ezekiel said slowly, and slouched in his chair. ''You want to be rich, I gather?''

''I *need* to become rich.''

''Explain,'' Zeke directed.

So Nathaniel did, spending the better part of an hour relating his relationship with Adeline, his choice of a career as an accountant, and his marriage prospects without the wealth Adeline required.

Ezekiel King rarely interrupted, venturing a few questions now and then, listening to his favorite nephew with an air of sadness about him. Toward the end of Nathaniel's discourse, when Nate mentioned how much Adeline loved him, Zeke had to feign a sudden interest in his moccasins to conceal the scowl that automatically twisted his mouth.

''Now you understand the reason I must acquire the money necessary to support Adeline in the manner to which she is accustomed,'' Nathaniel mentioned.

''I understand perfectly.''

''Do you really intend to share your treasure with me?'' Nathaniel queried eagerly.

''I do.''

Overjoyed, Nathaniel beamed and glanced around the room. ''This is great news! By August I can be in New York again, proposing to Adeline.''

Zeke pursed his lips thoughtfully for a moment. ''Perhaps not.''

''What?''

''I didn't bring my treasure with me.''

Nathaniel was stunned. ''You didn't?''

''I couldn't,'' Zeke said.

''But you wrote in your letter that you would share it with me.''

"And I will, but to see my treasure you must return with me to my cabin in the Rocky Mountains."

The proposal shocked Nathaniel. He sank back in his chair, envisioning the dangers of a trek into the wild regions of the virtually unexplored Rocky Mountains. The risks were not his major concern. Rather, he was worried by the prospect of losing his life before he could return to civilization and his beloved Adeline.

"Does the idea bother you?" Ezekiel inquired.

"I was under the misimpression you were bringing your treasure to St. Louis," Nathaniel stated.

"I would if I could, nephew. But it would be impossible to transport such a treasure all the way from the Rockies to here."

"Couldn't you have brought a portion of it?"

"A portion would not be enough to satisfy you."

Nathaniel placed his elbows on his knees and rested his head in his hands. "I don't know what to do, Uncle Zeke. How long would such a trip take?"

"Months, at the very mimimum."

"How *many* months?"

"I doubt if you would be able to make it back here before winter sets in, so you would be obliged to wait until next spring. Ten months to a year, at least."

"A year?" Nathaniel exclaimed, and surged out of his chair. "I can't be away from Adeline for a year!"

"If she's truly the woman for you, she'll wait."

"But a *year!*" Nathaniel said, sitting down dejectedly.

Ezekiel sighed and stood. He crossed to a polished dresser and opened a drawer. "I'm sorry, Nate. I had no idea this would upset you so."

"I came so far," Nathaniel said softly.

"For which I'm grateful." Zeke removed a small leather pouch from the drawer and sat down again.

"My parents would be furious," Nathaniel predicted, and looked at his uncle. "Say, why haven't you asked any questions about Father or Mother or my brothers?"

"Your father and I parted ways years ago. Tell me. Does

he still refuse to talk about me to anyone?''

"Yes."

Zeke shrugged. "There. You see? As far as your father and mother are concerned, I might as well be dead. And your older brothers and I were never as close as the two of us. You were always special to me, Nate. And to be quite honest, you're the only relative I give a damn about.''

"Since you're being honest, so will I," Nathaniel said. "If you share your treasure with me, I intend to share with them. They're my family, after all.''

"I would expect no less from you," Zeke said, and smiled. "Here. Take a gander at this.'' He flipped the small pouch into the air.

Nathaniel deftly caught the pouch and placed it in his lap. He loosened the drawstring and upended the contents into his left palm, his eyes widening when out tumbled seven golden nuggets, each the size of his thumbnail, each glittering in the light. "Are these what I think they are?''

Ezekiel nodded. "Gold. From the Rocky Mountains.''

"And you have more?''

"The Rocky Mountains are filled with gold. The Spaniards mined the region extensively years ago. I've come across several of their diggings and arrastra ruins in my travels.''

Nathaniel glanced up from the nuggets. "Why haven't there been any reports in the newspapers?''

"There will be," Zeke said, and gazed out the window at the lights of St. Louis. A melancholy settled upon him and he spoke in a low tone. "Eventually the word will become common knowledge. Now, only a few men such as myself are aware of the riches waiting to be plucked from the land to the west. I know a trapper who has a cabin situated near a creek where the bed is dotted with nuggets. You can walk along the bank and see them sparkle. But he hasn't touched them.''

Incredulous, Nathaniel straightened. "Why not?''

"Gold doesn't interest him.''

"Is he in his right mind?''

Ezekiel chuckled and nodded. "As sane as they come.

Gold is not the most valuable commodity in life, nephew.''

"It is to anyone with intelligence," Nathaniel said. "Look at yourself. You know how to use your gold wisely. You're staying at the best establishment in all of St. Louis.''

A minute elasped before the frontiersman spoke, during which he regarded his nephew critically.

"Is something the matter?" Nathaniel inquired.

"Nothing that will not be remedied in due course.''

Nathaniel began replacing the nuggets into the pouch. "How much time will I have to decide whether to go with you?''

"I'll need to know tomorrow.''

A gleaming nugget almost dropped from Nathaniel's fingers. "Tomorrow? So soon? Surely you jest.''

Zeke shook his head. "I leave for the mountains the day after tomorrow. You're welcome to come with me, if you like. If not, feel free to take those few nuggets with you to reimburse you for the expenses of your journey.''

"But the treasure!"

"To see the treasure, you must see the Rockies.''

"I'm at a loss to know what to do," Nathaniel confessed.

Ezekiel rose and moved to the window. He clasped his hands behind his broad back and contemplated the flurry of activity below: the carriages, carts, and wagons going to and fro, the individuals hastening home from work or en route to their favorite tavern or other night spot, and the many horses ridden by men from all walks of life. "I can sympathize with you, nephew. A decade ago I was in the same boat you are in.''

"In what way, Uncle Zeke?''

"I had a similar decision to make. Whether to stay in New York or venture out west, whether to continue in the rut I was in or to take my life into my own hands and forge my own destiny.''

"Why did you come out west?''

"Has your father told you much about my early life?" Zeke asked, still gazing at the street.

"No. Whenever I've tried to talk about you, he always

changed the subject."

"How typical of Tom. He never could understand my reason for leaving. We argued for weeks before my departure and he accused me of abandoning the family, of losing my proper perspective. I'm five years older than your father, and yet he had the gall to say I was acting like a ten-year-old."

Nathaniel relaxed in the chair, listening attentively, intensely curious about his uncle's past. "You weren't married, were you?"

"No," Ezekiel said. "I almost married once, when I was twenty. Rebecca was her name, and she was the loveliest woman I ever laid eyes on. We courted and made plans to raise our own children. I was in business with Tom at the time, helping him launch the construction business." He paused, his shoulders slumping. "And then my world fell apart. Rebecca died."

"What happened?"

"Consumption. Can you believe it? A healthy young woman like her and she died from consumption."

"Consumption can strike anyone at any age," Nathaniel noted, then felt awkward over having made such a trite observation.

Ezekiel did not speak for a while, and when he did he seemed to be talking from a great distance, not literally but emotionally. "Rebecca's death crushed me. For years I drifted through life, going through the motions without bothering about the meaning of anything I did. I worked hard, putting in long hours, only because I had nothing else to do. Try as I might, I could not bring myself to court another woman. Rebecca was the only woman I've ever loved."

Nathaniel said nothing.

"I had often considered the notion of leaving New York, of heading for the frontier. I wanted to view the wonders of the unexplored lands for myself, but I kept concocting excuses for why I shouldn't go. When I'd bring the subject up to Tom, he'd always ridicule it as juvenile thinking." Zeke sighed. "I lost count of how many hours I spent reading about

Lewis and Clark and other explorers. I would often spend my days off in the woods, and I fancied myself as a bit of an outdoorsman.''

"And one day you just up and took off?''

"Yes. One day I cut out for the frontier. I had saved a fair sum of money with which to outfit myself, and I joined a group of settlers who were heading westward. This was in 1818, and we arrived in Missouri about the same time the territory was admitted to the Union. The fur trade is the state's most important industry, and I naturally became a trapper for the American Fur Company. That's how I met Shakespeare.''

"You mentioned him earlier. Who is he?''

"My best friend in all the world. Shakespeare McNair.''

"What a strange name.''

Ezekiel laughed. "Many of the men who live on the frontier have acquired unusual sobriquets. Shakespeare got his because he likes to quote Shakespeare all the time.''

"You wrote home once, didn't you?''

"Yes, about nine years ago. I told Tom about my employment with the American Fur Company and praised the new lands I had seen. I never received an answer.''

"I think Father tossed your letter out.''

"That would be Tom,'' Zeke said sadly. "Oh, well. He always was a stubborn cuss.''

"What happened next?''

"I trapped for the American Fur Company for two years, and then Shakespeare and I decided to become free trappers. We headed for the Rocky Mountains, and except for occasional treks to St. Louis and elsewhere, that's where I've made my home.''

"Did you ever have the desire to visit New York?''

The frontiersman turned. "Never.''

Nathaniel performed some mental calculations. "Only ten of your forty-eight years have been spent on the frontier, and yet you seem at home in the wilds.''

Zeke's eyes bored into his nephew's. "Out here, Nate, either you adjust and adapt or you die. It's as simple as that.''

"That man Osborne, where do you know him from?"

"I met him on the way to Missouri. We've been friends ever since."

"Why did he call you Firebrand?"

Ezekiel chuckled. "Think nothing of it. Firebrand is a nickname Osborne bestowed upon me when we had a slight misunderstanding with a band of Indians who refused to allow our wagons to pass through their territory unless we gave them two thirds of our horses and twelve rifles."

"What happened?"

A cloud seemed to descend over Ezekiel's countenance. "The red rascals didn't get one horse or rifle."

Nathaniel decided to ask Osborne for the particulars if ever the opportunity presented itself. "Here, Uncle," he said, and returned the pouch of gold nuggets.

"I'll be turning in early," Zeke announced. "I traveled long and hard to reach St. Louis today, and after that fracas in the alley I'm a mite tuckered out."

"Do you mind if I stay up for a while? I have a lot to think about," Nathaniel commented.

"Stay awake as long as you like, Nate," Zeke said, depositing the pouch in the dresser drawer. "You have the most important decision of your life to make."

"If I decide to stay, I'll have to write my family and Adeline and explain the situation."

"Go right ahead," Zeke responded, moving to the side of the bed. He noticed a book lying beside his nephew's open bags, which they had placed on the bed when they first arrived. "What's this?" he asked, and scooped the book into his right hand.

"*The Last of the Mohicans.*"

"James Fenimore Cooper," Zeke said thoughtfully. "I've heard of him. Isn't he the one who writes about Leatherskin?"

"That's Leatherstocking, Uncle Zeke."

"Whatever. Some of my friends have read his other books. They say he writes well."

"You're welcome to read it if you wish."

"Thanks. Perhaps I will. It has been a while since I've

read anything, and in New York I read all the time." Zeke wagged the book in his hand. "Oh, well. Reading always was a substitute for experience."

Nathaniel watched his uncle prepare the bed. He envisioned his darling Adeline, far, far away in New York, and he closed his eyes. A single question repeated itself over and over in his mind: *What am I going to do?*

Chapter Seven

What choice did he have?

If he wanted to please Adeline—and pleasing her was more important to him than breathing—he had to accumulate the fortune he would need to support her lavish style of life. He considered returning to New York City and going to work for her father, but the prospect of spending years in the mercantile profession did not appeal to him, especially as every moment would be spent under the watchful eyes of her stern father. If wealthy he must be, then he would acquire the wealth by his own initiative and not be dependent on another man for his livelihood. For the sake of Adeline, he convinced himself, he must make the journey to the Rocky Mountains and obtain his share of Ezekiel's treasure.

But there was another reason, a reason he scarcely admitted, although at the back of his mind he realized the truth. The idea of heading farther west, into the rugged, unmapped regions of the unknown, appealed to his adventurous spirit. He had supreme confidence in his Uncle Zeke, and believed that Ezekiel would see him safely through any ordeal. In addition, he kept thinking about the adventures of Leatherstocking, and he wondered if he just might, perhaps, have an adventure or two of his own before he saw St. Louis again.

Few men can resist the siren song of love and the dictates of the heart. Even fewer can resist the overpowering drives of human nature. So it was that with a clear conscience and a happy, expectant soul Nathaniel informed his uncle of his decision at first light the next morning. "I've decided to go with you."

Ezekiel bounded out of bed and pranced around like a panther dancing a jig, clapping his hands and cackling as if at a great triumph. After a couple of minutes he halted abruptly and beamed down at Nathaniel. "Nephew, you will never regret your decision. This I can promise you."

"I'll believe that when I see the light in Adeline's eyes as I show her my gold."

Zeke straightened, suddenly sober. "Of course. The gold. Well, we should have breakfast and commence outfitting you for the trip."

"I can buy my own supplies," Nathaniel offered.

"Nonsense. Since this was my idea, and since I'm the one with the gold nuggets, I insist on paying for your gear and clothes."

"Clothes? What's wrong with the clothes I already own?"

Zeke laughed and glanced at the apparel in question, draped over the back of a nearby chair. "Those clothes are all right for city life, even for travel east of the Mississippi, but you'll need far better if you want to be comfortable beyond the frontier."

"But I paid good money for them in New York," Nathaniel persisted.

"New York clothes are mainly for dandies and squires who don't know beans about life outdoors. Trust me," Zeke said.

"I trust you," Nathaniel replied, still not entirely convinced of his need for new clothing.

Ezekiel noticed and placed his hands on his hips. "What are your trousers made of?"

"Wool."

"And your coat?"

"Wool."

"And your hat?"

"Wool. But what does that matter?"

"If the Eternal had meant for man to wear wool, He would have made us sheep," Zeke stated. "Wool is fine for city uses or on a farm, but out west, where you'll be subjected to the worst weather Nature can throw at you, where you can start out hot at the base of a mountain and be in ten feet of snow by the time you reach the summit, you want buckskins. Wool can shrink, nephew. Wool falls to pieces after a month or two of mountain living. Buckskins do not."

"Are you saying I need buckskins?" Nathaniel inquired, secretly pleased by the idea.

"Buckskins and much more."

"Then I guess I'm in your hands."

"Have you ever fired a gun?"

The unexpected question gave Nathaniel pause. He almost lied, but changed his mind. "No."

"Not *ever*?"

"Never."

Ezekiel shook his head and clucked. "What has my brother done to you?"

"Don't blame my father. Why should I have fired a gun when there are no hostile Indians in New York and all the food we ate could be bought at the market or the butcher?"

"I can see your point, but it's still a tragedy when a boy has grown to manhood and hasn't learned to fire a rifle. How is a youngster to learn the qualities of self-reliance and independence if he doesn't know how to feed and clothe himself? If this is what cities do to our youth, then they are more vile than I imagined. Cities breed slaves to civilization, nephew, and produce men and women who are in bondage to the mercantile and the slaughterhouse."

"I never gave the matter much thought."

"I have. Did you know your father and I hunted quite avidly when we were young?"

Nathaniel's surprise showed. "No, I didn't. We don't even have a gun in the house now. He won't allow them."

"Probably because they remind him of me," Zeke speculated. He walked to the south wall, where he had propped his rifle, and held the gun out. "Do you know what this is, Nate?"

"A rifle."

"More than a rifle, nephew. It's a Hawken. The best damn gun ever made, and they're made right here in St. Louis by Jacob and Samuel Hawken, friends of mine. Mine is a .60-caliber, and I've knocked down a buffalo at two hundred yards with it."

"Two hundred yards?" Nathaniel repeated skeptically.

"One day maybe you'll do even better."

"Will you teach me to shoot yours?"

"No. I'll teach you to shoot yours."

Nathaniel came out of the bed so fast he stubbed his right foot on the night table. "You'll buy me a rifle of my very own?"

"That's the general idea, nephew. We'd be in a sorry state if two grizzlies decided that we were their tasty supper and we only had one rifle between us."

"My own rifle," Nathaniel said softly, thrilled.

Ezekiel smiled and nodded at his nephew's clothes. "Get your britches on, Nate. We have a lot to do today if we hope to leave this serpent's den tomorrow."

Nathaniel would always remember that day as long as he lived, the first of many memorable days he would experience in the months ahead. He followed his uncle from establishment to establishment like an eager young puppy anxious to please its new master, listening to tales about Zeke's years on the frontier, tales that prompted him, more than once, to gaze at the western horizon with longing in his eyes.

Ezekiel went on a buying spree, not only for the equipment and supplies his nephew would need, but for provisions he required to restock the depleted stores at his remote cabin. He paid for most of the items with cash or coin, although on two occasions, when he bought buckskins for Nathaniel and when he purchased three pistols, two for the youth and one for himself, he paid with a few of his gold nuggets.

The buckskins were obtained at a store named Farber's, where the owner, a former trapper himself, specialized in goods for those engaged in the fur trade. One of his employees was quite skilled at constructing custom-made garments from the many skins and furs the owner received in barter. Upon learning, however, that the employee had more work than he could handle and that buckskins for Nathaniel would take four days to be stitched together, Zeke became annoyed at the prospect of staying in St. Louis beyond his alloted departure date. The owner came to their rescue by suggesting Nathaniel try on one of the dozen or so sets of buckskins that had never been claimed by their purchasers and were gathering dust on a shelf at the back of the store.

To Nathaniel's delight, he found buckskins that fit him, although rather loosely. Once he donned the soft, pliable deerskin garments, including a pair of moccasins that rose almost to his knees, he felt as if he were a new man. He ran his fingers over the dressed deerskin again and again, thinking he should pinch himself to see if he was dreaming.

Ezekiel studied his nephew for a minute, then commented, "Not a bad fit. We'll make you another set after we reach my cabin."

"I don't know if I can thank you enough."

"Shucks, Nate. We're just getting started."

Next Nathaniel acquired a wide leather belt to which he attached a hunting knife sporting a 12-inch blade in a plain sheath. His uncle helped him select a powder horn, which he hung over his left shoulder by means of a thin strap, angling it across his chest to ride high on his right hip, within easy reach. He also obtained a large pouch for his bullets, bullet mould, ball screw, wiper, and awl. As he was adjusting the bullet pouch under the powder horn, his uncle approached bearing a red and black Mackinaw coat.

"Try this on for size," Zeke said.

"A red coat?" Nathaniel responded.

"What's wrong with it?"

"Won't Indians and game be able to spot me too easily?"

"Beaver, bear, and deer don't care if you're wearing red, blue, or purple. With a Hawken in your hands, it doesn't matter if the game spots you or not."

"But what about the Indians?"

"I've been wearing a red cap for years and I still have my scalp," Zeke said, then surreptitiously winked at Eugene Farber, who stood nearby. "But if it worries you, just remember the best method for getting out of Indian trouble. It never fails."

"What is it?"

"Run like hell."

After trying on the Mackinaw coat, which fit perfectly, Nathaniel added the garment to his growing collection. His uncle continued to buy provisions, some of which they were to pick up the next day on their way out of St. Louis. There were spare flints and locks, 200 pounds of lead, 60 pounds of powder, a few spare knives, two pipes and tobacco, and much more.

From Farber's they went to a small shop where Ezekiel bought the three pistols. He stuck two of them under his nephew's belt, stood back, studied the pistols and the knife, and nodded. "You look green, but I can guarantee no one will try to rob you now."

Their last visit of the day was to the Hawken brothers, Jacob and Samuel, who were kept busy meeting the great demand for their superb rifles. Both men were soft-spoken and dedicated to their craft. They greeted Ezekiel warmly and listened to his request for a rifle for Nathaniel.

"What caliber would you prefer?" Samuel inquired, scrutinizing Nathaniel closely. "Since it's his first plains rifle, I would recommend a .40-caliber."

"If a man is going to carry a rifle, he should carry one that will stop any brute or hostile he meets," Zeke declared. "Give Nate a .60-caliber."

The Hawken brothers glanced at one another, and Jacob shrugged and said, "As you wish. Would you care for us to instruct him in its use?"

"Go right ahead."

Into Nathaniel's tingling hands was delivered a heavy .60-caliber Hawken. He hefted the rifle, admiring the smooth 34-inch octagonal barrel, the sturdy stock with its cresent-shaped butt plate, the low sights, and the percussion lock.

Samuel Hawken smiled. "This rifle will serve you in good stead, young man. But you must always remember that a rifle is only as good as the man who uses it. A rifle is a tool, nothing more. Keep it clean and protect it from the elements, and you may find that it rewards you by saving your life."

"I'll take good care of it," Nathaniel promised.

Samuel nodded knowingly. "I expect you will. I can recall how I felt about my first rifle. Now allow me to show you how to load and fire it."

For 20 minutes Nathaniel was instructed in the proper use of a plains rifle by the two brothers, who seemed to derive considerable enjoyment from the teaching. They showed him how to load the ball, how to use the ramrod properly, and gave him tips on priming. They advised him that there would be a slight kick to the .60-caliber, a negligible recoil that would not hamper a fast reload in an emergency. Nathaniel thanked them for their kindness and walked out the front door feeling strangely euphoric.

"We'll need to find a cover for your rifle," Zeke mentioned as they headed for The Chouteau House. "You'll want to keep it dry and handy at all times once we're on the prairie."

Staring at his new gun, his forehead creased as he remembered the duel between Tyler and Clancy, Nathaniel voiced a question. "Have you killed a *lot* of men, Uncle Zeke?"

"Killing is part and parcel of frontier life. You might never need to kill a white man, but as sure as the sun rises and sets every day you'll have to kill an Indian or two," the frontiersman said. "And yes, I've killed my fair share. Why?"

"Oh, nothing."

"Don't you think you could shoot another human being?"

"I don't know."

"When the time comes to do it, you'll do it."

Nathaniel glanced at his uncle. "How can you be so certain?"

"Because when the time comes, it will either be you or the other fellow, whether white or Indian. And when someone is about to knife you, or scalp you, or put a ball in your head, you'll find that the Good Lord put a sense of self-preservation in us for a reason. Only a fool or a weakling rolls over and dies without giving a good account of himself. On the frontier and in the unexplored regions it's often kill or be killed."

"I don't want to die," Nathaniel said softly.

"Who does?"

Chapter Eight

Ezekiel and Nathaniel King rode out of St. Louis on the morning of May 6 under a sunny sky and with a light breeze from the northwest to cool their faces. Nathaniel rode his mare, Zeke a roan gelding, and both led pack horses loaded with their provisions. They followed the winding course of the Missouri River along a well-used dirt road. The state of Missouri had been admitted to the Union in 1821 as a slave state, and there were already 70,000 people living in the westernmost frontier of the nation.

Nathaniel soaked up the sights and sounds with a keen relish. They were not in any danger from the Indians in Missouri, who had signed a peace treaty with the U.S. government some years back, so he could relax and enjoy the trip. He noticed that his uncle seemed to be in a hurry; they only spent two hours in Independence. Eight days after they left St. Louis they came to the farthest outpost of civilization, Westport Landing, near the point where the Missouri and Kansas Rivers met. The trading post there, founded by a Frenchman in 1821, did a bustling business with trappers, hunters, and Indians, and served as a stopping-off point for the traders from Missouri en route to Santa Fe to do business with the Spanish.

Two hours after they arrived, an incident occurred that Nathaniel would have reason to reflect on later. His uncle had selected a campsite to the southeast of the trading post, and they were busily engaged in bedding down for the night, when Nathaniel saw his uncle straighten and stare intently at three men who were riding toward the post. Puzzled, he looked at the riders, all three of whom were hulking, unkempt types attired in shabby buckskins. None of the men so much as glanced in their direction. He shrugged and went back to unfolding a blanket.

At first light they were packed and off, heading west across the rolling prairie, staying close to the Kansas River. In front of them stretched more than two million square miles of pristine wilderness.

Nathaniel cradled his rifle in the crook of his right arm and admired the scenery. Low grass covered the ground for as far as the eye could see, interspersed with colorful, beautiful flowers. Now and then they would come across a small brook that intersected the river. Cedar trees and others grew along the banks. Occasionally a large fish would leap out of the water and splash down again.

At midday Ezekiel called a halt. He dismounted and stood staring along their back trail for several minutes.

"Is something wrong?" Nathaniel asked.

Zeke frowned. "I'm the biggest fool who ever lived."

"I don't understand."

"By the Eternal, I should have known better!" Zeke snapped angrily.

Nathaniel gazed eastward and saw nothing but the picturesque expanse of prairie. "Known better about what?"

"About paying for the pistols and the buckskins with gold."

"Why?"

"Because gold loosens lips. Folks start to talk. And then the wrong people hear about it."

"Like robbers?"

"And worse," Ezekiel said, and sighed. "We're being followed, nephew."

Nathaniel looked eastward again. "I don't see anyone."

"Keep watching."

Squinting in the warm sunlight, Nathaniel fixed his eyes on the eastern horizon. To his surprise, barely perceptible figures materialized in the distance, and he guessed they were three men on horseback. "I see three riders."

Zeke nodded. "The same ones who were at Westport Landing, no doubt."

"They've trailed us all the way from St. Louis?"

"I reckon they have."

"If they want your nuggets, why didn't they jump us sooner?"

"They're hoping we'll lead them to where I found the gold," Zeke said. "They'll trail us all the way to the Rocky Mountains if I let them."

"How can we stop them?"

Ezekiel vented a harsh laugh. "There are all sorts of ways, nephew."

"Should we keep going then?"

"No. We'll take a break and rest the horses. We don't want the varmints to know we're on to them."

Nathaniel had lost much of his appetite. He kept glancing at the eastern horizon, hoping his uncle was mistaken, and wondering how he would fare when the confrontation came. Since leaving New York he had seen three men die, and the future, as Zeke had indicated, promised to hold more death in store for him. But could he squeeze the trigger when the time came? His uncle believed he could, but Ezekiel had spent a decade living as a savage lived. For Zeke killing must be easy.

"You have nothing to be nervous about yet, Nate," Zeke commented.

"Will they try to kill us?"

"Not until they're convinced I won't lead them to the gold. They're fools, in addition to being worthless vermin. They probably make a living by robbing other trappers and traders.''

"What will you do to them?"

"Wait and see."

In 20 minutes they were mounted and resuming their journey. To take his mind off the men shadowing them, Nathaniel concentrated on the wildlife they encountered and asked his uncle about each species, learning the habits of all the game on the plains. They saw deer and antelope in abundance, and several days later spied the first of many elk. There were birds and hawks, eagles and owls. But Nathaniel had yet to spy the animal he most wanted to see.

"Uncle Zeke, where are all the buffalo?" he inquired when they turned up the Republican Fork of the Kansas River.

"We're not quite to buffalo country yet," Ezekiel answered. "They don't quite range this far east, although I was told by a Caw chief that they did graze in this vicinity many years ago."

"Why haven't we seen any Indians yet either? I was under the impression they are all over these plains."

"They are. A small band was watching us about three hours ago."

Nathaniel stiffened in the saddle. "They were?"

"Calm down, nephew. Not all Indians are hostile. The main ones to worry about are the Blackfeet, the Arikara, the Sioux, and the Cheyenne. That's just on the plains. If you ever head to the Old Southwest, down Santa Fe way, you'll have to guard your scalp against the Comanches, Kiowas, and the Apaches."

"Have you fought many Indians, Uncle Zeke?"

"More than I care to remember."

"How do you feel about them?"

"Feel about them?"

"Yes. Do you hate the Indians?"

Ezekiel glanced at his kin. "Now why would I hate them?"

"There have been a lot of stories in the press back east about what to do with the Indians. Some folks think we should let them live on their lands in peace. Others, those who seem to despise the Indians, want to force them out of the way by having the government relocate them," Nathaniel mentioned. "Andrew Jackson, who's running for President again, says the Indians are an inferior race and that we have an obligation to reorganize them according to our way of doing things."

"Jackson said that, did he?"

"Yes. I read about it in the paper. A lot of people agree with him."

Ezekiel gazed westward and sighed. "I know about Old Hickory, Nate. Why do you think he acquired a nickname like that? Because he's an unyielding bastard who can not abide another point of view than his own. He always believes he's right and the rest of the world is wrong. Mark my words. If that pompous ass is elected, there will be hell to pay with the Indians."

Nathaniel pondered those words as they rode onward. Five days later he encountered his first tribe when they rode to the sloping crest of a low hill and there, encamped near the Republican river, were dozens of Indians.

"Otos," Zeke declared.

"Are they friendly?"

"As friendly as they come."

Reassured but still anxious, Nathaniel retained a firm grip on his rifle as he followed his uncle down to the Indian camp. He saw that the tribe lived in pole huts covered with straw and dirt. The women hung back while the men advanced to meet Zeke and him. There were few guns in evidence, and most of the men wore little more than a buckskin loincloth, if that. They impressed him as being a poor clan, not one of the great warlike plains tribes he had heard so much about.

A stocky Indian stepped in front of the rest and moved his hands and arms in a peculiar series of gestures.

Nathaniel was about to inquire as to the meaning when his uncle responded with a similar sequence. Perplexed, he surveyed the Otos, relieved to see none of them displayed the slightest hostility.

Ezekiel dismounted and walked to his pack horse. He extracted a hunting knife and presented it to the stocky Indian. After a few more hand gestures he climbed aboard his stallion, smiled and nodded, and rode through the clan.

Amused, Nathaniel observed the stocky Indian proudly displaying the hunting knife. He stayed on his uncle's heels and didn't speak until they had passed the village. "What was that all about, Uncle Zeke?"

"Their chief wanted us to smoke with them."

"Smoke?"

"Smoke a pipe, nephew. Do you know how to smoke?"

"No."

"Then you'd best learn. Every Indian tribe I know has a smoking ceremony. When an Indian offers to smoke with you, it means he has no intention of doing you harm. The ceremony is supposed to mean that your hearts and minds are one."

"Why didn't you smoke with him?"

"Because of those sons of bitches after us. I told him there were bad white men on our trail and we couldn't afford to stop. To show I was sincere and not offering an insult, I gave him that knife."

"You talked to him with your hands?" Nathaniel inquired in amazement.

Zeke nodded. "They call it sign language. Every Indian uses it. Learn sigh language and you can parley with any tribe on the plains, no matter what language they may speak."

"Who taught sign language to you?"

"Shakespeare. And I'll teach you. By the time we reach my cabin, you'll be an old hand at it."

"How long will it take us to reach your cabin, anyway?"

"If we're lucky, about four weeks. Maybe a bit less. We'll follow the Republican to within seventy-five miles or so of the Rockies. Then we have quite a haul up to the high country. We could shave time by cutting straight across instead of sticking with the river, but there's more game this way," Zeke explained, and smiled. "And I wouldn't want you to starve to death before you see the treasure."

"I can hardly wait," Nathaniel admitted.

"We won't be spending much time at the cabin when we get there," Zeke remarked.

The statement surprised Nathaniel. "Why not?"

"Because if we don't run into any problems, if we don't get sick or snake-bit or scalped, I want to push on to the rendezvous."

"The what?"

Ezekiel stared at his young nephew and shook his head. "It's hard to believe I was as green as you once. The rendezvous is held each summer. Practically everybody involved in the fur trade shows up for a month or so of the wildest goings-on you'll ever see. This year the rendezvous is to be held at Bear Lake, up in the same neck of the woods as the Great Salt Lake."

"I read about the Great Salt Lake in the papers."

"You sure must read those newspapers a lot."

"Why shouldn't I?"

"Newspapers are like a gabby gossip. They're just so much hot air."

In another mile they came to a stand of thick cedar and pine trees. Zeke took a faint trail running along the bank of the river, and when they passed the trees he suddenly wheeled his mount. "This will do," he announced.

"Are we making camp already?"

"No," Zeke said, and rode into the thickest part of the stand. He dropped to the ground and secured the reins to a firm limb.

Nathaniel followed suit, wondering what his uncle could be up to now. He tied his horses, then walked with Zeke to the Republican.

"Water, nephew, is the key to survival in the wilderness. Learn to sniff out water and you'll never need to worry about thirst or starvation. Every living beast needs water to survive. Deer, elk, buffalo. Find the water and you find them," Ezekiel stated, and stared at the surrounding plains with admiration reflected in his eyes. "Some folks happen to think that game is scarce in these parts, but it isn't unless you're with a big party that scares every living critter within miles into hiding. The Otos and the Caws make a living hereabouts, and so can a white man if he learns their secret. The Indians learned to live the natural way ages ago, and they have a lot to teach us if we'll just give a listen."

"Are we going to fish here?" Nathaniel inquired, watching the sluggush flow of water.

"No." Ezekiel faced east. "I asked the Oto chief to delay those three varmints trailing us as long as he could. If they smoke with him, they'll be hell-bent for leather to catch up with us. They'll come along our back trail as fast as they can, and they won't be as cautious as they might be otherwise."

"If the Otos are going to delay them, shouldn't we be making tracks? Maybe we can lose them."

"We're not going anywhere, Nate," Zeke said slowly, and motioned at the trees. "We'll wait right here until those snakes-in-the-grass show their ugly faces, and then we'll put all that target-shooting you've been doing every time we stop to good use." He grinned. "We'll kill them."

Chapter Nine

"We can't just kill them, Uncle."

"Watch me," Zeke said, walking into the trees.

"But we don't really know that they're after us," Nathaniel said, staying one step behind. "They could be on their way to the Rocky Mountains, same as us."

"They're not."

Nathaniel took hold of his uncle's right arm and swung Zeke around. "You don't *know* that!"

"I know it," Zeke maintained obstinately.

"I can't believe you would murder someone in cold blood."

"Better I do unto them before they do unto me."

His anger mounting, Nathaniel glanced eastward, relieved the trio weren't in sight, then tore into his uncle again. "How do you plan to kill them? Shoot them from ambush?"

"I'll ask them to turn around and smile before I squeeze the trigger," Zeke said sarcastically. He frowned and studied the younger man for a minute, noting the set of Nate's jaw and the fire in his nephew's eyes.

"If you do this," Nathaniel warned, "I'll return to St. Louis."

"All by yourself?"

"With or without your assistance."

Ezekiel rested the barrel of his Hawken on his right shoulder. "You'd go back without seeing the treasure?"

Nathaniel nodded.

"Then this must mean more to you than I figured," Zeke said. "How would you feel if I can prove those men aim to kill us or rob us?"

"I'd stand by your side come what may."

"Fair enough," Zeke said, and scrutinized the lay of the land. He pointed at two cedar trees growing close to one another 30 feet to the south. "Those trees should do you."

"For what?"

"As a shield. Hunker down in the grass behind those trees and wait until they go for their guns."

Nathaniel glanced at the trees. "What do you have in mind?"

"You don't trust me, Nate, and that cuts me to the quick. If you won't accept my leadership now, what are you going to do later, when we run into unfriendly Indians or some other danger? I can't afford to argue with you every time there's killing to be done. Out here, killing is just part of staying alive."

"You still haven't told your plan."

"It's simple. You'll wait behind those trees and I'll wait by the river. When those three upstanding citizens catch up with us, we'll play it by ear. If they're friendly, as you claim, then we won't raise a hand against them. But if they're not, if they try to kill me, I'll be counting on you to back my play."

"Shoot them?"

"You can club them to death for all I care. Just don't let them do me in."

Nathaniel licked his lips, nervousness seizing him, and fidgeted. "I don't know if I can," he confessed.

"Now is a hell of a time to turn Quaker on me."

"I've never shot anyone before."

"I know. You told me, remember? Well, nephew, as the saying goes, there's a first time for everything," Zeke said, and chuckled. He strolled toward the bank. "Now remember, if one of those rascals takes a bead on me, you can pretty much take it for granted he doesn't have peaceful intentions."

"Uncle Zeke, let's keep riding," Nathaniel urged.

"Another rule to remember is this, nephew. If you can't avoid a fight, then be damn sure you get in the first lick. A word to the wise," Zeke stated. He reached the bank and squatted down, facing to the east.

Stunned at the likelihood of imminent violence, Nathaniel shuffled to the cedar trees and knelt in the soft grass to their rear. He fingered the Hawken and gulped. Despite the seasoned reasoning of his uncle, he couldn't shake a gnawing, growing feeling of outright fear. Not fear for his personal safety, but fear over the inner consequences of slaying a fellow human being. He knew he wasn't the most devoutly religious person on the continent, but his parents had raised him to attend church every week and to respect the Ten Commandments. And one of those commandments was as plain as the nose on his face: Thou shalt not kill.

Not ever.

So what would happen to his soul if he slew one of the three men, even if they were robbers or killers? What were the eternal consequences of violating the commandment not to take a life? His uncle had taken the lives of two men back in St. Louis and had hardly given the matter a second thought. And Tyler, the gambler, had been all too ready to take Clancy's life on the field of honor. But they were grown men. They'd already made their peace with the world, or at least they had rated their priorities and adhered to their own personal code of conduct.

But what about me? Nathaniel asked himself. He would be 20 in November. By Eastern standards he was already a man. By the values practiced on the frontier he was still a green kid, wet behind the ears. He'd already taken the first step toward manhood by asserting his independence. Over what mysterious threshold would killing another man take him? Did he automatically become a man by the standards of the West if he participated in bloodshed? Jim Bowie was widely considered to be a brave man, and yet what was he

most noted for? Killing with his famous knife. Andrew
Jackson had acquired a reputation as a fearless man. And
how? By killing Creek and Seminole Indians in the South,
and by killing the British at New Orleans. Killing one's
enemies, it seemed, constituted a badge of courage in the
eyes of most men.

But was it *right*?

Nathaniel touched his pistols, working them up and down
under his belt to ensure they were loose and ready to be used.
His mouth felt extremely dry and he craved a sip of water.

"Here they come!" Ezekiel suddenly called out.

Startled, Nathaniel glanced to the east. Through the trees
he glimpsed them in the distance, riding hard, approaching
rapidly. Even at that range he recognized them as the same
three hulking riders he had seen at Westport Landing, and
a chill rippled down his spine. He promptly drew his pistols
and placed them to his right, then flattened and extended the
Hawken between the cedar trees.

Ezekiel stood and cradled his rifle across his waist. He
watched the trio draw ever nearer, his visage calm, his hands
steady.

How does he do it? Nathaniel marveled, and placed his
right thumb on the hammer, his finger already lightly
caressing the trigger. He heard the sound of hooves
drumming on the hard earth, and the sound grew louder and
louder. Then the cadence abruptly slackened off.

The three riders had spotted Ezekiel. They immediately
slowed to a walk, less than 100 yards from the stand of trees,
and began conversing animatedly.

Nathaniel pressed the Hawken to his shoulder and glued
his eyes to the three scruffy men, breathing shallowly, his
pulse quickening.

After a brief discussion the trio advanced in a line with
the largest man in the middle. All three carried rifles and
had pistols stuck in their belts. All three appeared capable
of giving a baby nightmares.

Please let them be peaceful! Nathaniel thought, his
abdomen tightening into a knot. When they were 20 yards
from his uncle, so close that he could see the nostrils of the

large man's horse flare, he cocked his rifle.

Displaying an attitude of complete unconcern, Ezekiel smiled and gave a little wave with his left hand. "Howdy, strangers!" he hailed them. "Am I pleased to see you."

Nathaniel saw the three men exchange glances, and the one on the right grinned slyly for a few seconds until he realized what he was doing and sobered. The grin was a bad omen. Nathaniel's instincts told him that his uncle had been right, that the trio were up to no good, and he realized there would be violence without a doubt. The certainty shook him.

"Hello, friend," the large rider declared when the trio was 40 feet from Ezekiel. They approached to within two yards before stopping. All three were glancing every which way, as if they suspected a trap. "This is a bad land in which to be afoot."

"You've hit the nail on the head there, stranger," Ezekiel agreed, just as friendly as a minister.

"Where's your horse?"

"Wouldn't you know it?" Zeke said and laughed. "My horse and my pack animal both lit out. I'd stopped for a rest and they were spooked by a damn snake."

The large man gazed into the densest section of the trees. "Are you alone, then?"

"No," Zeke replied. "My partner is out trying to round up the horses."

"Which way did your horses run?" the large man inquired.

Ezekiel pointed to the west. "In the direction I want to go, but unfortunately without me in the saddle." He laughed again. "I'm hoping you'll be kind enough to lend my partner a hand. I hate to be standing about in Indian country."

"I know what you mean," the large man agreed. "My name is Gant, by the way."

"My friends call me Zeke."

"Well, Zeke, we wouldn't want to leave you alone in your time of need. My partner here, Madison, will head out and help your friend while we stay here in case any Indians should show up." Gant nodded at the man on his left, who urged his animal past Zeke and rode off at a leisurely pace.

Nathaniel did not bother to watch the man depart. He

trained his rifle on the larger rider, Gant.

"This is right neighborly of you," Zeke mentioned.

Gant shrugged. "A white man should always look out for another white man, eh?"

"Ain't that the truth."

"Where are you heading?"

"To the Rockies," Zeke revealed.

"Is that a fact?" Gant responded in apparent surprise. "Why, so are we."

"Are you heading for the rendezvous?"

Gant blinked a few times, as if the idea had never occurred to him, then smiled broadly. "We sure are. We hope to get there before all the whiskey is gone. You know how trappers are."

"I guess I do," Zeke said, and studied the men and their mounts. "Are you trappers?"

"How did you guess?" Gant replied jokingly.

"Where are your traps?"

Gant seemed to tense. "What?"

"It's odd to see trappers without their traps," Zeke remarked, still in his brotherly vein. "For that matter, I'm surprised to see you don't have any pack animals."

"We're living off the land as we go," Gant said stiffly. "Pickings are slim, but we get by. As for our traps, they're stored at our cabin on the Green River."

"The Green River?" Zeke said. "I know that country well. Some prime beaver skins have come out of that vicinity."

"We had us a good season last," Gant mentioned. "Took in near three thousand skins."

Zeke whistled in appreciation. "That's a heap of pelts. What, about a thousand a man?"

"Pretty near," Gant said. "I did a little better than my partners."

"What did you do with your windfall?"

"What else? We've spent the past month in St. Louis doing what comes naturally."

Ezekiel chuckled. "Those St. Louis women know how to treat a man right."

Perplexed by his uncle's friendliness, his nerves frayed to the limit, Nathaniel held the barrel fixed on the large man and wondered what was going on. Why didn't Zeke simply challenge Gant and get it over with? Why were they being so nice when each would just as soon shoot the other? He observed his uncle glance westward, and he risked a hasty look in the same direction. The other rider, Madison, was nowhere in sight. Could that be what Zeke was waiting for?

"I hope they find my horses soon," Zeke commented. "It was my own fault. I should have tied them up."

"You know what they say," Gant responded. "Count ribs or count tracks."

Now what in the world did that mean? Nathaniel speculated. His skin felt clammy and cold.

"Care for some jerky?" Gant asked.

"Don't mind if I do."

The large man climbed down and stuck his right hand in a blanket tied behind his saddle.

Nathaniel saw Ezekiel get a firmer grip on his rifle. He braced for the worst, thinking that Gant would pull a pistol from the blanket. Instead, out came a wide strip of jerky.

"Here we go," the large man stated. He wedged his rifle between his legs and drew his knife, then proceeded to cut several pieces of dried meat from the strip and handed a morsel to Zeke.

"I thank you kindly."

"We have some to spare in case you don't find your pack animal."

Hidden by the trees and the grass, Nathaniel listened attentively. He shifted his aim from the large man to the one still in the saddle. Zeke and Gant were now two yards apart, and he counted on his uncle to handle Gant when the time came. *If* it ever came.

"All this kindness has me a mite confused," Ezekiel said while chewing on the jerky.

"Why's that?" Gant replied.

"Because if you're aiming to rob and kill a man, you ought to come right out and do it instead of talking him to death."

Nathaniel suddenly felt light-headed. His uncle had thrown

down the gauntlet, and if Gant and the other man were
innocent of any wrongful intent they were bound to become
rather mad. But if they were, as Zeke asserted, cutthroats,
how would they react? He received an answer an instant later
when Gant went for his gun.

Chapter Ten

It all happened so incredibly fast.

Nathaniel saw the mounted man snap a rifle up, and without any regard for the consequences, thinking only of his uncle's safety, he sighted on the man's chest and squeezed the trigger. The boom of the Hawken produced a cloud of smoke and slapped the butt plate against his right shoulder.

A surprised grunt came from the rider as the ball bored through his torso and knocked him from his horse.

Ezekiel and Gant were bringing their rifles to bear, and Zeke was a shade quicker. He fired, the ball striking the larger man high in the chest and causing Gant to stumble backwards and drop to one knee.

Alarmed, well aware that both men could still pose a threat, Nathaniel released his rifle, scooped up his pistols, and sprinted toward the river bank. Zeke had already drawn his pistol and fired into Gant's chest, and this time the big man toppled onto his back.

Just then, while Zeke held his smoking pistol trained on Gant, the other rider stepped unsteadily into view near the head of his skittish horse. He pointed his rifle, the barrel swaying from side to side.

"Uncle Zeke!" Nathaniel cried, his fear lending Mercury's wings to his feet, running as he had never run before, and his shout served a twofold purpose.

Ezekiel frantically threw himself backwards, out of the line of fire.

The rider hesitated, swinging in the direction of the yell, still unable to hold the barrel straight.

Again Nathaniel gave no thought to the repercussions of his act. He extended both arms and fired while on the run, figuring at such close range he was bound to hit his target. And he did.

The robber staggered as a ball smacked into his right side, piercing the flesh and shattering a rib bone, even as the second ball struck him at the base of the throat, passed clear through his neck, and shattered the top of his spine. His arms waving wildly, spitting blood as he gurgled, he reeled backwards and tumbled into the river with a loud splash.

Nathaniel reached his uncle's side and halted, staring in disbelief at the pair of motionless bodies. "Dear Lord," he gasped. "What have I done?"

"We're not finished yet," Ezekiel said. He was reloading his rifle, his hands flying, and glancing repeatedly to the west.

"We're not?" Nathaniel asked, not quite comprehending, his arms still extended, breathing in the acrid gun smoke.

"No," Zeke reiterated, ramming a ball home.

And suddenly Nathaniel remembered the man who had ridden off to assist in rounding up the fictitious strays. He swung around and spied a lone rider galloping toward the stand of trees, a rifle held aloft, 300 yards distant.

"Keep coming, you son of a bitch," Zeke said, raising the rifle to his shoulder.

Nathaniel opened his mouth to protest, then changed his mind. What good would it do? His uncle had no intention of letting the man live, and who was he to dispute Zeke? Which one of them knew best how to survive on the frontier? Certainly not him with his New York City upbringing, which had emphasized living by the rules of polite society, according to the structured laws of civilization. He glanced at the dead man in the river, who was floating within inches of the bank. What rules prevailed here? Survival of the fittest? Civilization lay far to the east, and the laws imposed by those in power no longer applied. Out here, out in the untrammeled wilderness, every man appeared to be a law unto himself.

"Keep coming," Zeke repeated.

Lowering his arms, Nathaniel looked to the west. The third man was now only 200 yards off, racing toward them, evidently oblivious to the fact his companions were dead. Couldn't he see them? Didn't he—

The sharp crack of Zeke's rifle punctuated Nathaniel's thought, and the onrushing rider suddenly swayed in the saddle, then toppled off his horse, landing headfirst, his rifle sailing through the air to clatter a dozen yards from his lifeless form.

"Got him," Ezekiel stated happily, and lowered his Hawken. "So much for those three."

"We killed them," Nathaniel said softly.

Zeke nodded. "We sure as hell did. It was either them or us, nephew. And I'm right proud of the job you done."

"I shot a man," Nathaniel said lamely.

"And a smart rifle shot it was," Zeke stated, and clapped the young man on the back. "I couldn't have done any better. And the way you finished him off with the pistols!" He laughed heartily. "You're a natural-born fighter."

Nathaniel looked at Gant and saw blood oozing from the big man's chest. "Should I be proud of the fact?" he asked.

"Certainly," Ezekiel responded, at work loading his rifle once again. "You're proven you're a man after all, not one of those dandified sissies the cities breed like rats."

"I don't feel very manly," Nathaniel divulged, striving to come to terms with his feelings. "I feel . . . strange," he said, for want of a better word.

"It'll pass, nephew," Zeke assured him. "I felt the same way when I killed my first man. But the feeling goes away. Eventually you'll regard the killing of a bad man in the same light as killing any vermin."

"I will?" Nathaniel responded, and the notion shocked him. If he ever became that callous, what would serve to distinguish him from the lower animals?

"We must each live according to our nature, Nate," Zeke said solemnly. "There's no getting around the fact. Try, and you're doomed for a life of misery."

A listless sensation crept through Nathaniel's veins, and he regarded his pistols as if they were alien objects he'd never beheld before. "What is my nature?" he queried absently.

"That's what I hope you'll discover before this treasure hunt of ours is over," Zeke said. "Now you'd best reload your guns in case any unfriendly sorts heard our shots."

"Unfriendly sorts?"

"Indians, nephew. Indians."

Nathaniel needed no further prompting. The thought of hostile Indians dispelled his moodiness, and he hastily retrieved his rifle and reloaded all three guns. Once the pistols were again secure under his leather belt and he had his rifle grasped firmly in his hands, he turned to his uncle.

Zeke was already busily at work. He had hauled the dead rider from the river and aligned the body next to Gant's. Then he had stripped each man of their guns, knives, powder horns, and bullet pouches. Now he was about to mount Gant's sturdy animal.

"Do you want me to bury them?" Nathaniel queried.

The question gave Zeke pause. He glanced over his shoulder. "Whatever for?"

"So the beasts don't devour them."

"Why deprive the beasts of a meal?"

Nathaniel envisioned a pack of wolves tearing into the corpses, and swallowed. "But that's not proper."

"Why do you think the Good Lord created vultures? It's not proper to deprive the buzzards of their meal. So just drag the bodies into the trees and we'll leave them there."

"Just like that?"

"Nephew, I wasn't joking about Indians. I've seen sign of some in this vicinity, and I don't mean Otos. Now get cracking." So saying, Zeke mounted and rode toward the third corpse.

Nathaniel gazed skyward, his soul in torment. He'd killed! Violated one of the Ten Commandments! So what happened now? Would he spent eternity in Hell, tortured for the deed he had done? Or would a bolt of lightning flash from the clear sky and fry him to a cinder? He scanned the heavens, almost disappointed when nothing transpired. Yes, he had killed, but the world went on. The sun still shone and birds still sang and fish swam in the river. Was the passing of a human life of such inconsequence, then? Bothered by his train of thought, he shook his head and propped his rifle against a nearby tree. Working laboriously, he dragged the man he'd shot deep into the cedar trees, then returned for Gant.

Ezekiel was riding up with the third man's horse in tow and the robber's body draped over the saddle. "Wait until I tell Shakespeare about this," he said, in high spirits. "He'll enjoy a laugh at the way I skunked these scoundrels."

"Skunked them?"

"Didn't you hear me?" Zeke asked, dismounting. "Oh, that's right. You wouldn't have understood. Nephew, those men weren't trappers. They were fixing to kill us for my gold. I tricked them into confessing as much."

"How?"

"By getting them to talk about their so-called trapping activities. Did you hear the big one tell me they caught three thousand beaver in a season?"

"Yes."

"That came to a thousand per man."

"So?"

"So there ain't a man alive who has caught one thousand beaver in a single season. It's not humanly possible. Why, Jeb Smith himself caught only six hundred and sixty-eight in a whole year, not just one season."

Nathaniel had heard of Jebediah Smith, who in 1826 had led a party of fur trappers from the Great Salt Lake all the way to the Mission San Gabriel in California, the first to successfully do so. "How many seasons are there?" he queried.

"Two. The first is in the fall when the fur has reached its prime and runs until the ice makes trapping out of the question. The second starts in springtime and goes until about June, when the warm weather means the fur is real thin."

"Do you know Jeb Smith?" Nathaniel thought to inquire.

"I've met him a few times," Zeke disclosed. "He's got the mountains in his blood, and every mountain man in the wilderness recognizes him as one of the best who ever lived. And did you know he's only around twenty-eight years old?"

"No, I didn't," Nathaniel confessed. "Somehow, I figured he would be older."

Zeke locked his eyes on his nephew. "Out here, Nate, it's not a man's years that count. It's his experience. You're only nineteen. Why, if you were of a mind to stay out in the west, you could be as highly regarded as Jeb Smith by the time you're twenty-eight."

"Stay out here?" Nathaniel said, and snorted at the idea. "Not when I have Adeline waiting for me."

Ezekiel's fine spirits abruptly dissipated. "That's right. I plumb forgot about Adeline."

"I never will," Nathaniel vowed.

Zeke turned to the body draped over the horse. "Give me a hand."

Together they dragged the man named Madison into the brush with his fellows, then covered all three with limbs and greenery.

"Why go to all this bother if the vultures are going to eat them?" Nathaniel asked.

"The scavengers will find them soon enough. In a few days they'll be ripe enough to draw flies and coyotes from miles around. In the meantime, we want to put as much distance between them and us as we can. And we don't want anyone to find them right away," Zeke explained.

They walked back to their horses.

"What will we do with their animals?" Nathaniel questioned.

"What do you think? We'll keep them."

"We just take their animals? Doesn't that make us the same as the men we killed?"

"No."

"Why not?"

Zeke chuckled. "We're alive. They're not."

They mounted and rode westward, Ezekiel leading three

horses, Nathaniel only two. Except when spoken to, for the next five days Nathaniel hardly uttered a word, immersed in reflection on his part in the slayings of the would-be gold robbers. Zeke kept to himself, recognizing his nephew's agitated state of mind and respectfully allowing the youth to sort the matter out, vividly recalling how he'd felt when he killed his first foe.

On the fifth day, as he lay on his blanket not far from their smoldering fire, gazing in awe at the celestial display overhead, dazzled by the sheer number of stars, Nathaniel came to terms with himself. Since he wanted to return to Adeline at all costs, and since he wouldn't be able to see her again if he was dead, he logically concluded that staying alive was a foremost priority. And since in this great, sprawling wilderness where the men were often every bit as savage as the beasts they were trying to subdue, killing for food or simply in self-defense was an accepted practice, then if he was forced to kill to preserve his life, so be it. He believed his Maker would judge him in mercy and with compassion. And surely the Lord didn't intend for a man to stand idly by while another took his life! With such thoughts of personal absolution soothing his soul, he drifted into peaceful slumber.

The next morning the warmth of the rising sun on his upturned cheeks roused Nathaniel to wakefulness, and he sat up to discover his uncle already awake and packing their gear.

"Well, sleepyhead, it's nice to see you're not going to sleep the day away," Zeke joked.

"How do you do it? No matter how early I rise, you're always up before me," Nathaniel commented, rubbing his eyes and yawning.

"Life is meant for living, nephew. I don't believe in wasting a minute. I've trained myself to wake at the first streak of light on the eastern horizon. You might practice doing the same."

"I'll try," Nathaniel said halfheartedly.

Ezekiel grinned. "Why don't you splash some life into you, Nate?"

Nodding, Nathaniel rose and shuffled toward the Republican River, a distance of 30 yards. They had taken shelter for the night in a small clearing in the center of a ring of trees and scrub brush. His moccasins crunched on twigs as he ambled along. Still fatigued, his body sluggish to respond to the demands of a new day, he traversed the 30 yards in a daze. Only when he reached the south side of the river and knelt to dip his hands in the chilly water did he finally come to his full senses. And even then the water had nothing to do with his rude awakening. It was the guttural growl that emanated from off to his left, and the huge brute he spied when he swung in that direction.

Not 25 feet away, illuminated in all its primal ferocity by the increasing sunlight, stood an enormous grizzly bear.

Chapter Eleven

Stark, unadulterated terror welled within Nathaniel's breast at the sight of the monster. His mind and body were suddenly numb; he couldn't think, couldn't will himself to move, and he stayed there on his knees with his fingers in the water while the bruin lumbered slowly toward him.

Seven feet in length from the tip of its nose to its bobbed tail and weighing over 1200 pounds, the grizzly loomed in the dawn like one of the prehistoric mammoths unearthed in New York 20-odd years ago. Rippling with powerful muscles and steely sinews, the telltale hump bulging between its massive shoulders, the bear drew nearer and nearer, swinging its extremely wide head from side to side and sniffing the cool air. Its coat was primarily brown, but all the hairs were white-tipped, giving the beast its grizzled aspect.

Nathaniel finally recovered his presence of mind and glanced toward the camp. There was no sign of Ezekiel, and if he yelled to attract his uncle the bear might charge. He looked down at his belt, thinking of the pistols and rifle he had left lying next to his blanket, and chided himself for being so stupid as to traipse off without a gun.

The grizzly bear was now only 15 feet away.

What do I do? Nathaniel mentally screamed. He couldn't just kneel there like a bump on a log and let the bear get within striking range. He could see the grizzly's four-inch claws on its forefeet, and he could well imagine what a swipe from one of those gigantic paws would do to him.

Only 12 feet separated the two.

Girding his courage, Nathaniel abruptly stood erect, his hands at his sides, and faced the bear.

The grizzly drew up short, raising its head and sniffing even louder.

Nathaniel's mind raced as he debated the wisest course of action. Should he stand still and hope the bear would leave, or should he make a run for it? And if he ran, should he head for the camp and shout for his uncle, hoping he was fleeter of foot than the bruin? Or should he retreat into the river where the bear might not follow? Did grizzly bears like to enter water? Ezekiel had told him all about deer and antelope and elk and other animals, but never once had Nathaniel thought to inquire about bears for the simple reason he hadn't seen any. Until now.

Without any warning of its intent, the colossal grizzly reared upright, its front paws held with the claws extended, its mouth hanging wide to reveal its long, sturdy teeth. The beast growled again.

His fear getting the better of his reason, Nathaniel instinctively backed away from the bear, retreating into the shallow water at the edge of the river.

The grizzly dropped onto all fours and ponderously advanced, rumbling deep in its chest, its eyes fixed on the man.

Nathaniel could stand the strain no longer. He cupped his hands to his mouth and bellowed at the top of his lungs. ''Zeke! A grizzly!'' Then he retreated several more strides. His left hand bumped a hard object on his hip, and all of a sudden he remembered the 12-inch hunting knife he carried. He drew the blade with his right hand and held the weapon at waist level. Compared to the size of the mighty bruin, the hunting knife seemed puny indeed, but it was all he had and he refused to go down without a fight.

The shout prompted the grizzly to growl louder, and it stepped to the river's edge, then hesitated for a moment.

Nathaniel glanced over the bear's back, and his hopes soared when he spotted his uncle sprinting toward the Republican, a rifle in each hand. He began to think he would survive his first encounter with a grizzly without receiving so much as a scratch, that perhaps the reputation of the species for ferocity was vastly overestimated, when the bear proved him wrong.

The grizzly attacked.

Nathaniel's eyes widened as the bear waded into the Republican, splashing water in all directions, and came for him, its enormous jaws opening and closing. He frantically backed farther away, until the water rose to his waist, and thinking that he might be safer if he could reach the opposite shore, he spun and was about to swim for it when the unexpected occurred. He slipped, his left moccasin sliding off an unseen rock underwater, and stumbled forward a pace, sinking onto his left knee, the water rising almost to his chin.

A bestial growl sounded right behind him.

Panic gripping him, Nathaniel straightened and whirled and found himself staring straight into the eyes of the horrendous brute. A paw streaked out of nowhere and caught him on the left shoulder, the claws ripping his buckskin shirt and tearing into his flesh, and the force of the blow knocked him backwards. He nearly lost his footing and went under, his arms swinging wildly, but at the last instant he regained his balance and surged erect.

And there was the grizzly, coming at him again, its gaping maw about to bite.

Nathaniel twisted and sidestepped to the right. His left shoulder throbbed and his entire arm arched. Ignoring the agony, he swung his right hand in an arc, striking in frenzied desperation, and stabbed the bruin in the head. Once, twice, three times he struck, and the third time the blade speared into the grizzly's left eye and held fast in the socket. Before he could wrench the knife free, a reverse swipe of the bear's paw connected with his chest and sent him sailing into the river. He went under, forgetting to close his mouth, and water poured down his throat. *I'm drowning!* he thought, and thrashed his legs, seeking a firm footing, completely disoriented. His moccasins found a purchase on the bottom and he pushed upward, his head breaking the surface, the water up to his chin. He sputtered and gasped, then stiffened when he saw the grizzly not six feet away.

The bear had reared onto its hind legs again, and was uttering the most savage sounds while shaking its head and pawing at the knife imbedded in its socket.

Nathaniel braced for another attack, when to his astonishment the bruin dropped onto all fours, turned, and made for the shore, continuing to vigorously sweep its head to the right and the left, as if the agitated motion might cause the knife to slip out and end its agonized torment. No sooner had all four feet touched solid ground, however, than a solitary shot rent the morning air and the grizzly pitched onto its face, then rolled onto its right side and was still.

"Nate! Nate! Did he get you?"

Dazed by the attack, feeling oddly sluggish, Nathaniel glanced to the right and spied his uncle, a smoking Hawken in his hands. He moved forward, keenly desirous of reaching the bank, afraid he might pass out.

Ezekiel had placed his Hawken on the ground and picked up the second rifle he'd carried from the camp, a gun that formerly belonged to Gant. He warily stepped over to the grizzly and poked its head with the barrel. After satisfying himself that the brute was indeed dead, he laid the rifle down and came into the water to assist his nephew. He saw the torn buckskin shirt and blood trickling down, and swore. "Damn! He did get you!"

Nathaniel heard the words, but they were strangely distorted. He blinked and swallowed, struggling to stay alert, and took one leaden stride after another. A moment later strong arms gripped him under the arms and he felt himself being propelled to the gently sloping bank.

"I have you, Nate," Zeke said. "We'll have that shirt off in no time."

"Is it really dead?" Nathaniel mumbled, staring at the beast in disbelief.

"As dead as they come," Zeke assured him.

"Thanks," Nathaniel said weakly.

"For what? You did most of the work. He was on his last legs when I shot him."

They reached the shore and Ezekiel gently deposited Nathaniel on the ground not six feet from the bear. "Let's remove that shirt," he suggested, and squatted to help remove his garment.

His fingers seemingly composed of mush, Nathaniel fumbled with his belt. Dizziness assailed him, and he was worried he might humiliate himself by fainting.

"I'll do it," Zeke offered, and quickly undid the belt.

Nathaniel left the task to his uncle. He struggled to comprehend why everything was distorted, why he couldn't concentrate. Had he lost too much blood? Would he die here on the prairie? Would Adeline mourn his passing when she learned the news? His head sagged and he saw the bear, the knife jutting from its ruptured eye, blood flowing over its facial fur. Did *I* do that? he marveled. "Dumb luck," he muttered.

"By the Eternal, I only know of one other man who has killed a grizzly with a knife," Zeke declared proudly while stripping off the shirt. He raised Nathaniel's head into his lap so he could slide the soggy buckskin over his nephew's head. "Wait until the word gets out! I'll tell Shakespeare and he'll tell everyone else in the Rockies. That man can gab up a storm."

Nathaniel closed his eyes and breathed deeply, relieved the queasy sensation was subsiding. He debated whether he should look at the wound. The horrible sight of so much gore might be more than his shattered senses could handle.

"Nephew, you are the luckiest man who ever lived. All you've got is a little scratch," Zeke stated, lowering Nathaniel's head.

Surprised, Nathaniel opened his eyes and glanced at his left shoulder. The "scratch" turned out to be three claw marks, three neat incisions in his flesh, the longest several inches in length, starting just below his collarbone and extending to where his arm joined the shoulder. The furrows were no more than half an inch deep and there was scant blood in evidence.

"I'll have you on your feet in an hour," Zeke predicted.

Nathaniel looked up at him. "An hour? Couldn't I rest until at least noon?"

"Whatever for? If you were seriously injured I'd let you rest, but these tiny cuts are hardly worth the bother of patching together."

"Tiny cuts?" Nathaniel retorted indignantly.

Zeke nodded. "Compared to some folks I've see who were attacked by a grizzly, you came off in fine form. Why, once about seven years ago it was, a Canadian trapper I knew stumbled on a she-bear and her cubs. Before he knew what hit him, that bear rammed into him and started ripping him to pieces with her teeth and her claws. By the time she was done, his legs were nearly severed from his body and the right side of his face had been chewed to the bone."

The queasy sensation returned and Nathaniel blanched. "I'd rather not hear about it, if you don't mind."

"Grizzlies are the most unpredictable critters the Good Lord ever put on the face of this earth," Zeke went on philosophically. "You never know if they'll turn tail or try to eat you, and they can be regular devils to kill when their dander is up. I've known of grizzlies who were shot ten to fifteen times and they still wouldn't keel over. Take my word for it. You want to avoid grizzly bears at all costs."

Nathaniel almost laughed. "I'll try to keep it in mind," he said dryly.

Ezekiel grinned and studied his nephew's face for several seconds. "There. I guess you're out of your shock. Now stay put while I go to camp and fetch my bag. But first—" he said, and rose. In seconds he was back with Gant's rifle. "Hold onto this in case your bear has a friend lurking about."

"A friend?"

"Sometimes they roam in pairs. Not often, but sometimes," Zeke said. He hurried off, retrieved his Hawken and ran toward their camp.

Gritting his teeth, Nathaniel used his right elbow to prop himself off the ground, then straightened in a sitting posture. He wasn't about to lay on his back when there might be another of those monsters in the vicinity. A survey of his surroundings assured him he was alone, and he expelled a breath in relief. The dead bear drew his attention. How could he have survived an attack from such an awesome creature? If he hadn't actually lived through the experience, he would doubt such a feat was possible.

Something caused a splash in the river.

Startled, Nathaniel stared at the Republican, but all he saw were ripples on the water. A fish, he figured, and happened to gaze at the plain beyond the Republican. The figure he spotted less than 100 yards away prompted him to leap to his feet in astonishment, momentarily forgetting all about the bear and his shoulder wound, forgetting everything except the man astride the horse.

An Indian.

He sat astride his horse in an attitude of casual curiosity, wearing only a breechcloth and moccasins. Over his back hung a quiver of arrows. In his left hand he held a short bow. His dark hair hung down on both sides of his head to his naked shoulders.

Nathaniel started to raise the rifle, then thought better of the idea. The Indian had not displayed any hostility, and he doubted his uncle would be pleased if he shot a friendly warrior. So he simply returned the other's stare and waited for the Indian to make the first move.

After a minute the warrior made a gesture with his right hand, then nodded and wheeled his mount. Without a backward glance he rode to the north, sitting tall and easy, riding bareback. Soon he was out of sight, disappearing in a small cluster of trees far off.

Abruptly feeling weak, Nathaniel sank to his knees and

pursed his lips. There was so much he had yet to learn about
life in the West, he wondered if he would live long enough
to learn it all. He had no idea to which tribe the Indian might
belong; for all he knew, the warrior might return with others
of his tribe to slay Zeke and him. He began to realize that
making a mistake in the wilderness, even the smallest, most
inconsequential error such as leaving camp without a gun,
could have a fatal outcome. How different life here was from
New York City, where a man could leave his house forgetting
to take along one of his personal effects, such as his overcoat,
and experience nothing more than a minor inconvenience.
Apparently civilization cushioned people from the harsher
realities of life.

"Here we go."

Nathaniel shifted, relieved to find his uncle returning so
quickly. "I saw an Indian," he blurted.

Ezekiel halted in midstride and scanned the surrounding
expanse of grass and flowers. "Where?"

"There," Nathaniel said, and pointed. "He watched me
for a bit, then rode off."

"Describe him."

"He was sort of tall and had a bow and arrows," Nathaniel
replied, uncertain as to which details his uncle wanted to
know. There wasn't many he could provide, in any event.
"I don't know what else to say."

"Was his hair shaved?"

"No. Why?"

"If his hair had been shaved except for a strip from the
forehead to the neck, then he would have been Pawnee. Their
villages are north of us a ways. They don't give white men
much trouble," Zeke said, and frowned. "But since his hair
wasn't shaved, then my guess is the warrior was part of a
Cheyenne war party. The area we're in is at the eastern edge
of their territory."

"Are the Cheyenne friendly?"

"Sometimes yes. Sometimes no."

"That's not very reassuring."

"It's not meant to be," Ezekiel said, and squatted

alongside his nephew. "I'll dress those cuts and we'll be on our way. If there is a Cheyenne war party hereabouts, we want to get somewhere else as fast as we can." He paused and grinned. "I'm rather fond of my scalp and I hope to keep it a spell."

Chapter Twelve

Ezekiel followed the Republican for another two miles, then struck a course to the northwest, pushing the horses, his alert gaze constantly roving over the prairie. He repeatedly glanced over his shoulder, watching their back trail.

His left shoulder throbbing, Nathaniel was hard pressed to keep up. He looked forward with keen anticipation to stopping for the night so he could rest. The thought of nine or ten more hours in the saddle did not appeal to him in the least.

After they had traveled four miles, Ezekiel relaxed a bit and slowed down. "I don't see any sign of pursuit," he announced.

"Good. Maybe we can stop soon and take a break," Nathaniel suggested.

"Not on your life. Not until we've put a goodly distance between any Indians and us."

Nathaniel was holding the reins in his right hand. His left arm he held bent at the elbow and tucked in to his side, with the Hawken barrel wedged into the crook of his arm. Carrying the rifle was painful, but he wasn't about to ride unarmed through country brimming with hostile Indians. He started a conversation to take his mind off his discomfort. "Have you ever killed a grizzly bear?"

"More times than I could count."

"And you were never hurt?"

"A few nicks and bites," Zeke disclosed. "I know as much about grizzlies as any man living, I reckon, except for Shakespeare. So pay attention. Grizzlies might be unpredictable, but they'll usually leave a man alone unless you get too close or it's a she-bear with cubs. *Never* go near a bear with cubs. You're just asking for trouble."

"Why didn't that bear leave me alone? I did nothing to provoke it, yet it kept coming closer and closer and sniffing as if it liked my scent."

"There's the key. Your scent. Grizzlies live by their nose. They go from scent to scent like a butterfly from flower to flower, looking for something tasty to eat. Shakespeare says a grizzly doesn't have the best eyesight in the world, but it damn sure has the best nose," Zeke said, and chuckled. "There's a saying the trappers have about the grizzly. If a pine needle falls in the woods, the eagle will see it, the deer will hear it, and the bear will smell it. Nine times out of ten, when a bear gets your scent, it'll head for the hills. But if the wind is blowing your scent away from the bear, or if you surprise it, then watch out."

"Do you think the bear that attacked me had my scent?"

"Hard to say, nephew. But I suspect the bear was more curious about you than crazed with the killing lust, or you wouldn't be alive right now."

"The next time I see one I'll run like hell," Nathaniel mentioned, thinking of the advice Zeke had given him concerning Indians.

"That's one thing you never want to do with a bear."

"No?" Nathaniel asked in surprise.

"Not unless the bear is already after you. Grizzlies are as thick as fleas on a mangy dog in some parts of this country. You'll be running into them all the time, so you'd better learn the basics now. If a grizzly does come after you, hold your ground. Face the bear down. Most of the time they'll run up to within a few yards of you, stand up, and glare into your eyes, as if they're taking your measure. If you run, they'll chase you and tear you to pieces. This advice holds for most any critter in God's creation. The Good Lord made us to be the masters of the brutes, and most beasts won't attack unless you show cowardice," Zeke asserted.

Nathaniel digested the information thoughtfully. So he had committed two blunders that morning. The first was leaving the camp without his rifle, which he would never do again. And the second had been in retreating from the bear and entering the river.

"Actually, the same advice holds true for Indians," Ezekiel went on. "Never let on that you're afraid of them or you'll be sorry. The Indians respect bravery above all else. That's why they attach so much importance to counting *coup*."

"To what?"

"*Coup*, Nate. Counting *coup* is how an Indian warrior proves his manhood. For a warrior to win glory, he has to touch his enemy. Each time he does, he counts *coup*. Some of the tribes even have special sticks for just that purpose."

"I don't get it," Nathaniel ssid. "What's so important about touching an enemy?"

"The way the Indian looks at war, it takes no great courage to kill an enemy from afar, to shoot him with a bow or a rifle from a hundred yards away. But it does take considerable courage to face an enemy up close and strike him with a hand or a stick or a lance," Zeke explained. "That's why the bravest warriors are always those who have counted the most *coup*."

"I had no idea. I thought they just killed for the sheer sake of killing."

Ezekiel looked at his nephew. "Indians might be savage, but they're not savages, no matter what you've read in the press."

"You sound as if you admire them."

"There's a lot to admire about the Indian way of life. You'll discover the truth for yourself."

"I will?"

Zeke nodded and rode a little faster.

Two hours later they came to a brook and halted to refresh their horses. A few cedar trees grew near the water's edge, and Nathaniel sat down and leaned his back against one of them, relieved to be sitting still.

Zeke stared to the east, his hand over his eyes, peering intently at the horizon.

"Have any of your friends ever been killed by Indians?" Nathaniel inquired.

"Why do you ask?"

"Just curious."

"Yes, I've lost a few to Indians. The Blackfeet ambushed three of my closest friends near the Jefferson Fork of the upper Missouri River about a year and a half ago. Shot two of them so full of arrows they looked like porcupines. The third they tortured, then scalped."

"How did you find out about it?"

"The third man, Grignon, was released because they couldn't make him cry out even under the worse torments they could devise. So they sent him packing, stark naked, without so much as a knife. They told him to warn all whites to stay away from their land or else."

"What happened to your friend?"

"He stumbled into the camp of another group of trappers about three days later, his feet torn to ribbons, on his last legs. They tried to save him but there was little they could do. He died after two days."

Nathaniel blinked a few times. "Wait a minute. He was still alive after being scalped?"

"Losing your hair doesn't kill you, Nate. It's what happens to you before or after that'll determine whether you live or die."

"How horrible."

"There are worse fates than being scalped."

"I can't imagine what they could be," Nathaniel commented, and closed his eyes. He imagined what it would be like to lose his own hair, and the prospect revolted him.

"Actually, being killed by Indians is just one of the hazards of living in the wilderness. Two years ago one hundred and sixteen men left Santa Fe to trap the southern Rockies and other parts. Only sixteen came back."

Nathaniel straightened. "Sixteen? What happened to the rest?"

"Some were probably killed by Indians. Some likely died from disease. Others were snake-bit or mauled by a grizzly. There are all sorts of things that can happen to a man living in the mountains."

"Why would anyone want to put up with such hardships just to live in the wilderness?"

Zeke sighed. "That's a question many a man has asked himself. The answer might surprise you."

"I don't intend to stay out here long enough to learn the answer."

"You never know, nephew."

Nathaniel closed his eyes and thought of Adeline. Spending a year away from her, spending 12 whole months in the mountains with his uncle, appealed to him less and less with each passing day. The farther they went, the more convinced he became that it would be a miracle if he lived to see his sweetheart again. True, he wanted to be rich, but was wealth worth his life? Was Adeline's love worth such a cost? Was he—

"Nate!"

The harsh word brought Nathaniel out of his reverie. He opened his eyes and saw his uncle gazing at a distant point to the east. "What is it?"

"Get mounted. There are Indians on our trail."

Even with his injured shoulder, Nathaniel climbed on his horse faster than he ever had before. The pain was momentarily forgotten in the urgency of the moment.

Zeke stared eastward for a few more seconds, then mounted and headed due west, crossing the shallow brook.

"Are they Cheyenne?" Nathaniel asked, riding on his uncle's left.

"They're too far away to tell," Zeke said. "And we don't

want them to get any closer if we can help it."

They rode hard for 20 minutes, passing several dozen antelope and a solitary wolf that bounded away at their approach. A low hill appeared ahead, not much more than a mound of dirt and wispy grass, yet still the highest elevation for miles around. Ezekiel made straight for the rise and reined up at the top, swinging his roan around.

Nathaniel did the same, and far to the east he saw the band of horsemen coming after them. He counted eight riders, and even to his untrained eye they were clearly not white men.

"Damn!" Zeke declared angrily. "We're in for it now."

"Do we make a stand?"

"Not if I can help it," Zeke replied. "I'd prefer to outrun them, but with all these extra horses we don't stand a prayer."

"What if we leave the horses we took from Gant and the others here? Maybe the Indians will be satisfied with them," Nathaniel proposed.

"I wouldn't count on it. I know one man who tried that trick once, and the Indians took his spare animals and still chased him for over a day. He barely got away with his life."

"Then what do we do?"

Ezekiel pursed his lips and surveyed the countryside in every direction. For miles around lay rolling prairie, a seemingly endless expanse of thin grass, with not so much as a tree to afford a hiding place. "I reckon we make that stand after all." He slid down and inspected his Hawken.

Nathaniel dismounted and stood regarding the figures on the plain, calculating that the Indians would reach the hill within five minutes at the most.

"If worse comes to worst, we'll shoot the horses we took from those vermin and use them as a breastwork," Zeke proposed.

"Shoot the horses?"

"Would you rather have the Indians shoot us? Out here horses aren't pets, Nate. Never become too attached to your animal because you may have to eat it."

"Never," Nathaniel stated, glancing at his mare.

"If you're hungry enough, you'll eat anything," Zeke

stated. "And horse meat beats starvation any day."

"I hope I'm never that hungry."

Ezekiel took several paces and cradled his rifle in his arms. "We'll have an advantage over those devils if they try to take us. They'll see just the two of us and expect us to have only two rifles. But we have five, plus our pistols and the extra pistols we took from Gant and his partners." He chuckled. "Yes, sir. We could give those Indians a powerful surprise."

"But what if they all have rifles?"

"Not very likely. Most warriors prefer a bow, lance, or tomahawk to a rifle when it comes to killing. And those who do own rifles are not always the best shots in the world."

"I hope you're right."

"Don't be such a worrywart, Nate. You'll live longer."

Nathaniel absently nodded, but inwardly he felt a gnawing knot of fear at the likelihood of fighting Indians. *Indians!* He had read about the atrocities attributed to the red man, about the scalpings and other revolting horrors allegedly practiced by the barbaric tribes in the vast unexplored lands west of the Mississippi. Never in his wildest dreams had he expected to be contending with them in a fight for his life. What *am* I doing here? he asked himself again and again, watching the warriors draw closer and closer.

"Remember, put on a brave front," Zeke advised.

Troubled, Nathaniel looked at his uncle. "Are you afraid to die?"

"Afraid? No, I wouldn't say that. You grow to accept death as your constant companion out here, Nate. Once you know it can happen at any time, you sort of resign yourself to that fact. Oh, I don't *want* to die, and I'll do my best to stay alive. But no, I can't honestly say I'm afraid right at this moment."

"I am," Nate said softly.

"Fear is nothing to be ashamed of, not so long as you don't let it get the better of you. You can conquer fear with your mind if you give it a try," Zeke said. "Besides, didn't you learn your lesson from what happened with Gant?"

"Which lesson?"

"That when the chips are down, when your life is in danger, when you have no choice but to kill or be killed, your fear evaporates like dew under a hot sun." Ezekiel glanced at the horses. "Fetch the other rifles and pistols and lay them here so they'll be handy when the shooting commences."

Nathaniel hastily complied, and as he deposited the last of the rifles on the ground at his feet he looked up to discover the band of Indians within 500 yards of the hill.

"Damn!" Zeke exclaimed.

"What is it?"

"Those aren't Cheyenne, Nate."

"What are they?"

"Kiowa," Zeke said, almost spitting the word out, his features hardening. "Their usual range is far to the south of here. They must be looking for a Cheyenne camp to raid and they came across us instead."

"Are they friendly?"

"Let me put it this way. Never turn your back on a Kiowa unless you aim to commit suicide."

Nathaniel licked his suddenly dry lips and nervously fingered the trigger on his Hawken.

"There has been bad blood between the Cheyennes and the Kiowas for years," Zeke went on. "They raid each other all the time. The Cheyenne will kill a few Kiowas, so naturally the Kiowas have to strike back." He paused. "Mark my words. Sooner or later the two tribes will declare war, and they might not stop until one or the other has been destroyed."

Listening with only half an ear to the news, Nathaniel anxiously watched the eight Indians ride nearer.

"That's what will do the Indians in, you know," Zeke mentioned thoughtfully.

"What?"

"The fact that they're always so busy killing each other off. They'll never be able to stand together against the whites."

Nathaniel opened his mouth to ask why the Indians should have to band together when there were so few whites west of the Mississippi, but the question died in his throat as the eight warriors abruptly halted. A second later one of the Kiowas rode straight for the hill.

"Remember, Nate," Zeke admonished. "This is your survival that's at stake. Any mistakes now, and you'll wish that bear had got you first."

Chapter Thirteen

Two hundred yards off the Kiowa slowed his horse to a walk and came on cautiously, a lance held in his right hand.

Nathaniel impulsively raised his rifle to his shoulder, but a firm hand pushed the barrel down again.

"Not yet, Nate," Zeke directed. "This one wants to talk. I'll ride down and see what he wants."

"Is that wise?"

"He won't try anything," Zeke said, walking to his roan. "It won't hurt to find out what he has on his mind." He swung into the saddle and headed down the sloping incline.

For the first time since leaving St. Louis, Nathaniel appreciated how dependent he was on his uncle. If anything happened to Zeke, he wouldn't last a week. His apprehension climbing, he glued his eyes to the two men and held his rifle at chest height, ready to fire if need be. He saw them ride to within ten yards of one another and begin communicating in sign language. Their exchange went on for minutes. Finally, the Kiowa warrior made an angry gesture and turned his horse around, then rode briskly toward his fellows.

Ezekiel returned to the top of the hill.

"What happened?" Nathaniel inquired anxiously.

"I just had the honor of meeting Thunder Rider, a Kiowa warrior of some distinction," Zeke said, climbing down. "He told me, as I suspected, that his raiding party is searching for a Cheyenne camp. He was surprised to find any white men in this vicinity and kept asking me if there are any more about. I don't think he believes there are just the two of us."

"Was that all?"

Zeke frowned. "No. He wanted us to trade our guns for horses."

"What did you tell him?"

"What else? To go eat bear."

"Eat bear?" Nathaniel repeated, perplexed.

"The Kiowas never eat bear meat. It's taboo for them, just like eating a dog is taboo for the Cheyenne. So telling Thunder Rider to go eat bear was the same as telling a white man to go to hell."

"How did he take it?"

"Get set for a fight."

Nathaniel gazed at the Kiowa war party. Thunder Rider was talking to the other warriors and making sharp motions toward the hill. He looked down at the extra rifles on the ground, then at the two pistols tucked under his belt, and pondered the fact that he was about to kill again. At that moment, he fervently wished he had never left New York.

"Here they come," Zeke said calmly.

Thunder Rider and the seven other warriors were riding swiftly toward the hill. They started yelling at the top of their lungs, voicing piercing, wild shouts as they waved their weapons in the air.

"Take your time when you aim," Zeke instructed. "We can't afford to waste a shot."

Nathaniel pressed the Hawken to his shoulder, marveling at how composed his uncle could be under the circumstances. He sighted on one of the warriors and waited for them to get within range. The Kiowas were still over 200 yards out, and he wanted them a lot closer to ensure he wouldn't miss.

Ezekiel's rifle cracked.

One of the charging Kiowas flung his arms out and toppled

from his horse. The others immediately checked their charge and rode to the fallen warrior.

"Maybe that will discourage them," Zeke said, although his tone did not convey much confidence. He began reloading.

"Why do they yell like that?" Nathaniel asked absently.

"Those war whoops? Warriors from different tribes all yell like banshees sometimes. It's supposed to unnerve their enemies."

"It works."

Zeke smiled. "You're doing fine."

"I haven't done anything yet."

"Here's your chance," Zeke stated, and nodded at the Kiowas.

Nathaniel turned, scarcely breathing at the sight of the warriors renewing their attack. Again he took aim, selecting a Kiowa with several feathers in his hair. He held the barrel as steady as he could, trying to compensate for the elevation and the trajectory as his uncle had taught him, afraid his lack of experience would cause him to miss. He was about to squeeze the trigger when the Kiowas adopted a wily strategem.

The warriors suddenly slid onto the sides of their horses, each man lying in a horizontal position along the length of his racing animal, with one heel hanging on the horse's back for support, presenting the smallest possible target.

Ezekiel fired.

Trying to get a bead on the Kiowas, Nathaniel was surprised when none of the Indians fell. His uncle had missed!

"Damn!" Zeke fumed, lowering his Hawken to the ground and grabbing one of the extra rifles. "Go for their horses, Nate! Their horses!"

Kill a horse? Nathaniel hesitated for all of three seconds. He thought of the fate in store for him if those warriors reached the top of the hill, and he aimed the barrel at an onrushing animal and squeezed the trigger.

The horse stumbled and almost went down, and the Kiowa on its back was forced to swing up in order to avoid being tossed onto the ground. The animal recovered, though, and surged onward.

"Keep shooting!" Ezekiel urged, raising a rifle to his shoulder and sighting on the foremost steed. His gun belched lead and smoke, and the horse abruptly catapulted forward, hit the earth hard, and rolled, throwing its rider in the process.

The six other Kiowas came on at full speed, undeterred. As if on an unseen cue, they fanned out and began weaving their mounts from side to side. Slightly more than 100 yards separated the warriors from their quarry.

"Fire, Nate! Fire!" Zeke prompted.

Nathaniel seized one of the other rifles and aimed at the Kiowa on the right, but the constant changing of direction disconcerted him. Just when he had the horse in his sights the animal would change course.

Ezekiel got off his third shot, and the horse he'd targeted went down in a disjointed whirl of legs, mane, and tail. "Cut one down, Nate!" he bellowed. "They'll be on us soon!"

Taking a breath and holding it, Nathaniel risked a shot, and he grinned in delight when the horse on the right seemed to trip over its own hooves and crashed to the ground. His elation was short-lived however.

Four of the Kiowas were almost upon them.

Nathaniel glanced down at his feet and was startled to realize they had fired all of the rifles. He looked at his uncle, who was quickly reloading, then at the charging Indians. Knowing he couldn't possibly reload before the warriors reached them, he discarded his rifle and drew his two pistols. He saw Thunder Rider and the three others angle their animals toward Zeke and him, and he took several steps toward them, determined to buy his uncle time, to sell his life dearly if necessary. He didn't think of Adeline, or the treasure, or of his family back in New York. He didn't think about whether killing was right or wrong. He didn't think about the odds or the danger. All he thought about was slaying those Indians before they slew him, and he focused his total concentration on the warrior in the lead, trained both pistols on the Kiowa, and waited until the Indian was only

15 feet away and had risen to an upright posture before squeezing both triggers.

Both balls struck the Kiowa in the chest and hurled him from his animal to fall flat on his back in the dirt.

And then the three remaining Kiowas were there, two armed with lances, the third with a bow.

Nathaniel dodged to the right as Thunder Rider's horse barreled toward him and the Kiowa tried to impale him on a lance. The point narrowly missed his chest. He turned toward the spare pistols lying six feet away, and as he did he saw his uncle fire a rifle at the warrior armed with the bow at the very same instant the Kiowa released a shaft. To his horror, both men scored a hit.

The Indian flipped backward from his mount and sprawled onto the hill.

Ezekiel staggered as the arrow penetrated his right side, the tip passing completely through his body and slicing out his back. He sank to his left knee, gripping the shaft, his face ashen from the shock.

"Uncle Zeke!" Nathaniel cried, and took several strides toward his relative, forgetting about the extra pistols.

Ezekiel swung around, his eyes widening. "Behind you, Nate!"

The warning saved Nathaniel's life. He spun, and not 20 feet distant was the second Kiowa with a lance, the Indian's horse kicking up dirt and grass as it pounded toward him. The Kiowa drew back his right arm to throw his weapon, and Nathaniel threw himself to the left.

Just as the warrior started to hurl his weapon, the sharp retort of a pistol sounded and a ball hit him squarely in the forehead and he toppled backward.

Nathaniel spun, stunned to see that his uncle had gotten off a pistol shot even with an arrow imbedded in him. He ran for the spare pistols, glancing down the hill as he did, consternation seizing him when he beheld two Kiowas sprinting toward the rise on foot. And where was Thunder Rider?

A loud drumming of hooves arose on his right.

Nathaniel looked around in time to see the leader of the

war party closing in on him again, trying to run him through with the lance. He frantically twisted aside and the lance missed him by a hair, and as it did his hands flashed out and took hold of the weapon. Digging in his heels, he held fast with all of his might, and to his astonishment unhorsed the warrior.

Thunder Rider fell on his left side, letting go of the lance as he dropped. Displaying pantherish reflexes, he jumped to his feet in an instant and drew a tomahawk.

There was no time to try for the pistols. Nathaniel adjusted his grip on the lance and whipped the point at the warrior.

Strangely, Thunder Rider grinned and bounded forward, swinging the tomahawk, batting the lance aside.

Nathaniel furiously backpedaled and tried to bring the lance to bear again, hoping to keep the Kiowa at bay, but Thunder Rider swatted the lance to the left and pounced. In desperation Nathaniel swept the blunt end of the lance into the warrior's abdomen, doubling the Kiowa over. He arced the lance upward, using both arms, and the heavy wood caught Thunder Rider on the jaw and rocked him backwards.

Somewhere a pistol fired.

An Indian shouted words in the Kiowa tongue.

Ignoring both distractions, Nathaniel reversed his grasp and speared the point at Thunder Rider's chest.

The warrior evaded the lance, skipping to the right. And then he did a most peculiar thing. He ignored his intended victim and dashed toward his horse, which had halted a dozen yards away.

Nathaniel scanned the hill, expecting to find other Kiowas charging him or attacking Zeke. Instead he saw a lone Kiowa fleeing on foot down the hill, and the bodies of four warriors lying nearby.

Thunder Rider leaped astride his horse in a smooth, graceful motion, and in the blink of an eye he was riding as fast as he could to the east.

"Nate!"

The agonized dry drew Nate around, and he gasped when he spotted his uncle doubled over next to the extra pistols. He ran to Zeke's side and knelt. "I'm here!"

Ezekiel lifted his head. Blood trickled from the right corner of his mouth. "The Kiowa?" he asked faintly.

"We've beaten them. They're leaving," Nate said, staring at the arrow, noting the spreading crimson stain on his uncle's buckskin shirt.

"Sure?" Zeke mumbled, his eyelids fluttering.

"I'm sure," Nathaniel replied, but he glanced over his right shoulder to verify the Kiowas were, indeed, fleeing. He saw Thunder Rider leading a riderless horse to the warrior on foot. Neither was paying any attention to his uncle and himself.

"The others?" Zeke queried, the words barely audible.

"They're all dead, near as I can tell," Nathaniel replied.

"Not the Kiowas," Zeke said, struggling to straighten, his visage contorted in anguish.

"What?"

"The others. Where are the others?" Zeke groaned and almost collapsed.

Nathaniel placed his hands on his uncle's shoulders to keep Zeke from falling. "What others are you talking about?"

The beating of many hooves suddenly filled the air, and over the west rim of the hill rode 15 more Indians.

Chapter Fourteen

Nathaniel impulsively snatched up two pistols and stood. He stepped around his uncle, placing himself between the Indians and Zeke, and grimly cocked both weapons.

The 15 warriors rode to within a few yards of the Kings and stopped, spread out in a line, staring at the white men without a trace of hostility in their expressions. None went to employ a weapon.

"Come on, damn you!" Nathaniel cried defiantly, flushed with the excitement of the battle and enraged that victory should be torn from him just when he thought the Kiowas had been sent packing. He pointed the pistols at the warrior in the center, who had halted a couple of feet in front of the rest. As he gazed into the Indian's disquieting eyes, recognition dawned.

It was the same one as before.

The warrior he had seen near the Republican.

Close up, the Indian showed a handsome countenance and luxuriant, dark hair. He was muscular and endowed with a robust build. His gaze, even with the pistols trained on him, was unflinching and fearless. Four eagle feathers, not visible previously because of the distance involved, adorned his head.

A hand fell on Nathaniel's leg and he glanced down.

"Don't shoot," Zeke said, still on his knees, staying as straight as he could. "They're not Kiowas."

"They're not?" Nathaniel responded, keeping the pistols extended and ready to fire at the slighest provocation.

"No," Zeke stated. "They're Cheyennes."

The warrior in the center surveyed the hilltop, his eyes lingering on each body, and then he gazed to the east at the rapidly departing pair of Kiowas. He barked a few words. Immediately eight of the Cheyenne lit out in pursuit.

"Lower the guns, Nate," Zeke directed.

"I don't trust them."

"If they'd wanted our scalps, we'd already be dead," Zeke said. "Lower the pistols."

Reluctantly, Nathaniel obeyed.

The Cheyennes began talking amongst themselves in low tones. Finally the warrior in the center stared down at Ezekiel, at the arrow jutting from the frontiersman's torso, and slid to the ground.

Nathaniel tensed and started to raise the pistols.

"Don't!" Zeke said. He grunted and bowed his head, his mouth curled in a grimace.

The warrior stepped up to Ezekiel and squatted. He reached out and gingerly touched the shaft, then leaned to the side so he could see the tip protruding from Zeke's back.

"What can I do?" Nathaniel queried, feeling totally helpless, conscious of the stares of the other Cheyennes.

"Nothing," Zeke replied, looking at the warrior in front of him.

The apparent head of the band made a gesture.

Zeke nodded, his lips compressing.

Before Nathaniel could intervene, while he stared in perplexity at his uncle and the warrior, the Cheyenne clasped the arrow firmly, his hands next to Zeke's chest, and with a short, sharp jerk, he snapped the shaft.

Ezekiel's head reared skyward and his mouth widened, but he didn't utter a sound.

The warrior stood and moved around behind Zeke. He knelt, gripped the protruding section of the arrow just above the triangular metal tip, and slowly pulled the rest of the shaft all the way out. A faint sucking noise announced the arrow's extraction.

Disregarding the Indians, Nathaniel knelt next to his uncle. "There must be something I can do," he offered.

"Not yet," Zeke replied.

The warrior stepped in front of them and began using sign language.

Nathaniel watched his uncle respond sluggishly. A few of the signs Zeke had taught him, but the Cheyenne's hands flew too fast for him to follow the exchange. After a few minutes the warrior glanced at him and smiled. Not knowing what else to do, Nathaniel smiled back.

The Cheyenne touched his own chest, then launched into a series of signs.

"What's he saying?" Nathaniel asked.

"He's thanking you for your part in killing his enemies, the Kiowa," Zeke said softly.

"But you did most of the killing."

"He's also telling you that you're welcome in his lodge any time," Zeke translated. The removal of the arrow appeared to have revitalized him to a small degree, and he observed the warrior while pressing his right elbow against the wound.

"Thank him for me."

Zeke relayed the message, then, surprisingly, grinned. "His name is White Eagle. Remember that, Nate."

"I will."

"He says that he hopes to be able to repay you one day for the favor you've done his people, Grizzly Killer."

Nathaniel glanced at his uncle. "Grizzly Killer?"

"Oh, did I forget to mention that?" Ezekiel said, and grinned again. "White Eagle saw you fight the bear. Grizzly Killer is the name he's given you, and from now on that's how every Cheyenne will know you."

"You're kidding?"

"Nope."

"What do I do now?"

"Leave it to me," Zeke said, and executed more hand signs.

After a bit White Eagle responded, then pointed at Nathaniel and added a few sentences in Cheyenne.

"He says that he believes the Master of Life will guide your footsteps in all that you do, that some men are touched in this way and you are one of them, which is rare in a white. He says he knows this because of the way you defeated the bear, that the Master of Life directed your hand," Zeke translated.

"Who is the Master of Life?" Nathaniel inquired.

"Some of the tribes worship a sort of creator force, a Supreme Being. The best I can interpret it, the closest I can come to the meaning of his words, is to call it the Master of Life."

"Thank him again."

"I have a better idea. Give him one of the extra pistols."

"What?"

"Give White Eagle a gun."

"Are you sure?" Nathaniel responded, balking at the idea of supplying a firearm to an Indian who might later use the gun against a trapper or even a soldier from Fort Leavenworth.

"Which one of us has lived out here for ten years? Which one of us knows these people like the back of my hand?" Zeke asked testily. "Give him a pistol and you'll have a friend for life."

Nathaniel eased the hammer down on both pistols and extended his left arm. "Here. Take this as a token of my friendship."

"You learn fast," Zeke said, grinning.

White Eagle looked at the pistol, then at Nathaniel. He took the weapon and inspected the gun carefully, then slid the barrel under the top of his breechcloth. After a moment's consideration, he reached up and removed one of the eagle feathers from his hair and offered the feather to the younger King.

"Do I take it?" Nathaniel queried.

"You'd better, or he'll be insulted," Zeke said.

Nathaniel took the feather into his right hand and admired the excellent state in which the plume had been preserved. "Thanks," he said, and smiled.

"Put it in your hair," Zeke directed.

"Are you serious?"

"Damn it, Nate. Why must you question everything? An Indian doesn't wear a feather just for decoration. A feather is a badge of distinction, just like the medals given to those in the military. White Eagle is showing his gratitude for the pistol by bestowing a great honor on you. Only warriors who have performed bravely in battle get to wear them."

Nathaniel twirled the quill in his fingers. "How do I attach it?"

"Use your noggin, nephew. Cut a piece of fringe from your shirt and tie the feather to the back of your head."

Aware that White Eagle and the other Cheyenne were watching his every move, Nathaniel drew his knife, trimmed a short length of buckskin fringe from his shirt, and secured the eagle feather to his hair. He felt ridiculous doing so, imagining how heartily Adeline would laugh if she could see him now. But then he pondered the fact that she was about two thousand miles away, that adopting to the frontier style of dress made prudent sense, and that White Eagle must figure the feather was a gift equal in value, or maybe even better in a certain respect, than the pistol. He smoothed the feather down, letting it hang to his neck, and regarded the warrior solemnly. "Again I thank you."

White Eagle nodded and used sign language again, his gaze on Ezekiel.

Zeke answered the warrior.

Annoyed at not being able to understand them, Nathaniel vowed to learn sign language at the first opportunity. He glanced at his uncle's wound, wondering how Zeke could withstand the pain.

With a curt nod, White Eagle turned and mounted his horse. In moments the rest of the band was riding hard to the east after their companions.

Nathaniel sighed, amazed at the encounter, gratified to be

alive. He knelt next to Zeke. "Tell me what to do and I'll take care of you."

Ezekiel nodded at their horses, which had skittishly strayed 40 yards to the southwest during the fight with the Kiowas and were now nipping contentedly at the grass. "First catch them, then we'll tend to me."

The catching proved to be an easy task. Nathaniel caught his horse first, then rounded up his uncle's roan, their pack animals, and the three horses they had taken from Gant and his friends. In short order he was back at his uncle's side.

"Now comes the tough part," Zeke said. He began to peel his shirt off, moving laboriously, grimacing in torment.

"Here. Let me," Nathaniel declared, and assisted in removing the bloodstained garment. The arrow had left a finger-sized hole in the flesh, and both the entry and exit points were rimmed with drying blood.

"I was lucky," Zeke commented. "I don't think it hit an organ and I haven't lost too much blood. Once I cauterize the hole, I should be able to manage."

"How will we do that?"

"Since there isn't enough wood around here for a fire, we'll have to make do. Look in the large bag on my pack animals. You'll find a bottle of whiskey."

Nathaniel did as requested and returned with the bottle. He watched in fascination as his uncle poured a large portion of the contents directly into the hole, and he shuddered when he heard Zeke grunt, thinking of the distress his relative must be suffering.

Ezekiel straightened and held out the bottle. "Here. Pour some down the hole in my back."

His stomach feeling queasy, Nathanial took the whiskey and walked around his uncle.

Zeke bent over to make the job easier. "Try not to spill any. This is a terrible waste of good liquor."

"I didn't know you were a drinking man."

"When I'm in the mood, I can drink anyone else under the table except for Shakespeare."

"I'm looking forward to meeting him," Nathaniel mentioned, and slowly upended the bottle over the exit hole.

Zeke stiffened and snorted.

"It must hurt like the dickens," Nathaniel remarked.

"No worse than having your innards torn out by a grizzly."

"How much should I use?"

"That's enough," Zeke declared, and straightened. He took the bottle and swallowed thirstily.

Nathaniel gazed at the bodies of the Kiowas. "Should I bury them?" he inquired.

"You never bury an enemy, Nate. Leave them for the buzzards and the coyotes. But you can do the scalping, if you want."

"The scalping?" Nathaniel repeated, uncertain if he had heard correctly.

Ezekiel nodded. "Those scalps are ours. We took those Kiowas fair and square, and their hair is worth its weight in gold. You can have the honor."

Emotionally dazed by the suggestion, Nathaniel looked at the corpses, then at his uncle, blinking a few times, seeing his relative in a whole new light. He'd noticed a certain change in Zeke's character as they traveled westward, a subtle hardening, a rougher demeanor than his uncle had exhibited in St. Louis. And now he fully appreciated how much Zeke had changed since the lazy days they had enjoyed back in New York. "I don't think I could," he said.

"Give it a try. It's easy. Just pull up on the hair and insert the tip of the knife under the skin. I've seen Indians take off scalps in two or three swipes."

"No," Nathaniel said firmly. "I won't do it."

"You can't afford to be squeamish out here, Nate. A man does what he has to do."

"But to take a scalp!"

"Indians and whites have been doing it for decades," Zeke said. "Why, at one time bounties were paid for Indian scalps in New York. And the Mexican authorities have put bounties on Apache scalps. Almost every tribe I know of takes the scalps of their enemies. A scalp is a symbol of success, nephew, nothing to be ashamed of."

"I won't do it," Nathaniel reiterated.

Ezekiel struggled to his feet. "Oh, well. I can't expect you to see the light yet. I'll do the scalping." He shuffled to the nearest body and sank onto his right knee, then drew his hunting knife.

Nathaniel watched, aghast, as his uncle took hold of the warrior's hair and sliced the knife into the skin at the top of the forehead. Blood started to flow, and Nathaniel turned away and gazed to the west, in the direction they were heading, wondering if he had made a major mistake in agreeing to accompanying Zeke into the wilderness. After all, how much did he truly know about the man other than the fond memories of his childhood? Or was he merely becoming agitated over nothing? If scalping was a way of life out here, and if he intended to stick it out for the whole year, then he should try and accept the practice. He glanced at the scalping in progress, then shook his head.

Accept such a savage custom?

Never!

Chapter Fifteen

For someone who had been shot with an arrow, Ezekiel remained in exceptionally high spirits. He recovered quickly. For two days he required frequent stops to relieve the pain, but by the third day he could ride for six hours at a stretch without seeming to be bothered by the discomfort.

Nathaniel became subdued, often riding in silence for miles, moodily reflecting on his situation. He wished he had never departed New York, never left his loved ones, especially Adeline. All he could think about was her. He saw her in his mind's eye in the beautiful splendor of every sunrise and in the radiant hues of each sunset. He felt her gentle touch in the lingering caress of the westerly breeze. And at night he gazed at the sparkling heavens and remembered the many hours they had shared together. He longed to see her again, and only one inducement served to keep him riding ever westward, only one lure drew him like a fish to a hook away from the woman of his dreams.

The treasure.

He thought of the gold often, and idly speculated on the amount he would possess after Zeke gave him his share. On several occasions he attempted to sound his uncle out about the treasure, but Zeke always responded in the same fashion: "Once we're at the Rockies, you'll see the treasure. Be patient."

Easy for him to say.

After five days Nathaniel began to shake off his troubled disposition. They were encountering more and more game the farther west they progressed, and he besieged Zeke with questions about the habits of each animal. He also pestered his uncle to teach him sign language, and he readily learned every gesture Zeke knew. They would practice by conducting conversations in sign language. On one such occasion, a week and a half after the battle with the Kiowas, they were riding over a knoll when Ezekiel abruptly reined up.

"Supper!"

In the act of signing a question concerning White Eagle, Nathaniel halted and stared straight ahead, his eyes widening in astonishment. "I never would have believed it!" he exclaimed.

"There's your buffalo, Nate."

Buffalo there were, thousands and thousands of them, covering the plain for as far as the eye could see. The males stood six feet high at the shoulders, the females slightly less. They were dark brown in color and possessed shaggy manes and scruffy beards. Black horns curved out from their broad, massive heads, with a spread of three feet from horn tip to horn tip. There were a score or so of calves in evidence, distinguished by their diminutive size and their reddish hair.

Nathaniel gaped at the great humped beasts, flabbergasted by the immense brutes and the magnitude of the herd. He saw several of the herd gaze in his direction, but none of them displayed any alarm.

"You're in for the treat of your life," Zeke said. "Leave the pack animals here and come with me." He started forward, his Hawken in his right hand.

"You could pick one off from here," Nathaniel commented, riding on his uncle's left.

"I could, but I won't. Where's your sense of sport? Taking a buffalo from horseback is the thrill of a lifetime."

Nathaniel glanced at a huge bull standing proudly at the front of the herd. "Isn't it dangerous?"

"Only if you're careless. Buffalo are the dumbest brutes in creation. They'll let you run them in circles or off of cliffs. But they're also fierce when riled, and they can gore you or your horse to death in the time it takes to spit."

"I see some of them looking at us."

"They know we're coming, but they haven't figured out what we are yet. We're about three hundred yards away, and buffao have pitiful eyesight."

Nathaniel checked his Hawkin, experiencing an odd commingling of excitement and dread.

"These critters supply everything the Indian needs to live," Ezekiel mentioned. "If the buffalo ever die out, the Indians are finished. Not that it will ever happen. There are millions of the brutes. Did you know that each one of those big males weigh about two thousand pounds?"

"No, I didn't."

"That's a lot of meat on the hoof, and the best-tasting meat on God's green earth."

"What if they charge?"

"Get somewhere else right quick," Zeke said, and angled toward the foremost bull. "There's a trick to killing a buffalo. Their skulls are so thick that trying to shoot one in the brain is a waste of time. Your best bet is to always go for a lung shot. Aim just behind the last rib."

Nathaniel stared at the bull, noting the thickness of its hide. "How do I know where the last rib is located?"

"Once you've skinned and butchered one, you'll know exactly where to find the ribs."

"What do I do in the meantime?"

"Guess.

"Oh. There's one other thing to remember. If you ever come across buffalo that have been butchered by Indians, don't take one of the hearts. The Indians will be extremely upset, and the last thing you want is for a tribe to be out for your blood."

"I don't understand. What do the hearts have to do with

anything?''

"Some of the tribes leave the hearts behind. They think that if they leave the hearts where the buffalo have fallen, it helps the herd to grow so they'll have more buffalo to kill later on.''

Nathaniel envisioned a green field littered with buffalo bones and hearts, and shook his head. Was there no end to the wonders of the West?

"We'll take this bull together," Zeke stated. "You ride on the left, I'll stay on the right. Remember, go for the lungs. And try not to shoot me or my horse by mistake.''

"Are you sure you're up to this?''

"I wouldn't miss your first buffalo kill for the world.''

"But your wound hasn't healed yet.''

"It will eventually. For now, I'll act as if it's already healed," Zeke said, grinning. He glanced at Nate. "Out here, nephew, when you're knocked off a horse you get right back up in the saddle.''

"Meaning?''

"If you roll over and whine and moan every time you're hurt, you won't last a year. You've got to be tough, to think tough. This kind of life is no life for a quitter. I know back in the States a lot of parents spoil their youngsters to the point where the children grow into adults and can't do much of anything because the parents didn't teach much of anything worthwhile. Spoiling breeds weaklings, and out here a man and a woman have got to be as strong as catgut.''

They were drawing nearer to the herd. Some of the bulls snorted and fidgeted nervously, while the cows began to move away.

"The herd will likely stampede as soon as we cut out after that bull," Zeke said. "Keep a tight rein on your horse. If you go down, you could be trampled to death.''

Nathaniel licked his lips. "Do you do this often?''

"Every chance I get.''

"And this is your idea of fun?''

"It beats wrestling a grizzly.''

More and more of the herd were moving to the southwest, lumbering rapidly, the calves struggling to keep up with their mothers. The bulls, always more belligerent, gave ground reluctantly.

"Are you ready, Nate?" Zeke asked.

"As ready as I'll ever be."

"Then let's get us some buffalo steak," Zeke said, and uttered a piercing shriek while urging his horse toward the bull he'd selected.

Nathaniel kept abreast of his uncle, his heart seemingly pounding in rhythm to the beating of his mare's hooves. He gripped the rifle and concentrated on the bull, which had suddenly spun and was racing to the southwest with the rest of the herd.

"Get as close as you can before you fire!" Zeke shouted.

Nathaniel barely heard him. Hundreds of buffaloes were now in motion, fleeing mindlessly from two riders they could crush in an instant, and more joined the general rout every second. Evidently if one buffalo bolted, they all did, and the sound made by the drumming of thousands of heavy hooves resembled the booming of thunder during a spring storm. The din climbed to a throbbing crescendo, and the passage of the buffaloes sent a billowing cloud of dust into the air.

Whooping and hollering like an Indian, Ezekiel closed on the bull.

They were fast approaching the herd, and Nathaniel could see the thick haunches and the swaying tails of the tremendous beasts. He inhaled the swirling dust and coughed, then squinted to prevent his eyes from watering. As they narrowed the distance his mare became difficult to control. The sight and noise of so many strange creatures terrified her, but she sped gamely onward.

Ezekiel was cackling and waving his rifle.

Bewildered, Nathaniel continued the chase although every instinct told him it would be infinitely safer if he simply stopped and let Zeke enjoy all the "sport." The bull was now at the trailing end of the herd, but there were other buffaloes bolting along on both sides of him. To get close enough for a shot, Nathaniel would have to ride in between the bull and a cow on the left, and with his mare already excitable and balking at drawing any nearer to the fearsome beasts, maneuvering her was a challenge that demanded all of his attention and riding skill.

Zeke had no such problem. His roan readily plunged into the herd, apparently trained for just such a hunting tactic, and Zeke tried to get a bead on the bull while racing at full speed, a difficult task in itself.

The pounding roar of the fleeing buffaloes and the increasingly dense cloud of dust, combined with the ever-present prospect of being pitched from his horse and gored or trampeled, made the initial minutes of the chase a nightmare for Nathaniel. As the pursuit continued, though, he began to think less of the danger and more about the job at hand. After all the trouble he was going to, he wanted that bull, wanted to put a ball into that huge bulk and see the brute crash to the ground. He focused on the beast's body, trying to estimate the point he should aim at.

For over half a mile the chase continued. The major part of the herd was obscured by the dust cloud, but the thudding of the thousands of hooves could be clearly heard.

Ezekiel rode into position first, his roan only four feet from the bull and abreast of its rear legs. He suddenly released the reins, pressed the Hawken to his shoulder, took but a moment to sight the rifle, and fired.

The ball had no effect.

Nathaniel barely heard the crack of the Hawken above the thundering of the herd, but he saw the smoke discharged by the shot and knew his uncle could hardly miss at such close range. He was astonished that the bull appeared to be unaffected, and he goaded his mare closer, held his rifle as tightly against his shoulder as he could under the circumstances, and tried to hold the barrel steady long enough to squeeze the trigger.

The bull gave no sign of slowing.

Although he was impatient to snap off a shot, Nathaniel forced himself to stay calm, to wait for the right moment. So engrossed was he in aiming, that he failed to detect any movement to his left and had no idea the cow had changed position until he felt something brush against his left leg. He glanced down.

The cow was within an inch of his foot!

Nathaniel almost panicked. His mare had edged to within a hand's-breadth of the bull, and now he was riding between both buffalo, hemmed in, trapped with no room to turn or evade those wicked horns if either brute tried to gore him. And sooner or later, if he didn't do something, one of them was bound to go for him or the mare.

What should he do?

The urgent question brought an automatic response born of desperation and intuition. Nathaniel simply lowered the Hawken barrel to the bull's side and squeezed the trigger at the same instant that he kicked at the cow and hauled on the reins, bringing the mare to an abrupt stop.

Without breaking her stride, the cow raced onward.

The bull, however, suddenly slowed to an unsteady walk and shook its massive head from side to side. It tottered, then halted as the rest of the herd sped to the southwest.

Nathaniel sat on his mare not 30 feet from the beast, wondering why the bull had stopped. Maybe, he reasoned, one of the balls had finally taken effect. Only when the buffalo turned toward him did he realize his time would be better spent in reloading than in speculation. He groped for his powder horn.

Too late.

The bull lowered its head, elevated its tail, and charged.

Move! Nathaniel's mind screamed, and he wheeled the mare and took off, unsure of the direction he was going and not really caring. The horrific vision of over two thousand pounds of enraged buffalo bearing down on him filled him with dread and he fled for his life, glancing over his right shoulder.

Amazingly, the bull was gaining!

Nathanial clutched at one of his pistols, doubtful the smaller piece would have enough stopping power to deter the bull. As his hand closed on the walnut grip a shot rang out, and he looked to his left to observe Zeke and the smoking Hawken, then back at the buffalo in time to see the bull go down.

Its bearded chin sagging and tucking underneath its head,

the buffalo executed a forward rolling flip, its legs and tail flying, and came down on its left side. For a few seconds the beast thrashed and kicked feebly, raising its head and snorting, and then it went limp and collapsed.

Nathaniel rode back toward the bull slowly, astounded he had survived, feeling keenly thrilled at their success. He stared at his uncle, who was riding over, noting Zeke's beaming smile and gleaming eyes.

Any vestige of the former cultured New Yorker was gone. His features flushed from the stimulation of the pursuit, elated at the slaying of the bull, his long hair tousled, his face covered with dust, Ezekiel threw back his head and laughed uproariously. He indicated the buffalo with a jab of his Hawken while looking at Nathaniel. "Ain't this the life, nephew! Out here, a man can *be* a man!"

"Provided he lives long enough."

The comment caused Zeke to laugh even harder.

Chapter Sixteen

The next couple of weeks passed without any life-threatening incident occurring.

Ezekiel skillfully guided them on a northwesternly bearing, going from one watercourse to another. He seemed to know the location of every stream, river, and spring on their route. Game at times was scarce, but they never went hungry thanks to the buffalo meat Zeke had carved from the bull and dried.

Nathaniel used the opportunity to question his uncle more about the wildlife on the plains and in the mountains, as well as to elicit information about the various Indian tribes inhabiting the country. When they stopped to rest the horses or eat he would invariably practice with his Hawken, and he became quite adept at hitting small targets, such as clumps of earth or thin twigs stripped from the brush, at considerable distances. His best shot, though, entailed the downing of an antelope at 150 yards. He killed the animal with one shot through the head, and Zeke praised him highly.

Three times they came across Indian sign. Each time Zeke examined the ground carefully and announced that the sign was a day or two old. He taught Nathaniel the basics of reading tracks, of judging the weight from the depth of the impression and determining the age by the consistency of the soil and the degree of erosion.

One night, eight days after the buffalo chase, a strange incident transpired that Nathaniel would have reason to recall and regret later. They were seated around their fire, and Ezekiel was discoursing on the relative beauty of the women in the various Indians tribes, when he abruptly ceased speaking and straightened. ''Did you hear that?''

''What?'' Nathaniel responded, tensing, his right hand creeping to his Hawken.

''I don't know. A faint noise.''

''What did it sound like?''

''Like the snap of a twig, only different.''

''I didn't hear anything unusual.''

Ezekiel stood and scanned the prairie to the southeast. ''I'm sure I heard it.''

Puzzled, Nathaniel also stood, his rifle at his waist. They heard so many sounds at any given time of the day: the cries of birds, including the piercing calls of certain hawks; the growls and snarls of the predators, including grizzlies and panthers; the howling and yipping of wolves and coyotes; the whistles and chattering of ground squirrels and prairie dogs; and, infrequently, the far-off war whoop of an Indian. In addition, at times the wind intensified and rustled the grass and the tumbleweeds. So why would Zeke become concerned at the snap of a mere twig?

''I must be getting jumpy in my old age,'' Zeke joked, and sat back down.

Eager to learn more about the Indian women his uncle had known, Nathaniel sank onto the ground, forgetting about the queer noise. The next day, though, he noticed that Zeke kept looking to the southeast, as if there might be someone or something out there, but Zeke never expressed any undue concern. Nathaniel dismissed the matter as unimportant.

Days later one of the most exciting events of the whole trip took place.

They came within sight of the Rocky Mountains.

Zeke spied them first, and pointed with his right hand. ''There they are, nephew. The top of the world.''

Squinting, Nathaniel shielded his eyes from the sun with his right palm and gazed at the distant peaks. Silhouetted on the far horizon, the mountains at first resembled low-flying clouds. As they trekked westward the range grew in size and grandeur, each peak acquiring an individuality of its very own, a unique, stark symmetry onto itself.

Ezekiel picked up the pace. They reached a shallow river and followed the waterway across the last stretch of plain to the foothills bordering the towering Rockies.

Never in his wildest imaginings had Nathaniel envisioned the mountains would be so awesome. The tallest of the peaks reared many thousands of feet into the air and were shrouded in caps of white snow. One of the mountains, in particular, the highest of the lot, looked like the father of all mountains, its lofty summit visible for dozens of miles out on the plains. The upper third of its towering slopes were covered in a mantle of white, layered with more snow than any other mountain. Another slightly smaller peak stood close by. Gazing at the highest mountain in reverent admiration, Nathaniel said softly, "I had no idea."

Zeke nodded. "It's beautiful, isn't it?"

"Does the tall one have a name?"

"A lot of the trappers and traders have taken to calling it Long's Peak after that crazy fellow who headed the Yellowstone Expedition."

The name jarred a memory. Nathaniel recalled reading about the Yellowstone Expedition of 1819 and 1820 while still in school. The leader had been a military man, a Major Stephen Long, and the press had reported extensively on his observations and conclusions regarding the plains. "Major Long? Why was he crazy?"

"I heard tell that the idiot claimed the prairies were unfit for settlement, that he called the country we just passed through the Great American Desert."

Nathaniel nodded. "I saw that on a map."

"The man didn't know what he was talking about."

"But you'd have to admit it would be difficult for farmers to make a living on the prairie. The soil isn't rich enough to support crops or livestock."

Zeke snorted. "Tell that to the millions of buffalo."

They rode higher, climbing deeper into the foothills, and the going was not as rough as Nathaniel anticipated would be the case. Game, particularly deer and elk, abounded. The hills became steeper. They skirted the higher peaks and loftier bluffs. After 12 miles of arduous travel they passed through a broad opening between two mountain ridges, and there below them, extending for many miles, lay a large valley replete with ample timber and meandering watercourses and rife with wildlife. The valley was almost completely ringed by mountains and hills. Long's Peak was now southwest of their location.

"As far as I know, nephew, no white men other than you, me, and Shakespeare have ever set foot in this valley," Zeke mentioned with pride in his tone, as if he had discovered a natural jewel others had missed.

"Is your cabin in this valley?" Nathaniel inquired.

Zeke started forward. "On the other side of the lake."

"What lake?"

"You'll see in a bit."

They descended to the valley floor, and once clear of the forest they had an unobstructed view for miles.

Nathaniel spied the large lake, toward which they rode rapidly, and he marveled at the profusion of wild fowl. Ducks, geese, gulls, and brants, among others, crowded the water to such an extent they appeared to barely have room to flap their wings. He saw a herd of blacktail deer to the south, and soaring high in the azure sky were several eagles and hawks. "This is a Garden of Eden," he breathed in fascination.

Ezekiel was studying his nephew intently. "I was hoping you'd like it."

"Does Shakespeare live here too?"

Zeke shook his head. "He's my nearest neighbor. His cabin is about twenty-five miles north of here."

"What about Indians?"

"You already know about the Cheyennes. They tend to stick to the prairie where most of the buffalo are found. Another tribe you're bound to meet are the Arapahos, the dog-eaters. They live on the plains too, but you'll find them hunting game in the foothills quite often. Their territory is just north of the Cheyenne hunting ground. The two tribes get along like two peas in a pod. They have an alliance. If you make an enemy of the Cheyenne, then you become an enemy of the Arapaho," Zeke detailed, then frowned. "The Cheyenne and the Arapaho will leave you alone. It's the Utes you have to worry about."

"Are they the ones who live on the west slope of the Rockies?"

Zeke nodded. "And the central Rockies. They've been at war with the Cheyenne and the Arapaho for decades. And the Utes will kill any white man they come across. Mark my words, nephew. Never trust a Ute. If you see one, shoot first and admire his buckskins later. I doubt if they'll ever learn to live at peace with anyone, let alone us whites."

"Have you had run-ins with them?"

"I've been obliged to kill about fifteen."

Nathaniel's eyebrow arched. "Fifteen?"

"Which is why they tend to leave me alone. A few years back they sent a war party to wipe me out. I was lucky. Shakespeare was paying a visit. I took an arrow in the thigh, and he pulled me into the cabin to safety. Those red devils tried every trick they could think of to force us out, even setting fire to my cabin, but our rifles taught them the error of their ways." Zeke chuckled. "I haven't seen hide nor hair of them varmints since."

"They'll be back one day," Nathaniel predicted.

"You think so, Mister Indian Expert?"

"Would you let it rest if you were them?"

Ezekiel regarded his relative thoughtfully and smiled. "No, I wouldn't. You're learning, Nathaniel. You'll make a great mountain man."

"I'll be back in civilization in a year, remember? I doubt anyone will ever know I was here."

Zeke did not respond. He pursed his lips and rode along the south shore of the lake, musing.

"Why did you call the Arapahos the dog eaters?" Nathaniel inquired out of curiosity.

"Because they eat dogs, nephew. They consider dog meat a real delicacy. They'll fatten their mongrels until the dogs are plump as a buffalo, then butcher them and have a fine meal."

Nathaniel scrunched up his nose at the idea of eating a dog. "Have you ever eaten dog meat?"

"On several occasions. If you ever visit an Arapaho camp, they'll likely offer you some. You'll insult them if you refuse."

"Remind me to never visit an Arapaho camp."

Zeke laughed. "If you stay out here long enough, you'll get over your finicky stomach."

"If you say so."

"Just don't take to eating people."

"Now you're joshing me."

"Nope. There are some folks who think human flesh is downright tasty. If you ever meet up with Old Bill, watch your hide."

"Who is he?"

"Old Bill Williams. He's a weird one. Lives all alone somewhere way up in the Rockies, but he comes down every now and then to socialize. You might bump into him at a rendezvous."

"And he eats people?"

"So they say."

"Surely you don't believe the stories?"

"I wouldn't, except for a little fact."

"What's that?"

"I had a talk with Old Bill two years ago, and I asked him point-blank if the tales were true, if he was partial to human flesh."

Nathaniel leaned forward, half expecting this to be another of Zeke's wild yarns. "And?"

"He looked me right in the eye and smacked his lips, then cackled like he was out of his mind. I believe the stories, and you'd be well advised to do the same."

Cannabalism? Nathaniel thought the very idea repugnant. He shook his head, stared ahead, and saw the cabin, a low log structure situated approximately 40 feet from the west end of the sparkling lake. He glanced to the north and spotted a river flowing into the lake, and traced the course of the river back into the higher country to the west.

"There's where I hang my leggings."

"How long have you lived there?"

"I built the place about five years ago."

"And you've lived there all alone?"

"Do you remember those Indian women I was telling you about?"

"Of course."

"Three of them were my wives, and they lived there in my cabin with me for a season or two of trapping."

"You have three wives!" Nathaniel exclaimed.

"Had, nephew. Had. And I didn't have them all at once, either. I haven't gone Indian that much," Zeke said, smirking. "I usually buy a wife at the rendezvous, keep her for a year, then take her back to her tribe to sell her once the attraction wears off."

Nathaniel almost reined up. "You *buy* your wives?"

"Of course. Why get hitched for the long haul when you can dally for the short term, if you get my drift."

"How can you *buy* a woman?"

"It's easy. A lot of Indians show up at the rendezvous, and they're more than happy to sell their women to whoever wants them. The ugly ones are right cheap, but the pretty ones will cost you a couple of horses, a gun with powder and ball, and a half-dozen pounds of beans or some whiskey. I know one joker who paid two thousand dollars in beaver skins for a chief's daughter. Talk about overpriced goods!" He chuckled.

Nathaniel was dazed. It never occurred to him that Indian women could be bought, could be paid for much like those slaves he had seen. The practice went against the moral fiber of his being. He stared at his uncle, amazed again at the uncanny transformation his uncle had undergone since leaving St. Louis. Zeke's outlook on life, his mannerisms, even his speech had slowly altered, as if St. Louis had temporarily drawn the old Ezekiel King to the surface and now the wilderness had reclaimed the man who had been molded in its own image.

"Here we are," Zeke announced, halting within five yards of the cabin door, which stood slightly ajar. "That's odd. I distinctly remember closing that door. I hope Silver Tip did't get in there or my goods will be in a shambles."

"Silver Tip?"

"A grizzly that lives in these parts. I've tried to kill him several times, but he's been too slippery for me," Zeke said, dismounting.

"How would a grizzly get in a locked door?"

"This isn't New York, nephew. Out here folks don't have to worry about locking—" Zeke began, then suddenly froze, staring at the cabin wall.

Nathaniel gazed in the same direction, at the logs to the left of the door, and saw it.

A tomahawk was imbedded in the wall.

"Utes!" Zeke declared.

Chapter Seventeen

Nathaniel quickly dropped to the ground and scanned the valley. "Do you think they're still around?"

"I don't see any fresh sign," Zeke said. "I've been gone for months. They probably came to scalp me, then left this message when they found I wasn't home." He walked to the cabin, set down his rifle, and wrenched the tomahawk loose.

"Message?"

"No two tribes make their weapons alike," Zeke disclosed while inspecting the tomahawk. "This is definitely Ute. They wanted me to know they were here, to rub my nose in it, to show they're not afraid of me and to let me know they'll be back."

"Why didn't they burn your cabin?"

"This is personal between them and me. They want my hair hanging in one of their lodges. Maybe they figured I'd leave if they razed the cabin. I don't know."

They cautiously edged to the doorway. Zeke shoved the heavy door inward and they peered inside.

"Damn!"

"What a mess," Nathaniel commented, eyeing the

ransacked interior. Furniture had been broken. Blankets had been ripped to shreds. Pots and pans were scattered about, and numerous personal effects had been shattered to bits.

"They'll pay for this," Zeke vowed. He entered and kicked angrily at a busted chair. "I made that myself."

"We'll have this cleaned up in no time," Nathaniel said.

Ezekiel scowled. "I don't mind the mess so much. I can always replace the things the vermin broke. But they took all the meat I had cut and dried."

"What do you want me to do?"

"Tie up the horses. We'll tidy the cabin, unpack, and go fishing in the lake. You've never tasted fish so good as the trout in these mountains."

Nathaniel nodded and went to turn when a horrifying thought struck him. "The treasure!" he blurted anxiously.

"What about it?" Zeke replied. bending down to pick up the leg from a smashed table.

"Did the Utes find your treasure?"

"No."

"But you haven't checked."

"The treasure isn't in the cabin," Zeke assured him. "I know they didn't find it."

"When will I get to see it?"

"Soon enough. Now get busy with those horses."

Nathaniel strolled to his mare, mystified by his uncle's nonchalant attitude. If *he* had a treasure cached nearby, it would be the first thing he checked. A squirrel chattered at him from a nearby pine tree, and he halted to gaze at the beautiful scenery all around him. This was so different from New York City. He remembered the sooty air, the crowds, and the grimy streets, and slowly shook his head. Perhaps Zeke was right. Compared to the pristine purity of the virgin wilderness, city life seemed unnatural. All those people crammed into a limited space, fouling the air with soot and the ground with their excrement, seemed vile and gross. Cities were breeding grounds for rats of the four-legged and the two-legged variety.

But out here!

He inhaled deeply, invigorated by the crisp air, and stared at the snow-capped peaks in the distance. A man could easily become addicted to such splendor, he mused. No wonder his uncle had never returned, and how wrong his father had been to condemn Zeke for choosing to live in harmony with Nature. Which, after all, *was* more natural? To live and work in cramped confines, to have walls and buildings limit the view, to breathe fouled air and eat overly salted meat? Or to have the far horizon be your wall and the sky your ceiling, to breathe in air as fresh as that on the day the world was created, and to eat the still-warm flesh of an animal recently slain?

Nathaniel grinned and took hold of the mare's reins. If he didn't know better, he'd swear he was beginning to thoroughly enjoy the wilderness life. If he wasn't careful, he might wind up like his uncle.

The thought made him laugh.

That afternoon, after the cabin had been cleaned out and their provisions stored inside, they went down to the lake to fish. Zeke constructed a pair of makeshift poles from the thin limbs of a tree. Within half an hour they had seven large trout on the bank.

"Tomorrow we'll go after an elk," Zeke mentioned as they ambled toward the cabin. He carried his rifle in his right hand, their poles in his left. "We'll gorge ourselves and dry some of the meat before we head out for the rendezvous."

"When do I get to see the treasure?" Nathaniel asked, hefting the string of fish in his left hand. Slanted over his right shoulder was his Hawken.

Ezekiel looked at his nephew. "Is that all you think about?"

"Wouldn't you if you were in my shoes?"

"I reckon I would," Zeke conceded, his features clouding. "Very well. Tomorrow morning I'll show you the treasure."

Nathaniel beamed. He could hardly wait! At last he would have the wealth he needed to woo Adeline properly! Elated, he gazed idly at the cabin, and as he did he heard an unusual swishing noise, and then a pronounced thump and a grunt. He glanced at his uncle and instantly halted, transfixed by the sight of a lance protruding from Zeke's chest.

Ezekiel was standing stock still, regarding the lance in bewilderment, his shoulders sagging. "Damn! Not again!" he exclaimed, and fell to his knees, releasing the poles but not his rifle.

"Uncle Zeke!" Nathaniel cried. He dropped the fish and looped his left arm around his uncle's shoulders.

"Get us inside, quick," Zeke urged.

Nathaniel scanned the forest, expecting a lance or an arrow to streak out of nowhere at him. He detected movement in the brush to the left of the cabin, approximately 20 feet from the door, and he let go of Zeke, whipped the Hawken up, and fired at a vague figure in the shadows. The figure promptly vanished.

"Inside," Zeke reiterated weakly. "Hurry, nephew."

The hair at the nape of his neck prickling, Nathaniel supported his uncle with his left arm and together they made for the shelter of the log structure. Zeke walked unsteadily and breathed loudly. Constantly surveying the woods for Indians, dreading another attack before they could reach safety, Nathaniel resisted an urge to dash inside. He assisted Zeke in reaching the cabin, and once they were there he lowered his uncle to the floor and immediately closed the door.

"I sure am having a pitiful run of luck," Zeke quipped, sitting stooped over. The lance had passed completely through his body, entering just an inch to the right of his sternum and exiting low down on his back, above the hip bone.

"The Utes must have been waiting for you to return," Nathaniel mentioned, kneeling next to Zeke.

"It's not the Utes."

"What?"

Zeke bobbed his chin lower. "This lance isn't a Ute lance."

"Then who—?" Nathaniel began.

"It's a Kiowa lance."

"But you told me the Kiowa don't range this far," Nathaniel commented while examining the shaft. He remembered how the Cheyenne, White Eagle, had extracted the arrow, and he reached for the lance, intending to do the same.

"Don't bother," Zeke said.

"But we can't leave it in."

"Check the window," Zeke advised.

Nathaniel propped his rifle against the wall and took his uncle's Hawken. He stepped to the only window, located to the right of the door. There was no glass, but a deerskin flap had been tacked to the top, rolled up, and then tied to afford a passage for the breeze. Inching his head to the sill, he peeked outside and saw only the trees, the lake, and the fowl. "I don't see anyone," he whispered.

"The savage is playing a game with us."

"Who is?"

"Thunder Rider."

"Do you mean he followed us all the way here?"

"That'd be my guess, nephew."

"But White Eagle and those other Cheyenne went after him."

"He got away from them."

Nathaniel still couldn't believe that the Kiowa warrior had trailed them so far. "How could he follow us without you spotting him?"

"He's an Indian, Nate, not a clumsy white man like Gant and those others."

Perplexed, Nathanial scurried back to his uncle. "But why would he come all this way? Why didn't he ambush us earlier?"

"I don't know why he waited so long. Maybe he felt he couldn't get close enough to us on the prairie. Or maybe he just wanted to learn where we were headed," Zeke said. "But I do know he's out for revenge. We shamed him, and he won't rest until he's taken our hair."

Nathaniel stared at the lance, alarmed at the red stain

developing on his uncle's shirt. "How do I remove the damn thing?"

"You don't."

"We've got to do something," Nathaniel insisted. "Tell me how to remove the lance."

Ezekiel looked into his nephew's eyes. "There's no need," he responded, the words barely audible.

"Why not?" Nathaniel queried, instinctively sensing the answer, filled with fear at what his uncle might say next.

"I'm dying, Nate."

The statement resounded in Nathaniel's mind with all the force of a thunderclap, and he stared at his uncle in disbelief. "You can't die."

"We all do eventually," Zeke said, and gave a wan smile.

"But you don't know for a fact that you're dying. If I take out the lance and dress the wound, you could live."

"I know it, Nate. I can feel it. I'm all torn up inside. I'm leaking like a sieve."

"You don't know that!" Nathaniel insisted, a tinge of desperation to his voice.

"I do. It feels like I have an itch inside, only I can't scratch it."

Nathaniel swallowed hard and felt tears in his eyes. "You can't die! I won't accept it!" He glanced wildly about the cabin. "There must be *something* I can do!"

"There is."

"What?" Nathaniel queried eagerly, leaning forward. "I'll do anything. What do you want done?"

"I want you to take Thunder Rider's hair."

Nathaniel recoiled. "You want me to scalp him?"

"Yep. But kill the son of a bitch first. He might object, otherwise," Zeke said, and grinned. Suddenly he coughed violently and put his left hand over his mouth. When the fit subsided and he removed his hand, both his lips and his palm were covered with blood.

"Dear God!" Nathaniel declared. "This can't be happening."

"Get a grip on yourself, Grizzly Killer," Zeke stated.

"This is survival, remember? Either you kill the Kiowa or he'll kill you."

"I won't leave your side."

"You don't have any choice. Listen, Nate. Thunder Rider was leading that war party. When a warrior leads a raid and doesn't lose a man, he's honored by his tribe. If the war party suffers a loss, though, that's considered bad medicine. Thunder Rider must avenge the warriors we killed and take our scalps back to his tribe to erase his shame."

"He won't live that long," Nathaniel vowed gruffly.

"That's the King spirit," Zeke said, and erupted into another fit of coughing. Blood spilled from the corners of his mouth and he gasped for air.

Terrified of losing his uncle, Nathaniel placed his left hand on Zeke's shoulder, wishing there was something he could do to relieve Zeke's suffering. "Please, no," he said.

A shadow flitted across the window, momentarily blocking off the sunlight.

Nathaniel tensed, gripped the Hawken in both hands, and moved toward the window. He had to be extremely wary. The Kiowa warrior was out there somewhere, waiting for him to make a mistake. He had to remember everything Zeke had taught him and finish off the warrior quickly. The sooner Thunder Rider was dead, the sooner he could tend to his uncle. He glanced out the window but saw no one.

There was only one way to get the job done.

Looking one last time at Zeke, who had closed his eyes and was wheezing, Nathaniel walked to the door. If he stayed inside, the warrior would simply wait him out or set fire to the cabin. He had to go out, to meet Thunder Rider in the open, to draw the Indian to him.

"Nate?" Zeke said huskily, his eyes still shut.

"I'm here," Nathaniel replied.

A protracted sigh issued from Zeke's crimson flecked lips. "I'm so—sorry."

"Don't talk. Save your breath. I'll be right back," Nathaniel stated. He faced the door, squared his shoulders, and gripped the latch.

"So sorry," Zeke repeated.

Nathaniel opened the door and pulled it inward, standing behind the wooden panel for protection, scrutinizing the terrain between the cabin and the lake. Where would Thunder Rider be hiding? In the trees on either side most likely, he deduced, and wondered if the warrior possessed another lance or bow. He heard a faint scratching noise and stiffened. What was that?

The scratching ceased.

"Never expected this," Zeke said.

Girding his courage, Nathaniel slipped outside and flattened against the outer wall. The air felt cool and clammy on his face, and he realized he'd been sweating profusely. He looked to the right and the left, cocked the Hawken, and edged to the southeast corner.

Somewhere in the forest a bird was singing.

The ducks and geese were swimming sedately on the lake.

Off to the south stood a solitary black-tailed doe.

Who would guess that death lurked in the trees? Nathaniel thought, then frowned at his lapse in concentration. To survive he must focus all of his attention on the present. He must be guided by his eyes and ears and act on impulse rather than reason.

Where was Thunder Rider?

Nathaniel studied the forest, checking every tree, every boulder, any place the warrior might be hiding. Another thought occurred to him and gave him pause.

What if Thunder Rider had obtained a rifle?

He dismissed the idea as unlikely. If the Kiowa had a rifle, Thunder Rider would have used it instead of a lance. Or so he hoped. After a minute, satisfied the warrior was not on that side of the cabin, Nathaniel moved to the northeast corner. Again he scrutinized the tall timber, and again he failed to detect the Indian.

A loud groan came from inside the cabin.

Nathaniel frowned and stepped back toward the doorway, thinking of Zeke alone and in exquisite agony. Uncertainty seized him, and he wavered between staying outside and searching for the warrior or going in to comfort his uncle.

Distracted by his thoughts, he scarcely noticed when a few pieces of dirt or splinters of wood fell onto his shoulders. Not until a flake landed on his nose did he finally look up, and by then it was too late.

Because he had found Thunder Rider.

Uttering a piercing screech, a knife clutched in his right hand, the Kiowa warrior launched himself from the roof.

Chapter Eighteen

Nathaniel tried to bring the Hawken to bear, sweeping the barrel upward, but the Indian's hurtling form struck the rifle and sent it flying even as Thunder Rider landed on top of his shoulders, driving Nathaniel forward, away from the cabin. He felt the weight of the warrior on his back, felt a hand brutally yank on his hair, and the force of the impact knocked him to his knees. He arced his body down, lowering his forehead to the ground, attempting to flip the Indian off. He succeeded.

Thunder Rider hit the grass and rolled, displaying the reflexes of a panther. He leaped to his feet, still brandishing the knife, a wicked grin twisting his countenance, apparently confident of victory.

A shade slower in rising, Nathaniel clawed for his right pistol. His fingers were just closing on the grip when the warrior came at him again, slashing that gleaming blade back and forth, forcing him to retreat and to release the pistol or have his hand sliced open.

Thunder Rider vented a war whoop and sprang.

Frantically backpedaling to evade the knife, Nathaniel abruptly bumped into the cabin wall. He started to dodge to the right, intending to dart inside, but somehow the warrior anticipated his move and skipped between the door and him. Frustrated, he retreated toward the northeast corner, never turning his back to the Indian for fear of being knifed. He managed only four strides when the unforeseen transpired.

He tripped.

Nathaniel felt an object under his left heel and began to lose his balance. He threw his arms out, flapping them in an effort to stay upright, and in that instant when he was most vulnerable, the warrior pounced.

Thunder Rider lowered his head and charged, his left hand going for his victim's throat, his right arm swinging the knife in a vicious arc.

Flailing recklessly as he fell, Nathaniel blocked the knife swing. But he couldn't prevent the warrior's left hand from clamping onto his throat, and he landed on his back with the Kiowa astride his chest and the knife already spearing in at his neck. His eyes wide, he snatched at the Indian's wrist and held on for precious life, all the while prying at the fingers on his throat, trying to breathe.

A feral gleam lit up the warrior's eyes. His maniacal thirst for revenge had supplanted all conscious thought. He lived only to kill the men who had slain his fellows, and he would achieve his goal or perish in the attempt.

Nathaniel experienced more difficulty in breathing. He couldn't tear the Indian's fingers from his throat, and the razor point of the knife was slowly descending closer and closer. If he didn't break free in the next few seconds, he would die. And so would Zeke if he wasn't already dead.

Ezekiel!

The thought of his dying, helpless uncle spurred Nathaniel into action. He bucked and thrashed, then drove his right knee up into the warrior's back. Once. Twice. And again for good measure, and on the third blow the Kiowa's visage contorted in pain and Thunder Rider threw himself to the right. Nathaniel heaved to his feet, his left hand finding the left pistol and drawing as he rose.

The warrior also leaped erect.

Nathaniel pointed the pistol at Thunder Rider and cocked the hammer. He saw the warrior's look of stunned surprise, and he allowed himself the luxury of a smile, knowing he had won, knowing he was about to pay the Kiowa back in kind for Zeke. And then he squeezed the trigger.

Nothing happened.

Except for the ticking sound of the flint, absolutely nothing happened.

The pistol had misfired.

Thunder Rider vented a triumphant scream and closed in again, batting the pistol from his foe's hand with the blade of his knife.

Nathaniel recovered quickly and took several swift steps toward the northeast corner. His gaze alighted on the rifle, lying at the base of the cabin wall, and he angled for it, diving and gripping the barrel in both hands. He twisted onto his side and saw the warrior already in midair, that glistening blade extended, and he did the only thing he could. He swung the Hawken like a club, whipping the heavy stock in a circle, catching the Indian full on the face, the wood crushing Thunder Rider's nostrils and the force of the blow knocking the Indian to the ground. Nathaniel adjusted his grip and pressed the rifle to his right shoulder, about to fire.

The Kiowa warrior rolled to the right, then surged to his feet and did the unexpected. He threw his knife.

Nathaniel jerked his head to the right, but it wasn't enough to completely dodge the weapon. The blade bit into his left temple and sliced open a shallow groove, causing a lancing pang in his head. He ignored the feeling and sighted on the Indian's head, smack between the eyes.

Thunder Rider shrieked and attacked one more time.

Cooly, calmly, Nathaniel fired, wondering in the back of his mind if using the rifle like a club might have damaged the gun in some way, if it would misfire as the pistol had done. He needn't have worried. The Hawken belched smoke and lead, and never in all his life had Nathaniel heard any sound as sweet as the sharp retort of the rifle.

The ball struck the warrior at the top of the nose and

snapped his head back, spinning him in his tracks. He stopped and blinked once or twice, as if astounded at the outcome, and slowly sank to his knees, then pitched onto his stomach, his arms outflung.

Nathaniel took a deep breath, striving to soothe his suddenly fluttering nerves. Now that the fight was over, his blood seemed to be racing through his body of its own volition. He stared at the lifeless warrior and dropped the Hawken, his hands trembling.

What was wrong with him?

Why couldn't he concentrate?

An unexpected exhaustion made Nathaniel slump onto his back for a few seconds. He stared at the blue sky and spotted an eagle soaring far, far overhead. Putting his palms on the ground, he pushed himself up and stood. His knees were unaccountably wobbly and he leaned on the cabin for support.

A pool of blood was forming under Thunder Rider's head.

Nathaniel gazed at the warrior for a full minute. He'd killed again. How many did that make now? There had been the man with Gant at the Republican River. There had been that Indian during the battle on the hill. Maybe several Indians. So he'd slain at least three men, perhaps more, since leaving St. Louis. To his pleasant surprise, he did not feel any degree of remorse this time. Thunder Rider had needed killing.

It was as simple as that.

His strength returning, Nathaniel pivoted and hastened into the cabin. He almost cried out when he saw his uncle lying on the floor.

Ezekiel had collapsed onto his left side, his hands clasping the lance. Blood caked his chin and neck and coated his hands.

"Zeke!" Nathaniel shouted, reaching his uncle in a bound and kneeling alongside him.

There was no response.

Nathaniel leaned over and gingerly touched his uncle's chest. Relief brought moisture to his eyes when Zeke's eyelids fluttered.

"Nate? Is that you?"

"It's me."

"Did you kill him?"

"He won't be bothering us ever again."

Zeke coughed lightly. "Where's the scalp you promised me?"

"I—I haven't taken it yet."

"No hurry, I reckon," Zeke said. His voice rasped when he spoke, and tiny red bubbles formed on his lips.

Overcome with emotion at the impending loss of his uncle, Nathaniel placed his right hand on Zeke's shoulder. "Please don't die."

"I don't have much choice in the matter."

"There must be *something* I can do!"

"There is. Take me outdoors."

"What?"

Zeke twisted his head a few inches, grimacing with the effort. "I don't want to die in a building. Please, Nate. Carry me outside."

A knot seemed to have formed in Nathaniel's throat. He nodded and eased his arms under his uncle, then straightened, his face turning red from the strain, trying to be as gentle as possible. "Where outside?"

"Anywhere I can see the mountains."

Nathaniel conveyed his uncle out the door and several yards into the open, then tenderly deposited Ezekiel on the cool grass, laying the frontiersman down on his left side so Zeke could gaze to the south and see Long's Peak.

"Thank you, nephew."

"Is there anything else I can do?"

"You can listen."

"Why don't you save your breath?" Nathaniel suggested, sinking onto his right knee.

"For what? Eternity?"

Nathaniel bowed his head.

"I have to tell you," Zeke said. "You need to know about the treasure."

"I don't care about the treasure now," Nathaniel stated, and he meant it. What did wealth matter when he was about to lose a man he had grown to deeply respect and love?

Zeke, strangely, smiled. "That's good. Because there isn't any."

"What?"

"There isn't any treasure, at least not in the way you think there is."

Confused, his brow furrowed, Nathaniel bent over his uncle, trying to read Zeke's expression. "I don't understand. You told me there's a treasure. And you had all those gold nuggets."

"If you trap beaver in these mountains long enough, you'll find a few nuggets too. As for the greatest treasure in the world, I've already shared it with you."

"You have?"

"Look at those mountains," Zeke said, then added forcefully when his nephew didn't comply, "*Look* at them, Nate!"

Nathaniel stared at the majestic peaks, confounded by the revelation, at a loss for words.

"Now look at the lake," Zeke directed. "Do it."

Shifting on his knee, Nathaniel gazed at the sparkling water.

"Take a good look at this valley, Nate. Look at the wildlife, at the deer and the elk and the other game. Think about the fact that all this is now yours. My cabin, my rifle, my clothes, everything I leave to you," Zeke said. "And I leave you with one more thing. The greatest treasure in the world. The treasure that I found when I came out to the Rockies. The treasure I wanted to share with the only relative I give a damn about. The treasure I wanted to share with you, Nate."

Nathaniel looked down. "What treasure?"

"Freedom."

Dazed, Nathaniel shook his head and pressed his right hand to his forehead. "You brought me all the way out here to give me something I already had?"

"Did you? Do you call sitting behind a desk all day, scribbling numbers with a pencil and taking orders from a man who probably considers himself your better, *freedom*? Do you call marrying a woman who is more interested in money than in your happiness *freedom*? Do you call letting your life be run by others *freedom*?"

"But it's not as if I was in chains."

"There are visible and invisible chains, Nate. You told me about those slaves you saw. They wore visible chains. But you were wearing the worst kind. You were wearing invisible chains, the chains of laws and rules and regulations imposed by others who want to control your life for their own selfish ends," Zeke stated passionately, and the exertion cost him. His chin sagged and he groaned.

Nathaniel rested his hand on his uncle's arm. "I don't know what to say."

Zeke's lips barely moved. "Tell me you'll stay out here. Live in my cabin. Learn to trap. Make your mark in the world, but do it your way."

"I don't know how to trap."

"Shakespeare will teach you."

"How do I find him?"

"He should be here in a few days. We were going to the rendezvous together. He'll take you."

"But what if I want to go home?"

"You can trust Shakespeare, Nate," Zeke said, as if he hadn't heard.

"What if the Utes come before he shows up?"

"Then show them that you're a man. Show them that you're the lord of this valley, that you're the king of the mountains." Zeke grinned, then gasped.

"Oh, God, Uncle Zeke!"

Ezekiel glanced up, his eyes startlingly clear. "You're a man, now. You have to give up your boyish ways. In the city you can still be a boy at nineteen. Out here you can't. You're Nate King, free trapper, mountain man, and the master of your own destiny." He inhaled noisily and struggled to speak one more time. "I've done all I can. The rest is up to you. Make me proud, Nate. I'm going to meet the Eternal."

"Zeke!"

A soft whisper came from Ezekiel King's lips. He stiffened, straightening to his full length, and then went limp, his head settling on the green carpet underneath his cheek, his eyes closing, a curious smile creasing his lips.

Far overhead the eagle soared.

Epilogue

He rode into the valley through the broad opening between the ridges, sitting astride a white horse, a Hawken cradled in his big arms. His shoulder-length hair, his beard, and his mustache were all a striking white, his eyes a sea blue. He wore buckskins and a brown beaver hat, and slanted across his chest were his powder horn and his bullet pouch.

The valley appeared tranquil.

Accustomed to the path he followed, he rode down to the valley floor and toward the lake teeming with geese and ducks. Beyond the lake stood the familiar cabin, and the rider smiled in anticipation. He goaded his horse to go a little faster, taking the south bank, watching gray smoke curl upward from the narrow chimney. Not until he was 20 yards from his destination did he spy the freshly dug grave and reined up.

The low mound of earth was situated ten yards to the south of the cabin, in an open area.

The rider took a firmer grip of his rifle and rode closer. That was when he saw the Indian and his eyes widened.

Someone had placed the body 30 yards away, simply

dumped it on the hard ground and left it there to rot. The warrior lay on his back. He had been scalped.

"Can I help you?"

The hard tone drew the rider around to the north. A man was standing at the northeast corner, a rifle in his hands, a man with green eyes and black hair, wearing buckskins and a red Mackinaw coat. "Howdy, neighbor," the rider said in a friendly fashion. "Who might you be?"

"You're the one who's trespassing in my valley," the man responded. "Who are you?"

"Folks hereabouts call me Shakespeare."

"You're Shakespeare?" the man in red replied, and took several strides forward. "Zeke told me to expect you."

"And who are you?"

"His nephew."

Shakespeare scarcely concealed his surprise. "*You're* Nathaniel?"

"*Nate*. Nate King."

"Well, I'm right pleased to meet you." Shakespeare glanced at the grave. "Is that who I think it is?"

"Zeke was killed by a Kiowa."

Sadness etched the rugged mountain man's features. "Alas, poor Ezekiel. I knew him well. A fellow of infinite jest, of most excellent fancy; he bore me on his back a thousand times."

"What?"

The mountain man stared at the man in red. "That's Shakespeare, Nate. Of a sort, anyway. And that's why folks call me by that name." He reached back and thumped a rolled blanket tied behind his saddle. "I never go anywhere without my book on old William S."

"I'm pleased to make your acquaintance," Nate said. "Why don't you climb down and share some elk meat with me?"

"I don't mind if I do," Shakespeare answered. He rode up to the cabin and dismounted.

"We can leave for the rendezvous in the morning," Nate stated.

"You want to go to the rendezvous?"

"I do. My uncle told me I can trust you, that you'll teach me everything I need to know."

The mountain man grinned. "It seems like I'm making it my life's business to teach Kings the facts of life."

"I already know them," Nate said, and motioned at the open door. "Come on in. I want you to tell me all about Zeke."

Shakespeare laughed. "That'd take a year."

"I have the time." Nate turned and entered the cabin.

Chuckling, Shakespeare took a step, about to go in, when his gaze fell on the scalp nailed to the front of the door, a scalp recently removed. He looked back at the dead Indian, then at the hair hanging in front of him. "What's this?" he asked.

The reply was a full ten seconds in coming.

"Nothing. Nothing at all."

LURE OF THE WILD

Dedicated to...
Judy, Joshua, and Shane.

And to all those in the black powder fraternity who know that shooting a hawken ranks right up there with wild onions and fresh venison.

Chapter One

"Indians," the lead rider said softly.

Both men immediately reined up.

The second rider, the younger of the duo, sat anxiously astride his mare and took a firmer grip on the Hawken in his right hand. He scanned the surrounding forest, his keen eyes scouring every shadow and possible place of concealment, the northwesterly breeze stirring his long black hair. Like his companion, he wore buckskins. A knife with a 12-inch blade rested in a sheath on his left hip. Slanted across his broad chest were his powder horn and bullet pouch. Tucked under his belt were two pistols. "Where?" he asked.

"Over yonder," the first man said, and nodded at the mountain slope to the southwest. In contrast to his youthful companion, the lead rider sported shoulder-length hair, a beard, and a mustache that were all as white as the snow capping the towering peaks to their rear. His eyes were a striking sea blue. A brown beaver hat adorned his head, and cradled in his big arms was a Hawken.

"I don't see them," the younger man commented.

"Keep looking, Nate."

His eyes narrowing, Nate scrutinized the slope carefully, estimating they were at least a half mile from the mountain in question. Large boulders dotted the slope, interspersed with stands of evergreen trees, typical terrain for the west slope of the Rocky Mountains. "I still don't see any Indians, Shakespeare."

The older man chuckled. "You're just like your uncle was when he first came out to the Rockies, Nathaniel King. You're blind as a bat and have the ears of a worm."

"Worms don't have ears."

"You're learning."

Nate started to smile, but he froze when he detected movement on the mountain slope and spied the five Indians riding at a leisurely pace from west to east, apparently using a narrow trail running from the top of the mountain to the bottom.

"Don't move," Shakespeare advised. "They haven't seen us yet. If we're lucky, they won't." He paused. "Those Devils are Utes."

The name jarred Nate's memory. "My uncle told me the Utes kill every white man they come across."

"And Zeke was right."

"What do we do if they see us?"

"Tuck our tails between our legs and cut out."

His skin tingling, Nate watched the five Utes ride lower down the mountain. The distance was too great for him to distinguish the details of their dress and the weapons they carried, but he had no doubt that each warrior was well armed.

"They're probably heading over the Continental Divide to the Plains," Shakespeare mentioned. "Going to do a little buffalo hunting, or maybe raid the Cheyennes or the Arapahos."

"Will they use the same pass we did?"

"Most likely."

"Then they'll see our tracks in the snow."

"So? By the time the Utes reach that pass, we'll be long gone. And even if they do try to trail us, they won't follow us very far," Shakespeare predicted.

"Why not?" Nate asked.

"Because they're not stupid. They'll figure that we're white men because that horse you bought in New York is shod. Then they'll work it out in their heads that we must be heading for the rendezvous at Bear Lake."

"The Utes know about the rendezvous?"

Shakespeare snickered. "Every tribe in these parts knows about the get-together of all the trappers and the fur traders. A lot of the tribes sends groups to the rendezvous to trade, sell their women, and such."

"And the Utes won't follow us there?"

"No. For two very important reasons. First, they'd be shot on sight. Second, we'll be passing through the Green River country, and no Ute in his right mind wants to go there."

Nate saw the five Utes disappear behind a cluster of trees. "Why not?"

"Because the Blackfeet roam that area."

That name sparked another memory. Nate glanced at his companion. "Uncle Zeke told me that the Blackfeet are one tribe I should avoid at all costs."

"And Zeke spoke the truth, as always. The damn Blackfeet are the most warlike tribe west of the Mississippi. They fight everyone. Even the other tribes think they're war crazy and that says a lot because most tribes like going to war."

"They do?"

"Sure. Why, there's hardly three tribes in the whole Indian Country that are friendly to one another, except for the Cheyennes and the Arapahos. They just can't get along. And the Blackfeet are the most feared of the lot,"

Shakespeare disclosed.

"Have you ever run into them?" Nate inquired.

"A few times."

"What happened?"

"Let me put it this way. The Blackfoot warrior who hangs my scalp in his lodge will be the envy of the tribe."

Aligning his Hawken across his thighs, Nate surveyed the mountain slope. "I don't see the Utes."

"We can keep going," Shakespeare said, and rode onward. "I want to cover as much ground as we can today."

Nate followed. "How long will it take us to reach Bear Lake?"

"About a week, if we're lucky and push it. The rendezvous will be in full swing when we get there. I'm taking the shortest route I know of. If we'd had the time to spare, I would have gone up the Sweetwater Valley and then over the Divide at South Pass. It's a lot easier that way, but we'd miss almost all of the rendezvous," Shakespeare detailed.

Nate glanced over his right shoulder at the rim of snow-covered peaks behind them, to the east. "What was the name of that pass we used?"

"It doesn't have a name. Not many folks know it exists. The Indians do, of course. You and me. And Zeke did."

The mention of his uncle brought a frown to Nate's face and he stared glumly at the terrain, thinking of the man who had lured him to the West under false pretenses, the man he had grown to care for as much as he did his own father. By all rights he should despise Zeke for the dirty trick he had played on him, but he couldn't bring himself to feel angry, not when the six weeks or so he had spent in Zeke's company had been the six happiest weeks of his entire life.

Nate shook his head in disbelief. Had it only been about

three months ago that he had departed New York City in response to the letter sent by Ezekiel? The time seemed longer. Much, much longer. So much had happened. He'd nearly been robbed and killed. He'd crossed the prairie in company with his uncle, surviving encounters with cut-throats, a grizzly bear, and a war party of Kiowas. He'd made it all the way to the uncharted vastness of the Rocky Mountains, to his uncle's cabin high up in the rugged wilderness, only to see his uncle slain at the hands of an avenging Kiowa warrior.

All that, and for what?

For a treasure that never existed, at least not in the way he had anticipated.

Zeke's letter had hinted at great riches. His uncle had extended an invitation to meet him in St. Louis, and promised to share "the greatest treasure in the world." Believing that Zeke had found gold or made a fortune in the fur trade, hoping to use his share of the wealth to woo his beloved Adeline Van Buren, Nate had decided to take Zeke up on the offer.

How was he to know the offer had been a sham?

Nate sighed and watched a squirrel scamper from branch to branch in a nearby tree. He'd traveled almost a thousand miles to St. Louis and met his uncle, only to have Zeke inform him that he must venture all the way to the Rocky Mountains if he wanted to see Zeke's "treasure." The prospect of being away from Adeline for a year had troubled Nate immensely, but he had justified going with Zeke on the pretext that the wealth he would obtain would make the separation and hardships entailed worthwhile.

But was that the real reason?

Quite often of late, Nate found himself speculating that there might be another, underlying reason why he had allowed himself to be duped. True, he'd genuinely liked Ezekiel. True, he had wanted to impress Adeline by acquiring riches beyond her wildest dreams. Also true, however, was the fact that he had been thrilled at having the opportunity to journey into a savage realm few white men had ever penetrated. In his youth he had read countless stories about the fierce Indians and the wild beasts inhabiting the unmapped lands beyond the frontier, and had often imagined the adventures he would have if he was to go west.

Now his dreams were coming true.

Nate's reflection was interrupted by a question from his companion.

"Did you bring that scalp along?"

The corners of Nate's mouth curled downward slightly as he thought of the Kiowa warrior he had slain, the Indian whose scalp he had taken to fulfill a promise made to his dying uncle. He glanced at the pack horse he was leading, at the blanket in which he had rolled up the scalp, then looked at Shakespeare. "I brought it."

"Good."

"What's good about it?"

"The Indians and quite a few of the whites out here place a lot of stock in taking the hair of an enemy. It marks you as a man."

"Have you taken any scalps?"

"Thirty-two."

The number staggered Nate. He'd taken the Kiowa warrior's hair in the heat of a burning rage over his uncle's death. Without that fury to act as a stimulus, he doubted whether he could have performed the grisly task. "I don't know if I can ever take another one," he commented.

"You will."

"How can you be so sure?"

"To be, or not to be. That's the question. Whether it's nobler in the mind to suffer the slings and arrows of outrageous fortune, or to take arms against a sea of troubles, and by opposing end them,'' the white-haired mountain man replied.

"Shakespeare again?"

"Sort of."

"Why do you like him so much? I struggled through some of his works in school, and I never could understand half of what I read."

"Old William S. was one of the wisest mothers' sons who ever lived. I picked up a book of his plays about thirty years ago, and I've been reading him ever since. It's gotten so that I'm a fair hand at quoting him. I reckon that's why everyone now calls me Shakespeare."

Nate stared at the roll tied behind Shakespeare's saddle, where the frontiersman kept his book on the English playright, and thought of his own affinity for the works of James Fenimore Cooper. "What's your real name?"

Shakespeare unexpectedly halted and twisted. "Let me give you a word of advice, Nate. You're the nephew of the best friend I ever had, and I've made it my business to teach you how to survive out here. One thing you must never do is pry into another man's personal affairs. If a man volunteers information about himself, about his past or whatever, all well and good. But don't go poking your nose in where it doesn't belong or someone is likely to try and shoot it off."

"All I did was ask your name," Note noted defensively.

"And if I ever figure I can trust you enough, I'll tell you my name," Shakespeare said.

Nate's forehead furrowed in confusion as he mulled the implications of the other man's remarks. What possible motive could Shakespeare have for not revealing his own name? Was he embarrassed by it, as some people occasionally were? Or could there be a darker motive? Was Shakespeare wanted by the authorities somewhere? Did the mountain man have an evil secret buried somewhere in his past he wanted no one to know? "Sorry I asked," he commented. "I meant no offense."

"None taken," Shakespeare said, and resumed riding in a northwesterly direction.

Nate lapsed into silence, mentally debating whether he had made another mistake by deciding to remain in the West for a spell instead of returning to the States. After Zeke had died, he'd spent a sleepless night sitting out under the star-filled firmament, pondering the course he should take, weighing the pros and cons, trying to gauge the consequences of both options.

One factor had stood out above the others. He had informed Adeline that he would be acquiring great wealth. In the letter he'd composed to her before leaving New York City, and again in the epistle he'd sent from St. Louis, he'd related Zeke's pledge to share the "treasure" and promised to return to New York incredibly rich. What would Adeline think when she learned the truth? How would she react when she discovered he had been duped? How would she feel towards him when she found out there never had been any gold or silver or money garnered in the lucrative fur trade? Would she think him a fool, or worse?

He couldn't blame her if she did.

How was he to know that Ezekiel King's treasure wasn't anything material, wasn't anything he could hold in his hands or hoard at the bank? He could still vividly remember the earnest expression on his uncle's face as Zeke lay dying, and the words Zeke spoke that seared into his brain and struck a responsive chord.

"Take a good look at this valley, Nate," Zeke had said. "Look at the wildlife, at the deer and the elk and the other game. Think about the fact that all this is now yours. My cabin, my rifle, my clothes, everything I leave to you. And I leave you with one more thing. The greatest treasure

in the world. The treasure that I found when I came out
to the Rockies. The treasure I wanted to share with the
only relative I give a damn about. The treasure I wanted
to share with you, Nate.''

"What treasure?" Nate had asked.

"Freedom."

The one word had provoked a peculiar response. Nate
had later gazed at the majestic mountain peaks ringing
the valley, at the abundant wildlife, at a sparkling lake
situated not far from his uncle's cabin, a lake swarming
with ducks and geese and fowl of every description; he
had stared overhead at the brilliant blue sky, and inhaled
the crisp, invigorating high-altitude air; and for a brief,
insightful moment, a few seconds of lucid contemplation,
he had actually felt that distinctive, transcendent freedom
his uncle had alluded to, the pure, pristine freedom of a
soul unfettered by the restraints of civilization.

Nate cherished that feeling, an exquisite sensation he
had never known before. How could he return to New
York now, after tasting a morsel of genuine freedom? New
more importantly, how could he return to Adeline without
the wealth he had promised? How could he go back a
failure? Both reasons for remaining in the Rockies vied
with one another for dominance, and he had yet to resolve
his true motivation for staying and for deciding to go to
the rendezvous. He had—

"It appears I've miscalculated a mite," Shakespeare
intruded on Nate's rumination.

"How so?"

Shakespeare pointed to the southwest. "Here come the
Utes."

Chapter Two

Nate shifted and glanced to the left, and there were the five Ute warriors bearing down on them at breakneck speed. Even as he spied them, his eyes widening in alarm, they uttered loud war whoops and one of them foolishly snapped off a rifle shot.

"Stay close!" Shakespeare bellowed, and took off to the right, angling across the narrow valley they had been following, his white horse throwing up clods of earth with its hooves.

Expecting to feel an arrow penetrate his back at any moment, Nate kept as close to Shakespeare as he could, his mare pounding under him, the pack horse only a few feet to the rear of his mount.

The piercing shrieks of the Utes rose in volume.

They're gaining! Nate realized, and swallowed hard. He saw that his companion was making for a stand of trees several hundred yards off, and he risked a hasty look over his left shoulder to determine the position of the warriors.

Riding as if they were born on the back of a horse, their animals flying over the ground, the Utes were approximately five hundred yards to the southwest, waving their weapons and bellowing in anticipation of slaying the intruders into their territory.

Nate rode as he had never ridden before, his body rising and falling with the rhythm of his mare, his left hand holding the reins, his right hand clutching the Hawken and the lead to the pack animal, his blood coursing through his body even faster than the mare was running. He concentrated on the stand of trees, struggling to suppress the panic welling within him, knowing if he lost his head he would lose his life.

The Utes whooped and hollered, giving the impression there were scores of them instead of only five.

Shakespeare glanced back once, a devilish grin creasing his visage.

What did he find so humorous? Nate wondered, licking his dry lips, remembering how his Uncle Zeke had demonstrated the same peculiar, lighthearted attitude when confronted with danger, as if a life-and-death situation were a mere game of some sort. He doubted if he would ever understand these rugged, individualistic men who inhabited the unknown regions of the West. They seemed to possess an outlook on life that differed greatly from their cultured cousins in the States.

For a tense minute the race continued, the Utes doing their utmost to close on their quarry before the mountain men could reach the trees, but they were still a hundred yards away when the white-haired man reached the stand, practically leaped from his horse, and whirled.

Nate saw Shakespeare whip the Hawken up and fire, apparently without taking deliberate aim, and yet when Nate glanced back he beheld one of the Utes pitching to the ground.

Shakespeare voiced a whoop at his own.

And now Nate smiled as he reined up and vaulted to Shakespeare's side. ''Nice shooting,'' he commented, keeping his voice as calm as he could. He raised his Hawken and took careful aim, not wanting to waste the shot, sighting on the Indian riding on the right, scarcely breathing. He waited several seconds to be certain, then fired.

Eighty yards out the Ute threw his arms in the air and toppled backwards.

"We'll teach those savages a thing or two," Shakespeare remarked, in the process of reloading, his practiced fingers performing the task with astonishing speed.

Nate began to reload his rifle.

The three remaining Utes were still coming on strong. One of them unleashed an arrow.

"Watch out!" Shakespeare warned, and gave Nate a shove.

Startled, Nate looked up in time to see the arrow hurtling out of the blue. The shaft whizzed through the air and thudded into the ground at the exact spot where he had been standing.

"Quills are for porcupines," Shakespeare quipped, and aimed at the Ute with the bow. An instant later his rifle cracked and belched a ball and smoke.

The bow-wielder was in the act of drawing back the buffalo-sinew string when the shot hit him high on the chest and flung him over his mount's rump. In concert the remaining pair of warriors swung to the left, hunching low, glaring at the whites, racing for cover.

Nate finished reloading and lifted the Hawken to fire again.

"Don't bother," Shakespeare advised, watching the Utes depart. "We don't want to kill them all."

"We don't?" Nate declared in astonishment. "But they were trying to kill us."

Shakespeare glanced at the younger man and chuckled.

"Bloodthirsty son of a gun, aren't you? No, we don't want to kill all of them and I'll tell you why." He paused and stared at the fleeing Indians. "Out here, Nate, a man's reputation is as important as the man himself. Those two will go back to their tribe and report that they tried to take the hair of old Carcajou and failed. They'll embellish the story a bit, and make me out to be a fire-breathing demon who can down an enemy at a thousand yards. Now that will add considerably to my reputation, and the next time some Utes stumble across me they'll likely think twice before attempting to take my hair. Understand?"

"I believe so," Nate said. He observed the Utes vanish in the forest. "What was that name you mentioned? Carcajou?"

Shakespeare nodded. "If you live out here long enough, and if you become acquainted with the friendly Indians, you might acquire an Indian name of your own. Long ago the Flatheads gave me the name Carcajou."

"What does it mean?"

"It's another name for the wolverine."

"What's a wolverine?"

The frontiersman looked at Nate and laughed. "You'll learn soon enough."

Puzzled by the answer, Nate cradled his rifle. "I already have an Indian name of my own," he mentioned.

"You do?" Shakespeare responded in surprise.

"Yes. A Cheyenne named White Eagle gave it to me."

"I know him. He's a member of their Bow String Society."

"Their what?"

Shakespeare chortled. "You have so much to learn, it's pitiful. Most of the tribes living on the Plains have what they call soldier or warrior societies. They're a lot like those fancy, exclusive clubs for the rich back in the States, only the soldier societies have as their members the bravest men, the best fighters. The Cheyennes, as I recollect, have six societies." He paused, then began counting them off on his fingers. "The Bow String, the Crazy Dogs, the Red Shields, the Fox Soldiers, the Elk Soldiers, and the Dog Soldiers."

"So White Eagle must be an important man in their tribe?" Nate inquired.

"I'll say. He's one of their top war chiefs."

The news staggered Nate. He recalled the first time he'd seen White Eagle, shortly after being mauled by the grizzly that had surprised him when he wasn't carrying his rifle. He'd managed to plunge his butcher knife into the bear's head, and his uncle had finished the bruin off with a well-placed shot from a Hawken.

Later, during the battle with the Kiowas war party, White Eagle and other Cheyennes had arrived and rendered assistance. Before riding off, White Eagle had bestowed a gift and the name on Nate, and only now was he truly beginning to appreciate the significance of both acts. "I had no idea," he mumbled.

"What name did White Eagle give you?" Shakespeare asked.

"Grizzly Killer."

The corners of Shakespeare's mouth started to curl upward, and he looked as if he was about to burst out laughing. He scrutinized Nate for a moment, then suddenly sobered. "You're not pulling my leg?"

"Nope."

"Well, I'll be," Shakespeare said, his brow knitting. "A true knight, not yet mature, yet matchless, firm of word, speaking in deeds and deedless in his tongue, not soon provoked nor being provoked soon calmed, his heart and hand both open and both free."

"What?"

"Never mind," Shakespeare replied. He scanned the

distant trees, ensuring the Utes were indeed gone.

"White Eagle also gave me an eagle feather," Nate mentioned.

"Where is it?"

"In my pack."

Shakespeare regarded his companion carefully. "Why aren't you wearing it?"

"I removed the feather from my hair after the first day because I couldn't sleep with it tied behind my head," Nate explained. "I haven't worn the thing since."

"I'm not one to offer advice unless asked, but if I were you I'd consider wearing the feather. They're marks of distinction for an Indian, and in some tribes you can't wear one unless you've killed an enemy," Shakespeare commented, his eyes narrowing. "Who did White Eagle see you kill?"

"A Kiowa warrior."

Shakespeare nodded. "White Eagle must regard you highly. If you're ever in Cheyenne country again, you'd best wear that feather. If you bump into him and you're not wearing it, he'll be offended."

"I'll keep that in mind," Nate promised. He glanced down at the arrow imbedded in the earth and bent over to pull the shaft out. "Another second and I'd have been a goner," he commented.

"Never underestimate an Indian with a bow," Shakespeare admonished. "They learn to shoot while standing, running, or from horseback when they're young boys, and they're accurate at over a hundred yards."

Nate studied the shaft thoughtfully.

"Not only that," Shakespeare went on, "they can fire arrows faster than you or I can load and fire a rifle. I saw a contest once between a trapper, a fellow who could shoot an acorn off a limb at fifty yards, and a Crow warrior. In the time it took the trapper to fire, reload, and fire again, that Crow got off twenty arrows.''

''Twenty?'' Nate repeated skeptically.

Shakespeare nodded. ''And about ten years ago I spent some time in a Mandan village. The Mandans had this game they played, where the warriors tried to see which one of them could keep the most arrows in the air at the same time. Their best bowman, the best damn archer I ever saw, could keep nine arrows in the air all at once.''

Nate whistled. The more he learned about the prowess of the Indians, the more amazed he became that any white men managed to survive in the wilderness.

''Let's mount up and skedaddle,'' Shakespeare suggested. He walked to his horse, which stood patiently nibbling at grass several yards away.

''You're certain those Utes won't try to circle around and ambush us?'' Nate asked, moving toward his mare.

''As certain as I was they hadn't spotted us earlier,'' Shakespeare said, and laughed.

''Well, now I'm relieved,'' Nate quipped.

Minutes later they were mounted and riding to the northwest across an open, grassy expanse stretching to more mountains ten miles away.

''Let this incident be a lesson to you,'' Shakespeare said after they had traveled a quarter of a mile without seeing any sign of the Utes.

''Let me guess. I should never turn my back on an Ute.''

''No. You should always trust your own instincts, no matter what someone else with more experience might tell you. Go with your gut, as I like to say. My gut has saved my hide more times than I care to recollect.''

''But your instincts didn't warn you about those Utes,'' Nate noted.

Shakespeare chuckled. ''Which brings to mind another saying I'm fond of. Most folks have no more brains in their head than they do in their elbow.''

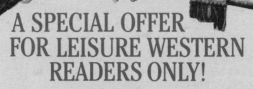

A SPECIAL OFFER FOR LEISURE WESTERN READERS ONLY!

Get FOUR FREE Western Novels

Travel to the Old West in all its glory and drama—without leaving your home!

Plus, you'll save between $3.00 and $6.00 every time you buy!

EXPERIENCE THE ADVENTURE AND THE DRAMA OF THE OLD WEST WITH THE GREATEST WESTERNS ON THE MARKET TODAY...FROM LEISURE BOOKS

GET YOUR 4 FREE BOOKS NOW—
A VALUE BETWEEN $16 AND $20
Mail the Free Book Certificate Today!

FREE BOOKS CERTIFICATE!

YES! I want to subscribe to the Leisure Western Book Club. Please send my 4 FREE BOOKS. Then, each month, I'll preview the four newest Leisure Western Selections to preview FREE for 10 days. If I decide to keep them, I will pay the Special Members Only discounted price of just $3.36 each, a total of $13.44. This saves me between $3 and $6 off the bookstore price. There are no shipping, handling or other charges. There is no minimum number of books I must buy and I may cancel the program at any time. In any case, the 4 FREE BOOKS are mine to keep—at a value of between $17 and $20! Offer valid only in the USA.

Name_____

Address_____

City_____ State_____

Zip_____ Phone_____

Biggest Savings Offer!

For those of you who would like to pay us in advance by check or credit card—we've got an even bigger savings in mind. Interested? Check here. ☐

If under 18, parent or guardian must sign.
Terms, prices and conditions subject to change. Subscription subject to acceptance. Leisure Books reserves the right to reject any order or cancel any subscription.

"I like that," Nate said cheerfully, beginning to relax, already filing the fight with the Utes in the back of his mind as just another wilderness memory.

"That saying is taken straight from old William S."

"You're kidding me?"

"Nope. *Troilus and Cressida.* Act Two, Scene One."

Nate shook his head in astonishment. "You sure know your Shakespeare."

"I guess I do. Who would ever have figured I'd acquire such a classical education in the Rocky Mountain College."

"The what?"

"The Rocky Mountain College. That's the term us mountain folk use to describe all those long winter nights when it's too cold to trap and we're sitting around the fire in our toasty lodge debating everything under the sun."

"Zeke didn't tell me about it."

"Your uncle didn't have time to tell you about every aspect of life out here before he died. Give yourself a while. In a few years you won't be a greenhorn any longer."

"I don't know if I'll stay out here that long," Nate confided.

"You will."

"How can you be so certain?"

"You're a King."

"So? I have brothers back in the States who will never venture out of New York."

Shakespeare glanced at Nate. "You're different. You're like your uncle was, filled with the urge to roam, to see new lands and have adventures. That's what brought me out here ages ago."

"Ages?"

"It seems that long, sometimes," Shakespeare said wistfully. "The years are longer when you cram them with experience, when you live life to the fullest like the Good Lord intended. In the States, especially in the cities, most people go from day to day doing exactly the same thing they did the day before. They get up at the same time every morning, go to the same job each day, come home to the same house at night, and sleep in the same bed under the same covers. Their lives streak past like a shooting star, and before they know it someone is dropping dirt on their coffin and they haven't experienced one damn thing life has to offer."

"I never thought of it that way."

"You'll see. In a year from now you'll agree with me."

Nate thought of the Utes, the Blackfeet, and the Kiowas. "If I live that long."

Chapter Three

Several days later, after crossing another mountain range, they came to a remarkable expanse of arid, steep canyons totally different from the Rockies. Columns of red sandstone reared everywhere. Game became scarce and vegetation virtually nonexistent.

Nate took advantage of the trip to pepper Shakespeare with countless questions concerning the wildlife, the Indians, the general known geography of the land west of the Mississippi, and any other subject he could think of, adding substantially to the lore he had learned from Zeke. The aged frontiersman was a virtual fount of knowledge and wisdom, and Nate soaked up the information like a human sponge.

Shakespeare continued in a northwesterly direction, pushing their mounts as hard as he dared, eager to reach the rendezvous.

Nate found the older man's uncharacteristic hurry amusing. In every other aspect to Shakespeare's life, the man never displayed the slightest inclination to rush, but he was bound and determined to reach the annual gathering of trappers, traders, and friendly Indians while it was still in progress.

On the third day after the incident with the Utes, Shakespeare called a midday halt at a spring situated at the base of a steep plateau. They watered their animals and sat down to enjoy strips of jerked venison.

"Do you realize that not five white men in the whole world have been within ten miles of this spot?" Shakespeare asked. He took a bite of jerky and chewed vigorously.

"Really?" Nate responded absently, gazing out over the barren terrain.

"Prime beaver country is north of here. Few trappers ever bother to pass through this region because it's a waste of their time."

"Reminds me of a desert."

Shakespeare snorted. "If you want to see a real desert, you should travel into the territory west of the Great Salt Lake. There isn't a drop of water to be had anywhere, and your throat becomes so parched you drink your own sweat just to survive."

"You've been there?" Nate inquired.

"A few times."

"Is there any part of the land between the Mississippi and the Pacific you haven't seen?"

"There's more country I haven't seen than country I have," Shakespeare said. "And some of the parts I have laid eyes on were downright amazing."

"For instance?"

Shakespeare tilted his head and pondered for a full ten seconds. "Well, the most amazing wonders of all are located north of here a ways. There are boiling mud holes, geysers that shoot hundreds of feet in the air, and natural hot springs where the water is hot enough to scald you."

"Boiling mud holes?" Nate repeated skeptically. "Geysers?"

"Don't you believe me?"

"Of course. I know you're not one to invent tall tales. But still, boiling mud holes, you must admit, seem a little preposterous. I hope I see them myself, one day."

The frontiersman regarded the younger man for a minute, then broke into a grin and nodded. "Yep. If I hadn't of seen those geysers and mud holes, I'd probably say the same thing. I hope you do get to see them, Nate. If the land gets into your blood, you will."

"Into my blood?"

Shakespeare gestured at the far horizon. "The wilderness has a way of growing on a man. Those who come out west intending to spend a year or so trapping wind up staying four or five years. Some stay longer. Once you start traveling and beholding all the marvels, once you can live off the land like an Indian, and once you realize that life in the States is akin to being penned in a cage, you can't leave." He chuckled. "Once you've tasted genuine freedom, it's a mite hard to settle for anything less."

"There's that word again," Nate commented.

"Which word?"

"Freedom. Uncle Zeke said practically the same thing."

"He knew what he was talking about. Out here, where you don't have to answer to anyone, where you don't have taxes to pay or the government breathing down your back, where you don't have politicians trying to tell you how to live, is where you find the freedom our forefathers fought and died for."

"I didn't realize you're so political-minded," Nate said.

Shakespeare's eyes narrowed. "Don't you ever insult me like that again. Implying a man is like a politician is as bad as calling him a liar and a thief. There's hardly a politician alive worth his salt, and rare are those who knowing the true meaning of the word honor." He paused.

"Mine honor keeps the weather of my fate: Life every man holds dear, but the dear man holds honor far more precious-dear than life."

"Let me guess. More of your William S."

Shakespeare nodded. "I don't give a tinker's damn about politics, Nate, except when some dignified, vote-begging leach tries to take my freedom away. Then I can get riled."

"I've never paid much attention to politics," Nate mentioned.

"Good. Don't. The more you think about it, the more agitated you'll become," Shakespeare predicted. He placed his hands on the hard ground and pushed to his feet.

"Going somewhere?"

"Nature calls. I'll be back in a bit."

Nate watched his companion walk to a cluster of huge boulders to the south. Moments later Shakespeare disappeared among the rocks. He squinted up at the bright sun, then stood and stretched. After all that riding a little exercise seemed to be in order. He turned and strolled casually along the edge of the spring, gazing idly into the crystal-clear water while finishing his dried venison.

How strange fate could be.

Who would ever have thought that one day he would be standing next to a spring in the heart of an unexplored wildnerness? Or that he would be traveling with an old man who was as tough as leather and who could quote Shakespeare by the hour?

Nate grinned.

Who would ever have thought that he would have the courage to leave New York City and venture into the Great West? Who would ever have guessed that in the breast of an accountant lurked the heart of an adventurer? Which brought a pertinent question to mind. How far was he willing to go, both physically and personally? How much longer would he remain in the wilderness? What about beautiful Adeline, awaiting his return? How long could he reasonably expect her to wait for him? He'd told her in his letter from St. Louis that he would be gone about a year. Did she possess the patience to hold out for a year? Or would she grow lonely and bored and seek out other male suitors?

The realizataion sobered him.

He had to face facts. Adeline could have her pick of practically any man in New York. In the States, for that matter. And he wouldn't be justified in blaming her if she did acquire a new beau, not after he had up and left her without more than a day's notice.

What had he done?

Upset by his train of thought, Nate stopped and licked his dry lips. The water beckoned, and he knelt and dipped his right hand in the cool liquid. That jerked meat had made him extremely thirsty. Eager to drink, he flattened on his stomach and touched his mouth to the spring.

A strange rattling noise arose on his right.

Nate took a sip, puzzled by the rattling. He glanced at a pile of fair-sized stones within inches of his right arm, and froze.

Lying coiled under a large flat stone, its stout body tensed and ready to spring, its wide head hovering motionless, its eerie eyes with their vertical pupils fixed on his neck, was an enormous rattlesnake.

Petrified, Nate didn't move a muscle. He scarcely breathed, his gaze riveted on those alien, wicked eyes. What should he do? Would the rattlesnake strike if he tried to rise and flee? Would the reptile slither away if he simply stayed glued to that spot?

The rattling continued unabated and the snake remained coiled, its long, forked black tongue flicking out and in.

Nate's initial panic began to subside. He concentrated

on keeping perfectly still. Sooner or later, he hoped, the reptile would leave. He'd heard somewhere, probably in school many years ago, that a rattlesnake wouldn't strike unless directly threatened, and he had no intention of posing the slightest possible threat.

A minute elapsed.

Two.

Sweat formed on Nate's brow and trickled down his back. He ignored the sensation. Don't move! he told himself over and over. Don't twitch a muscle!

The peculiar buzzing from the snake's rattles abruptly ceased.

Nate almost forgot himself, almost smiled in triumph. The rattler must be about to slide off to hunt or return to whatever hole it used as a den. He saw the reptile begin to glide forward. Elated, he watched the rattlesnake carefully, expecting it to turn to the left, away from the spring.

Instead, to his utter horror, the rattler came straight toward him!

Nate's terror returned in a rush, and only with a supreme effort could he prevent himself from trembling. The rattlesnake angled at his head, and for a heart stopping instant he thought it would bite his face. But the reptile slid up and over his neck, moving slowly, its cool scales rubbing against his flesh.

Dear God!

Nate wanted to scream. He gritted his teeth until they hurt and clenched his fists, wishing the rattler would pass completely over him quickly and go on its way.

The snake unexpectedly stopped.

No! No! No! Nate shrieked in his mind. Keep going! He could feel the weight of the reptile on his neck. The strain on his nerves was tremendous. What was it doing? Why had it stopped? He detected a flickering motion out of the corner of his left eye, and without moving his head he swiveled his eyes and caught sight of the cause.

The rattlesnake had turned. Its squat head was now near the water, its tongue continuing to dart out and back again.

What was it *doing*? Nate nearly bolted, but he willed himself to relax, to remain calm, certain the reptile would leave soon. The seconds dragged by. Beads of sweat dribbled down his cheeks and dripped from his chin. The pistols were gouging him in the abdomen. If only he dared make a grab for them!

A second later the rattler began to move away, its head weaving from side to side.

Nate felt the scales scraping his skin.

In another few seconds the snake would be gone!

A tingling sensation suddenly developed in Nate's nostrils and he experienced an urge to sneeze. Not now! He wiggled his nose, trying to suppress the impulse, to no avail. The tingling grew more intense. He went to lift his right hand, to clamp his fingers on his nostrils, but he was too late.

The sneeze, to his agitated mind, sounded like a gunshot.

Nate tensed and glanced at the rattlesnake, his blood racing when he saw the reptile snap around and stare directly at him. He expected to hear the rattling again, but the snake was motionless except for the constant flicking of its forked tongue.

What *now*?

Had the rattler realized he wasn't a log or a rock? Would it strike without warning? A quick roll to the left might enable him to escape. It also might trigger an attack. So his best bet appeared to be to stay still and do nothing.

The snake, apparently, had other ideas.

It started to crawl toward him.

Nate's eyes inadvertently widened and his breath caught in his throat. If the rattler sank its fangs into his face, he'd be a goner within minutes.

The rattlesnake glided slowly nearer.

Goose bumps erupted all over Nate's body. He watched the reptile draw to within six inches of his face, then stop, and he became acutely conscious of the rattler's eyes boring into his own. It knew! It knew he was something alive! Perhaps the snake was puzzled because he hadn't moved. Another thought occurred to him.

Maybe the rattlesnake was sizing him up before striking.

Nate decided he couldn't afford to lie still any longer. The rattler wasn't coiled, which should give him a few seonds of precious time to get out of the way before it could attack. Unless the rattlesnake didn't *need* to coil before launching itself, in which case he would be dead soon and Shakespeare would bury him just as he'd buried his uncle.

Shakespeare!

Where *was* he?

The rattler edged forward again.

Nate felt something rough pass over his neck and then the weight of the snake was gone. Unable to endure another moment of suspense, his nerves stretched to the breaking point, he uttered an inarticulate bellow and shoved upward, scrambling away from the reptile as he moved.

In a flash the rattlesnake coiled.

Acting on pure instinct, Nate grabbed at his pistols. His left moccasin stepped on a loose rock and he tripped, starting to fall backwards onto the very stones the rattler had been concealed under.

The venomous reptile's tail began to buzz loudly.

Nate came down hard on his back, wincing when the sharp edges of several jagged rocks lanced into his body. He pulled the pistols free and cocked them at the same instant the rattler struck.

The snake speared its head at his right foot.

As if in slow motion, Nate saw the rattler open its mouth, saw the snake's long, hooked fangs ready to tear into his skin, and he jerked his leg away from the deadly maw. He saw the reptile miss by the merest fraction, and then he had the pistols extended and pointed at the rattlesnake. His fingers tightened and both guns cracked and belched smoke. For several anxious seconds he couldn't see the serpent.

Had he hit it?

He listened for the buzzing, but the rattles were no longer shaking. Bracing his elbows against the rocks, he rose to a sitting posture and peered intently at the last spot where the snake had been.

The breeze dispersed the smoke.

And there lay the snake, its head severed from its body, the tongue jutting from its thin lips, those unnatural orbs still fixed in his direction.

Nate slowly stood, feeling suddenly limp. That had been too close for comfort! He licked his lips and took a step, then became aware of someone standing off to his left. Startled, he spun.

"Not bad," Shakespeare commented, his arms folded across his chest. "I couldn't have done better myself."

"How long have you been there?"

"A few minutes."

"A few minutes!" Nate snapped angrily. "Why didn't you do something?"

"What could I do? That snake was too close to you for me to risk a shot."

"You could have tried!" Nate declared.

"And deprive you of that valuable experience? I should say not," Shakespeare said, clucking his tongue. He strolled over to the rattler.

Nate wasn't certain he'd heard correctly. "Experience?

I was almost killed.''

The frontiersman turned a kindly gaze on his protégé. "You have a lot to learn about life in the wilderness, Nate. The best teacher I know of is experience." He nodded at the reptile. "Now you have experience with rattlesnakes.''

"But I could have been killed!" Nate reiterated.

"No one ever claimed the lessons you have to learn would be easy.''

Nate glanced at the snake's head and inadvertently shuddered, his indignation beginning to dissipate.

"No hard feelings?" Shakespeare asked.

"I guess not.''

"Good.''

"I'm just glad I already have experience with grizzlies.''

Chapter Four

Over the next few days they continued on their northwesterly course. They left the barren canyons far behind and entered country where the mountains were covered with thick stands of pine and the valleys were verdant. Game abounded. Buffalo, elk, deer, and antelope were everywhere. Bighorn sheep were visible on the higher rocky peaks. Eagle and hawks soared on the air currents.

Nate gradually forgave Shakespeare for the rattlesnake incident, but he vowed to keep a watchful eye on his companion in the future. If the older man had it in his head to teach a few more lessons, there was no telling what might be in store.

They were crossing a low knoll one afternoon when Shakespeare made an announcement. "We'll be at the rendezvous the day after tomorrow."

"I'm looking forward to it."

"Are you?"

Nate's eyes narrowed at the peculiar tone Shakespeare used. "Shouldn't I be?"

"Just be on your guard."

"Why? What could happen to me?"

"If you're not careful, I could be riding back alone."

"You're kidding me," Nate declared.

"Am I?"

"Quit talking in riddles."

"Fair enough," Shakespeare said, watching a raven wing to the north and listening to the swishing beat of its flapping wings. "Any old hand at the rendezvous will mark you as a greenhorn the moment they lay eyes on you. Most of the men will accept you and leave you alone. But there are a few troublemakers who may take it into their heads to test you."

"Test me?"

"Test your mettle. See if they can rile you. If they find they can get your goat just once, you won't know a minute's peace."

"Their behavior sounds childish to me," Nate commented.

Shakespeare grinned. "If you're going to survive the rendezvous, I'd better fill you in on what to expect." He paused. "To understand the goings on, you have to understand more about the life of a trapper. For an entire year these men are roaming the West, traveling from stream to stream, catching as many beaver as they can and getting their peltries ready for the annual get-together. Except for those who take up with a squaw, they live a pretty lonely life. They work from dawn to dusk every day when the weather permits, and you don't know what real work is until you spend most of the day working a trap line in ice-cold water and lugging around beaver that can weigh up to sixty pounds until you skin them."

Nate listened attentively.

"A trapper has to always be on the watch for hostiles. If caught, he'll be subjected to indescribable tortures. Things like having his ears and nose cut off, or his

privates. Or maybe he'll be scalped and stuck in the ground
up to his neck for the animals to finish off."

Imagining the fate of such a hapless man, Nate
grimaced.

"And if the Indians aren't enough to worry about, there
are always the grizzlies. They've torn many a trapper up
beyond recognition and left him to bleed to death. Then
there's the chance of being caught in a flood or a snow-
slide."

"It sounds like a dangerous life," Nate acknowledged.

Shakespeare snorted. "Now there's an understatement
if ever I heard one. Did you know that a couple of years
ago over one hundred trappers left Santa Fe to spend a
year in the mountains, and only sixteen made it back?"

"Sixteen?" Nate repeated in surprise.

"So now you have some idea of the life a trapper leads.
And you can see how much they look forward to the
rendezvous. After a year of doing without, a year of facing
hardship after hardship, they're definitely ready to
celebrate. To tell you the truth, most of them live for the
few weeks each summer when they can drink and brawl
and brag to their heart's content," Shakespeare related.

"How many of these rendezvous have you been to?"

"Three."

"That's all?"

"There's only *been* three."

"Oh."

"A gent by the name of Ashley started them back in
'25. The first one was at Henry's Fork on the Green River.
In '26 it was held at Cache Valley. Last year was at Bear
Lake, the same as this year."

"How many trappers will be there?" Nate inquired.

"Depends. Somewhere between one and two hundred."

Nate blinked a few times. "Two hundred?"

"And that doesn't count the breeds—"

"Breeds?" Nate interrupted.

The aged mountain man sighed. "Half-breeds. Born of white and Indian parents. I feel sorry for most of them."

"Why?"

"Because both the whites and the Indians tend to look down their noses at the mongrels. The breeds know better than to try and mingle in polite white society, and most of the tribes don't treat them much better."

"That's not fair."

"How green you are and fresh in this old world," Shakespeare quoted. "Who ever claimed life is fair? Is it fair for a fawn to be torn to pieces by a pack of starving wolves? Is it fair for trappers to be caught and mutilated by the Blackfeet? Is it fair for the owners of the fur-trading companies to get rich off the sweat and labor of honest trappers?"

Nate said nothing.

"Life is seldom fair," Shakespeare stressed. "Now where was I? Oh, yes. There might be upwards of two hundred trappers at the rendezvous, half as many breeds, and a goodly amount of Indians. The Snakes, the Flatheads, the Nez Perce, the Crows, and the Bannocks will likely show up. Maybe a couple of thousand, all told."

"I had no idea."

"What did you expect? A dozen old farts sitting around telling tall tales about their adventures in the Rockies?"

"No," Nate said defensively.

"Keep your eyes and ears open at the rendezvous and you'll learn more in a couple of weeks about life out here than I could teach you in a month."

"I will."

They rode in silence for over five miles, paralleling a stream winding through a wide valley.

"Can I ask you a question?" Nate inquired.

"Go ahead."

"It might be too personal."

"Don't worry. I'm not about to shoot you for prying into my personal life," Shakespeare said, and grinned.

"Have you ever bought an Indian woman?"

Shakespeare glanced at the younger man, his brow furrowed. "That bothers you, does it?"

"A little," Nate conceded.

"Why?"

"I regard buying an Indian woman the same as buying a Negro slave. You might have heard that the state of New York abolished slavery last year. There are a lot of people back in the East who consider slavery an abomination. The minister at our church called slavery a moral and spiritual evil."

"Do tell."

"That's right. I just don't think it's decent to treat another human being like a piece of property."

"Correct me if I'm wrong, but aren't most of those Negroes brought to the States on ships from some far-off country like Africa?"

"Yes," Nate answered.

"And the Negroes are brought over whether they want to come or not?"

"That's what everyone says."

Shakespeare nodded. "I thought so. To you the practice might appear the same, but there's a world of difference between buying an Indian woman and buying a Negro slave."

"In what respect?"

"For one thing, most of the time the Indian women want to be bought."

"They do?" Nate queried skeptically.

"The height of any Indian woman's ambition is to get herself married off, and to the Indians buying a woman is the same as marrying her off. You get all upset at the notion of white men purchasing an Indian girl. I'll bet you don't even know that Indian men do the same thing.''

''I didn't know.''

''There. See? Ignorance is its own worst enemy. Yes, Indian men buy their wives. The usual way is for the warrior to offer a certain number of good horses, and maybe other items besides. Let's say, for instance, that a Sioux warrior has his sights set on a pretty girl. He sends the horses to her lodge and has a friend or a relative announce his intention to marry her. If she accepts the horses, then they hold a big feast in a day or so and the marriage is sealed,'' Shakespeare detailed.

''And all the Indian men pay for the brides?'' Nate inquired.

''Pretty near. So is it any wonder the white men do the same? If a white man tried to marry an Indian woman without purchasing her, there'd be hell to pay. The woman's father would be insulted, and the entire tribe might decide to teach him some manners. If you ever fall for an Indian woman, make sure you court her properly.''

Nate laughed at the idea. ''That will never happen.''

Now it was Shakespeare's turn to say nothing.

''Tell me more,'' Nate urged after a minute.

''Well, I can give you some pointers on Indian women in general. I've seen some real beauties in my time. Some trappers believe the Flathead women are the prettiest in general. Others think the Nez Perce women are the most beautiful. And I know quite a few who will swear by the Mandan women.''

''What about Cheyenne women?''

''Oh, they're right pretty in their own way. But everyone regards them most for their chastity. Unmarried Cheyenne women wear a leather chastity belt.''

Nate's mouth dropped, and he took several seconds to recover from the surprise. ''They do?''

"Yep. The Cheyenne are firm believers in no sex before marriage. If a girl makes a mistake and lets herself be fondled beforehand, she earns a reputation for being immoral. And no Cheyenne girl wants that," Shakespeare related.

"But a chastity belt? They went out with the Middle Ages."

"I'd wager there are quite a number of white women back in the States who would have liked to be wearing a chastity belt at one time or another."

Nate shook his head in amazement. Would the wonders never cease? Who would have thought that Indian women would wear chastity belts? Yet, at the same time, they allowed themselves to be bought like an item of merchandise in a trading post. What a land of incredible contradictions!

"I was married to a Flathead woman about twenty years ago," Shakespeare mentioned. "And I always thought she was the loveliest creature ever put on this planet."

"What happened to her? Did you divorce her?"

"The damn Blackfeet killed her."

"Oh. I'm sorry to hear that," Nate said.

Shakespeare shrugged. "It was a long time ago. Of course, I've never forgiven the Blackfeet, and exterminate the savages every chance I get." He paused. "And about divorce. The Indians have a different attitude about it than the whites do."

"Do they allow divorce?"

"Sure do. In fact, it's a lot easier for an Indian to divorce than it is for those upright folks back in the States. If an Indian man wants a divorce, he goes through a ceremony and publicly announces he doesn't want her any more. All the woman has to do to be divorced is move back into her parents' lodge."

"An Indian woman can leave her husband?"

"If she wants. Few do." Shakespeare scratched his beard. "Even fewer fool around with other men."

"They must have high morals," Nate remarked.

"That, and the fact that any wife caught in the arms of another warrior has her nose cut off."

"Isn't that a bit extreme?"

"Not to the Indian way of thinking. You see, Indians put a lot of stock in public opinion. Most of them are scared to death at the notion of acquiring a bad reputation. Every warrior and maiden knows that if they get too far out of line, if they break the rules of the tribe, they could well have to walk about in shame for the rest of their lives."

"Every tribe is the same way?"

"The rules vary from tribe to tribe, and some are more severe than others. The Utes, for instance, don't cut off the nose of a woman found guilty of adultery."

"Now they sound civilized."

"Sometimes they whip her."

Nate began to suspect that Shakespeare was deliberately disclosing customs certain to shock him. "You make Indians out to be rather cruel," he commented to test his theory.

"Do I? That's certainly not my intention. Some of their practices are harsh by our standards, but Indians are not cruel by nature. In fact, I admire them highly. If I didn't, I wouldn't have spent the better part of my life living among them." He gazed at the ridge to their right. "For instance, Indians rarely spank their children."

Memories of all the beatings he had received as a youngster flashed through Nate's mind. "How do they discipline their children then?"

"By always instructing them in the right way to do things. Where a white parent might slap a child's face for not doing chores or whatever, an Indian parent will sit the child down and explain about the importance of always doing one's work and being honest and diligent. They're always loooking at the positive side of things.''

"There must be some instances where they punish their children," Nate said.

"When the kids cry they're punished."

"Why? Aren't they allowed to cry?" Nate queried, half in jest.

"No."

"What harm can crying do?"

"Crying can get the whole tribe killed. Out here sounds can travel a long ways. An enemy war party could hear a child crying from far off and know where to find the camp. So Indian mothers are real strict about crying. They teach their babies not to cry at an early age.''

Nate envisioned such a task as being impossible. "How can they stop a baby from crying? Crying is as natural as eating and sleeping."

"It's easy. Whenever a baby starts bawling, and if there's no apparent reason for it, the mother takes the baby away from the camp and hangs the cradleboard in a bush or on a tree. She leaves the baby there until the crying stops.''

Nate thought of the grizzly he'd encountered. "That's heartless. What happens if a wild animal stumbles on the baby?"

"Rarely happens. Besides, most babies stop crying after two or three times out in the brush."

"I'd never do that to my child," Nate asserted.

Shakespeare abruptly reined up. "We sure are having a pitiful run of luck this trip."

"What do you mean?"

The frontiersman pointed at the ridge to the east. "Blackfeet."

Chapter Five

Nate twisted in his saddle and scanned the ridge, immediately spotting a large group of Indians who were riding over the crest, heading eastward. "They're going in the opposite direction," he declared in relief. "I don't think they saw us."

"Neither do I," Shakespeare agreed. "Keep your fingers crossed that none of those savages look back."

Nate watched the Blackfeet with bated breath, hoping there wouldn't be a repeat of their experience with the Utes. He was elated when the last warrior disappeared on the far side. "They're gone, and good riddance!"

"My sentiments exactly," Shakespeare said. "Although I could use a few more Blackfeet scalps to add to my collection." He chuckled and rode onward.

Pleased at their narrow escape from a potentially deadly encounter, Nate grinned as he followed his companion. He found himself speculating on why so many white men enjoyed the mountaineering life when there were so many varied and lethal dangers associated with such a hazardous existence. Was unbridled freedom that valuable? He'd enjoyed just a fleeting taste of wilderness life, and he had to admit he found the life appealing, infinitely more so than the drab routine of a bookkeeper in New York City. He stared at a golden eagle off to the west and marveled that he had once sought to have a career as a successful accountant.

They traveled for five hundred yards, and were angling into dense timber when a succession of gunshots arose to the east, from the other side of the ridge.

Shakespeare reined up and cocked his head. "Damn. Those Blackfeet must be after someone."

"Buffalo or elk maybe," Nate suggested. A second later he detected the faint sound of war whoops and realized he was wrong.

"Those Blackfeet aren't after game," Shakespeare said, turning his horse.

"What are you planning to do?"

"Go have a look-see."

Nate began to protest, but Shakespeare's next words caused him to hold his tongue.

"Those vermin could be attacking trappers en route to the rendezvous. Let's go."

"I'll be right behind you," Nate vowed, and let the older man lead the way. If white men were being attacked, then he had a duty to try and help them. He kept the mare close to the white horse as they galloped toward the ridge, the pack animal trailing behind them, amazed at his friend's horsemanship.

Shakespeare could ride as proficiently as an Indian, and his nimble mount took every obstacle in stride. He sped up the west slope of the ridge, using a narrow game trail, the same trail the Blackfeet had taken. Ten yards from the top he slowed his horse to a walk and cautiously approached the crest.

Nate nervously surveyed the rim, the Hawken in his right hand. What if the Blackfeet had posted a lookout?

The pressure of his pistols against his midriff was mildly reassuring. If worse came to worst, the Blackfeet would know they'd been in a fight. He saw Shakespeare stop and slip to the ground, and he did likewise.

The mountain man, keeping low, stepped to the rim.

Nate came up on Shakespeare's right and gazed at the scene below.

A beautiful valley about six miles long 'and three miles wide ran from the southeast to the northwest. Although trees were thick on the slopes of the surrounding mountains, in the valley there were few. The ground was covered with lush grass and herbage. Approximately a quarter of a mile from the west ridge was an Indian encampment consisting of 15 lodges, and the inhabitants of the village were now industriously engaged in defending themselves from the onslaught of 19 screeching Blackfeet.

Even as Nate watched, one of the defenders loosed an arrow and struck a Blackfoot warrior in the chest, toppling the attacker to the turf. But in the next few seconds he realized the defenders were hopelessly outnumbered. There only appeared to be three or four men in the whole village; the rest were women and children who were bravely assisting the few defending warriors as best they could.

"Damn!" Shakespeare exclaimed angrily. "I know them. You can stay here if you want." He wheeled and sprinted to his horse.

"I'm not staying put," Nate said, running to the mare. "Where you go, I go."

Shakespeare chuckled as he swung into the saddle. "If you make that your life's ambition, you might not live to see your hair turn gray."

"Are those Indians in the village friends of yours?" Nate asked as he climbed on his animal.

"Yep. They're Shoshones." Shakespeare urged his

mount upward. "Stay close and make every shot count."

Nate took a firm hold on his rifle and rode forward, feeling an equal mixture of excitement and trepidation. He resolved to give a good account of himself and not let Shakespeare down.

"Yell your lungs out once we hit the bottom," the frontiesman directed as he went over the crest.

"Why?"

"The more noise we create, the more we'll confuse those Blackfeet. They may get the notion that there's more of us than there are."

"But they'll see there's just the two of us."

"What they see doesn't matter. It's what we can make them *think* that counts. And they're bound to figure two white men wouldn't be crazy enough to attack them alone. They may jump to the conclusion there's more of us."

"Sounds awful risky," Nate noted, shifting his weight to compensate for the sharp slant of the slope.

"Not really. We'll be taking them by surprise. Out here, when a person is taken unawares, the best policy is to make tracks and count the enemy later. You live longer that way."

Nate glanced at the village. Several Blackfeet were already down, and one of the Shoshone warriors was on the ground, impaled by a lance. Two of the Shoshone women were also dead. The Blackfeet galloped around and through the encampment, firing their rifles and bows, but their elusive adversaries were difficult to hit. The Shoshones darted from lodge to lodge, dodging and weaving, always on the move.

Shakespeare broke his white horse into a gallop 15 yards from the base of the ridge and hit the valley floor in full stride. He uttered a piercing shriek that would have done justice to any Indian on the continent, and waved his rifle in the air.

Feeling as if his heart was in his throat, Nate followed suit, his left hand holding the lead to the pack animal. He glued his eyes to the battle, expecting the Blackfeet to spot them at any moment.

Embroiled in their intense conflict, none of the Indians were paying the slightest attention to the plain around the village.

Nate smiled grimly. This was perfect. The Blackfeet were too occupied to notice. If only the fight would continue for another minute.

A cluster of Shoshone women and children suddenly broke from the encampment, racing to the south, making toward the gully 40 yards distant. In the lead, urging on the others, was a young woman with flowing black hair down to her hips.

Five of the Blackfeet turned from the village, pursuing the women and children.

Nate released the pack horse and swerved to the right, forgetting all about staying close to Shakespeare in his concern for the Shoshones. He angled to intercept the Blackfeet, knowing full well he wouldn't arrive in time.

The young woman abruptly halted, motioned for the others to continue without her, and stooped to grab a rock. She faced the onrushing Blackfeet, her posture radiating defiance, and raised the rock overhead.

Admiration welled within Nate. What could she hope to accomplish wielding such a puny weapon other than to temporarily delay the warriors long enough for the rest of the women and the children to reach the gully? Bravery and pride were reflected in her carriage. His heart went out to her and he whipped the Hawken to his right shoulder.

The foremost Blackfoot, a husky warrior armed with a bow, approached the woman at an almost leisurely pace, smirking as he trained an arrow on her.

Would the warrior really fire? Nate wondered. Did Indian men slay the maidens in other tribes or merely take them captive? He couldn't afford to risk the woman's life on the chance the warrior might be bluffing, so he attempted to get a bead on the Blackfoot. The rocking motion of the mare made the task extremely difficult and he held off firing, covering another 30 yards in the process.

Laughing, the warrior lowered the bow.

The young woman shouted a word and hurled the rock.

Nate saw the Blackfoot rein sharply to the right, and the projectile missed. Clearly furious, the Shoshone woman scanned the grass near her feet for another stone.

Moving methodically, the warrior made a show of sighting another arrow on her breast.

It's now or never! Nate told himself. He fixed the front of the barrel on the Blackfoot, held his breath, and squeezed the trigger. Smoke and lead belched from the end of the Hawken.

One hundred and twenty yards distant, the warrior's mount unexpectedly buckled and pitched the Blackfoot onto the grass.

What a blockhead! Nate lowered the rifle and frowned. He'd missed the Indian and hit the horse! Now he'd wasted the shot, and he wasn't fast enough nor skilled enough to reload while riding at a full gallop before he reached the Blackfeet.

The warrior on the ground had risen to his knees and was recovering his bow. The other four had turned their animals at the retort of the Hawken and were gawking in frank astonishment.

Nate voiced a war whoop of his own, clutched the rifle and the reins in his left hand, and drew one of his pistols. He observed the Blackfeet glance to the north, where Shakespeare was bearing down on the village, and then look at him. The next few moments were crucial. Would the Blackfeet cut out or stay and fight?

One of the warriors hefted a war club and charged.

So much for Shakespeare's bright idea! Nate swung the mare to meet the Blackfoot head-on and made straight for him. Pistols were designed for short-range use, and unless he wanted to hazard wasting another ball, he had to get as close as practical to his opponent.

Whooping and swinging the club, the Blackfoot rapidly advanced.

The pounding of the mare's hooves drummed in Nate's ears as he closed. He kept the pistol next to his waist, screened by the animal's neck, his thumb on the hammer, his finger on the trigger. There was no sense in advertising how he intended to dispatch his adversary.

Two other warriors started toward him.

Nate focused on the first warrior to the exclusion of all else, acutely conscious of the shrinking yardage between them, anxious to fire but restraining the impulse until the proper moment. In the back of his mind he wondered if Shakespeare was faring all right. He couldn't venture a glance at the village to find out.

The Blackfoot vented his war cry once more and rose slightly on his mount, holding the club steady, ready to launch a downward stroke. Like most Indian weapons, the club had been embellished to suit the personal tastes of its owner. A sharp metal spoke projected from the blunt, rounded head, and the wooden handle was covered with elaborately decorated buckskin stitched together with sinew.

All of Nate's self-control barely sufficed to prevent him from shooting prematurely. At a distance of 20 yards the urge caused his fingers to twitch. At 15 yards, when he could clearly see the warrior's blazing eyes and flaring nostrils, he almost lifted the pistol from concealment. At ten yards he tensed, and at eight he swept his right arm up, extended the pistol, and fired.

The ball caught the Blackfoot at the base of his throat and propelled him over the rear of his animal to fall onto the hard earth with a thud. The war club went flying.

Nate looked down at his foe and saw the warrior thrashing violently, and then he had to stare straight ahead at the pair of Blackfeet converging on him. The one on the left reined up, but the warrior on the right came on strong.

This second warrior was armed with a fusee. Such rifles were smooth-bored flintlocks the Indians received in trade with the Hudson's Bay Company. The fusee the Blackfoot held had been shortened, as were many of the trade guns, to make the weapon easier to use while on horseback.

Nate remembered Shakespeare telling him that fusees were cheap, inferior weapons and no match for the rifles of the trappers and mountaineers. In fact, many Indians held the fusees in disdain and preferred to employ the traditional bow. At close range, though, a fuseee could be every bit as deadly as a Hawken even if it did lack the Hawken's accuracy and superb craftsmanship.

Gunshots were still sounding from the village.

Somewhere a woman screamed.

Alarmed, Nate looked at the young maiden with the flowing hair, relieved to see she wasn't being attacked. The Shoshone woman was simply standing there, watching him, perhaps astounded he had interjected himself into the battle or hoping he would emerge victorious. Her left hand was pressed to her neck. He spotted the warrior he had unhorsed standing a few dozen yards to the north, observing the progress of the fight.

The fight!

Startled by his lapse, Nate glanced at the charging Blackfoot who was now only 30 yards away. He quickly slid the empty pistol under his belt and drew the second one.

Both were smoothbore single-shot .55 caliber flintlocks, a matched set selected for him by his Uncle Zeke in St. Louis. They were powerful, but he had to get close to use them.

Apparently the Blackfoot had no intention of letting him come within range, because the warrior suddenly raised the fusee to his shoulder.

Chapter Six

Nate knew the Blackfoot would fire in the next few seconds. His pistol was no match for even the unreliable fusee at such a distance. He had to do something, and do it fast, or be shot.

But what?

What could he possibly do?

He saw the warrior smile and expected to hear the fusee crack, and at that instant a flash of inspiration galvanized him into prompt action. He recalled the time he and Zeke had fought a party of marauding Kiowas, remembering the technique the Kiowa warriors had used to minimize the targets they'd presented. At the time he'd been taking a bead on one of them, and he'd been amazed to see the warrior slide onto the side of the galloping horse, using just a heel and a hooked arm to stay on board.

Could he do the same thing?

There was no time to debate the issue. He swung to the right, flattening against the mare, his left arm looped over the saddle, grasping the Hawken in his left hand. For added support he braced his left leg on the animal's broad back. The swaying motion threatened to dislodge him, but he held on for dear life.

He'd done it!

The Blackfoot couldn't see him, couldn't get a clear shot.

Nate gripped the pistol tightly, elated. Then a thought occurred to him and his exhilaration evaporated.

Yes, the Blackfoot couldn't see him.

But he couldn't see the warrior either.

Just great!

How was he supposed to defend himself? What if the Blackfoot changed direction? What if—and the idea brought goose bumps to his flesh—what if the warrior shot the mare instead? He eased forward as far as he could and peered under the mare's neck.

The Blackfoot was only 15 yards off. He'd slowed and straightened, striving to see over the side of the mare, the fusee flush with his shoulder.

Nate observed the warrior sight down the gun, and he realized the Blackfoot was going to shoot him in the arm or the leg to bring him down. He swiftly extended his arm, angled the pistol under the mare's neck, and fired.

A strident howl attended the blast as the ball hit the warrior in the left cheek and slammed the man from his mount.

Pulling himself up, Nate sat erect and glanced over his left shoulder. The Indian lay motionless on the ground. Two down and three to go, and that didn't include the Blackfeet attacking the village. To complicate matters, all three of his firearms were now empty.

Another warrior whooped and came on at a full charge.

Nate tucked the second pistol under his belt and slipped his butcher knife from its sheath. The knife was all he had left.

The third Blackfoot held a lance.

Nate recollected the tales Shakespeare and Zeke had

told him about the uncanny accuracy Indians could achieve with their slim spearlike weapons. They were trained in its use from boyhood, and a full-grown warrior could cast a lance 20 to 25 yards and consistently hit a target the size of a man's head, even when riding at full speed. He didn't stand a prayer armed with just a knife.

The warrior waved his lance and voiced a defiant challenge.

Nate urged the mare to go faster. He couldn't hope to outrun the Blackfoot. And the slower he went, the better target he would make. So his best bet seemed to be to gallop at the warrior and try to dodge the lance. Perhaps he could deflect the tip with his rifle. With that in mind he replaced the knife in its sheath and elevated the Hawken.

Wait a minute.

He knew the Hawken wasn't loaded, but the Blackfoot didn't. What would happen if he sighted on the warrior, if he pretended he was going to fire? There was only one way to find out. He pressed the stock to his shoulder and aimed at his enemy.

Executing an abupt turn, the Blackfoot lowered his lance and raced away to the south.

The ploy had worked!

Nate beamed and let the Hawken drop, overjoyed, congratulating himself on his cleverness. He saw the other Blackfeet hasten southward, including the warrior whose horse he'd accidentally killed, and his forehead creased in perplexity.

Why were they *all* running away?

He slowed, puzzled, and gazed at the maiden. She was beaming happily and staring past him, to the northwest. Was Shakespeare coming to his rescue? He looked over his left shoulder and tensed.

More Indians were rushing toward the village, 12 warriors bearing from the northwest, and in the lead rode a strapping warrior who wore only a breechcloth and carried a bow with a shaft at the ready. He led the band directly at the few Blackfeet still lingering in the vicinity of the lodges.

Nate reined up and swung the mare to view the conflict. He realized the dozen newcomers must be Shoshone warriors, returned to defend their families.

The majority of the Blackfeet had spied the Shoshones and fled, but three of the former were riding among the lodges, firing and hollering, oblivious to the fact the tide of battle had turned. They discovered their error seconds later.

Like a storm-tossed wave pounding the rocky shore of the Atlantic Ocean, the Shoshones fanned out and swept into their village. The tall leader drew his bowstring all the way back, sighting on a Blackfoot who was about to bash his war club against a boy's head, and let the arrow fly.

The shaft caught the Blackfoot between his shoulder blades, and the triangular tip and six inches of shaft burst out the center of his chest. He arched his back when he was struck, his mouth forming an oval, his eyes wide, then silently toppled to the ground.

In moments the other Shoshones dispatched the remaining Blackfeet. In one instance the Blackfoot was surrounded by seven Shoshones and brutally clubbed to death.

Absorbed in watching the battle, Nate nearly jumped out of the saddle when a hand fell on his right leg. He glanced down to find the young woman with the long hair.

She smiled up at him, her brown eyes studying him intently. Her dark tresses framed a face of uncommon beauty and accented her prominent cheekbones. A beaded buckskin dress covered her trim figure and moccasins adorned her feet.

"Hello," Nate said.

The woman spoke a sentence in the Shoshone tongue and regarded him inquisitively, apparently anticipating a reply.

Frustrated by his failure to understand, and wanting very much to communicate with her, Nate recalled the many lessons Zeke and Shakespeare had given him in Indian sign language, the universal means of exchanging information used by practically every tribe in the West. He extended the thumb and index finger on his right hand, curled the other fingers, then held the hand near his left breast. Next he moved his hand out and slightly up, turning his wrist as he did so, his palm becoming vertical. He was careful to have his thumb pointing to the front and the index finger pointing to the left. Keenly aware of her eyes on his hand, and hoping he was doing the sign language properly, he finished the response by opening his hand and sweeping it to the right and back again. There. If his memory had served him in good stead, he'd just told her that he didn't understand her language.

But what if he'd made a mistake?

What if he'd just stated that she looked like a fat buffalo cow?

The woman nodded, then pointed at the nearest Blackfoot he had shot. She extended both of her slender hands and held them flat, palms down. Sweeping them upward, she angled them down toward Nate.

She was saying thank you! Incredibly relieved, Nate grinned and made the proper signs to ask her name.

"Winona," she revealed.

"Nate," he said, tapping his chest. "Nate King."

"Nate King," Winona repeated slowly, speaking each word crisply, duplicating his pronunciation with remarkable facility. "Nate King. Nate King."

Her melodic voice thrilled Nate to his core. He tried

to think of something else he could say, feeling oddly self-conscious about his inexperience and ignorance.

Winona's hands began making signs at a rapid clip.

Struggling to keep up, Nate leaned down to catch every movement. Some of the signs she used were foreign to him. He gathered that she was telling him his medicine must be very great to have slain so many Blackfeet, but he couldn't be certain. She stopped and looked at him as if awaiting a reply, and at that awkward moment he heard the drumming of hooves and straightened to face the village.

Shakespeare, the tall Shoshone, and five other warriors were riding toward them.

Nate became aware of the tall Shoshone's gaze focused on himself, and he wondered why he should be the object of such an intense scrutiny. He realized he'd neglected to reload and chided himself for being a dunderhead.

"Well, well, well," Shakespeare said as he drew to a stop. He gazed at the dead Blackfeet. "You've been a mite busy, I see."

"And what about you?"

"I took care of three of the rascals, and good riddance," Shakespeare said. "Strike! Down with them! Cut the villains' throats! Ah! Whoreson caterpillars! Bacon-fed knaves! They hate us, youth. Down with them! Fleece them!" He gestered wildly as he spoke.

"What?" Nate asked, wondering if the frontiersman was putting on an act.

"William S."

"Oh."

The strapping Shoshone abruptly addressed Winona, and she answered with a torrent of words, gesturing repeatedly at the slain Blackfeet and at Nate. After a minute the tall warrior looked solemnly at Shakepeare and spoke a few words.

"What did they say?" Nate queried.

Shakespeare chuckled. "You never cease to amaze me."

"I do?"

"Yep." The frontiersman indicated the tall Shoshone. "This here is Black Kettle, a prominent man in the Shoshone nation. Winona there is his daughter. She just gave him a blow-by-blow description of your fight. Says you saved her life and the lives of the women and children with her." He snickered. "She also says you are the bravest fighter who ever lived and the second greatest man in existence, her father being the greatest, of course."

Nate didn't know what to say.

"Yes, sir," Shakespeare commented. "You've made quite a mark."

"I was just trying to stay alive."

Black Kettle glanced at the mountain man and voiced an extended discourse.

"He says he is in your debt," Shakespeare translated after the Shoshone finished. "He says he owes you for the life of his precious daughter and his beloved people."

"I did what I had to," Nate said. "He doesn't owe me a thing."

"Don't expect me to tell him that."

"Why not?"

"Remember what I told you about being mighty careful not to insult an Indian? If he wants to be in your debt, let him. Having an Indian be in your debt is a lot better than having an Indian try to scalp you," Shakespeare observed.

"What do I do? What do I tell him?"

"I'll handle the conversation," Shakespeare declared. "He wants to know your name. Now let me see." His forehead furrowed and he scratched his head. "What was that name the Cheyennes gave you?"

"You can quote Shakespeare but you can't remember

a simple thing like that?''

"Oh. Now I remember. Grizzly Killer." Shakespeare turned to Black Kettle and went on at length in the Shoshone tongue.

Again Nate was the object of the tall warrior's undivided attention. To cover his embarrassment, Nate gazed at the village and sw a party of six Shoshones ride off in pursuit of the fleeing Blackfeet. The women and children were returning to their lodges. He glanced down at Winona and gave her his friendliest smile.

Black Kettle replied to Shakespeare, who then interpreted.

"If it will make you feel any better, he says he's in debt to both of us. His family is on their way to the rendezvous and he's invited us to tag along. How does the notion strike you?''

"Just fine."

"I figured it might."

"I'll have the opportunity to learn some of their language."

"And I admire a man who's never too old to learn," Shakespeare said with a twinkle in his eyes.

"Would you accept his invitation and thank him for his kindness?''

"Now why didn't I think of that?" Shakespeare spoke to Black Kettle for half a minute, listened to the Shoshone's response, and stared at his companion. "He's delighted. He plans to have us for supper."

"Tell him not to bother going to so much trouble."

"There you go again."

"What do you mean?" Nate queried, and insight dawned. "Oh, Sorry. It's just force of habit."

"I know, but it's a habit you'd better break and fast. When you live with the Indians, you live by Indian rules."

"There's so much to know."

"Let me give you some sound advice," Shakespeare offered. "When in doubt, keep your mouth shut and your ears open. You'll live longer that way."

"I'll do my best," Nate vowed.

"Oh. And one more thing."

"What?"

"How do you feel about getting married?"

Chapter Seven

"What's that supposed to mean?" Nate demanded.

Shakespeare grinned. "The young filly you saved has her sights set on you."

Nate looked down at Winona, who smiled sweetly at him, then at the frontiersman. "You're crazy."

"You are already Love's firm votary, and cannot soon revolt and change your mind."

"What?"

Shakespeare chuckled and quoted more of his favorite author. "But love, first learned in a lady's eyes, lives not alone immured in the brain. But, with the motion of all elements, courses as swift as thought in every power, and gives to every power a double power, above their functions andd offices."

"Sometimes I don't understand a word you say," Nate said testily. "Why can't you use English like everyone else?"

"Use English?" Shakespeare repeated, and erupted into a fit of laughter, rocking back and forth in the saddle, his eyes closed. "Use English!" he roared, and laughed harder.

The Shoshones stared at the mountain man as if he were a madman.

Annoyed, Nate occupied his time by reloading the Hawken. He wedged the rifle under his left leg, poured the amount of black powder he would need from the powder horn into the palm of his left hand, then fed the powder down the muzzle. Next he took a ball from his bullet pouch, wrapped the ball in a patch and used his thumb to start both down the barrel, and concluded by shoving the ball the rest of the way down with the ramrod. When he finished and glanced up he was surprised to find all of the Shoshones watching him. He smiled at them and gazed at Shakespeare, who was still smiling. "Why are they all looking at me?"

"They don't own many guns. They're just curious."

Black Kettle pointed at the Blackfeet Nate had slain and addressed the frontiersman.

"This should be interesting," Shakespeare said when the warrior was done.

"Does he want us to bury them?" Nate guessed.

"No, nothing like that," Shakespeare replied. "He'll have the bodies taken into the village, but first he figured you'd want to scalp the ones you killed."

Nate inadvertently tensed. "Scalp them?"

"Yep. What's wrong? You scalped that Kiowa warrior who killed your Uncle Zeke."

"I told you I didn't know if I could ever take another," Nate reminded him.

"Don't be squeamish now. If you don't take the hair off those Blackfeet, the Shoshones will think you're less than a man."

"Just because I don't want to slice someone's hair off?"

"You know how important scalps are to these people. Some tribes are downright fanatical about it. The Crows, for instance, consider a man who won't kill and scalp his enemies as a weakling and an insult to the tribe. He's not allowed to carry weapons or take part in any of the activities the men do. Instead he's made a slave of the women. He has to do anything the women tell him. Tote water. Chop wood. Dress hides. You name it. Believe me, Nate, any Crow warrior who falls into the womens' ranks can't wait to be given the chance to prove himself and regain his manhood.''

"They're not going to make a slave of me."

"No, but they'll tell everybody they meet about the white man who wouldn't scalp an enemy he bested in fair combat, and you'll acquire a reputation worse than a polecat's.''

Nate tried to keep his features inscrutable as he looked at Black Kettle. He was trapped by Indian custom. He didn't necessarily want to scalp the Blackfeet, but he'd learned enough about life in the wilderness to appreciate the critical importance of an unsullied reputation. "Tell Black Kettle I thank him. Yes, I would like to scalp the warriors I killed."

Shakespeare nodded slowly. "Figured you would." He spoke to Black Kettle.

Cradling the Hawken in his left arm, Nate wheeled the mare and rode to the closest Blackfoot, the one he had shot in the cheek. He dismounted, placed the Hawken on the ground, and drew his butcher knife.

The warrior lay on his back, his eyes wide and glazing.

Nate took a deep breath, knelt, and grasped the Blackfoot's hair in his left hand. He tilted the head and carefully inserted the tip of the knife at the hairline above the forehead. Blood trickled onto the blade and down over the warrior's eyes. Working swiftly, he pried the knife under the hair and neatly separated the scalp from the head. He studiously avoided staring at the grisly, crimson-splotched pate underneath, and instead grabbed his

Hawken, stood, and led the mare to the Blackfoot he had shot in the throat.

A pool of bright blood had collected about the warrior's head, forming a liquid halo, and more blood continued to seep from the hole. The Blackfoot's mouth was opened wide, and he seemed to have died when about to scream his vented terror to the impassive heavens.

This time Nate worked even faster, and in less than a minute he held both scalps in his left hand. He wiped the knife clean on the grass, replaced the weapon in its sheath, clutched the Hawken in his right hand and mounted the mare.

Shakespeare and the Shoshones were waiting for him.

"Smartly done," the mountain man observed as Nate rode up.

"I didn't realize I'd have an audience."'

"You've impressed Black Kettle. He just told me he thinks you have the makings of a mighty warrior."

"If he only knew."

"Don't sell yourself short, Nate. Stranger things have happened."

Black Kettle said a few words to Winona, then motioned with his right arm and headed for the village, trailed by the five warriors.

"What did he say to her?" Nate said.

Shakespeare laughed lightly. "He instructed her to remember she's a lady."

"Why in the world would he tell her that?"

A peculiar snort, much like the noise made by a young bull frolicking in a pasture with a bovine playmate, issued from the frontiersman. "I hope you won't mind me saying this, and please don't take offense, but you are downright pitiful."

"In what way?"

"In every way, my young friend." Shakespeare nodded

at the Shoshone village. "Let's go to Black Kettle's lodge. His people will tend to the mess. One of his warriors is fetching our pack horse."

Perplexed and feeling slightly hurt, Nate rode along slowly with Shakespeare on his left and Winona walking beside his mare on the right. "I'll expect a full explanation later," he stated peevishly.

"Life will be your explanation."

"Sometimes you make no sense whatsoever."

"Never forget, Nate, that one man's ignorance is another man's past."

Nate sighed. "I'll remember it, but I'll be damned if I know what it means."

Winona interjected a string of remarks in Shoshone, directing them at Shakespeare.

"Anything I should know?" Nate inquired when he finished.

"She wants to know if you're married."

Nate almost dropped the scalps.

"I warned you. She's got the notion into her dainty head that you're the rip-roaringest thing in pants, and if there's one fact I've learned during my long and eventful life, it's this: Women never give up once they've fixed their sights on a man. Nine times out of ten they'll bag the man they want, and the one exception can usually be blamed on circumstances they can't control. I don't care if it's a white woman or an Indian, a black or a Chinese, an Egyptian or Helen of Troy, they get the man they want." He chuckled and shook his head. "Of course, another fact I've learned is that women are never satisfied once they have their men. Remember this, Nate. There's no pleasing a woman. Anyone who tries to tell you different has his brains below his belt."

Nate smiled down at Winona, and there was no denying the incipient affection in her lively eyes. "Somehow I had the idea Indian woman were shy and retiring."

"The shy ones are the worst. They lay the cleverest traps."

"You seem to equate romance with hunting and going after game."

"You've just hit the nail on the head. Romance is a hunt, and for a woman it's the grandest hunt of all. She throws her wits and her charms into the chase, and the lure she uses is practically irresistible."

"I think you're exaggerating."

"Time will tell."

"You can let her know I'm not married," Nate said. "And whatever else she wants to know."

"As you wish, young squire."

"Huh?"

"Remind me to find you a book on Shakespeare. You could use a little of William S.'s wisdom."

"I could use a drink."

They came to the edge of the village. Bodies lay scattered about, the corpses of men, women, and a few children. The Blackfeet had been relentlessly ruthless in their attack. With sorrow lining their features the Shoshones were going about the miserable business of attending to their dead.

"Shouldn't we help them?" Nate inquired.

"They wouldn't want our help. This is a private matter to them."

Winona unexpectedly dashed off to aid an elderly woman who had sustained a scalp wound and was shuffling around a nearby lodge.

"Why did the Blackfeet kill women and children? What honor could there be in slaying those who are defenseless?"

"Defenseless?" Shakespeare repeated, and snorted. "Where'd you ever get a notion like that? It's true the men do most of the warring, but the women and young'uns are far from defenseless. Both will defend their village when it's attacked. Indian boys can shoot a bow as soon as they're old enough to hold one, and Indian women are no slouches when they're riled. In some tribes women are even allowed to go on raids. The Utes let a woman go along if she wants.''

"They do?'' Nate said in surprise.

"Yep. Remember that. You might find yourself on the business end of a lance held by a pretty woman some day. What would you do if it happens?''

"I'd do everything in my power not to harm the woman.''

Shakespeare smiled. "You would, huh?''

"I don't know if I could help myself. I was raised to be a gentleman around ladies.''

"Ladies are nothing but ordinary women with high airs and fancy clothes. And if you don't change that attitude of yours, you could end up as a *dead* gentleman.''

"Have you ever killed a woman?''

Shakespeare glanced sharply at his companion. "There are some questions you should never ask a man, not even a friend.''

"Sorry.''

"Here we are,'' Shakespeare announced, and reined up in front of one of the lodges. "This is Black Kettle's teepee.''

"His what?''

"Teepee. It's a Sioux word for lodge.''

Nate studied the structure before them. The general shape reminded him of the haystacks he had seen on farms. A number of pine poles had been placed on end in the shape of a large circle, then secured together at the top. Dressed buffalo hides served as the outer covering; they had been sewn together and stretched over the pole framework. He estimated the height to be 25 or 30 feet and the diameter of the base to be 20 feet.

"We'll have to wait for Black Kettle before we can go in," Shakespeare mentioned. "In the meantime I'll fill you in on how to behave."

"What do you mean?"

"There are certain rules you need to know. Do you see that door there?" Shakespeare asked, and nodded at a closed flap.

"Yes."

"If the door is open you can enter a lodge without bothering about formality, but if the door is closed you can't go in until after you let those inside know you're there and get an invite. Understand?"

"Yes."

"Once you're in, go to the right and wait for the man of the lodge to ask you to sit down."

"Go to the right? Why can't I go to the left?"

Shakespeare sighed. "Because the women go to the left. Are you a woman?"

"No, of course not."

"Then go to the right. The head of the lodge will likely want you to sit on his left. On your way to the spot never pass between the fire and another person."

"Why not?"

"The Indians consider it rude and a bad sign."

"You're kidding?"

"Where's a war club when I need one?"

"What?"

"Just pay attention. Always walk behind people seated around a fire. If you're invited to eat, eat. And you'd damn well better eat every morsel. Don't leave a crumb or you'll insult your host."

Nate shook his head in amazement. "I had no idea."

"I'm not done yet. If the head of the lodge taps his pipe

on the ground or asks his woman to unroll his blanket, it's the signal to leave.''

"Do I leave on the right side?"

"No. You fly out the ventilation flap at the top," Shakespeare answered, and cackled. He slid to the ground and turned.

Nate climbed down, his mouth twisted in a wry smile. He heard a mournful wail, and pivoted to behold three Shoshone warriors bearing a fourth between them. Walking alongside was a woman with tears pouring from her eyes. Her hands were pressed to her cheeks and she sobbed pitiably.

"I'm glad you've gotten over your squeamishness," Shakespeare commented.

"Why's that?" Nate inquired.

"Because you're about to see some sights that can freeze your blood in your veins."

Chapter Eight

Shakespeare, as it turned out, had uttered the understatement of the century.

While some Shoshones tended to the wounded, others gathered the dead. Three slain Shoshone warriors, five women, and three young boys were laid out in a row near Black Kettle's lodge. Then the dead Blackfeet were collected, 11 in all, and arranged in a line ten yards to the south.

Nate observed the proceedings expectantly. He saw the wives of the three deceased warriors throw themselves on the bodies of their husbands, where the women lamented their fate to the heavens and sobbed profusely. The mothers and sisters of the young boys likewise displayed their anguish. But the men vented their sorrow differently.

Black Kettle and the other Shoshone warriors walked to their fallen foes, took out knives, and commenced to cutting out the hearts, livers, and other organs, all the while voicing piercing yells and howls.

Aghast at the atrocity he was witnessing, Nate leaned close to Shakespeare. "Why are they mutilating the

Blackfeet?''

"They're taking revenge for their own people who were killed."

"But the Blackfeet are already dead."

"Doesn't matter a lick to them."

Nate recoiled in revulsion when the Shoshones began to cut the organs into bits and pieces and then tossed the chunks to the village dogs, which had materialized as if out of nowhere after the battle ended. He bowed his head, feeling a bitter bile rise in his mouth, and when he looked up again the horror had worsened.

The Shoshones were hacking off the heads of the Blackfeet.

"This is the part I like the best," Shakespeare commented.

Slicing methodically, the Shoshones severed every last Blackfoot head. They each grabbed a grisly trophy in each hand and began to dance and prance, triumphantly waving the heads, shouting in exultation. The women and the children watched happily, beaming in innocent delight.

"Dear God in heaven!" Nate breathed.

Shakespeare heard and glanced at his companion. "The white man's God don't count for much west of the Mississippi. Most of the tribes believe in the Great Spirit or the Great Medicine. They're very religious in their way."

Nate stared at the Shoshones gloating and cavorting in primitive abandon. "You call these people religious?"

"You've got to remember that one man's God is another man's devil."

"Meaning what?"

"Don't judge Indians by our values."

"They're savage by any standard."

"So what if they are? Who's to say white men are any better than them just because the whites are supposedly civilized?''

Appalled, Nate looked at the frontiersman. ''Do you approve of this barbaric conduct?''

''I won't lie to you. Yes, I do.''

Nate took a half step backwards, his abhorrence transparent. *''How can you?''*

''It's the call of the wild.''

''The what?''

''The call of the wild. The lure of the wilderness. A zest for life. Whatever you want to call the feeling that grows inside a man if he stays out here long enough. You label the Shoshones as barbaric for defeating their enemies in fair combat and then taking pride in their accomplishment. At least they're open about it. They're honestly in touch with their inner feelings,'' Shakespeare said. ''That's more than I can say for the white man. Our kind hide their feelings behind a wall of laws, or they deny their feelings rather than offend someone else. If two whites have a dispute, and if they're too cowardly to settle the issue with a duel, one might sue the other and let a court settle the affair. They never really face their enemy or their own emotions. If they lose, they act as if it doesn't matter when deep down they want to beat the other fellow to a pulp.''

Nate gazed at the Shoshones and said nothing.

''Out here a man enjoys true freedom, the freedom of the wilderness. And if there's one lesson the wilderness teaches every mother's son, it's this: If you bite off more than you can chew, you pay the price. Big bite, little bite, it doesn't matter. Those Blackfeet bit off more than they could chew, and now the Shoshones are doing what comes naturally.'' Shakespeare paused. ''Do you understand what I'm trying to tell you?''

''I think so.''

''Civilization cushions folks from their own mistakes, Nate. Someone in St. Louis or New York doesn't have to worry about going hungry if they miss a deer or an elk. They can walk down to the corner market and buy all the food they need. And they don't have to fret about dying of thirst if they get lost and can't find a spring or a stream. They can get a drink just about anywhere.''

Nate listened with half an ear, his gaze on the Shoshones as they scalped the heads of the Blackfeet.

''Civilization is the haven of bullies and the weak,'' Shakespeare went on. ''A bully can get away with pushing folks around in a big city because he knows few of them will have the gumption to stand up to him. But any man who tries to impose on another out here is likely as not to be shot for his effort.''

The Shoshone warriors were now impaling the heads on lances and proudly swinging the lances in the air.

''And in the wilderness a man can't afford to be weak. It's true what they say about only the strong surviving, and sometimes even the strong ones don't make it. Look at what happened to your Uncle Zeke,'' Shakespeare mentioned.

Nate glanced at the mountain man. ''Then why bother?''

''Beg pardon?''

''Why do so many white men come west of the Mississippi to live, to hunt and trap and mingle with the Indians, if life here is so hard and filled with danger? If one little mistake, like leaning down to get a drink from a spring and not checking the rocks for rattlesnakes, can get you killed, why bother staying? Is the freedom you keep talking about worth all the trouble?''

''That's a decision you'll have to make on your own. It's worth more than all the gold in Creation to me, but it might not be worth a cent to you.''

''I just don't know,'' Nate said slowly.

The Shoshone warriors carried the impaled heads to the southern edge of the camp. Once there, they proceeded to dash the heads to the ground repeatedly, smashing the faces to a pulp and splitting several of the Blackfeet craniums. Brains and gore spattered the earth.

"Why don't they just bury the bodies and be done with it?" Nate asked distastefully.

"Indians never bury the dead of their enemies. Why should they send a foe off in style into the Great Mystery? Besides, you've got to bear in mind that Indians don't view dead bodies the same way whites do."

"So I've noticed."

"Let me explain. It's possible for a warrior to count coup on a dead body—"

"What?" Nate interrupted in surprise. "I thought they counted coup by touching live foes or killing them."

"It's more complicated than that. Some tribes let up to four men count coup on the same enemy. The Crow and Arapahoe do. The Cheyenne, on the other hand, only allow three men to count coup. And the Assiniboin won't permit the counting of any coup unless the body has been touched, whether it's alive or dead."

Nate shook his head. "I'm confused," he admitted.

"Let me try to clear it up for you," Shakespeare offered in the manner of a schoolteacher. "Let's say two tribes are fighting, the Crow and the Blackfeet. One of the Crows strikes one of the Blackfeet with his war club, and the Crow gets to claim first coup, the highest honor, because he struck the Blackfoot while the man was still alive. Then let's say another Crow comes along while the Blackfoot is lying wounded and this second Crow actually kills the Blackfoot. This second Crow can claim second coup, a lesser honor. Follow me so far?"

"So far."

"All right. Then let's say yet a third Crow comes along, and he's the one who scalps the dead Blackfoot. The third Crow can claim third coup, an even lesser honor but still a coup. To round this up, a fourth Crow comes by and cuts the heart out of the Blackfoot. He has fourth coup, which isn't much, but a warrior will take every coup he gets.''

"Why didn't the first Crow do the killing and the scalping and all the rest?" Nate questioned.

"You've been in a few scrapes now. You know how hectic a fight can be. Sometimes a warrior will wound an enemy but doesn't have the time to finish the job," Shakespeare said.

"The way you explain it all makes perfect sense," Nate stated. "But I still don't much like the notion of carving an enemy into pieces. That's the work of a butcher."

"War is butchery. Don't let anyone tell you different."

The Shoshone men reentered the village and joined the women and children around their fallen tribe members. The warriors went to their fallen companions and addressed the three dead Shoshone warriors in the most earnest terms.

"What are they doing?" Nate asked, thoroughly perplexed by the sight of grown men talking to lifeless corpses.

"They're letting their friends know that they took revenge on the Blackfeet."

"But their friends are dead."

"There you go again, thinking in white man's terms," Shakespeare admonished the younger man. "If the Indians view everything from eating to fighting differently than us, doesn't it stand to reason they'd view the dead differently too?"

Nate simply nodded.

"You've got to remember that most Indians believe in an afterlife. These Snakes believe that the souls of the dead watch over the living. Each warrior has his own guardian angel, as it were."

"Wait a minute. You just called them Snakes. I thought they were the Shoshones."

"Shoshone is their own word for their tribe. Most whites call them the Snakes, probably because they spend a lot of the year in the regions around the head branches of the Snake River, although they'll travel all the way over the Divide to the Plains for buffalo when they're in the need."

The sound of approaching horses drew the attention of everyone in the camp to the southeast, and moments later the six Shoshones who had raced in pursuit of the Blackfeet rode into view from a stand of trees.

"We might as well get comfortable," Shakespeare advised. "This will take a while." He sat down on the ground cross-legged and placed his rifle across his lap.

Nate remained standing, not wanting to miss a single moment of the spectacle. In his mind's eye he saw himself back in the comfort and safety of New York, relating to Adeline and his family the many harrowing experiences he'd survived while living in the wilderness. Being Easterners born and bred, they would undoubtedly be particularly interested in any and all Indian customs, and here was a firsthand opportunity to observe those practices often held in mystified dread by the whites.

The six warriors pounded into the village and promptly dismounted. One of them whooped while proudly displaying the body of a Blackfoot he'd ridden down and killed. He held the body erect with his left arm and hit it several times with his war club while reciting his coup.

Nate's eyes narrowed at the sight of the Blackfoot. He recognized the enemy warrior as the same one he'd unhorsed by accidentally shooting the man's animal. So indirectly he was responsible for that Blackfoot's death. Add another life to the tally! he thought bitterly. He was still troubled by shadowy notions of what would happen to his own soul after all the killing he had done. He'd never been excessively religious, but he'd attended church regularly in his younger years and he could quote the Ten Commandments by rote. Thou shalt not kill.

Couldn't get much clearer than that.

Nate looked down at his hands. Strange, though, how with all the death on his hands they were still the same hands and he was still basically the same person. Taking the lives of others hadn't resulted in any great, profound, or terrible insights of self-discovery. Slaying them hadn't altered him one bit as far as he could see. Although, deep down, he'd realized that taking the lives of the last two Blackfeet had been emotionally easier to do than taking the life of the first man he'd killed.

Was that the way it happened?

The idea troubled him. What if each killing became easier and easier? What was to stop him from shooting people for the sheer spiteful meanness of the deed? What separated a basically decent, honest peson like him from cold-blooded murderers? There must be some higher quality or capacity he possessed that served to distinguish him morally and spiritually from common, vile killers?

But what?

A sharp cry came from the Shoshones.

Nate glanced up, startled.

Apparently the Snakes did not intend to make the burial of their dead an elaborate ritual. Some of them had gone to the east side of the village and were busily engaged in digging graves. Others were collecting buffalo robes and other items. Those women connected by blood or marriage to the deceased were clinging to the corpses and wailing pitiably, seemingly striving to attest to the depth of their love by the volume of their cries.

"I heard one of them talking," Shakespeare mentioned loudly to be heard over the crying. "Ordinarily they'd wait a day to plant the bodies in the ground, but when Black Kettle and his hunting party were out earlier they found sign of a large number of Blackfeet in the area. That's why they came back when they did. They're fixing to leave first thing tomorrow morning."

"How many Blackfeet?" Nate asked absently.

"About fifty."

"Fifty?" Nate repeated, glancing at the mountain man. "Why would there be so many Blackfeet in this area now of all times? They must know that every white man in the country and many of the friendly tribes are gathering for the annual rendezvous?"

"That's *why* the Blackfeet are here," Shakespeare stressed. "They roam around the countryside like vultures, preying on any small groups of whites or Indians they find. They know about the rendezvous and they figure this is a golden opportunity to settle old scores."

Nate envisioned hordes of savage Blackfeet descending upon helpless travelers, slaughtering the innocents in droves. "Can't anything be done about them?"

Shakespeare chuckled. "Well, a lot of folks, whites and Indians, are doing a right smart job of exterminating the varmints every chance they get."

"I'm serious."

"What would you do then?"

"Why, I'd raise an army and wipe them out or drive them all the way into Canada if need be."

"There you go again. You really are a bloodthirsty cub. Where do you think you're going to get this army of yours? From the other Indian tribes? How do you think the Blackfeet got to be the top dogs in the northern Rockies and on the high plains? They whipped every other tribe, that's how. The Blackfeet have beaten the Nez Perce, the Flatheads, the Crow, and the Shoshones time and time again. They've taken the choicest land for themselves and driven the others into the high valleys. There isn't a tribe north of the Yellowstone River that would stand a snowball's chance in Hades of defeating the Blackfeet.''

"Then what about the whites? Why do they tolerate the situation?''

"Probably because there aren't more than four or five hundred white men scattered about the entire West from the Mississippi to the Pacific Ocean and from Canada to Santa Fe, not counting the state of Missouri."

"So how many Blackfeet are there?''

"I don't know exactly. Thousands, at least. I'd guess eight or ten thousand.''

"I didn't realize,'' Nate said blankly.

Shakespeare glanced at the Shoshones, who were busily attending to their burial preparations, and faced his friend. "Let me tell you a story. About five years ago someone had the exact same notion you did about raising an army, only they were going after the Rickarees, not the Blackfeet.''

"Someone really raised an army?''

"Let me finish, will you? Early in '23 a gent by the name of Ashley led about seventy men out of St. Louis on his way into trapping country. He got as far as the Rickaree villages way up on the Missouri River. There his men were attacked by six hundred warriors, and he lost twelve before he could cut out and head back downstream. He sent a letter to good old Colonel Henry Leavenworth, old blood and guts himself,'' Shakespeare related. "Well, the colonel got together about two hundred white men, rounded up a pair of cannons and some swivel guns, and marched north to pit his army against the Rickarees and teach those heathens a lesson.'' Here the frontiersman stopped and laughed.

"What's so funny?''

"Never mind. Now where was I? Oh, yes. Along the

way the colonel was joined by pretty near seven hundred Sioux. The Sioux, you see, can't abide the Rickarees, so they were right eager to help give their enemies a licking. Colonel Leavenworth named his army the Missouri Legion, and before the Legion finally showed up outside the Rickaree villages, he'd collected more whites and stray Indians until he had well over a thousand fighting men under his command.''

"The Rickarees must have been destroyed," Nate predicted.

Again Shakespeare laughed. "You'd think so, wouldn't you? Well, the Rickarees couldn't help but notice an army that size approaching their village, so they did the only sensible thing they could do."

"They fought to the last warrior."

"No. They ran."

"The cowards!" Nate opined.

"Cowardice is like bravery, Nate. Sometimes it's relative to the occasion. What good would it have done those Rickarees to be wiped out to the last man, or to have their wives and children slaughtered by the Sioux?"

Nate didn't respond. The answer was obvious.

"So the Rickarees retreated under the cover of darkness and left their village unattended."

"And Colonel Leavenworth burned the villages and returned without a decisive victory," Nate concluded, deducing the rest of the tale. Or so he thought.

"Wrong. Colonel Leavenworth laid siege to the empty villages. For days his Legion tippy-toed around the villages, just out of rifle and bow range, while he bombarded them with cannon rounds to convince them he was deadly serious."

"You're joking me."

Shakespeare snorted. "The joke was on Colonel Leavenworth and the Missouri Legion. They made complete and utter fools of themselves. The white man became the laughingstock of the Rickarees and their allies, and the whites lost prestige in the eyes of every other tribe who heard the report, even the friendly tribes. The upper Missouri has been pretty much closed to white trappers ever since because the Rickarees are no longer afraid of us.''

''But the idea for an army is still sound. It would have worked if Leavenworth had defeated the Rickarees.''

''Even if he had, he certainly didn't have enough men to conquer the Blackfeet. No, you might as well get used to the notion that the Blackfeet will be around for years to come. If you should decide to stay out here, they'll be your worst enemies.''

Nate was about to make a comment when a piercing wail drew his attention to the Shoshone women gathered around the fallen warriors.

One of them had just hacked off the tip of her finger.

Chapter Nine

"Dear Lord!" Nate exclaimed.

Someone had brought a large, flat rock and placed it on the ground near the three deceased Shoshone warriors. Five women were gathered around the rock, and one of them, the woman who had just sliced off the end of her left forefinger at the first joint, was on her knees, a bloody hunting knife clutched in her right hand.

"Why?" Nate blurted.

The woman lowered the knife onto the rock, then used the stump of her left forefinger to smear streaks of blood on her cheeks. The entire time her face radiated supreme pride in her accomplishment. She slowly stood and stepped aside so another woman could kneel.

"They're the wives of the dead men," Shakespeare explained reverently. "They're mourning the loss of their husbands and showing their devotion."

Stunned by the sight, and not knowing what else to say, Nate commented on the obvious. "But there are five women."

"Many tribes believe in plural marriages. What with all the warfare and the dangers entailed in just going hunting, there's a regular shortage of men.''

The second woman now applied the knife to the tip of one of her fingers and cut the digit off without betraying the slightest qualm. It was another of the attending women who let out a wail as if in commiseration. One by one the five women each severed part of a finger and painted their faces with their own blood.

''They keep that blood on until it wears off,'' Shakespeare remarked.

Next the Shoshones wrapped the dead in buffalo robes and carried the bodies to the freshly dug graves. First the three warriors were lowered into the earth, then the five women and the boys.

Nate expected the graves to be promptly filled, but he was mistaken.

The Shoshones began depositing items in the holes: weapons in the case of the men, bows and arrows and war clubs—and one man even had a clipped horse's tail added to the pile; blankets, trinkets, and porcupine-tail hairbrushes were laid to rest with the women; and the boys were the recipients of weapons or other effects.

''What are they doing?'' Nate inquired.

''When Indians are buried, their favorite personal possessions and talismans get buried with them.''

''Why?''

''They believe that the dead wake up in the next world with whatever is buried with the departed. Did you see that horse's tail they put in one of the graves?''

''Yes.''

''They hold that each of those hairs will change into a sturdy steed in the spirit land.''

Nate regarded the Shoshones critically. ''I'll never understand the Indian way of life if I live to be a hundred.''

A wry smile creased the frontiersman's lips. ''Therefore, good Nate, be prepared to hear this. Since you cannot see yourself so well as by reflection, I your glass will modestly discover to yourself that of yourself which you yet know not of." He paused. "With apologies to Brutus."

"What?"

"I'll talk to you again in a year or so."

Mystified by the mountain man's words, Nate shook his head and observed the conclusion of the burial ceremony.

A number of Shoshones began beating drums and sticks while several warriors attended to filling in the graves. The rest of the tribe began a short procession, with the tribal members singing, yelling, and dancing in a slow, shuffling step. They made three circuits of the graves, then halted and gave voice to a melodic chant.

"We're lucky in a way," Shakespeare mentioned.

"How so?"

"These affairs can drag on for days. If Black Kettle wasn't concerned about the Blackfeet, we'd miss even more of the rendezvous than we already will."

"Can't we just leave when we feel so inclined?"

"We could, if you don't care about insulting Black Kettle. I'll wait this out. He'll probably be leaving tomorrow morning and we can ride along with his band."

"Safety in numbers."

"There's that, plus I don't want to get Winona mad at me if I take off with you before she has a chance to make her pitch."

Nate stared at the older man. "I really think you're exaggerating this out of all proportion."

"Much ado about nothing, eh?" Shakespeare retorted, and his shoulders shook with suppressed mirth.

Stung by his friend's baiting, Nate fell silent and thoughtfully watched the burial procession wind into the village.

Black Kettle was in the lead. The tall warrior halted

a dozen yards from his lodge and turned to address his people. For a minute he talked, and when he finished they dispersed to their respective lodges. Black Kettle came toward his guests.

"Be on your best behavior now," Shakespeare said in an aside to Nate. Then he straightened and stepped to meet the warrior, speaking in the Snake tongue.

Nate decided to occupy his time by reloading his pistols. He happened to glance at the crimson-coated rock the women had used as a chopping block, and his brow knit in confusion. How could anyone simply hack off a piece of finger as casually as he might pry a sliver from his skin? Did the gesture truly qualify as an act of sterling devotion, as Shakespeare maintained, or was the ritual another example of the crass behavior so typical of barbaric savages? He couldn't quite make up his mind one way or another.

And what should he make of this business concernng Winona? They hardly knew each other. The very idea that she might sincerely care for him was patently ridiculous. True, his heart seemed to flutter whenever he was in her presence, but his feelings could merely be confused physical attraction and nothing more. His one true love, Adeline Van Buren, was far off in New York City, awaiting his return. How could he even contemplate tarnishing her sterling memory by dwelling on the Shoshone maiden?

A sparkling voice spoke within inches of his left arm.

Startled, Nate looked up to find the lady in question regarding him quizzically. "Hello," he blurted out.

"Hello," Winona repeated precisely, and then indicated the pistol in his hand. Using sign language, she asked him to show her how to load the piece.

Feeling guilty over his line of thought and clearly self-conscious of her proximity to his person, Nate complied.

He patiently instructed her in how to check the vent leading from the pan to the barrel to ensure it wasn't blocked and would cause a misfire. With Winona brushing lightly against his arm, and distracting him terribly, he demonstrated the proper technique for measuring the charge of black powder. His nostrils detected a sweet scent emanating from her tresses as he showed her the way to hold the butt of the pistol against her hip with the muzzle slanted away from the body while doing the actual loading.

Winona appeared genuinely fascinated by the procedure. She was particularly interested in the means of inserting the patch and ball. Once, when his nervous thumb slipped as he tried to push the ball into the bore, she glanced at him knowingly and said a few soothing words in the Shoshone tongue.

Nate felt as if every square inch of his body was tingling by the time he finished his lesson. He tucked both pistols under his belt, hefted the Hawken, and stood as straight and true as his physique could accommodate.

Winona used sign to thank him, and also inquired if he would be staying the night.

Nate responded in the affirmative.

Smiling happily, Winona let him know she would be eager to talk with him later, then excused herself to go help her mother prepare the meal. She darted into her lodge, her long hair swirling, her lithe form moving with surpassing grace.

A lump had formed in Nate's throat. He swallowed hard and gazed out over the village, only to see Shakespeare eyeing him humorously. To his utter chagrin, Nate felt certain he inadvertently blushed. To cover his dis- comfiture, he pretended to be inordinately interested in a flock of startlings winging to the east. He heard footsteps and looked down.

"It's all settled," Shakespeare announced. "We'll stay

the night with Black Kettle, and at first light we're getting the hell out of here before the main body of Blackfeet show up.''

Hoping to avoid discussing Winona at all costs, Nate kept the conversation going. ''Do the dogs sleep outside at night?''

Shakespeare was surprised by the question. ''Yes. Why?''

Nate shrugged. ''I just wondered if they'd bother us, is all.''

The frontiersman's mouth twitched upward. ''No, the dogs won't bother us because we're sleeping in Black Kettle's lodge.''

''What?''

''When you're friends with an Indian, Nate, their home is your home. They'll give you the clothes off their back and the food off their table if you need it. When it comes to outright friendliness, the Indians have us whites beat all hollow.''

''Oh.''

Shakespeare nodded at three camp dogs standing ten feet away. ''Those mongrels stay out to keep watch. They'll bark like mad if anyone comes around.'' He laughed. ''They'd better bark. If a dog doesn't do its duty, it's usually eaten.''

The statement made Nate's head snap up. ''Will they serve dog at this feast we're attending?''

''They might,'' Shakespeare said, and had to turn away to conceal his merriment at the pained expression on his young associate.

''I can hardly wait,'' Nate said dryly.

The mountain man faced around. ''I wouldn't get too excited about the prospect. It's doubtful Black Kettle will serve us a prime dish like dog. That's for special occasions. Since I'm just like one of the family, we'll probably end up with deer or elk." He allowed himself to reflect the proper dregree of sorrow.

Nate brightened considerably. "I suppose I could make do with deer or elk meat. Besides, we wouldn't want to put them to any special bother on our account."

"Perish the thought."

"What should we do about our horses?" Nate inquired.

"We'll let them out to graze until dusk, then we'll tie them near the lodge for the night. You know the old saying. It's better to count ribs than tracks."

Nate knew the saying. It referred to the fact horses were more likely to wander off or be stolen if they weren't secured for the night, and although the animals might put on a little weight by roaming and grazing, a wise horseman would rather count his mount's ribs in the morning than the tracks made during its nocturnal wanderings. "Do you mind if I ask you a question?"

"I can't promise I'll answer it, but go right ahead."

"Do you have any close relatives back in the States?"

"Interesting question," Shakespeare commented, and glanced at Black Kettle's lodge. "Yep, as a matter of fact, I do. Two brothers and a sister. All three are doing quite fine. At least, they were the last I heard from them."

"How long ago was that?"

"Seven years."

"Isn't that a long time to go without hearing from your own relatives?" Nate queried.

"Not really. You may not have noticed, but I'm not a spring chicken any more. My kin and I pretty much parted ways about thirty years ago. If I make it back to Pennsylvania every ten years or so, I figure I'm doing okay."

"Don't you miss them?"

"Every now and then. But I wouldn't have left if there hadn't been some serious problems we couldn't work out, and whenever I get to missing them I just remember how big a pain they could be,'' Shakespeare said.

''I don't know if I could go that long without seeing my family,'' Nate mentioned.

''That's something you have to settle to your own satisfaction. We're not all cut from the same cloth.''

Nate mulled those words as they engaged in casual conversation for the next 25 minutes. All the while as they conversed about the various Indian tribes and the rendezvous, he was thinking about his family and Adeline. How long could he abide being separated from them? When he'd first ventured west to St. Louis, he'd regarded the trip as a terrific adventure, a wonderful opportunity the likes of which he would never see again. But now he had already stayed in the wilderness for a lengthier period than he had dreamt would ever be the case, and the odds were that he would stay for quite a while longer.

Could he take the strain?

He'd told his folks and Adeline he would be gone for a year, but such an extended interval now seemed excessively long. Three months, yes. Maybe six months. But an entire year?

In due course Black Kettle emerged from the lodge and engaged Shakespeare in an animated discussion using sign language and the Shoshone tongue.

Nate understood snatches of their talk. They were merely swapping tales about their exploits since last they had seen one another. Black Kettle, apparently, had been in three battles with the Blackfeet, and the warrior expressed the opinion the Blackfeet were out to get him and had placed him near the top of their long list of enemies on whom they wanted to take revenge for past indignities they had suffered.

The mouth-watering aroma of cooking food wafted from the open lodge flap.

Nate smiled when he recognized the scent of deer meat. His mouth watered in anticipation, and he spent the next half-hour impatiently waiting for the meal to begin.

Finally an attractive woman who wore her hair in braids poked her head out of the doorway and said a few words.

Shakespeare looked at Nate. "Here we go. Now remember what I told you about your manners. If you become confused, just do like I do."

"I'll keep my eyes glued to you."

"I'll bet."

Black Kettle led them into the lodge and strode directly to his customary seat near the rear.

A cursory glance sufficed to show Nate that Winona was not anywhere in sight, and he repressed his disappointment while wondering where she could be. He dutifully followed Shakespeare around to the right, and they both paused while Black Kettle graciously indicated their seats on the warrior's left. Nate took his and studied the interior of the first lodge he had ever been inside.

At the very center, underneath the ventillation flap, was the cooking fire. A stack of firewood had been placed to the right of the doorway. To the left of the door, where they could be grabbed quickly in an emergency, were Black Kettle's weapons. The thick buffalo robes used for beds had been rolled up and positioned along the east wall. Personal effects were arranged along the west wall.

All in all, Nate was very favorably impressed. The cleanliness and warmth gave the dwelling a respectable, homey atmosphere he found quite appealing. His heart began to beat faster moments later when Winona entered the lodge and began assisting her mother in dispensing the food.

The meal turned out to be an education in itself.

To Nate's surprise, the first course was a large tin pan heaped high with boiled deer meat. He took a juicy chunk of venison, and the moment he did Winona placed a flat piece of bark in front of him to serve as his plate. He beamed at her, then leaned to his left and whispered to Shakespeare, "A tin pan?"

"Black Kettle picked it up in trade at the rendezvous last year," the mountain man explained. "Indians are real partial to our pots and pans."

Other courses were distributed. One consisted of a delicious flour pudding that had been prepared using dried fruit and the juice from various berries. After being mixed, the pudding had been boiled to the proper consistency and set to cool. Cakes and strong coffee were also passed out.

Nate saw Shakespeare draw his butcher knife and did the same. Eating utensils were restricted to knives and fingers, a practice Nate didn't mind in the least. He dug into his meal with gusto, surreptitiously watching Winona whenever he felt no one was looking.

Black Kettle and Shakespeare engaged in a running conversation during the entire meal. When they spoke in sign language, which they resorted to frequently, their greasy fingers fairly flew.

Nate tried to follow the gist of their discussion. He gathered they were talking about the general state of affairs in the region west of the Mississippi, but the particulars eluded him. He glanced at Black Kettle's wife a few times, noting her happy, contented expression, and heard her humming softly to herself while she worked. What did she have to be so gay about? he wondered. For that matter, Winona also seemed to be in exceptionally fine spirits. Why? Perhaps, he reasoned, they were overjoyed because they had been spared the ordeal of slicing off part of a finger. At the thought he gazed at the mother's hands and almost lost his appetite.

Black Kettle's wife had the tips of three fingers missing. Troubled, Nate chewed on a cake and took a swallow

of hot coffee from a tin cup. He'd never understand the
savage mentality. An elbow nudged him in the left side
and he turned.

"Our host would like to talk to you," Shakespeare said.
"I've told him that you're still trying to get the hang of
sign, so he'll go slow. And I'll translate where necessary."

Nate deposited the rest of the cake on his plate and wiped
his hands on his pants. He smiled at the warrior, keenly
eager to make a favorable impression, and sensed
Winona's eyes on him.

Black Kettle nodded and moved his hands and arms
slowly, making a series of signs at a snail's pace.

Flooded with relief, Nate found he could understand
the questions the warrior posed, queries concerning where
Nate's parents lived, what Nate thought of the West, and
whether or not Nate was married.

Shakespeare almost choked on his coffee at the last one.

Although he had to struggle to recall several of the signs
he needed, Nate answered all of the questions adequately
and honestly. He grinned, pleased at his performance.

Black Kettle then asked one more.

For a second Nate sat perfectly still, shocked, afraid
he had interpreted correctly.

"Answer the man," Shakespeare prompted, a twinkle
in his eyes. "Do you want to court his daughter or not?"

Chapter Ten

Nate was too flabbergasted to speak for a full 30 seconds. He glanced at Winona and saw her smiling at him expectantly, then looked at her father and inwardly recoiled at the warrior's stern visage.

"Cat got your tongue?" Shakespeare quipped, then became serious. "Remember what I told you about insulting an Indian."

Nate's emotions were swirling in a whirlpool of indecision. He wanted to say yes, but his memories of Adeline prompted him to decline. On the other hand, he certainly didn't want to offend Black Kettle or hurt Shakespeare's feelings, and he adopted the latter justification as the motivation for his answer. "Tell Black Kettle I find his daughter extremely attractive."

Grinning impishly, Shakespeare complied.

"Also explain to him that my knowledge of Indian ways is very limited. Let him know I'm unaware of the proper way to court an Indian maiden," Nate said slowly, selecting his words carefully.

Again the frontiersman translated.

Nate wasn't finished. "Tell him that for the white man

courtship can be a long, drawn-out affair. A man and a woman should get to know one another before they become involved.''

Shakespeare faced his companion. "You expect me to tell him that?''

"Yes," Nate declared. "And that I'm asking you to relay my words beause I want to be sure they are spoken perfectly. I respect him highly and would not want to accidentally insult him through my ignorance.''

An appreciative smile creased Shakespeare's weathered visage. "You're a lot like your Uncle Zeke.''

"I am?''

"Yep. You pack more wisdom between your ears than most men have in their little finger," Shakespeare said. He turned to the warrior and spoke at length.

Nate waited anxiously for Black Kettle's response. He studiously avoided gazing at Winona. What would his family think if they could see him now, discussing the courtship of an Indian woman with her father? His father and mother would probably throw a fit.

The warrior held forth next, speaking in a somber tone.

"He says he's not offended in the least," Shakespeare related. "In fact, he's pleased that you're so considerate of his feelings. He also believes a man and a woman should get to know each other. The Shoshones have a custom they adhere to in courtship, and he believes the custom will serve you well.''

"What custom?''

Shakespeare twisted and pointed at a rolled-up buffalo robe lying against the side of the lodge. "A courting couple throw a robe over themselves for privacy and take a stroll in the moonlight.''

"He wants me to take a stroll with Winona?'' Nate asked, slightly shocked at the father's brazen attitude toward romance with his daughter.

"Whether you go or not is up to you," Shakespeare said. "All he's saying is you've got his permission."

Nate made the sign for "thank you" and indicated he would be delighted to walk with Winona.

Smiling contentedly, Black Kettle grunted and said several words to the frontiersman.

"What did he say?" Nate's curiosity impelled him to inquire.

Shakespeare smiled. "Why not now?"

"Now?"

"There's no time like the present."

"Just like that?"

Lines furrowed the mountain man's forehead. "What is the problem? You want to go walking with Winona. Go. Shoo!"

Nate started to rise, then hesitated.

"Now what's the matter?"

"I just had a thought."

"Uh-oh."

"We'll both be under the same buffalo robe, right?"

"That's the general idea. It's a bit difficult to get to know one another if you're under separate robes," Shakespeare quipped.

Nate saw Winona walk to the wall and pick up the rolled robe. He leaned toward his white-haired mentor. "What happens if I accidentally touch her?"

For a moment genuine astonishment caused Shakespeare's mouth to drop open, but he recovered and slapped his thigh in merriment.

"What's so funny?" Nate demanded uncomfortably.

"If you touch her, I doubt it'll be an accident," Shakespeare said, and cackled.

"You know what I mean. I don't want to be scalped for taking liberties with Black Kettle's daughter."

The frontiersman looked the younger man in the eyes. "Don't you know *anything* about women?"

"A little," Nate replied testily.

"Damn little," Shakespeare declared. "Now listen. No man can take liberties with a woman if she doesn't want them to be taken. Nine times out of ten it's the woman who fans the flames and in the bargain gives the man the mistaken notion that it was all his idea."

"But what about rape?"

Shakespeare blinked a few times. "Good Lord. You aren't fixing to rape her, are you?"

"Of course not."

"Rape is for weaklings. It's for men who don't have the gumption to face a woman in fair combat and lose honorably," Shakespeare said. "Now quit stalling."

"I'm not stalling."

"What would you call it? Babbling like an idiot?"

Nate slowly straightened.

"If it'll make you feel any better, no Indian woman has to stay under a buffalo robe if she doesn't want to," Shakespeare mentioned. "If you overstep yourself she'll just leave."

Winona stepped up to Nate and offered the robe.

Feeling as if he was moving in slow motion, a queasy feeling in his stomach, Nate took the robe and indicated the doorway.

Black Kettle addressed the mountain man, and received a response that made him burst out laughing.

"What did you say?" Nate asked.

"He wanted to know if you were ill. I told him you have water in your knees and mush between your ears," Shakespeare divulged, laughing.

"Thanks."

"Don't fret yourself. Romance has vanquished the mightiest of warriors."

"William S. again?"

"No. Me. Now get going before the sun comes up." Nate motioned once again at the doorway, puzzled that

Winona hadn't already started outside.

"No, you dummy!" Shakespeare cautioned. 'Indian men always take the lead."

"They do?"

"At least they think they do. Now go!"

Bowing graciously at Black Kettle and his wife, Nate backed toward the opening with Winona trailing him, a quizzical expression on her face.

Shakespeare gave a little wave and grinned. "This above all, young prince. To thine own self be true."

"What's that supposed to mean?" Nate asked, pausing near the flap.

"It means," Shakespeare answered, his eyes twinkling in their lined sockets, "you shouldn't light your wick until you can see the whites of her eyes." He threw back his head and convulsed in guffaws.

"The man is mad," Nate muttered, and exited the lodge. He halted in surprise at finding stars in the heavens and the sun long gone. A hand touched him lightly on the left shoulder. Inordinately startled, he turned.

Winona stood there calmly, her hands folded at her waist, her countenance most serious for someone about to go courting.

Nate smiled to reassure her, then proceeded to unwrap the robe, his fingers fumbling at the folds. To his consternation, he came across as a complete butterfingers. When the robe finally unfurled, inadvertently dragging in the dust before he could hold the hem aloft, he beckoned for her to step closer.

Obediently Winona took a short step and stood next to his left shoulder.

Mustering all the dignity at his disposal, Nate carefully draped the heavy robe over their shoulders. It covered both of them all the way down to their knees, screening them from public scrutiny, enshrouding them in a private

domain of intimate proximity although they weren't
actually touching. Nate found the experience discomfiting
and oddly stimulating. He cleared his throat and held his
head high, proud and self-assured.

Until he saw the warriors.

Nate froze when he beheld four young Shoshone
warriors standing 20 feet away near a camp fire. They
were all looking in his direction, and he wondered if they
were upset because he was with Winona. He chided
himself for leaving the Hawken in the lodge, but derived
comfort from the fact he still had his pistols tucked under
his belt.

One of the warriors suddenly came toward him.

Nate looked at Winona and smiled to reassure her that
he would handle any situation, then placed his right hand
on the corresponding flintlock.

The Shoshone, a tall warrior attired in a deerskin shirt
and leggings, approached within a yard and halted.
"Pardon," he said, his youthful voice betraying his age.
"So sorry, Grizzly Killer."

Nate's surprise at hearing English spoken, even if in
a halting fashion, was as nothing to his astonishment at
being called by his Indian name. How did the warrior
know? He remembered Shakespeare had told Black Kettle
and a few of the other men, and the word must have spread
through the village. "What do you want?" he demanded
quickly to cover his embarrassment.

"My name Drags the Rope. Much happy meeting you."

A smile started to curl Nate's lips, but he caught himself
and maintained a sober expression. Drags the Rope? What
kind of name was that? His prudence overrode his curiosity
and he asked a different question. "Where did you learn
the white man's tongue?"

"Trapper Pete teach little. Six winters past."

"Well, I'm pleased to meet you," Nate said, uncertain

of the young warrior's motivation in introducing himself.

"Friend of Shoshones. Friend of Drags the Rope."

"I'll always regard the Shoshones as my friends," Nate stated, for want of anything better to say.

Drags the Rope nodded and smiled. "Much friend. Always remember." He turned and walked happily back to his companions.

Now what was that all about? Nate wondered, and shook his head. He'd said it once, and he'd wind up saying it a hundred times: There was no understanding the Indian.

Winona spoke a few words and nudged his shoulder.

Bothered by guilt over his train of thought, Nate stared at her and realized she wanted to walk to the east. He stepped off slowly, carefully keeping his hands clasped behind his back, keenly aware of her shoulder repeatedly brushing his.

They covered ten yards in silence.

Nate gazed idly at the nearby lodges, wishing he knew the proper words to say. For that matter, he would have settled for knowing *any* words in her language that could help him convey his feelings. "I don't know what to say to you," he stated aloud, hoping she would derive his meaning from the tone he used.

Winona answered, her words almost musical.

"I've never felt so helpless," Nate informed her, staring into her eyes.

Their shoulders came together and stayed together.

Nate had an urge to mop at his brow. The temperature under the buffalo robe seemed to have risen a good deal in mere moments. He coughed to clear his throat, thankful Shakespeare couldn't see him now. The mountain man would laugh himself silly.

Winona began talking and went on at great length, her animated expression compensating somewhat for her unintelligible vocabulary.

Entranced, Nate gazed at her lovely features and simply

drifted with the words, nodding at points he perceived to be appropriate and smiling broadly whenever she deigned to look at him. He scarcely noticed when they went past the last of the lodges and halted a dozen yards beyond.

Winona ceased speaking and turned to face him.

"Nice night," Nate said lamely, though truth to tell he hardly noticed the bright stars overhead or the cool breeze caressing his brow. The sum total of his personal universe was reflected in the beautiful countenance before him. Dim, flickering firelight cast her skin in a faint golden glow and put a gleam in her eyes. She smiled and her teeth sparkled.

They stood stock still for over a minute, their warm breath touching each other's lips.

"I can't believe I'm doing this," Nate declared at last. He thought of Adeline and the memory pained him. How could he betray her like this? With an Indian, no less. The thought gave him pause. Were those the words, or the words of a mindless Easterner, someone who had been conditioned to view Indians with a limited regard by society and his peers? Because in his heart of hearts he couldn't bring himself to think less of Winona simply because of her Indian lineage. At that moment, as their eyes exchanged silently the words they longed to voice, he regarded her as the most wondrous woman of any race.

Somehow they inched closer together until they were nearly touching.

Nate's senses were swimming. His blood pounded in his veins. He licked his dry lips, and suddenly the impossible occurred. Before he could quite control himself, before the fading remembrance of Adeline could interfere, all of Creation was rendered immobile by a singular act.

They kissed.

Chapter Eleven

"What the dickens did you do to that girl last night?"

Nate's head snapped around to his right and he glared at the frontiersman riding beside him. "Just what do you mean by that?" he demanded testily, and gave the pack horse a vigorous yank.

"Simmer down, for crying out loud," Shakespeare said, grinning. "I'm not prying into your personal affairs. But I couldn't help but notice the way she waltzed around this morning all smiles, humming and whistling to beat the band. The whole time she was helping to take down the lodge and pack for the trip—the whole blamed time—all that girl did was show teeth. I don't reckon I've ever seen anyone so happy about doing work in all my born days."

"You're making fun of me again."

"Wouldn't think of it," Shakespeare stated seriously, although the corners of his mouth twitched.

Nate shifted in his saddle and gazed back at the column of Shoshones trailing behind them. Most of the warriors stayed off to one side or the other, ever vigilant for an attack. Some of the women rode horses, but most walked with the children and dogs. Every lodge had been quickly dismantled at first light and secured to horses by means of a travois. Consisting of two lengthy poles tied crosswise behind the horse's head using stout buffalo tendons, then secured in position with strips of rawhide that were lashed to the lower sections to form platforms, the travois sufficed to transport almost every article the Indians owned. With slight modifications, such as circular cages constructed from thin branches that were affixed to the rawhide platforms, they could even be used to convey small children.

All infants were carried on the back of their mothers in ingenious devices known as cradleboards. Simplicity incarnate, each cradleboard was composed of a carved wooden frame that supported a soft pouch. Every cradleboard was different, designed and embellished according to the mother's whim. And every one was a study in versatility. They could be tied onto a saddle or hooked on a travois. They could be leaned against any other object when the mother needed her hands free. And in the lodge they were frequently hung on pegs or hooks. Unlike their white counterparts, an Indian infant was rarely placed flat. The cradleboards were invariably positioned upright, and as a consequence the infant did everything in the same posture they would use once they learned to walk.

Nate scanned the Shoshones in the column, searching for Winona. Nearly a hundred horses were used to move the camp. The larger lodges alone, like Black Kettle's, required upwards of a dozen animals. Earlier he had noticed an interesting aspect of the move, one that surprised him unduly simply because he never expected it.

The Indians were class-conscious.

Those Shoshones who were wealthier, who owned more possessions, who had the biggest lodges and more horses, led the move. Next came those with smaller lodges and fewer horses. And in the rear, choking on the dust stirred by those in the lead, walked the poorer wives with their two or three beasts of burden, including their dogs.

Winona walked near the front, engaged in guiding the horses pulling her father's lodge. She saw Nate glance at her, smiled, and gave a little wave.

"Yep. There she goes again," Shakespeare remarked. "Worst case I've ever seen."

Nate turned his attention to the mountain man. "I want you to know something."

"What, pray tell?"

"I intend to get even. I don't know how and I don't know when, but one of these days when you least expect it, I *will* get even."

Shakespeare chuckled. "Fair enough, Nate. I admire a man who has spunk."

Nate chuckled and gazed ahead at Black Kettle, Drags the Rope, and five other warriors who were 40 feet in front of the column. He thought of the tender moments he'd shared with Winona and sighed. "I need your advice," he stated bluntly.

"I figured as much."

"I really like Winona—" Nate began.

"Remind me to buy you a dictionary one of these days," Shakespeare interrupted.

"What? Why?"

"A man should always say what he means and mean what he says."

"Huh?"

"For you to say you like Winona is the same as a Shoshone saying he's not particularly fond of the Blackfeet."

"I don't see the connection," Nate said.

"Sure you do. You're just hoping no one else does, but you're only fooling yourself," Shakespeare stated.

"Will you advise me or not?" Nate asked indignantly.

"That's what I'm here for."

Nate stared idly at the winding valley they were following to the northwest, mulling how best to present his problem. He observed a raven off to the left, winging on the wind over an expanse of verdant forest. "All right. I won't beat around the bush any longer."

"I wouldn't want you to break a habit on my account."

"Please, Shakespeare," Nate said earnestly, looking at his companion.

The frontiersman promptly sobered. "Fair enough. Flat-out serious. What can I do for you?"

"I think I'm falling in love."

Shakespeare opened his mouth to reply, then changed his mind and simply nodded. "Go on."

"I've fallen head over heels for Winona, and for the life of me I can't figure out why," Nate related, and went on before the mountaineer could interrupt. "Hear me out. I have a beautiful woman waiting for me back in New York City. At least I hope she's waiting." He paused. "Or I *was* hoping, anyway, before I met Winona. And now all I do is think about Winona. I want to be near her all the time. But how can I become involved with Winona when my heart is in New York with Adeline?"

"Before you get in any deeper, let's clear up a few things," Shakespeare said. "I know how it is when a man is in love. His brain is all addled. Or, as old William S. would say, when the blood burns, how prodigal the soul lends the tongue vows. To put it straight, a man can't think straight. Which certainly explains your raving."

"Raving?"

"What else would you call it? The last I knew, it's not possible for a man to be in one place and his heart to go its merry way somewhere else. So your heart can't be in New York if you're becoming involved with Winona. Maybe your memory is still lodged in New York and tugging on your heartstrings, but I daresay your soul has

succumbed to the lovely Winona's charms or I'm not the
most cantankerous cuss in the Rockies.''

Nate nodded slowly. ''What do I do?''

''What comes naturally.''

''That's not what I mean. How do I go about courting
her without getting in over my head before I'm ready?''

Shakespeare chuckled. ''It's a little late for that. You're
already in over your head. If you didn't want to get
involved, you should have declined to go for that walk
last night.''

''But I didn't want to offend her father,'' Nate said
quickly.

''Who are you trying to kid? I won't keep giving you
my advice if you keep insulting my intelligence. Never
label a gent as dumb just because he wears buckskins or
wears his hair longer than you do. And always remember
that experience has a way of sweating the fat from a brain,
which must rate me one of the smartest men around what
with all the gray hairs I've got.''

''Are you saying I'm committed to her whether I want
to be or not?'' Nate queried.

''You went and got her hopes all fired up, didn't you?
You sweet-talked her and stood under the same robe with
her. She made no secret of the fact she liked you, and
you receiprocated. Now Winona naturally figures you and
her are bound to be hitched before too long. Yeah, I'd
say you're committed.''

''But I honestly don't know if I want to marry her.''

''It's a mite late to be putting the horse behind the cart,
don't you think?''

''I don't know what to think,'' Nate said, and sighed.
His emotions were in keen turmoil. On the one hand there
was Adeline Van Buren, on the other Winona. On the one
hand a woman who enjoyed a prominent social position
and whose father possessed great wealth, on the other hand
a woman who was a member of a wandering Indian tribe

and whose father adorned the interior of his lodge with the scalps he had taken. They were as different as night from day, and he was caught in the middle. Correction. He had caught himself. Leaving a burning question in his mind. "What do I do?" he repeated softly.

"The decision is yours alone," Shakespeare commented, and stiffened in his saddle. He peered intently at the forest to the west.

Nate noticed and looked in the same direction. "What do you see?"

"I'm not sure," Shakespeare said, his forehead creased. "I thought I saw something move."

"What?" Nate asked, scanning the trees 30 yards distant. He failed to detect any motion whatsoever.

The frontiersman shook his head and started to relax. "Probably a deer or an elk."

"Why are you so jumpy?"

"Who's jumpy?"

"You are."

"I ate too much last night. I guess I'm still not over my indigestion."

Nate snorted. "Do you expect me to buy that? You have an iron gut. You told me so yourself."

"Believe a third of what you hear and half of what you see and you'll just about get the facts straight."

"Is that your motto?" Nate queried, grinning.

"You bet it—" Shakespeare began, and abruptly stopped, his gaze on the woods. He reined up and rested his right hand on the Hawken lying across his saddle. "Now I know I saw something."

Nate halted and stared into the shadows shrouding the base of the trees. He still saw nothing out of the ordinary.

"Let's take a look," Shakespeare proposed. He rode toward the forest without waiting for a response.

Puzzled by the mountain man's uncharacteristic nervousness, Nate quickly caught up, riding on his companion's right. In his right hand he held his rifle. He glanced to the northwest and saw Black Kettle and the other Shoshones had reined up and were watching intently. To his left the column of women, children, horses, and belongings still advanced.

"I could be making a fool of myself," Shakespeare remarked. "If so, it won't be the first time and I doubt it will be the last. But we can't afford to take any chances."

Twenty yards separated them from the treeline.

"Blackfeet, you think?" Nate asked.

"Some of that bunch got away yesterday, remember? I wouldn't put it past them to have gone after the rest of their war party, and then they swung around in front of us and set up an ambush."

"How would they know which direction we'd take?"

"They're not stupid. They've got to figure that Black Kettle's band is on the way to the rendezvous, and this is the shortest route," Shakespeare answered.

Nate looked at the woods. "I hope you're wrong."

"So do I."

But he wasn't.

Whooping and hollering, over three dozen Blackfeet emerged from concealment in the undergrowth. They waved their weapons in the air and broke into a gallop, heading straight for the column.

"We've got to turn them!" Shakespeare cried, and his white horse leaped to incercept the Blackfeet. "Leave our pack horse here!"

Winona was in danger! The thought spurred Nate to lash the reins and race even with the frontiersman. They angled to the left, listening to screams of alarm arising from the Shoshone women.

"They're going to try and drive off the horses!" Shakespeare shouted.

Nate nodded his understanding.

"And capture the women!" Shakespeare added.

Impulsively, Nate snapped the Hawken to his shoulder and took a bead on the foremost Blackfoot. He changed his mind at the last instant, preferring to save the shots for when he'd really need them.

The Shoshone women were trying to drive their animals to the east, away from the Blackfeet, while from all directions the Shoshone warriors converged on the column to protect their loved ones and property.

Nate hunched low in the saddle and the mare passed Shakespeare. He heard his name called but kept going. All he could think of was Winona, and his eyes strayed to the column where she was frantically striving to turn her father's horses. Attached to travois, and laden with lodge poles, robes, and every other item the Indians owned, the animals awkwardly heeded commands and prodding. They were packed close together, and many collided in their incipient panic.

A Blackfoot armed with a lance broke away from the main body and rode directly toward Nate, yipping like a coyote.

Undaunted, Nate never slowed. The warrior was obviously trying to cut him off. He'd let the Blackfoot get nearer before firing.

Someone beat him to the punch.

A rifle cracked to his rear and the Blackfoot reacted as if kicked in the forehead by a mule, catapulting backwards, arms flung outward.

Shakespeare! Nate knew, and grinned in appreciation. His elation lasted only a few seconds, however, just long enough for him to draw within ten yards of the milling column. He'd managed to outdistance the Blackfeet, but only by 30 or 40 feet, and now five of them shrieked and whooped and bore down in a compact group straight at him.

Chapter Twelve

Nate risked a glance to check on Winona and found her still struggling with the horses. He also glimpsed Shoshone warriors rushing to the rescue from all directions, but none of them were close enough to prevent the Blackfeet from reaching the column. Then there was no time for anything except simply staying alive. The five enemy warriors were 20 feet distant when he lifted the Hawken, aimed, and sent a ball into the chest of the only one of the five armed with a bow.

The shot struck him just as the warrior drew back the string, and knocked him from his mount. Prematurely released, the arrow flew wild at a downward angle to the left and the shaft sank into the neck of the horse galloping alongside the archer's. The wounded animal whinnied in torment and shied to the right, colliding with a third horse in the process, slowing down two of the warriors.

But two more came on fast and furious.

No sooner had Nate fired the Hawken than he wedged the barrel under his left leg and drew both pistols, one in each hand. He cocked them, keeping them next to his waist.

The two Blackfeet pounded toward him. A war club graced the upraised hand of the warrior on the left while the second Blackfoot held a lance.

Nate met them head-on, deliberately choosing a course that would take him between the pair of bloodthirsty warriors. He waited as long as he dared to fire, until the Blackfoot holding the lance drew the weapon back and tensed to hurl it. Then he extended both arms, pointed a pistol at each warrior, and squeezed both triggers.

The twin cracks and the discharge of lead and smoke resulted in both Blackfeet falling to the hard ground without uttering a word or cry.

Gloating was out of the question.

The fourth Blackfoot, a husky man bearing a tomahawk, had gotten his animal under control after colliding with the injured horse, and he screeched an inarticulate challenge as he now raced forward.

All three of Nate's guns were empty and he couldn't hope to reload before the husky warrior reached him. He had no doubt the Blackfoot could wield that tomahawk proficiently, and the odds against him surviving were astronomical unless he could concoct a clever ruse.

Desperate straits called for desperate measures.

Nate sat tall in the saddle, gripping both pistols tightly. He saw the warrior draw the tomahawk back when they were a paltry 15 feet apart, and to counter the anticipated blow he did the totally unexpected. He leaned *toward* the onrushing Blackfoot and hurled his left pistol at the man's startled face.

The warrior instinctively ducked and twisted to the side.

Which was exactly the reaction Nate wanted. He closed in next to the Blackfoot's horse and swung the right pistol, clubbing the warrior on the bridge of his nose. Blood gushed and the Blackfoot reeled. Nate hit him again, on the mouth, splitting the warrior's lips and breaking off two front teeth.

The Blackfoot swayed and almost fell.

In a flash of inspiration, realizing he needed a suitable weapon for up-close combat, Nate lunged, grabbed the tomahawk handle in his left hand, and wrested the aboriginal hatchet from the warrior's grasp. Instantly he tucked his remaining pistol under his belt, transferred the tomahawk to his right hand, and swung with all his might.

Finely crafted, with a triangular metal head fashioned in a white man's forge and a red, factory-made cloth covering the handle, the tomahawk had apparently been received in trade from French traders hailing from Canada, with whom the Blackfeet were known to conduct an extensive business. The weapon possessed a perfect balance, and Nate found he could use it with ease.

The sharpened edge bit deep into the warrior's brow above the right eye, and the Blackfoot clutched at the handle as he vented a strained, gurgling gasp.

Nate tore the tomahawk free and swung again, aiming at the warrior's neck, and the edge cut into the soft flesh as if it were penetrating an overripe melon. Skin and muscle were readily severed, as were veins and arteries, and a crimson spray gushed from the fatal wound.

His eyes and mouth both wide in shock, the Blackfoot futilely pressed his hands over the gash, then sagged and toppled to the grass.

Nate hefted the bloody tomahawk, feeling a surge of confidence, and looked around for other foes. He didn't have far to look.

The warrior astride the animal with the arrow jutting from its neck was bearing down on him, the wounded horse gamely responding to its master's unspoken directions. The Blackfoot waved a war club and vented a challenging cry.

For Nate, there was barely time to turn the mare to meet

the attack. He swung the tomahawk as the war club descended toward his skull, and just managed to deflect the weapon. The blow jarred his arm all the way to the shoulder.

Instantly the warrior swung again.

Nate blocked the strike, and then was forced to do so again and again as the Blackfoot tried to connect with increasingly reckless swings. All about him he could hear gunfire, shouts, screams, and the neighs of horses, but he couldn't dare take his gaze from his opponent for even a second. In the back of his mind he wondered what had happened to Winona and Shakespeare, and he wanted very much to dispose of the warrior so he could aid them if necessary.

The Blackfoot had other notions.

Whipping the tomahawk in a hasty sideways parry, Nate battered yet another blow aside. For a moment his arm was extended and he was slightly off balance, and in that moment the Blackfoot revealed himself to be a seasoned veteran of many clashes.

Instead of swinging one more time in vain, the warrior vented a bloodcurling screech and launched his body into the air.

Nate tried to land a backhand strike and send his foe sprawling, but muscular arms wrapped around his shoulders and he was driven to the right with the Blackfoot on top. They were almost face to face as they dropped, and Nate looked into a pair of hate-filled eyes that implacably promised the most horrific fate imaginable if he should succumb to the designs of their owner. He came down hard on his right shoulder, felt the encircling arms let go, and rolled to his feet.

The Blackfoot was already erect and trying to plant a terrific swipe of his war club on the top of Nate's head.

Only a reflexive counter-swipe with the tomahawk saved

Nate from certain death. He deflected the club from his cranium, but the stone had struck a glancing blow off his left arm, causing excruciating pain and compelling him to retreat to avoid being hit again.

Sensing he had the edge, the warrior pressed his advantage, raining blows.

Nate blocked a half dozen in rapid succession, gritting his teeth against the agony in his arm, and racked his brains for a means of dispatching the Blackfoot quickly. There had to be something he could do, some ruse that would work! He inadvertently stumbled on a way a few seconds later when his right foot slipped and he fell onto his right knee.

Bellowing in triumph, the Blackfoot streaked the war club in a vicious arc.

Nate threw himself to the right, onto the ground, and felt the passage of air past his ear as the war club narrowly missed. For a second he was on his side within arm's reach of the warrior's legs, and without conscious deliberation on his part, exhibiting a savagery that surprised even him, he buried the tomahawk in his enemy's left foot.

The Blackfoot voiced a wavering screech and lurched backwards, striving to yank his foot free.

Nate tore the tomahawk loose and surged to his knees, drawing his right arm to the left as he rose, then swung. The edge ripped into the warrior's abdomen before the Blackfoot could retreat out of harm's way.

Uttering a visceral grunt, the warrior doubled over, his dark eyes the size of walnuts.

Without a pause, his lips set in a thin line, Nate jerked the tomahawk out. A loud squishing noise and a gasp from the Blackfoot attended the motion. He happened to look at the warrior's face and saw displayed there, not fear or capitulation, but raw, spiteful defiance.

Somewhere nearby a woman wailed.

Winona! Was it her? Eager to go to her aid, Nate slashed

the tomahawk across the warrior's throat. The razor-edged steel sliced the Indian's throat from side to side, and a crimson torrent sprayed out over Nate and the ground. He elevated his right arm to shield his eyes from the sticky liquid and pushed to his feet.

Wheezing and sputtering, the warrior sprawled forward. There was no time to lose!

Nate spun, scanning the battlefield, seeking Winona and noting the flow of the fight. The action had already passed him by, and the main body of Blackfeet had reached the column and were now engaged in brutal, fierce combat with the Shoshone defenders. The Shoshone warriors had rallied to defend their loved ones, and although outnumbered, they were acquitting themselves admirably, Black Kettle foremost among them. The Shoshone leader was in the thick of the conflict, wielding a war club like a man possessed, striking madly at every adversary within range.

The din was deafening. Whoops, shouts, screams, gunshots, whinnies, and the frenzied barking of the Shoshone dogs commingled in a cacophonous uproar. Dust clouds swirled into the air, obscuring portions of the valley.

There was no sign of Winona. No Shakespeare, for that matter.

Alarmed, Nate spied his mare standing 20 feet away and ran toward the animal. En route he reclaimed his rifle, which had fallen when the Blackfoot knocked him from his horse, and the pistol he had thrown. The latter he crammed under his belt, then slid the tomahawk next to it. Torn between his eagerness to participate in the combat and the realization that carrying three empty guns into a fight qualified as a prime example of sheer stupidity, he took the time to quickly reload the Hawken and one of the pistols, his fingers flying faster than they ever had. In slightly over a minute both guns were ready to go and he climbed on the mare.

The clash still raged.

Nate rode into the dust cloud, toward where he'd last
seen Winona. He covered 15 yards without spying anyone,
just horses and dogs, and then the dust abruptly cleared
and he discovered a large party of Shoshones besieged
by the Blackfeet. Four Shoshone warriors were battling
seven Blackfeet, protecting a half-dozen women who were
fleeing eastward while driving horses laden with travois
ahead of them.

One of the women was Winona!

Even as Nate's gaze alighted on her, his blood seemed
to chill at the sight of a Blackfoot who had singled her
out and was trying to capture her.

Winona had a short pole in her hand. She was industriously swatting at the warrior in an attempt to drive him
off, but her blows had only sufficed to make him angry.

Nate urged the mare toward them, his concern for
Winona eclipsing all other considerations, even his own
safety. He ignored everyone and everything except the
struggle involving the woman whose lips tasted sweeter
than the richest honey, whose embraces had promised so
much the night before. An arrow whizzed past his head,
but he paid scant heed.

Winona stood in danger.

All else was insignificant.

Neither of them saw Nate approach. He drew within
two yards of the Blackfoot before the warrior awoke to
his presence and turned. "Take this!" Nate cried, and
extended the rifle barrel until the tip nearly touched the
Indian's nose. He instantly fired, holding the Hawken in
just his right hand.

The blast lifted the Blackfoot from his horse and
propelled him over eight feet to crash onto the unyielding
earth.

Nate almost went down himself. The recoil from the rifle, while negligible when the Hawken was held properly in both hands, almost tore the gun from his grasp, whipping his arm backward and rocking him in the saddle. He recovered, transferred the rifle to his left hand, and leaned down to offer his right arm to Winona. "Here!" he yelled. "Take my hand!"

She didn't understand his words, but his intent was clear, and she promptly took hold and allowed herself to be swung up behind him.

"Hold tight!" Nate advised, and pointed at his waist.

Winona nodded and banded her slim arms around his midriff.

Feeling strangely flushed, Nate wheeled the mare, about to speed Winona to safety far from the fight. He heard her cry out at the same moment he saw her father.

Forty feet to the west three Blackfeet had surrounded Black Kettle. He fought back valiantly, but they were clearly going to prevail unless he received assistance, and there were no other Shoshones close enough to lend a hand.

Winona shouted a word in Nate's ear and motioned at her father.

Did he really have any choice?

The question flickered across Nate's mind as he goaded the mare toward the unequal contest, drawing the loaded pistol and wishing he had taken the time to load both pistols.

Black Kettle had downed one of his opponents, bashing the man on the crown with a mighty swipe. As he twisted to confront the second Blackfoot, the third warrior, who held a slim lance, speared the shaft completely through Black Kettle's chest.

Winona screamed in terror.

Chapter Thirteen

Nate closed rapidly, cocking the pistol, filled with dread at the sight of thee Blackfoot yanking the lance out and Black Kettle pitching headfirst to the soil. Winona's arms tightened about his midsection, squeezing so hard it hurt.

The two Blackfeet weren't done with Black Kettle. The warrior holding the lance moved his horse next to the Shoshone's prone form and raised his arm for another thrust, evidently intending to be certain.

Winona sobbed.

Acting spontaneously, Nate pointed the pistol at the Blackfoot and at a distance of 25 feet squeezed the trigger. Much to his amazement, what with the range, the swaying of the mare, and the fact he had scarcely aimed, he scored.

The ball took the Blackfoot high in the right thigh, and in his shock and astonishment at being hit he dropped the lance.

At the retort the other warrior turned, a lean man holding a fusee. He took one look and raced off.

Nate stuck the pistol under his belt and drew the tomahawk, but the weapon wasn't needed. The injured Blackfoot reined his animal to the west and galloped away without a backward glance. Nate was strongly tempted to pursue the warrior and finish the man off, but he brought the mare to a precipitate stop next to Black Kettle.

In a bound Winona was on the ground and kneeling beside her father. She leaned down to inspect the hole.

Worried because they were in the open, exposed with nowhere to take cover if they should be attacked, Nate slid down and began loading the Hawken. He scanned their immediate vicinity, taking stock of the situation.

The dust had pretty much dissipated. Bodies were in evidence everywhere: men, women, children, horses, and even dogs. Shoshone possessions were scattered in profusion: lodge poles, many of them broken; buffalo robes, torn and lying in the dirt; baskets and bowls and blankets and dozens of items that had been crushed in the general stampede to escape.

Nate spotted a large band of Blackfeet departing to the east, taking scores of Shoshone horses with them. He saw no sign of Blackfeet warriors nearby, and he deduced the Shoshones must have driven the raiders off. A frantic woman ran toward them from the southeast, and he recognized her as Winona's mother.

Hoofbeats drummed to his rear.

Nate had just completed reloading. He whirled, bringing the barrel up.

"Whoa, there, Grizzly Killer! I'm on your side, remember?"

"Shakespeare!" Nate declared happily, overjoyed to find the mountain man alive. He tempered his excitement and stepped aside to reveal Black Kettle. "He took a lance."

"Damn!" Shakespeare exclaimed angrily, and dropped to the earth. He squatted next to Winona, examining the wound for himself. "This is bad. Very bad. He needs immediate medical attention."

Nate gestured at the retreating Blackfeet. "At least we won. We can give him the care he needs without fretting about them."

"That's where you're wrong, I'm afraid," Shakespeare said, looking up. "We're still in hot water."

"How so?"

"The Blackfeet will be back."

"They will?" Nate said, gazing after the war party.

At that moment Winona's mother reached them and sank down with a cry of anguish.

Shakespeare stood slowly, sorrow etching his craggy features. He stared eastward. "Those devils aren't about to let Black Kettle's band off the hook so easily. Unless I miss my guess, a third of his people are dead or dying."

"That many?" Nate stated in disbelief.

"And those bastards drove off almost all of the horses."

"Then why will they come back? They're already inflicted enough damage."

The frontiersman glanced at his companion. "Haven't you been paying attention? Indian warfare isn't like warfare among the whites. Rivals often fight until one side or the other is exterminated, even if it takes decades. At the very least they'll keep raiding each other until one side is driven hundreds of miles away." He paused. "The Blackfeet have been trying to kill Black Kettle for years. They want to wipe out his band, and they're not about to let this chance slip by."

Nate stared at the injured warrior, who lay unconscious with blood seeping from the cavity in his chest. "What do we do?"

"First we have to get everyone together, take stock, and see exactly how bad off we are. Then we've got to find a defensible position where we can hole up," Shakespeare said. He swung onto his white horse, looked at Winona's mother, and spoke several sentences in the Shoshone tongue.

The woman, whose normally stolid countenance radiated profound emotional misery, simply nodded in response.

Shakespeare glanced at Nate. "Stay here with Black Kettle. Morning Dew and Winona are going to rig up a travois we can use as a stretcher. There's not much else we can do for him for the time being." He frowned. "We've really got to get the hell out of here, pronto." So saying, he wheeled his mount and rode toward a group of five or six warriors 60 yards to the north.

Winona and her mother rose and hurried off.

So the mother's name was Morning Dew, Nate thought, realizing he had failed to inquire the night before. But then he had been rather preoccupied with musing about Winona. He studied Black Kettle for a minute, wondering if the warrior would live, noticing how shallowly the man breathed. The blood flow had reduced to a trickle. He could see the ring of pinkish flesh rimming the hole. Oddly, after all he had just been through, the sight made him squeamish and he quickly focused his attention elsewhere, watching the proceedings all about him.

Some of the Shoshones were going from body to body, ascertaining who was dead and who might only be injured. Others were industriously engaged in rounding up the scattered horses still in the vicinity, and a few were collecting undamaged personal items. The village dogs, temporarily left to their own devices, were lapping at puddles of blood, sniffing corpses, and to the south three of them were snapping at each other over which one would have the honor of tearing into a dead horse.

Nate used the opportunity to load both pistols and clean the tomahawk. The lethal effectiveness of the oversized hatchet had impressed him immensely and he decided to keep the weapon permanently. He tucked the handle under his belt at the small of his back where it was out of the way but handy in an emergency. What with the Hawken, the two flintlock pistols, the butcher knife, and the tomahawk, he was beginning to resemble a walking arsenal. He idly gazed northward.

Shakespeare had reached the group of warriors, five in number, and was addressing them. After a bit they spread out, going to their people and relaying instructions. One of the warriors turned out to be Drags the Rope.

A groan issued from Black Kettle's lips.

Nate glanced down, then over at the busy Shoshones, marveling at the rapport between the Indians and the mountain man. They appeared to trust Shakespeare implicitly and regarded his advice highly. This, despite the vast differences in their cultures and backgrounds. But was there really that great a difference? he speculated. If white men like Shakespeare could be so at home living as an Indian, if the frontiersmen who inhabited the wilderness could adopt Indian values so readily and be as much at ease experiencing life in the raw, were the differences between the whites and the Indians inherent or superficial? Or did the truth lie even deeper? Were some white men simply primitive at heart? Was that why they yielded to the call of the wild, as Shakespeare described it?

And what about his own feelings?

Nate had to admit that he found much to admire in Indian life, in the simplicity of existence they enjoyed and their affinity to Nature. He thought about life in New York City, about the hectic, frenetic, pace thousands upon thousands were caught up in each and every day, and he felt glad that he was out of that. All those years of contending with impolite people and carriage congestion, with overpriced goods and sooty air, seemed like the vague impressions of a bad dream. At least west of the Mississippi a man could set his own pace.

Provided he lived long enough.

Something touched his left leg.

Nate almost jumped out of his moccasins. He looked

at Black Kettle, shocked to find the warrior awake and gazing at him.

The Shoshone leader spoke a few words in his own language.

Shaking his head to signify he didn't comprehend, Nate squatted and scrutinized the area for Winona and Morning Dew, neither of whom were anywhere in sight.

Black Kettle coughed lightly and spoke again.

"Don't exert yourself," Nate said, and propped the rifle against his right shoulder so he could make the proper hand signs to tell the warrior not to talk.

Black Kettle motioned feebly, executing signs of his own, his hands barely moving.

"Must talk," Nate translated, and frowned. What could be so important that the warrior wouldn't lie still? Frustrated, he looked up and was relieved to spy his newly acquired friend from last night riding past 30 feet to the west. "Drags the Rope! Come here. I need you," he called out.

The young Shoshone warrior immediately turned his horse and hurried over. "Yes, friend Grizzly Killer?" he said as he slid to the ground. His eyes flicked to Black Kettle and he stiffened, then knelt and talked rapidly and softly in Shoshone.

Nate listened to Black Kettle reply, the words scarcely audible. He happened to glance to the southwest, and spotted Winona and Morning Dew over 150 yards distant. They appeared to be working at securing a travois to a brown horse they'd caught. He waved his arms overhead in an attempt to attract their attention, but neither one gazed in his direction.

"Black Kettle much words for you," Drags the Rope said.

Nate looked down. "For me?"

"Yes. Big words of heart."

"Are you sure he wouldn't rather talk to his wife or daughter? I can go fetch them."

Drags the Rope relayed the message to Black Kettle, who responded in a whisper. "No. Not wife. Not daughter. Words for your ears," the young warrior translated.

Perplexed, Nate squatted. "What could he possibly have to say to me?"

Again Drags the Rope passed on the question, and the answer he received clearly surprised him. He blinked, then stared at Nate. "Wants you take Winona."

"Take her where?"

"Wife her."

"What?" Nate asked in astonishment.

"So sorry. Wants you marry Winona."

"He said that!" Nate exclaimed, scrutinizing Black Kettle's inscrutable visage.

"Yes," Drags the Rope responded.

Black Kettle began speaking and went on at length.

"So much words," Drags the Rope stated uncertainly. "Hope speak rightly. My White Talk not best."

"What did he say?" Nate inquired apprehensively.

"Say he dying. Not long this world. Want know family fine before leave. Want you protect family."

"Me?"

"Yes. Want you marry Winna and have food and robes for Morning Dew."

"Food and robes?" Nate repeated in confusion.

"Yes. So sorry. Mean take care of her. Understand? Protect her. Take mother your lodge," Drags the Rope said.

Nate was at a loss for words. He cared for Winona unequivocally, but he wasn't ready to commit himself to her. Not in marriage anyway. Not until he knew her a lot better. But how could he tell that to a dying man?

Black Kettle talked to Drags the Rope, who then glanced at Nate. "Say you much like Winona, yes?"

"Yes," Nate admitted.

Drags the Rope relayed the word to the Shoshone leader and received more information to impart. "He say Winona like you much. Say you brave man. Say you be a good husband."

"But—" Nate began.

"Say Winona strong body. Much health. Have sons like bears. Many sons yours. She make good wife for warrior," Drags the Rope declared.

"I'm sure she would—" Nate began again, and was cut off a second time.

"Listen, please. Many words must say. I forget if not. Black Kettle know Shoshone warriors want marry Winona. Know many horses be his. But no need horses now. He want Winona happy, and she much want you. Much want. Understand?"

"I understand," Nate said, conscious of the leader's eyes on his face. He deliberately averted his gaze, troubled in his soul. Why didn't he just up and tell Black Kettle that he couldn't marry Winona at this time? He felt as if he was deceiving the man. Where was his courage? Why was he so tongue-tied? Could it be possible that deep, deep down he really liked the idea?

"Grizzly Killer?"

"What?" Nate snapped, forgetting himself.

"Something wrong?" Drags the Rope inquired.

"What could be wrong?"

"No idea. Black Kettle need answer. Need quick."

"An answer?" Nate said evasively, knowing the truth.

"Yes. Need know you will marry Winona. Please. Him not much time left. What say you?"

Nate shifted and locked his gaze on Black Kettle. He detected the fading expectancy in the warrior's eyes, and he intuitively perceived the critical importance of his response. The answer meant everything to the father and husband who would momentarily cast off his mortal shell and enter the vast unknown. Black Kettle wanted to die knowing his loved ones would be cared for, would be happy, and he was expending the last of his strength and energy while thinking only of Morning Dew and Winona. In light of so noble a sacrifice, Nate felt guilty about his own conflicting feelings.

How could he tell the man no?

How could he send Black Kettle into eternity in emotional distress?

Nate took a breath and voiced the single word that would link him indissolubly to the Shoshones and drastically alter all of his preconceived notions about his future, the momentous word that had changed more lives than any other in human history. "Yes."

Chapter Fourteen

"I can't leave you alone for two minutes."

"You would have done the same thing in my place."

"How do you know? It's risky trying to predict what another man will do in affairs of the heart because no two men are alike. I might have found a way out of it. I know I wouldn't have let myself be roped into a marriage I didn't want," Shakespeare stated testily.

Nate, in the act of arching his back to relieve a slight stiffness after three hours in the saddle, glanced at the frontiersman. "I don't see why you're so upset with me. You were the one who told me I was committed to Winona."

"Yeah, but I never claimed you had to up and agree to marry her out of pity."

"There's more to it than that."

"Oh?"

"I told you I think I'm falling in love with her," Nate reminded him.

"Getting married because you think you're in love is like wrestling a grizzly because you think you're bored and need a little excitement. In both cases a man winds up biting off more than he can chew.''

"It's too late for me to change my mind,'' Nate stated.

"Black Kettle is still alive,'' Shakespeare pointed out.

"But for how long?'' Nate countered, and twisted to survey the column behind them, a pale imitation of its former self. Where before there had been about a hundred horses laden with possessions, now there were 11 and all but two of them hauled injured Shoshones on makeshift hide platforms. Where before there had been almost 60 smiling, happy people, now there were 38 Indians, including those on the travois, and none were smiling or singing. Of that total, only nine were robust warriors capable of resisting another attack. Three of them trailed at the rear to cover the woman and children, while three rode on each side leaving Shakespeare and Nate to lead them to the northwest as swiftly as possible, which amounted to little better than a snail's pace. "I wish we could go faster,'' Nate remarked.

"We can't, not unless we don't care if some of the injured die on us,'' the frontiersman mentioned.

"I know.'' Nate stared ahead at a sloping hill they were slowly approaching. "What's your plan anyway? Other than putting as much distance as you can between us and the valley where we were attacked.''

"That's it.''

"You're kidding?''

"I wish I was. I know the Blackfeet will hit us again before nightfall, and I want to be ready for them.''

"Maybe you're wrong,'' Nate said hopefully. "Maybe they were satisfied with killing twenty-two Shoshones and stealing all those horses.'' He tugged on the lead to their pack animal.

"They won't be satisfied.''

"So you keep saying, but you don't know that for certain,'' Nate stated peevishly, annoyed that the mountain man kept harping on the worst likelihood.

Shakespeare sighed and looked at the strapping youth. "I know Mad Dog. He won't give up, believe me."

"Mad Dog?" Nate repeated, all attention.

"I recognized the Blackfoot bastard leading the war party," Shakespeare disclosed. "In his lifetime he's counted over eighty coup. Whites, Shoshones, Cheyennes, Arapahos, you name them, he hates them all. He had a run-in with Black Kettle about twelve years ago and came out on the losing end."

"Why didn't you tell me this before?"

Shakespeare shrugged. "I guess I didn't want you blabbing to Winona or Drags the Rope, although he might know. I think Black Kettle spotted Mad Dog, but he hasn't told anyone either. The Shoshones are brave, but the mere mention of Mad Dog's name would get them jumping at their own shadows."

"You're exaggerating."

"A little," Shakespeare conceded. "But the situation is bad enough without making it worse."

"So what can we do to stop this Mad Dog?"

"Pray."

Nate rode in silence for several minutes, pondering the information. One statement, in particular, galled him. "I'm not the blabbing type."

"I reckon I know that by now. My apologies then. I should have told you. But, if it's any excuse, you've got to admit I've been a mite busy and had a lot on my mind."

"You're forgiven," Nate said.

"Thanks," Shakespeare responded, and grinned. "Now I can sleep easier at night."

Nate looked over his left shoulder at Winona and Morning Dew, who were 15 feet behind him. The lovely woman he had agreed to marry mustered a wan smile. She was leading the horse pulling the travois on which her

father rested. Beside the platform walked his prospective
mother-in-law.

"I've been meaning to ask you something," Shakespeare mentioned.

"Ask."

The mountain man gestured at Nate's head. "What made
you decide to wear it?"

Nate reached up and touched the eagle feather he had
tied to the top of his head, at the back, using a short, thin
strip of buckskin. He'd arranged the feather so that the
flared end angled down and to the right, in the same
fashion as several Indians he had seen. "I don't rightly
know why I finally decided to put it on. Maybe because
I was bored standing around with nothing to do while you
were busy organizing our departure." He paused. "Or
maybe it's because I think I have some idea now of the
honor White Eagle bestowed on me."

Shakespeare nodded. "You're learning."

"Not fast enough to suit me."

"We have to take life at its own pace, Nate. Like the
Good Book says, to everything there's a season, and a
time to every purpose under the heaven."

"I don't believe it."

"What?"

"You quoted something besides Shakespeare."

The frontiersman made a show of slapping his forehead
in feigned amazement. "Did I? I must have received a
knock on the noggin and not realized it."

Nate chuckled and gazed up at the sun, which hung in
the blue sky two hours above the midday position. "Will
we stop before dark?"

"Not if I can help it. I don't care how tired the women
and children become, they've got to push themselves to
the limit. Once Mad Dog gets those horses he stole to
a safe spot, he'll be back. Following our trail will be easy.

I expect he'll overtake us in no time."

"What about those graves the Shoshones buried their dead in?"

"What about them?"

"They weren't very deep. Will Mad Dog dig up the bodies to take the scalps?"

Shakespeare looked at his friend. "Indians might be a tad bloodthirsty, but they're not morbid. They don't go around digging up corpses just to take the hair."

"Oh."

"Where do you come up with some of these wild notions of yours?"

Nate ignored the question and scanned the hill they were starting to ascend. Trees dotted the northern and southern slopes, but the crown and the central portion were relatively barren except for a circle of boulders at the very top.

"It must be all those books you read back in New York," Shakespeare went on in the same lighthearted vein. "Books can give a person powerful strange ideas."

"Like the works of William Shakespeare?"

"Old William S. wrote about life, not strange stuff like some of those Eastern writers."

"Life, huh? Correct me if I'm wrong, but wasn't Shakespeare the one who wrote about witches, ghosts, fairies, and such?"

"Well, yes, but—"

"I rest my case."

The mountain man's eyes narrowed. "You're getting a bit too upity for your own good."

"I suppose I've been hanging around you too long."

They wound up the hill toward the summit, picking their way carefully around sections of the hillside where large, flat rocks covered the ground.

"This is interesting," Shakespeare remarked.

Why would a bunch of loose rocks hold any attraction?
Nate wondered. He moved to one side and reined up,
waiting for Winona to draw abreast of his position and
thinking of the incredulous expression on her face earlier
when Drags the Rope had informed her about her father's
request. Black Kettle had passed out again by the time
mother and daughter returned with the travois, and Drags
the Rope had evidently gone into considerable detail in
reporting the conversation he'd translated. Nate held up
his left hand, recalling the warm pressure of her palm
against his during that special moment when she had
clasped his hands and turned to him the most wondrous
countenance imaginable, a fascinating combination of
affection and gratitude conveyed in an attitude of frank
bewilderment, as if she couldn't quite believe that he cared
for her and viewed his fondness as precious beyond words.

Shakespeare kept going. "We'll take a break at the top
of this hill," he announced.

"Fair enough," Nate replied.

Winona drew nearer, firmly holding the horse's bridle,
watching the animal's progress carefully to ensure her
father wasn't unduly jostled.

Morning Dew walked with her head bowed sadly, her
moist eyes fixed on her supine husband.

Would she cut off part of a finger if Black Kettle died?
Nate speculated. An unbidden, similar question rocked
his sensibilities. Would Winona hack off part of hers? The
prospect disturbed him greatly. Traditional ritual or not,
he didn't like the idea of Winona slicing a fingertip off,
and he resolved to prevent her somehow if the problem
arose.

Concentrating on the horse she led, the maiden had yet
to notice he'd stopped.

"Winona," Nate said softly.

She glanced up in surprise, then beamed a weary smile.

"Hello, Nate King."

Nate enjoyed hearing her speak his name. From her clipped, perfect English, no one could have guessed those were the only three words she knew. He leaned down to pat the horse she led, then straightened and used sign to inform her they would be stopping on the summit. They rode upward side by side. Nate asked her how her father was faring.

Frowning, Winona made signs to indicate Black Kettle was on the verge of dying. Her mother had cleaned the wound and applied herbal treatments, but the lance had passed quite close to the heart and the probability of a complete recovery was extremely slim.

Nate commiserated as best he could, and apologized profusely for his inability to adequately communicate his ideas.

Winona told him that he was doing fine. She said she looked forward to learning his language and teaching him hers.

Engrossed in their sign exchange, they came to the crown of the hill.

Nate glanced up to find Shakespeare dismounted and inspecting the terrain. Right away he perceived the reason for the frontiersman's interest. The circle of large boulders, which were actually aligned more in the shape of a horseshoe, formed a marvelous natural fortification ideally suited to their needs. The boulders, on average about four feet in height, were spaced close together, the typical gap being not more than 18 inches. The open end of the horseshoe faced to the northwest, and the slope there was steeper than elsewhere. The eastern opening, through which they entered, was four feet wide.

Shakespeare motioned for Nate to join him.

"Take care of your father. I will be back," Nate signed to Winona, and dismounted. He stepped over to the grizzled mountaineer, whose eyes were twinkling.

"What do you think?" Shakespeare inquired.

"About what?"

"The lay of the land here. What else?"

"We can defend it easily," Nate said.

"That we could," Shakespeare stated, nodding as he surveyed the perimeter of stony sentinels. "We could hold out here indefinitely, if need be."

"We'd need water," Nate observed.

"Didn't you see it?"

"What?"

Shakespeare smiled. "Follow me." He walked to the row of boulders on the north and pointed.

Only then did Nate behold the pool of water lying between a pair of squat boulders. Partly camouflaged by the shadow cast by the left-hand slab, the pool measured two feet across and enclosed a third of the bottom of the right-hand rock. Only someone endowed with exceptional eyesight could have spotted it. "A spring, you think?"

"Looks that way," Shakespeare said, and knelt to dip his right hand into the water. "It's cold enough to be a spring." He reached in as far as he could. "And it's too deep to be rain runoff."

Nate scrutinized the clear space enclosed by the boulders. "We'd still need food."

"Horse meat is right tasty in an emergency."

"I don't get it. Why all this talk of staying here? I thought you want to put as much distance behind us as we can."

"I did," Shakespeare said. Before he could elaborate, shouts broke out from those climbing the east slope.

Nate spun, the Hawken clutched in his left hand. "What is it?"

"Mad Dog."

Chapter Fifteen

Nate ran past the boulders and halted on the slope. He gazed to the southeast and saw them, dozens of riders coming on hard perhaps a mile and a half distant.

"They'll be here in less than ten minutes," Shakespeare commented.

"So much for taking a break."

Drags the Rope and the eight other uninjured warriors rode up. "We go fight," the former announced. "Hold Blackfeet back. You get away. Take wives, take children."

"Don't be hasty, my friend," Shakespeare said.

"We not fight?"

"There's no reason to get yourselves needlessly killed. We have time to execute a plan I have in mind," Shakespeare stated, and launched into an extended speech in Shoshone.

Nate wished he could understand the tongue. He watched the women and children move hastily onto the summit. Off to the southeast the cloud of dust raised by the horses of the Blackfeet drew slowly closer and closer.

At last Shakespeare concluded, then changed to English again. "You know what to do. Get busy."

"You foxy, Carcajou," Drags the Rope said, smiling
slyly, and spoke to two of the warriors. The pair
immediately turned their mounts and raced down the hill.

"Where are they going?" Nate inquired.

"They're ¯our bait," Shakespeare answered, and
chuckled.

Drags the Rope and the remaining warriors rode into
the trees on the south side of the hill.

"Are they bait too?" Nate asked.

"They're gathering branches for our breastwork."

"You have this all worked out, don't you?"

"In matters of life and death it doesn't pay to dawdle,"
Shakespeare remarked, and returned to their natural fort.
He began issuing instructions to the Shoshone women and
children, who galvanized into action, with as much alacrity
as if he had been one of their own.

What if he was? Nate wondered. He'd heard tell that
certain tribes adopted white men into their midst, and he
had never thought to ask if the Shoshones had adopted
Shakespeare. Glancing once more at the dust cloud and
the two warriors galloping toward it, he hefted his rifle
and went into the area enclosed by the boulders.

The women and older children were busily at work in
erecting a crude but creditable breastwork across the
opening to the northwest, using brush, manageable stone,
and logs. They left a three-foot gap in the center.

Shortly the warriors with Drags the Rope returned,
dragging stout limbs. These were passed to the women
and placed at appropriate points in the breastwork.

Other children herded the animals to the middle of the
cleared space, which encompassed 60 feet from one side
to the other, and went around tying the mouths of the dogs
shut so the canines couldn't bark.

Nate walked over to Winona and Morning Dew, who
were standing next to Black Kettle's travois located near

the spring. Both women looked at him expectantly.

"Are we making a stand?" Winona signed.

Nate responded in sign language, advising her they were indeed preparing to fight Mad Dog.

Mother and daughter exchanged startled glances, and it was Morning Dew who addressed him next, her hands and fingers flying almost too rapidly for him to follow.

Instantly Nate realized his mistake. He'd gone and done exactly what Shakespeare had been afraid he'd do. Morning Dew wanted to know how he knew Mad Dog led the Blackfeet. She demanded to be told why no one had informed her. Was the news a secret the men were keeping to themselves? He saw anger in her eyes, and he wanted to go over and beat his head against one of the boulders just so he could knock some sense into his skull.

"Don't tell me," a gruff voice stated sternly to his rear.

His face a study in embarrassment, Nate pivoted. "I'm afraid I'm the blabbing type after all."

Shakespeare shrugged. "Oh, well. Can't be helped. I reckon it's time they knew anyway." He spoke to the women in their own language for a minute.

"There's something I'd like to know," Nate stated when the frontiersman fell silent.

"What is it?"

"Why are the Shoshones following your instructions? Why aren't they listening to one of their own warriors?"

Shakespeare nodded at Black Kettle. "Because the best warrior in this band is out of commission, and Drags the Rope and the others know that I have experience along. these lines." He paused to regard the progress of the breastwork. "Let me fill you in on a secret, Nate. When it comes to one-on-one combat, Indians are able to hold thier own against anyone. But in general warfare they're not much for taking directions. They don't organize their attacks very well. A war chief might lead a raid, might lead the first assault, but after that it's every man for himself. They usually rely more on speed and force of numbers than strategy."

"Which still doesn't explain the reason they're listening to you."

"They trust me. I've lived among them off and on for years. They know I won't let them down," Shakespeare answered. "And too, they know there isn't time for them to squabble over the best tactics to use."

"Maybe they should make you their chief," Nate joked.

"I wouldn't accept the job."

"Why not?"

"Because I can't stand being tied down to any one place for very long. A chief has to stay with his people, to be there when they need him, to settle all the petty problems that crop up, to always be at their beck and call." Shakespeare shook his head. "That kind of life isn't for me, thank you very much."

Drags the Rope and the other warriors came over. They promptly dismounted and began checking their weapons: testing bow strings, verifying rifles were loaded, and loosening knives in their sheaths.

Shakespeare nudged Nate and pointed at the boulders rimming the east side of the hill. "Would you keep your eyes peeled for the two men we sent as decoys? I'm going to lend a hand with the breastwork."

"Sure," Nate said, and strolled over to the perimeter. He placed the Hawken on the flat top of a three-foot-high slab and leaned on the edge.

Approximately a mile off were the Blackfeet, still riding at a fast pace, sticking to the trail the Shoshones had made.

Nate began to speculate on whether he would ever reach the rendezvous. He would never desert Winona, and because of her his fate was inextricably bound to the whole band. A keen admiration for his hoary companion filled his heart. Shakespeare could leave any time he wanted, and yet the man had decided to stick with the Shoshones through thick and thin. The man had grit.

A golden eagle materialized to the south, flying from east to west.

Nate idely watched the big bird of prey and thought of the eagle feather in his hair, which belonged to a bald eagle, not the golden variety. How did the Indians obtain the feathers? He'd lost track of the number of warriors he'd seen who adorned their hair or shields or whatever with such feathers. They certainly couldn't collect so many feathers from birds that had died natural deaths. Did the Indians kill eagles? Or perhaps trap them? He decided he would ask Shakespeare when the right opportunity presented itself.

Mad Dog and his war party were continuing their steady advance.

It was funny, Nate mused. Here he was, intimately involved with a band of nomadic Plains Indians, prepared to give his all, if necessary, in their defense. Yet a year ago, even six months ago, he'd seldom given Indians more than a passing thought. When he had lived in New York City, in the throbbing hub of a mighty nation, surrounded by all the comforts and culture the metropolis had to offer, able to meet all of his needs by the flip of a coin or the exchange of a few bills, he'd never seriously pondered that fact that a thousand miles away dwelt hundreds of thousands of people who lived hand to mouth, who were dependent on the cycle of Nature for their existence, who went hungry when the game was scarce and thirsty during a drought, who knew no such constraints as those often meaningless rules and laws imposed on their so-called civilized counterparts, who roamed as free as the first man, Adam, must have been in the Garden of Eden.

There was that word again.

Freedom.

Many times he had asked himself why white men would

be willing to tolerate the hardships of the wilderness when life was so much easier back in the States. The answer became increasingly more apparent the longer he dwelled in the West.

Freedom.

For a man or woman to be able to live as they saw fit without harming others, to be able to put food on the table through their own efforts with a gun or a hoe, to be able to fabricate their own clothing and construct their own homes without having to rely on anyone else, to be totally self-sufficient, seemed to him to be the ideal way of living. The realization made him chuckle. He was thinking more and more like Shakespeare every day.

The Blackfeet were now three-quarters of a mile distant.

Nate gazed over his shoulder at the defensive preparations. Exercising remarkable zeal, the Shoshones had hastily erected the breastwork to a height of four feet. The women were ushering all of the children to the middle, where the men were already occupied in compelling each and every horse to lay down.

Now why were they doing that?

Shakespeare came toward him. "What's the status on those murdering savages?"

"They'll be here soon enough," Nate said.

"Good," Shakespeare declared, and grinned wickedly. "We'll have a little surprise for them."

"Aren't you taking a big risk?"

"Would you rather have Mad Dog overtake us somewhere else? Somewhere he'd have the advantage?"

"No," Nate admitted.

"Then this is where we'll make our stand," Shakespeare stated, halting next to a boulder on the left. "With any luck we'll give them such a licking they'll head for the hills and leave us alone."

"I hope you're right."

"Most Indians aren't fanatics about dying," Shakespeare mentioned. "When a battle goes against them, when there's no point to be made by needlessly wasting lives, they head for home."

"What about this Mad Dog? Is he a fanatic?"

"As loco as they come."

"How'd he ever get such a name, anyway?"

The frontiersman stared at the Blackfeet. "I heard tell he took it after a run-in with a rabid mutt."

"He took his own name?"

"It happens all the time. Indian babies are given their names right after birth. Sometimes they're named after animals, sometimes for something connected with nature that occurs the day they're born, like a thunderstorm, or else they get their name from a physical deformity they might have. Usually the women keep theirs throughout their lifetime, but the men often change the name they were given when they count their first coup, commit a brave act, have a vidid dream, or tangle with a wild beast."

"Like a mad dog?"

"Or a grizzly bear," Shakespeare said with a grin.

"And they even bestow such names on us," Nate commented thoughtfully, reflecting on the honor White Eagle had extended to him by giving him the name Grizzly Killer. The more he learned concerning Indian beliefs, the more he grew to value the singular distinction. He stared at the Shoshone warriors. "Why would a man take a name like Drags the Rope?"

Shakespeare chuckled. "Don't let the name fool you. He got it from one of the bravest acts I've ever seen."

"You were there?"

"Yep. About three winters ago," Shakespeare said, then corrected himself. "Sorry. Three years ago. It was during a buffalo surround."

"A what?"

"Indians have several ways of taking large number of buffalos. One of the tricks they use is for a lot of warriors to ride out on the plains, fan out around a herd, and drive all the animals into a circle. Then they take to killing the critters as fast as they can. It's damned dangerous work, though, because the buffalo, particularly the big bulls, will lash out with their horns and try to gore the horses and riders.''

Nate had hunted buffalo with his uncle, and he could envision the scene Shakespeare depicted. ''You'll never catch me hunting buffalo that way.''

''It's not for the faint of heart. The Indians have to get in close with their lances or bows to make the kill. Three years ago Drags the Rope was on a surround. One of his friends got knocked to the ground when a bull gutted the man's horse. That ornery bull would have gored the friend too, if not for Drags the Rope. He had a rope with him because he was planning to haul one of the cows he'd killed back to the camp for a feast. When he saw his friend go down, naturally he rode in to help. He'd thrown his lance into another buffalo and had no way to turn the bull except with the rope. So he started waving the rope in front of the bull, dragging it on the ground behind his horse and swinging it from side to side to get the bull's attention,'' Shakespeare detailed. ''And you know what? It worked. That fool bull took off after the rope. Trailed after Drags the Rope for hundreds of yards. Almost got his horse too. Finally another brave shot the thing. But if not for Drags the Rope's bravery, his friend surely would have died.''

''And that's how he acquired his name,'' Nate said.

Shakespeare nodded. ''Some Indian names might sound funny to you, but there's always a good reason for every name given.''

At that moment the warrior in question joined them, accompanied by the other Shoshone men. ''We ready fight,'' he announced boldly.

''Good,'' Shakespeare responded, facing eastward. ''Because here come your enemies.''

Chapter Sixteen

Mad Dog and the war party were only a quarter of a mile from the hill.

"Do you think they know we're here?" Nate asked.

"Not yet," Shakespeare said, and motioned for everyone to take cover behind the boulders.

Nate ducked down and peered at the valley below. The Blackfeet were coming up the center, following the tracks of the Shoshones. Bordering the valley on both sides was forest. "Where are your decoys?" he queried.

"Right there!" Shakespeare exclaimed, jabbing his right hand at a stretch of woods two hundred yards from the base of the hill.

Nate saw them. The pair of warriors broke from the trees and raced toward the hill, seemingly fleeing for their lives, their bodies hunched low over the backs of their mounts.

Instantly the Blackfeet voiced a collective whoop and took off in pursuit, waving their weapons in the air as they goaded their animals to top speed.

"Now we'll see how bright Mad Dog is," Shakespeare stated. "If he takes the bait, he'll pay."

Nate took hold of the Hawken in both hands and

nervously stroked the hammer. "Do we wait to fire until we can see the whites of their eyes?" he joked.

"Yep."

"You're kidding."

"Nope. I want those bastards so close that we can see the·sweat on their skin," Shakespeare said.

"But they outnumber us. How can we prevent them from overrunning our position if they're that close?"

"We shoot staight."

Nate didn't like the idea of permitting the Blackfeet to get very near to the fortification. He preferred to pick them off from long range. If the Blackfeet were ever able to breach the defenses and run amok within the circle of boulders, the poor Shoshones wouldn't stand a prayer.

Below the hill the race continued. With a six-hundred-foot lead on the Blackfeet, the two Shoshone warriors were easily holding their own. Mad Dog and his band screeched and vainly endeavored to narrow the range.

Nate glanced at the Shoshones crouched to his right and left. One held a rifle, five had bows, and one was armed with a lance. He remembered the information the mountain man had imparted about the accuracy of Indian archers, and he hoped it applied equally to the Shoshones.

A gunshot cracked in the valley.

Instinctively elevating the Hawken to his right shoulder, Nate looked down and deduced that one of the Blackfeet had foolishly fired and missed.

The pair of Shoshones were almost to the bottom of the hill.

"Remember, don't squeeze the trigger until I do," Shakespeare advised Nate, then repeated the order in the Shoshone language.

An air of tense expectancy gripped the defenders.

Although simmering with excitement inside, Nate casually glanced at the women and children huddled to his rear. Winona had her eyes on him and he smiled to express his reassurance that all would go well. Morning Dew was leaning over Black Kettle, apparently tending to his wound again. The children, horses, and dogs were all quiet, and he marveled at how disciplined the youngsters were, even the infants. Not one of them cried. Evidently the lessons the mothers imparted to instill obedience worked wonders.

The men acting as decoys were galloping up the slope.

"If you spot a Blackfoot wearing a dark beaver hat, that'll be Mad Dog," Shakespeare disclosed. "Don't hesitate to put a ball through him."

"I haven't seen many Indians wearing hats," Nate mentioned while watching the Blackfeet advance.

"A few are right partial to the hats white men wear," Shakespeare said conversationally, as if they didn't have a care in the world and weren't about to battle a band of bloodthirsty warriors. "I knew a Sioux once who took to wearing a top hat and a fancy coat. By the same token, there are white men who have gone over totally to the Indian way of living. They go around buck naked or wear only a breechcloth." He paused. "Never could see the sense in that. Had a spooked horse take me through a brier patch once. Just think what would have happened if I wasn't wearing clothes!"

Nate glanced at the frontiersman, amazed at his friend's easygoing attitude when they were literally staring death in the face. "I want you to know I've enjoyed our time together."

Shakespeare studied the younger man for a moment. "Don't be talking like that. We're not dead yet. And just between you and me, I have no intention of dying for another twenty or thirty years. When the Grim Reaper comes for Old Shakespeare McNair, he's going to have a tussle on his hands."

A pounding of hoofs heralded the arrival of the two decoys, who swept through the opening in the eastern line of boulders and abruptly reined up. They slid to the ground as two women came forward to take their perspiring animals. Doubling in half, the two men united with their fellows and crouched in the shelter of separate rocks.

Nate peeked over the top edge of the boulder and nervously licked his dry lips when he spied the Blackfeet starting up the hill. Quickly he conducted a count and pegged the tally at 31. Thirty one! Three times as many as the combined defending force!

"Hold your fire," Shakespeare directed, then repeated the command to the Shoshones.

Easy for him to say! Nate thought, nervously fingering the trigger. It took all of his self-control to refrain from leaping up and snapping off a hasty shot as the war party thundered ever closer to the crown. So intent were the Blackfeet on catching the decoys that they were uncharacteristically careless, goading their horses up the grade without pausing to survey the top.

Shakespeare chuckled. "I've always maintained that the Blackfeet sit on their brains," he quipped, and became serious. "Get ready."

"I'm as ready as I'll ever be," Nate muttered, and the act of speaking alleviated his tension somewhat.

The onrushing Blackfeet were now one hundred feet from the fortification, and the boulders, combined with the angle of the slope, prevented them from seeing the concealed Shoshones and animals.

"Where the dickens is Mad Dog?" Shakespeare asked, scanning the attackers intently.

Nate noticed a lot of bows and fusees in evidence.

Still whooping and hollering madly, the band raced higher. Only 80 feet remained to be covered.

Nate cocked the Hawken and heard a click as

Shakespeare did likewise.

The distance narrowed to 70 feet.

"Say, Nate," Shakespeare said.

"Yeah?" Nate responded without taking his eyes off the charging Blackfeet.

"It's too bad your Uncle Zeke went under. He'd be right proud of you if he could see how you've taken to life out here. He told me once that you were the only one of his relatives who was worth a damn."

Surprise almost caused Nate to glance at the mountain man, but he steeled his will and concentrated on their enemies. Why did Shakespeare mention such a fact at a time like this? he asked himself. And then there was no time left for idle reflection.

Forty feet of ground separated the two forces.

Thirty feet.

A mere 25.

"Give them hell!" Shakespeare bellowed, and rose from hiding with his rifle pressed to his right shoulder.

Nate stood and snapped the Hawken up. For a moment he had the impression a horde of Indians filled the slope. Astonishment rippled from visage to visage. He sighted on a warrior directly in front of him and squeezed the trigger. The blasting of the rifle and the Blackfoot toppling from his horse were nearly simultaneous.

Shakespeare's rifle boomed and another warrior went down.

The Shoshones were firing arrows as swiftly as they could notch their shafts and pull back their bow strings.

Taken completely unawares by the ambush, the Blackfeet lost eight of their men in the opening seconds of the conflict to well-placed balls or arrows. Two others were gravely wounded. Panic seized the majority, and they brought their animals to a sudden halt and attempted to turn their mounts and flee. Packed close together, their frantic efforts resulted in general confusion. Horses collided, men shouted and cursed, and dust swirled into the air.

Not all of the Blackfeet tried to retreat.

A pair of Warriors came straight for the boulders, each firing a bow.

Nate recoiled in alarm as a shaft buzzed past his head. He set down the Hawken and drew both pistols, but before he could fire someone else disposed of the duo.

Drags the Rope stepped into the wide opening, blocking the path of the pair, an arrow already fitted to his bow string. He aimed at one of the Blackfeet, who was drawing back a shaft, and let fly. His slim missile leaped to meet his foe, and the point ripped into the Blackfoot's throat.

Flinging his arms outward, the enemy fell.

Drags the Rope stayed rooted to the spot, his right hand flying as he swept a shaft from his quiver and placed the notch to the string.

The second Blackfoot loosed an arrow.

Unperturbed and unflinching, Drags the Rope was sighting along his shaft when the Blackfoot's arrow creased his left shoulder blade, gouging a shallow furrow in his skin but not imbedding itself in his flesh. His features shifted and hardened and he fired.

In the act of whipping another arrow from his quiver, the Blackfoot flew backwards when the tip penetrated his left eye and bored out the top of his cranium.

Nate glimpsed the exchange as he leveled both pistols at an adversary endeavoring to gain control of a recalcitrant animal. He squeezed off a shot from his right flintlock.

The ball hit the Blackfoot high on the left shoulder, passed through the fleshy part of his arm, and tore into his chest, drilling through his lungs before it came to a stop when it lodged against a lower rib bone. Twisting and clutching at his side, the warrior pitched forward.

One of the Shoshones darted from cover, a lance held in his right hand. He ran straight toward a Blackfoot and pumped his arm back for the toss.

Reacting instantaneously, the Blackfoot fired a fusee.

Nate saw the Shoshone's head snap around as the ball took him squarely in the forehead. He extended his left flintlock and sent a return shot into the Blackfoot's torso.

Having finally succeeded in disentangling themselves, the Blackfeet were beating a hurried retreat down the east slope. They cut to the right at the bottom and made for the nearest trees. A few shook their fists at the crest and uttered inaudible oaths.

The Shoshone warriors stepped into the open and voiced yips of delight at their victory, shaking their weapons overhead in triumph.

"Damn! We did it!" Shakespeare declared.

Nodding grimly, Nate surveyed the carnage. He counted 15 Blackfeet littering the ground, which meant there were 16 still alive. An improvement over the previous odds, but the defenders were still outnumberd. He glanced at the Shoshone who had been shot through the head, then glanced to his left and spotted another one lying flat on the earth with an arrow jutting skyward, its point apparently sunk in the warrior's heart. So there were nine left, including Shakespeare and himself.

"You don't look very happy," the mountain man observed.

"We're still outnumbered."

"True, but we gave those bastards a taste of their own medicine. They may change their minds about taking our scalps and head for home."

Nate looked at him. "Do you really believe that?"

A wry smile creased the frontiersman's lips. "No, but a man can always hope, can't he?"

"I didn't see Mad Dog," Nate commented as he began

reloading his guns.

"I spied the son of a bitch in the pack, but I couldn't get a bead on him," Shakespeare lamented.

"Do you think he got away?"

"Let's go check," Shakespeare proposed. "But first . . ." He clasped his powder-horn and proceeded to reload his rifle.

At least half of the downed Blackfeet were groaning in pain. Several were attempting to stand or crawl off. One stocky warrior, an arrow transfixing his neck from side to side, had risen to his knees and was bent over, coughing up blood.

"Let's finish those buggers off," Shakespeare suggested.

Four Shoshones had the same idea. They moved among the fallen, plunging their knives repeatedly into prone bodies until satisfied their foes were definitely dead.

Nate wedged his pistols under his belt and picked up his rifle. He gazed to the south at the forest but saw no sign of the Blackfeet. A commotion erupted on the slope and he spun.

A Shoshone had leaned down to plunge his knife into a Blackfoot, who had been lying face down, and when he gripped the Blackfoot's shoulder the man suddenly flipped over and buried a knife of his own in the Shoshone's groin. In a twinkling the Blackfoot stabbed the Shoshone twice more.

Shakespeare's rifle spoke.

The Blackfoot grunted as the ball punctured the base of his throat and he collapsed again, blood spurting from the cavity. He breathed in great, ragged gasps.

A trio of Shoshones pounced on the culprit and dispatched him with a series of blows, rendering his chest a pincushion for their blades. The Blackfoot's legs convulsed for a bit, then he was still.

Shakespeare ran to the Shoshone who had been stabbed and knelt down to examine him.

Warily watching the trees, Nate followed.

"He's done for," the frontiersman stated in disgust.

That leaves eight, Nate thought, and glanced at the Blackfoot transfixed by the arrow just as the warrior surged erect and bounded forward, a war club held in his upraised right hand.

Chapter Seventeen

Nate would have snapped off a shot while holding the Hawken at waist level, and he probably would have scored a hit at such close range, but Shakespeare suddenly stood, blocking his view of the Blackfoot and preventing him from firing.

The mountain man was straightening to his full height, his rifle coming up, when the unforeseen transpired. His left moccasin slipped on a slick spot of blood and his left foot buckled, sending him stumbling rearward.

Nate tried to sidestep, but Shakespeare slammed into him and knocked him to the right.

Before either man could recover his balance, the Blackfoot reached them and swung. Descending in a short, vicious arc, the war club connected, sriking the frontiersman on the left side of his chest as he tried to maintain his footing.

Shakespeare went down.

And at last Nate had a clear field of fire. He stopped stumbling, pointed the barrel at the Blackfoot, and got off a hurried shot that nailed the warrior full in the mouth and burst out the back of the Indian's cranium. The impact lifted the Blackfoot from his feet and propelled him a yard to crash onto a corpse. Nate whirled toward the mountain man. "Shakespeare!" he cried.

The grizzled frontiersman lay on his right side, blood seeping from the ragged tear in his buckskin shirt where the sharp stone head of the war club had connected. His rifle was beside him. Wincing, he looked up and shook his head. "Pitiful. I must be slowing down. Ten years ago he never would have touched me."

"Don't talk," Nate instructed him, kneeling. "Let me have a look at it."

"Just a scratch," Shakespeare mumbled.

"I'll be the judge of how severe it is," Nate admonished.

Drags the Rope and four of the warriors clustered around the mountain man. "Carcajou die?" asked the tall Shoshone.

"No, I'm not dying, you busybody," Shakespeare snapped. "It's just a damn scratch, is all."

"I told you not to talk," Nate said, and glanced at Drags the Rope. "Check the rest of the Blackfeet. Finish them off. But be careful! We can't afford to lose another man."

"We careful," Drags the Rope promised. He turned to go.

"Have someone keep an eye on those trees," Nate added. "The Blackfeet might try to spring a surprise attack on us."

"Watch with eyes of hawk," Drags the Rope said, and walked away while motioning for the other warriors to gather around him.

"That man has a way with words," Shakespeare remarked, then coughed violently.

"What does it take to shut you up?" Nate demanded. He went to loosen the shirt.

Shakespeare swatted his friend's hand aside. "I can

undress myself, thank you very much. And I don't understand why you're making such a fuss over such a tiny
bruise." He grimaced and sat up.

"Undo your shirt," Nate directed.

"Who appointed you chief?"

"If you don't, I will."

"You're becoming too nasty for your own good,"
Shakespeare groused, but he pulled the bottom hem of
the shirt from under his belt and lifted. "Do you know
anything about doctoring?"

Nate bent closer to inspect the wound. "Once, when
I was in my teens, I found a hurt sparrow and tried to
nurse the bird back to health."

"Tried?"

"It died."

Shakespeare regarded his grinning companion for a
moment, and laughed heartily. "You're learning, son.
You're learning."

"Keep quiet," Nate stated. The pointed tip had ripped
the material and penetrated over an inch into the soft tissue
underneath. No doubt the weakened state of the Blackfoot
had rendered the blow largely ineffectual. Had the warrior
been in prime form, the outcome would have been
drastically different. While blood continued to seep out
and the surrounding flesh was becoming discolored, the
wound did not appear to be life-threatening. "You'll live,"
he mentioned.

"I could have told you that."

"I'll have one of the women dress it for you."

In the act of lowering his shirt, Shakespeare paused and
snorted. "Like hell you will."

"Either one of them does it or I do," Nate informed
him.

Shakespeare opened his mouth, as if about to argue,
then evidently changed his mind and shook his head. "No.

I won't waste my breath. The more I get to know you, the more I find out you're like your Uncle Zeke."

"I'll take that as a compliment."

"Yep. Zeke was a hard-headed mule too." Shakespeare laughed, grabbed his rifle, and slowly stood. "Give me five minutes and I'll be back in action."

"Take it easy while we have a breather. As you pointed out, the Blackfeet are bound to be back sooner or later."

"Likely later."

"When?"

"My best guess would be right before sunset. If not then, you can expect Mad Dog to hit us at daybreak."

"Why daybreak?"

"Habit mostly. Indians are partial to surprise attacks at dawn, mainly because villages rarely post guards. Oh, they'll attack at any time if they think they have the edge, but dawn raids are their favorite."

Nate stared at the forest below, studying the wall of green vegetation that effectively screened their enemies. Were the Blackfeet watching the Shoshones at that very moment and planning their next attack? Most likely.

The layout of the hill favored the defenders. The barren central portion wouldn't hide the approach of a flea, let alone 16 warriors. Only to the south and the north, where the trees flanked the hill, could the Blackfeet draw near to the top without being spotted. Of the two, the south slope presented the greatest threat. The trees came to within 40 feet of the ring of boulders, well within rifle and bow range.

A gurgling whine came from behind Nate, and he turned to find the Shoshones dispatching the injured Blackfeet and taking scalps with unrestrained glee.

Drags the Rope was slicing the hair from a foe whose throat he'd just slit, grinning all the while.

Nate glanced at his companion. "Let's get your wound

tended." He walked toward the opening.

"Yep. A natural born leader," Shakespeare said, moving with less than his usual liveliness.

"Oh, please."

"I'm serious. You may turn out to be one of the great ones."

"That blow must have scrambled your brains."

"Scoff if you want, but old William S. put it best," Shakespeare responded. "Why, some are born great, some achieve greatness, and some have greatness thrown upon them. You could wind up in one of those categories."

"I'll settle for just staying alive," Nate said, reentering the fortification. The women and children were still huddled in the center. One of the warriors stood next to a boulder on the southern perimeter, staring at the shadowy, ominous woods.

Winona saw him and beamed happily.

Nate moved over to her. He made the appropriate signs to request that she minister to Shakespeare, and she gladly agreed.

Morning Dew volunteered to help.

"You sure got these womenfolk trained," the frontiersman remarked sarcastically. "And you aren't even part of the family yet."

Nate ignored the barb and gazed overhead at the sun, noting there were at least five hours of daylight remaining, maybe six. Hopefully in that time they could devise a strategy for escaping or defeating the Blackfeet. He glanced down at Black Kettle, and was surprised to discover the warrior's eyes were open and fixed on him. Feeling strangely uncomfortable under such intense scrutiny, he smiled and nodded.

Morning Dew had produced a leather pouch, and she was carefully applying an herbal powder to the mountain man's wound.

Black Kettle addressed Nate, his voice weak, speaking with clear effort.

"Oh, my," Shakespeare said when the warrior concluded.

"What did he say?" Nate inquired, and became aware of both Winona and Morning Dew contemplating him expectantly.

The mountain man chuckled. "He watched you fight the Blackfeet, and he says you truly are a natural-born warrior."

"Thank him for me."

"There's more."

"Oh?"

"Yep. He wants you to marry his daughter," Shakespeare said, and the tone he used indicated he might burst into laughter at any moment.

"I already know that," Nate reminded him.

"Right now," Shakespeare added, and made a choking noise as he suppressed his mirth.

Nate's mouth slackened in shock. He glanced from the frontiersman to the warrior. "Now?"

"Right this minute."

"Out of the question," Nate blurted.

"Give me one good reason."

"I'll give you plenty of reasons. For starters, we're pinned down by a bunch of hostile Blackfeet. They could attack at any minute. This is hardly the ideal time for a wedding."

"You know what they say. There's no time like the present," Shakespeare said good-naturedly.

Becoming angry, Nate glared at the mountain man. "Be serious, for crying out loud."

"I am," Shakespeare stated, and pointed at Black Kettle. "Look at him. Take a good look at him."

Puzzled, Nate grudgingly complied. "So?"

"So what do you see?"

Nate noticed the warrior's ashen complexion and labored breathing and saw blood trickling from the hole made by the lance. He frowned when he answered. "I see a man who is dying."

"Exactly. He knows he doesn't have much time left. Which is why he asked me to ask you to marry his daughter now. He wants to see the two of you hitched before he passes on," Shakespeare said with distinct reverence. "Can you blame him?"

"No," Nate replied softly. He swore he could almost feel Black Kettle's eyes boring into him, as if the warrior was striving to read his mind or plumb the depths of his very soul.

Winona spoke a sentence in Shoshone.

"She says she's ready if you are," Shakespeare translated, grinning. "You certainly can't fault her for being the bashful type."

"I don't know," Nate said hesitantly. He'd already told Black Kettle he would tie the knot, but now that the reality was staring him in the face, as it were, dozens of doubts flooded his mind and caused him to balk. They hardly knew each other. What if they turned out not to be compatible? What if their attraction was only physical? And what if, sometime down the road, he decided he'd made a mistake and elected to return to New York City and Adeline? How could he lead Winona on? Some men might, but it wasn't in his nature. He despised deceit.

Just then Winona went on at some length.

Shakespeare coughed lightly after she concluded and turned a peculiar expression toward his friend. "Well, Nathaniel, she said a mouthful. If you've changed your mind, she says she understands. She knows how hard marriages can be between Indians and whites, and she knows that many whites look down their noses at her people. She wouldn't want to be a burden to you. So there's no hard feelings on her part if you want to call it off, no matter what you may have promised her father."

Nate looked at Winona and was flabbergasted to observe fear in her lovely eyes, fear inspired by his possible refusal, fear that her heart would be crushed by the man to whom she had so openly and unconditionally given herself. Fear of him. The very last emotion he would ever want her to feel because of him. Before he even quite knew what he was doing, he had taken a step and tenderly caressed her cheek. "Tell her I'm a man of my word. I'll be her husband if she wants me."

Speaking in an unusually gravelly tone, Shakespeare relayed the message.

Conspicuous relief mellowed Winona's features and she clasped Nate's hand in her own.

"But I still don't see how we can get married here," Nate commented absently. "Don't we need a preacher to make it nice and legal?"

Shakespeare snorted. "There is no law west of the Mississippi. None that counts anyway. And as far as the ceremony goes, what were you expecting? A formal gown and organ music?"

"No," Nate said sheepishly.

"You'll get hitched Indian fashion, and even then you won't have the full affair," Shakespeare stated. He began tucking his shirt under his belt. "You stay put. I'll tend to the preparations." He hurried off, chuckling and muttering under his breath.

Nate stood next to Winona, at a loss for words, slightly dazed by the precipitous turn of events. He must be dreaming. Was he really about to tie the knot? To an Indian woman, no less? Was he in his right mind or had the sequence of harrowing experiences since he'd left St. Louis rattled his noggin?

The word spread quickly among the Shoshones. Drags
the Rope and the other warriors, having finished taking
scalps, took up guard positions around the rim. The
women and children gathered near Black Kettle's travois
to witness the event, many whispering and giggling. And
every one of them stared openly at the groom.

Nate felt as if he were under a microscope.

Shakespeare, adopting a solemn air belied by the way
the corners of his mouth continually curled upward, stood
to the right of the travois and had the couple stand in front
of Black Kettle. "Are you ready?" he asked Nate.

"Why do I feel like heading for the hills?"

"You're already *on* a hill, and you evaded the question.
Are you ready?"

"Is a man ever ready for marriage?"

"Now's not the time to wax philosophical. Are you
ready or not, damn it?"

Nate inhaled deeply and nodded. "Ready."

"Good." Shakespeare addressed Black Kettle, who had
managed to prop himself on his elbows. The warrior then
relayed a series of queries through the frontiersman. "Do
you want to take Winona as your wife?"

"You know I do."

"Do you promise to protect her, to treat her kindly,
to stay with her in good times and bad?"

"Yes," Nate said.

"Do you primise to carry on the line by having as many
sons as you can?"

"I'll do my best," Nate pledged.

"What do you offer to buy her with?"

Nate blinked and straightened in consternation. "Buy
her? No one said anything about buying her."

"Remember what I told you about how Indian men
purchase their brides? Normally, Black Kettle would
receive about six horses for a pretty thing like Winona.

But this is a special case. Still, you have to offer something. What will it be?''

''I don't have six horses,'' Nate said. ''All I have is my pack horse.''

''Done,'' Shakespeare stated, and conveyed the news to Black Kettle.

''Wait a minute!'' Nate exclaimed. ''I didn't mean—''

''Too late,'' Shakespeare interrupted. ''He accepts. Congratulations. You're now husband and wife.''

Stunned, Nate looked at his bride, who was standing coyly with her head bowed. ''What? Just like that? You're joking.''

''Nope,'' Shakespeare said, and grasped his friend's right hand in a firm shake. ''Let me be the first one to offer my condolences.''

''Condolences?''

''I've been married before, if you'll recollect.''

Peeved, Nate tore his hand free and gestured to Winona. ''And what about her? Doesn't she take part in the vows?''

''What vows? You gave Black Kettle your horse. She's yours. It's as simple as that.''

''But—''

''It's too late to change your mind,'' Shakespeare commented, his eyes twinkling. ''You're hitched.''

''But—''

''And I'm sorry to say that you don't even get to kiss the bride. The Shoshones don't go in for public displays of affection. So save your puckering for when you're alone.''

''There has to be more to it than this!'' Nate exploded.

''Well, if you want to be a stickler for formality, there's usually a big feast to celebrate. But under the circumstances, I reckon it's best if we hold off on the festivities. Don't you agree?''

Nate nodded blankly. His thoughts were whirling at a

cyclonic rate, yet his body was functioning in slow motion. He gazed at his bride in a dreamlike state, viewing her as an unreal vision of beauty and charm.

The next instant a strident scream brought him back to reality with a vengeance.

One of the Shoshone women staggered forward and stumbled, sinking to her knees, her torso pierced by an arrow, the bloody point jutting from between her breasts.

Chapter Eighteen

For a minute panic prevailed.

Everyone scrambled for cover, dashing for the shelter of the boulders. The woman who had been shot was supported by three others and half-carried to the slabs alongside the spring. At Morning Dew's urging, Shakespeare and Nate lifted Black Kettle from the platform and placed him at the base of the boulders. One of the warriors stationed along the southern perimeter began shouting excitedly, and all of the Shoshone men converged on him.

"Let's go," Shakespeare said, and hurried toward them.

Nate glanced at Winona, regretting they had married under such hazardous circumstances and wishing he could take her in his arms to express his affection. Instead, he gave her arm a tender squeeze and raced after the frontiersman.

Drags the Rope was peering at the forest below. He looked around and scowled. "Red Knife see Blackfeet there," he stated, and pointed at a point in the trees 50 feet from the rim.

"The bastards are going to pick us off," Shakespeare declared angrily. "They'll try and soften us up for their attack.''

As if in confirmation, a warrior yelled and jabbed his finger skyward.

Nate looked up in time to see the sunlight glinting off an arrow as the shaft arced high in the air and streaked down at the enclosed area on the summit.

Drags the Rope cried out a warning.

All eyes swung upward. The arrow descended in the center, missing the Shoshones huddled beside the rocks by a wide margin, but the tip still found a target. Purely by chance the arrow struck one of the horses, smacking into the animal's neck and burying itself to the feathers. The horse, neighing in torment and terror, scrambled erect and bolted for the eastern opening.

Several of the warriors endeavored to head the animal off, without success.

Snorting and whinnying, the horse galloped between the boulders and fled down the east slope.

''Damn their stinking bones!'' Shakespeare fumed, and brazenly stood to his full height so he could shake his left fist at the trees and curse the Blackfeet mightily.

''Get down!'' Nate snapped, grabbing the older man's leflt arm and hauling him safely behind the slab. ''What are you trying to do? Get yourself killed?''

A fit of coughing struck the frontiersman and he doubled over, his arms pressed against his left side. In a minute the paroxysm subsided and he leaned on the boulder. ''Whew! I'm not as spry as I used to be.''

''Not fifteen minutes ago you were bashed by a war club.''

''What's that got to do with anything? If you stay out here long enough, you learn to shrug those things off.''

''You're impossible,'' Nate mumbled, and scanned their immediate surroundings. The animals herded together in the middle were in grave peril, as were the Shoshones crouched behind boulders on the west, north, and east sides of the clearing, which included Winona and her family. "We have to get everyone on the south side," he stated urgently.

Drags the Rope nodded in agreement and started yelling for his people to move to safety.

"I'll be right back," Nate said. He propped the Hawken against a rock slab and sprinted toward his new in-laws. Halfway across the open track he heard Shakespeare voice a shout of alarm.

"Another arrow! Look out!"

Nate twisted and saw the incoming shaft, its metal point gleaming, on its downward sweep. He automatically calculated the trajectory, and in a flash perceived that one of the horses would be hit. He darted to his left, intending to pull the animal onto its feet and remove it from harm's way, but compared to a streaking arrow his speed was equivalent to that of a tortoise.

The Blackfoot shaft smacked into the brown stallion high on the animal's forehead, thrusting through skin, flesh, and even bone, drilling through to the cranial cavity and skewering the hapless horse's brain. It stiffened, opened its mouth, then convulsed silently for half a minute. Finally, its eyes rolling in their sockets, the stallion simply keeled over, blood and froth bubbling over its lips.

Nate didn't waste any more time on the animal. More arrows would be forthcoming. He sprinted to the north where Winona and Morning Dew were already turning the horse hauling the travois. Black Kettle had reclined on his back once again, exhausted by the energy he had expended during the wedding ceremony. "Let me," Nate said, and signed his desire to lead the horse. He grabbed the reins and headed to the south.

Winona and Morning Dew stepped to the travois, each on a different side, prepared to aid Black Kettle if needed.

The rest of the band was flocking to the boulders on the southern perimeter.

But what about the horses? Nate wondered as he hastened along. There was nowhere to shelter the mounts and the dogs from the rain of deadly missiles. So far the Blackfeet had fired a few shafts; soon they would unleash a dozen bolts at a time. The horses and dogs would be easy pickings. Mulling the predicament, he led the travois animal to within 15 feet of relative safety when Shakespeare yelled again.

"More arrows! Lots of them!"

Nate looked up, his breath catching in his throat at the sight of nine or ten shafts cleaving the air above the summit. Several were directly overhead. Spinning, he dashed to Black Kettle and hooked his left arm under the warrior's shoulder.

Winona and Morning Dew stepped in to help.

Resembling the spattering of heavy hail, the arrows thudded home. Many impaled victims. One found Morning Dew.

Nate would never forget the image of the shaft striking his mother-in-law on the left shoulder and protruding out her dress in the vicinity of her navel. He was staring into her eyes when she took the arrow, and he saw a flicker of exquisite anguish promptly replaced by something else—sorrow, he thought—and she collapsed.

Winona screamed and moved to her mother's side.

"There's nothing we can do for her," Nate said, but his words were meaningless to his wife and he couldn't execute sign language while holding Black Kettle in his arms. The warrior stared at his mate in silent horror.

Pandemonium reigned on the hill. Six Shoshones were down, dead or dying, and two women were screeching in the throes of agony. Injured horses were up and running wildly in circles, spooking other animals. And in the midst of the bedlam other Shoshones were trying to reach the south side before another volley descended.

"We've got to get out of the open," Nate told Winona. She leaned over her mother, oblivious to the world. He took a step and was about to snatch at her hair when a friendly voice sounded to his right.

"Let me take Black Kettle, Nate. You bring the missus."

Nate glanced at his friend. "Are you sure you're up to it?"

"Do you want to argue or become a porcupine?" Shakespeare countered, and grasped the warrior under the arms.

Inexpressibly grateful, Nate crouched next to Winona and placed his hands on her shoulders. "Come on," he urged. "Please."

She sobbed, tears flowing down her full cheeks.

"Hurry," Nate said, and tried to lift her. He glanced upward and felt a tingle run along his spine as he beheld yet another shower of shafts flying from the forest. His mind shrieked for him to move, and move he did, forcibly yanking Winona upright and propelling her toward the sheltering boulders. She meekly submitted to the leading. In five leaping strides he got them within reach of the perimeter, and he threw himself forward the last few yards, carrying her with him.

The volley thudded down. Four more Shoshones were hit, and three horses. One of the dogs was lanced clear through and fell without so much as a whimper.

Nate rose to his knees, pulling Winona with him.

Black Kettle rested with his back to the nearest boulder, his eyes still locked on Morning Dew, the smallest spark of vitality flickering in his sorrowful eyes.

"Those dirty vermin!" Shakespeare barked, surveying the slaughter.

Almost all of the Shoshones still alive had reached the haven of the southern rim. A few slow ones, the injured, were being assisted by others. Two horses took off down the east slope.

Drags the Rope and several warriors were firing arrows wildly at the forest.

"Save your shafts," Nate advised. "You'll need them."

The young warrior turned a visage full of rage and hatred toward the two white men. "Mad Dog's heart mine!" he growled.

"You may have to wait your turn," Nate said, gazing at Morning Dew.

"We need a plan," Shakespeare said, stating the obvious, and peeked over the boulder in front of him. "Damn! More arrows!"

Nate saw them too. Only four shafts this time, and miraculously each missed. He braced for others, but five minutes elapsed uneventfully.

"We can't make a run for it," Shakespeare remarked. "There aren't enough horses for everyone, and we'd be picked off before we covered a hundred yards."

"Charge trees then," Drags the Rope proposed.

"And commit suicide? No, thanks," Shakespeare replied. "We'd be lucky if any of us made it to the woods. And then what do you think would happen to the women and children? They'd be at the mercy of Mad Dog, and we both know what that son of a bitch would do to them."

Drags the Rope grunted.

The frontiersman swiveled toward Nate. "What about you? Have any brilliant ideas?"

"No."

"We've got to—" Shakespeare began, and looked skyward. "More arrows!" he announced.

Four slim missiles streaked out of the blue and plunged into the earth in the middle of the enclosed space. The remaining horses and dogs were milling near the spring, and they escaped being struck.

The mountain man cackled. "That's four more those buzzards have wasted."

Nate's forehead creased in contemplation. Once again the Blackfeet had fired only four shafts. Why? Were they conserving their arrows for their main assault?

"I propose we stick it out here until dark, then slip away," Shakespeare stated. "They can't hit us behind these boulders, so we're safe for the time being."

"I suppose," Nate said, bothered by a vague sensation of unease, his intuition telling him that there was an aspect to the battle he was overlooking. Something was not right, but he couldn't put his finger on it.

"Yes, sir," Shakespeare went on enthusiastically. "Even if the Blackfeet do post sentries around this hill, we can fight our way out and cover the women and youngsters."

"Women, children fight," Drags the Rope declared.

"I know they can," Shakespeare acknowledged. "Shoshone women are known for their courage."

Nate glanced at his wife, who had rested her head on her father's left shoulder and now weeped soundlessly. He wanted to embrace her, to soothe her, and he started to lift his right arm when Shakespeare uttered a remark that inexplicably troubled him immensely.

"If those mangy Blackfeet try to sneak up on us, we'll hear them. There's a lot of loose rock to give them away. We'll have to watch out for the same stuff when we cut out."

The frontiersman had a point. Nate recalled seeing the loose rock on the east and west side of the hill. But he hadn't noticed any to the south, where the Blackfeet were currently congregated, or to the north.

The north!

A cold wind seemed to tingle Nate's skin as he looked at the boulders on the north side of the summit. The arrows had driven all of the Shoshones away from those boulders, which overlooked the trees that came within 60 feet of the rim, leaving the north slope undefended, providing an undisputed approach route for the enemy.

What if forcing the defenders away from the north side had been a deliberate stratagem?

What if the Blackfeet were cleverer than anyone gave them credit for being?

What if Mad Dog had no intention of waiting until tomorrow morning to launch the attack? What if he wasn't even going to wait until sunset?

Why had the number of arrows drastically fallen off? And why had there been that five-minute span when no shafts were fired? What had the Blackfeet been doing during those five minutes?

"Shakespeare," Nate said softly, scanning the northern perimeter, filled with an equal measure of dread and doubt, wondering if perhaps he might be wrong, might be worried over nothing. He noticed his friend conversing with Drags the Rope, and realized the mountain man hadn't heard him. Instinctively he reached for his Hawken, and as he did he recalled the sage advice Shakespeare had dispensed after the incident with the Utes. "You should always trust your own instincts, no matter what someone else with more experience might tell you. Go with the gut, as I like to say." Well, his gut was telling him that they were in imminent danger, terrible danger, so he spoke louder and urgently. "Shakespeare!"

The frontiersman looked at him anxiously, alerted by his tone. "What is it?"

"The north rim—" Nate started to say, and then he saw them, saw the Blackfeet sweeping over and around the boulders to the north at the same moment they vented ear-splitting war whoops. He whipped up his rifle, snapped off a shot, and was gratified to see a Blackfoot drop.

A fraction of a second later Shakespeare's rifle cracked and a second attacker pitched onto his face.

The two shots, booming almost at the very instant they appeared, gave the Blackfeet brief pause as they ducked for cover or crouched to avoid being the next target. They had expected to take the defenders totally unawares, and they were collectively surprised that resistance should be so swift and lethal.

The two shots had another effect. By causing the Blackfeet to briefly check their rush, even for the short span of a few seconds, the Shoshones were given time to react to the startling discovery they were outflanked. The warriors gave tongue to soul-stirring challenges of their own, and charged.

Nate frantically reloaded his rifle and glimpsed Shakespeare doing the same.

Winona moved in front of her father, fury contorting her features, her fists clenched, prepared to defend his life with her own.

A fierce desperation pervaded the Shoshone warriors. Drags the Rope and the others were outnumbered, but they were fighting for the lives of their loved ones, for the very survival of their band, and such knowledge lent an inhuman savagery to their struggle. They unleashed a volley of their own, slaying six of their adversaries, and then closed in personal mortal combat.

Nate was raising the Hawken again when he realized very few of the Blackfeet carried rifles or bows. Most were armed with war clubs, tomahawks, and knifes, weapons best employed in close-in battle. Why hadn't they brought their fusees and bows and easily finished off the Shoshones? Nate asked himself. He percieved the answer as he took aim on a burly Blackfoot who had just stabbed a Shoshone warrior. Coup. The Blackfeet wanted to count the highest possible coup, and to do so they must engage the Shoshones man to man. Well, they could count all the coup they wanted. His main concern was staying alive. He squeezed the trigger, his ball catching the Blackfoot in the forehead and catapulting the man to the ground.

Now the center of the open track was a swirling melee of yelling and screaming Indians. Knives flashed. Clubs swung right and left. Tomahawks cleaved the air.

Nate saw Drags the Rope using a knife to hold off three foes. He leaned the rifle against the boulder, drew one of his pistols and gave it to Winona, then raced toward the conflict, drawing his other pistol. The confusing whirl of forms prevented him from determining which side was winning, although the Shoshones appeared to be holding their own. He came within ten feet of Drags the Rope, halted, and sighted on a Blackfoot swinging a club. His shot struck the warrior in the left cheek, spinning the man around and dropping him in his tracks.

A tall, screeching Blackfoot wearing buckskins and a dark hat ran directly at Nate, a tomahawk in his right hand.

There wasn't time to reload the pistol. Nate grasped his own tomahawk and tensed to meet the rush. He blocked a powerful swipe that would have split his skull wide open, then slashed at the warrior's midsection.

The Blackfoot skillfully danced aside and swung again.

Nate parried that blow, then another and another, put on the defensive by the warrior's adroit, unflagging onslaught. He retreated, the empty pistol still clutched in his left hand. A reverse thrust almost caught him in the neck, and he darted to the right.

The Blackfoot glanced down, then did a strange thing. He smiled. And lunged, his hat falling off in the process.

Stepping backwards, perplexed by the enigmatic glance, Nate apprehended its significance a heartbeat later when the heel of his right foot connected with a rock, throwing him off balance, and he fell.

Whooping triumphantly, the Blackfoot took a stride and raised his tomahawk for the death blow.

Flat on his back, his arms outflung, Nate stiffened in anticipation of the warrior's tomahawk slicing into his flesh. The glinting edge hung suspended in the air for a moment, and suddenly, incredibly, the Blackfoot looked up, looking at something or someone beyond Nate's line of vision.

Feral hatred etched the warrior's countenance, and he made a motion as if about to throw the tomahawk.

A shot rang out.

The Blackfoot's right eye was blown apart by the ball that penetrated his head and ruptured out the rear, showering hair, skin, and gore on the ground. His arms sagged, he swayed, and toppled over to the left.

Nate scrambled erect and turned, thinking he would find Shakespeare standing behind him. Instead, much to his astonishment, he discovered Black Kettle.

A pale shadow of his former self, a smoking pistol clutched in both hands, the leader of the band mustered a broad smile, cast a benign, almost grateful gaze at Nate, and sank slowly to his knees.

Heedless of his own safety, Nate bounded to Black Kettle's side. He recognized the pistol as his own and realized Winona had given the weapon to her father.

Winona!

Where was she?

Nate scanned the summit and recieved a shock. Eleven Shoshone women had entered the fray armed with knives, stones, and whatever else they could get their hands on. Five Shoshone boys, each between eight and 14 years of age, had also gone to the aid of the warriors. The Blackfeet were battling furiously, but now they were the ones who were outnumbered, and they were learning the hard way that a knife in the hands of an enraged woman or boy was every bit as deadly as a blade wielded by a man. The very existence of the Shoshone band was at stake, and every able-bodied member had rallied to the cause.

A figure materialized on Nate's right and he rotated, thinking it might be a Blackfoot.

Winona squatted next to her father, her countenance a mask of sadness.

Concerned that one of the Blackfeet might bear down on them, Nate quickly reloaded both pistols. As he took the one gun from Black Kettle, his father-in-law stared into his eyes and spoke a single word.

A tremendous cry of exultation shook the heavens.

Nate stood, both arms extended, but his further participation proved to be unnecessary.

Nine Blackfeet were dead, sprawled on the ground in spreading pools of their own blood, most bearing multiple wounds. The rest of the attackers had fled, barely escaping with their lives, clambering over the boulders or fleeing through the gaps as fast as their legs would carry them.

The carnage was appalling. Shoshone bodies dotted the enclosed area. Only five warriors were still standing, including Drags the Rope, and he had sustained a wicked gash on the right side of his chest. Most of the other warriors were also injured, but not as extensively, and many of the women bore cuts or bruises or both.

"We did it."

Nate turned to his left at the subdued words. There stood Shakespeare, his shoulders slumped, his face caked with sweat and dust. "Do you think the Blackfeet are gone for good?"

The frontiersman nodded wearily. "They took quite a licking. The bastards won't have anything to celebrate when they return to their village." He gazed at the

Blackfoot slain by Black Kettle. "Did you do this?"

"No. Black Kettle did."

"Well, I reckon he won't mind," Shakespeare said, and stepped to the dark hat lying in the dirt. He picked it up, smacked the fur against his leg a few times, and extended his arm to Nate. "Here. I don't like to see a good hat go to waste and I already have one."

"I don't need it."

"You will come winter," Shakespeare told him. "Don't argue. Black Kettle has no use for it. And he'd want you to have Mad Dog's hat."

"Mad Dog's?" Nate repeated in surprise. He took the handcrafted headgear in his right hand, feeling the soft texture of the fur. "Maybe Black Kettle would like to have this," he stated, and pivoted to offer the trophy to his father-in-law. Not until then did he understand Shakespeare's comment.

Winona was on her knees, her hands clasped under her chin, her eyes filled with tears. On his back in front of her, his eyes open but lifeless, his profile reflecting an attitude of profound peace, lay Black Kettle.

Epilogue

"You didn't make out so bad."

Nate looked to his right at his friend, frowning at the callousness of the comment, then stared straight ahead at the valley before them. He tightened his grip on the mare's reins and spoke sarcastically. "No, I didn't make out too bad. Both my wife's mother and father were killed, but other than that everything is just terrific."

"That isn't what I meant and you know it," Shakespeare countered. "I miss them more than you ever will. They were my close friends, remember?"

A twinge of guilt tweaked Nate's conscience. "Sorry. I guess I'm just taking out my frustration on you."

"Now that you're married, you're not supposed to get testy with your friends," Shakespeare noted, grinning impishly. "What do you think you have a wife for?"

"I'm beginning to wonder."

"Has anyone ever told you that you take life too seriously?" Shakespeare asked.

"I take life the only way I know how."

The rode in silence for a minute.

The frontiersman coughed lightly. "Actually, I was

referring to that fact that you received two of the horses the Blackfeet left behind. Now you have enough for your woman and all your goods.''

''Yes,'' Nate said dryly.

Shakepeare hissed in exasperation. ''I had no idea you can be so grumpy.''

''I have my reason,'' Nate stated obstinately. He shifted in the saddle and gazed back at the line of Shoshones trailing them, studiously refraining from looking at his wife, who was riding on a black gelding not two yards to his rear.

''Are you going to mope like this all the way to the rendezvous?'' the mountain man asked.

''I may,'' Nate said, facing front again.

''You're worse than a kid, you know that?''

Nate's anger got the better of him and he whirled on his friend. ''Damn it! She should have listened to me!''

A smile creased Shakespeare's mouth. ''Since when are wives supposed to listen to their husbands? You have a lot to learn about marriage. When a woman agrees to hitch herself to a man, she's not agreeing to do every little thing he wants. She reserves the right to disagree, and disagree she will. Every chance she gets. Sometimes I think women aren't satisfied unless they can bicker about an issue first.'' He paused and chuckled. ''Of course, they usually wind up doing what they want to anyway. Nine times out of ten a woman will outthink a man. Always remember that.''

''You're a big help.''

''I'm not done yet. I'm not suggesting you roll over and give in to your wife every time you have a spat. You can't be weak. A woman never respects a weakling. She'll pout and be bitchy and quarrel for the dumbest reasons in Creation, but through it all she expects her man to be strong,'' Shakespeare stated, and shook his head in amazement. ''Never did make much sense to me. They marry the strongest man they can find, then they get all hot under the collar when he stands by his own guns.''

"I'll be sure and write down your words of wisdom for posterity," Nate cracked.

"It's nice to see you can still make a joke."

Nate sighed and glanced at his friend. "Do you think I'm in the wrong?"

"Who's to judge? I do know she can't understand why you're so upset. To her it's the normal course of things. It's like eating and sleeping. Just has to be done."

"What have I gotten myself into?" Nate queried rhetorically.

"Ain't love grand?" Shakespeare responded, beaming.

"Love," Nate repeated softly, still immensely disturbed. But he did love her. That was the whole problem. He loved her so much, cared for her with all of his heart and soul, and he couldn't bear the thought of her being harmed in any way. Especially when he possessed the power to prevent it. And he'd tried. He'd really tried. Unfortunately, he couldn't keep his eyes on her 24 hours a day.

"We should be at the rendezvous in three hours," Shakespeare mentioned.

Nate nodded, then slowed the mare so his wife could ride alongside him. He smiled and stared at her, feasting his eyes on her loveliness.

Winona eagerly returned the smile.

Straining his self-control to the limit, Nate forced himself to keep smiling as his gaze drifted lower until he was looking at the strip of hide wrapped around her left hand, the hide that served as a bandage, the hide she had secured to staunch the flow of her blood after she chopped the tips off two of her fingers.

What *had* he gotten himself into?

Only time would tell.

TWICE THE FRONTIER ACTION AND ADVENTURE IN ONE GIANT EDITION!

GIANT SPECIAL EDITION:

THE TRAIL WEST
David Thompson

Far from the teeming streets of civilization, rugged pioneers dare to carve a life out of the savage frontier, but few have a prayer of surviving there. Bravest among the frontiersmen is Nathaniel King—loyal friend, master trapper, and grizzly killer. Then a rich Easterner hires Nate to guide him to the virgin lands west of the Rockies, and he finds his life threatened by hostile Indians, greedy backshooters, and renegade settlers. If Nate fails to defeat those vicious enemies, he'll wind up buried beneath six feet of dirt.

_3938-9 $5.99 US/$7.99 CAN